Praise for Ben Mezrich's fiction

'Like Crichton, Mezrich knows how to weave . . . a fast-paced story that's fun and irresistible.' —*People*

'On par with Robin Cook.' —*Kirkus*

'Ben Mezrich is a rising star whose name will become as well-known as Clancy, Koontz, Grisham, and others.' —*Tulsa World*

'Mezrich knows how to make science suspenseful.' —*Publishers Weekly*

Praise for *Bringing Down The House*:

'A book that will surely become a classic of its genre.' —*The Sunday Express*

'Part Tom Clancy, part Elmore Leonard . . . Gripping.' —*The Express*

'The reigning cowboy of creative nonfiction.' —*The Oregonian*

'What Mezrich has done, beautifully, is craft a riveting story about kids with excess brainpower taking on casinos with excess money. He has penned a gripping true-life adventure that will keep you reading well past your bedtime.' —*The Boston Globe*

'Mezrich manages to incorporate solid journalism into a narrative that just plain works.' —*Publishers Weekly*

SEVEN WONDERS

A NOVEL

BEN MEZRICH

WILLIAM HEINEMANN: LONDON

To my parents, on their fiftieth anniversary.
And to Asher, Arya, and Tonya, my eighth,
ninth, and tenth Wonders of the World.

Published by William Heinemann 2014

2 4 6 8 10 9 7 5 3 1

First published in the United States in 2014 by RatPac Press in collaboration with
Running Press, a member of the Perseus Books Group.

First published in Great Britain in 2014 by
William Heinemann
Random House, 20 Vauxhall Bridge Road,
London SW1V 2SA

A Penguin Random House Company

Penguin
Random House
UK

www.randomhouse.co.uk

Addresses for companies within The Random House Group Limited can be found at:
www.randomhouse.co.uk/offices.htm

The Random House Group Limited Reg. No. 954009

A CIP catalogue record for this book
is available from the British Library

ISBN 9780434023448

Interior illustrations © 2014 Gina and Matt

Printed and bound by CPI Group (UK) Ltd, Croydon, CR0 4YY

ACKNOWLEDGMENTS

First and foremost, I am grateful to Brett Ratner and Beau Flynn for sending me off on this amazing journey; this has truly been the best writing experience of my career. I am also indebted to my wonderful editor, Jennifer Kasius, and all the amazing folks at Perseus, Running Press, and RatPac. Special thanks to Chris Navratil and Allison Devlin, as well as Steve Asbell at 20th Century Fox. Thanks also for the encouragement, humor, and brilliance of John Cheng and Wendy Jacobson. Many thanks to the thorough and creative Dr. Daniel Friedman, my expert on too many things to mention, and to Gregg Selkoe, for some dancing bears. I am also eternally grateful to Eric Simonoff and Matt Snyder, the best agents in the business.

Most important, thank you Tonya, my incredible secret weapon. And to Asher, Arya, Bugsy, and my parents—you make it all worthwhile.

CHAPTER ONE

Three a.m.

It was five days into a fierce New England heat wave, the scattered trees lining Mass Avenue bowed and weeping, desolate sidewalks glistening, tar black asphalt leaking wisps of steam into the thick, humid air.

Fifty feet below, in a reverse-pressure, vacuum-sealed Level Four computer lab—two stairwells and one elevator ride beneath the famed, eight-hundred-and-twenty-five-foot-long Infinite Corridor that bisected the MIT campus in Cambridge, Massachusetts—Jeremy Grady's world had just turned upside down.

Impossible.

Jeremy staggered back from the flat-screen monitor on the glass desk in front of him, nearly upending his chair. The rubber of his sneakers shrieked against the vinyl floor panels, but he didn't take his eyes off the screen, didn't even blink as the brightly colored pixels continued to dagger out across the cave-like lab.

This has to be a mistake.

His fingers trembling, Jeremy yanked off his thick, plastic-rimmed glasses, hoping the blur of his poor vision would somehow change the image in front of him to something that made sense. But no amount of myopia could defang the electronic packets of light emanating from the screen. He considered running the program again, but he had already run it twice, and he knew that the results would be the same.

A bug? A problem with the code?

Jeremy put his glasses back on and then exhaled, letting the sound of his own breath compete with the hiss of the lab's high-powered ventilation system. Jeremy had written the code himself, had already combed through it a dozen times over the past two days. There was no bug. No mistake. The image on the screen, as impossible as it seemed, was as true and certain as math itself. After all, that's all the program really was, a complicated mathematical equation. Numbers turned into pixels. And numbers didn't lie. Numbers were safe and certain and sure.

At twenty-eight, Jeremy had built his entire life around numbers. Not by choice—it was simply the way he was wired. The various psychiatrists his mother had consulted over the years had always tried to couch it in the gentlest terms: a *special* child, with a *special* sort of mind. Anxious, socially awkward, and closed off, preternaturally obsessed with mathematical patterns, so wrapped up in his own internal compulsions that even the most normal, easy things in life often seemed like utter torture. A trip to the grocery store, a visit to a crowded park, an invite to a birthday party—from an early age, these were things that could leave Jeremy curled up in a corner of his bedroom, trembling and in tears.

There wasn't any one particular moment in Jeremy's past that he could point to when he'd realized that his faulty wiring was as much a boon as it was a disability. He'd hardly noticed when his middle school math teachers had stopped assigning him homework, because he was so far ahead of the class, they didn't have anything left to teach him. He hadn't felt left out when his twin brother Jack—his polar opposite, a thrill-seeking extrovert, a star in every sport he played—had headed off to the senior prom, because

Jeremy was too busy putting the finishing touches on a handheld computer he'd built in their basement from scratch.

But somewhere along the way, things *had* changed. Now that he was seven years into a PhD in applied math/computer science at MIT, his proclivities seemed little more than a nuisance. Besides, he wasn't the only doctoral candidate at the prestigious math-science mecca who chose to eat his meals in his studio apartment, meticulously stacking his silverware when he was done.

Nor, he assumed, was he the only programming guru to lock himself into his computer lab for two days crafting algorithms and running subroutines because of something he'd stumbled into that didn't seem quite right.

Though to be accurate, the Level Four security lab wasn't actually *Jeremy's*; even though he'd effectively moved in over the past forty-eight hours. He didn't actually have the proper clearance to be using such expensive and sensitive equipment. Especially on a project that had nothing to do with his PhD. But it had become evident that he didn't have access to enough processing power at his own workstation in a shared cubicle halfway across campus. On top of that, Jeremy had needed the satellite data; and everyone at MIT knew where you went when you needed satellite data.

The warren of underground labs tucked beneath the Infinite Corridor were one of the university's worst kept secrets—especially since some of the money the US Defense Department had set aside to fund the high-tech bunkers was earmarked to hire undergrads as lab techs and engineers. It was one of those undergrads who had loaned Jeremy his security ID to get past the guard manning the elevators that led down from the corridor. One geek with glasses looked much like the next, not that anyone treated this place like Area 51. MIT's relationship with the defense department went all the way back to before World War II, when radar had been developed in secret campus labs much like this one. At MIT, working on the next generation of missile defense systems was like playing in the marching band, an extracurricular to fatten up your résumé.

The last thing Jeremy was afraid of, staring at the image on the giant screen, was getting caught in the lab without the proper clearance. It was the nature of a university full of introverts that nobody knew what anyone else was doing.

To be fair, bathed in the glare of the impossible image on the screen, Jeremy was no longer sure he could even explain it to himself. Dr. Berman, the psychiatrist he'd most relied on through high school and college, might have insisted that Jeremy was having another one of his episodes—plunging deeper and deeper down the rabbit's hole of his mind, chasing patterns that only he could see. Even a perfectly normal human brain was built around a passion for patterns; it was part of the evolutionary process, a biological survival mechanism that had driven humanity to the top of the food chain. In Jeremy's case, the slightest hint of a numerical association could lead to near mental paralysis, as his obsessive mind searched for connections that may or may not actually exist.

And maybe in the beginning, Dr. Berman's diagnosis would have been correct. A normal person would not have turned what was essentially a stupid argument between brothers into a time-consuming diversion, employing enough computing power to launch a medium-size war. A disagreement so petty and bizarre, it wouldn't even make sense beyond the confines of the twins' dysfunctional relationship. Why his brother Jack even felt it necessary to return to Boston once a year, to mark the anniversary of their mother's death, was unfathomable to Jeremy. The two of them had so little in common, without an argument, they'd have nothing to say to each other at all.

This one had been as pointless as ever. Jack had barely stepped off the plane when he'd started going on about his latest excursion, some sort of field research study at an archaeological dig site in Turkey. An anthropology fellow at Princeton who spent more time getting his passport stamped than in any classroom, Jack was always prattling on about his latest adventures.

This time, he was particularly excited because the dig site was at one of the Ancient Seven Wonders of the World: the Temple of Artemis at Ephesus. Jeremy hadn't even realized there were two sets of Seven Wonders—Ancient and Modern—and when he'd casually mentioned that the Ancient Wonders couldn't have been all that impressive, since he doubted anyone could name three, let alone all seven, that was all Jack had needed to set him off on a lecture about the relative merits of the two lists that lasted until his flight back to Turkey.

Of course, that should have been the end of it. But the minute Jeremy had returned to campus, his mind started to spin. Subconsciously, he'd already begun trying to devise some sort of metric to compare modern and ancient architectural accomplishments. And just to get some sort of idea as to what he was even trying to compare, he'd pulled up maps of the various Wonders on his laptop. He wasn't sure what had made him start toying with the latitudes and longitudes, or what he'd been looking for when he'd started superimposing the various maps on top of one another, charting out geographical centers, functioning out elevations and topography—but certainly nothing could have prepared him for what he had found.

A pattern.

Mathematical, precise, and impossible.

At first, he'd refused to believe what he was seeing. The human mind searched for patterns, begged for patterns, often invented patterns when they couldn't be found in nature. He'd forced himself to approach it logically, treat what he was seeing as a mathematical anomaly he needed to disprove. When he'd realized his own facilities weren't enough, he'd gained access to everything he needed—holing up in the underground lab. All he'd brought with him were a change of clothes and his laptop, which was sitting next to the lab's supercomputer. Attached to his laptop was a small thumb drive hanging from a fairly unique keychain. He'd fashioned the keychain out of a souvenir his brother had given him years earlier. Maybe Jack had been going for something sentimental with the gift; Jeremy's Egyptology was rusty, so he wasn't sure what sort of message a gold-plated scarab was supposed to send. Hollowed out with a lathe from the mechanical engineering department, however, it made the perfect place to store a thumb drive.

There was no doubt now that Jeremy had uncovered something worth putting on that drive. Because based on the image on the screen, not only had he confirmed that the pattern wasn't a figment of his special mind, he'd now used satellite data to correct for the curvature of the Earth and immensely powerful data processors to rule out any other possibilities.

At its core, it was the same simple mind experiment he'd performed two days ago—superimposing maps of the Modern Seven Wonders of the World against maps of the Ancient Wonders of the World. First, he'd created a map of the Ancients: the Temple of Artemis at Ephesus, the Statue of Zeus at Olympia, the Mausoleum at Halicarnassus, the Colossus of Rhodes, the Lighthouse at Alexandria, the Pyramids, and the Hanging Gardens of Babylon. He'd had to look most of them up, and was surprised to learn that all were now little more than ruins, except for the Pyramids. One, the Hanging Gardens of Babylon, was even less than that; nobody was even certain where it might have once stood, or even if it was more than just a myth. After precisely mapping the rest, he'd connected the geographic center of each Wonder, correcting for topography and the Earth's curve. Then he'd created a similar map of the New Wonders of the World: Christ the Redeemer in Brazil, the Taj Mahal, Chichen Itza, Machu Picchu, the Colosseum, Petra, and the Great Wall of China. Together, they spanned a much larger distance, encompassing the entire globe rather than just the area surrounding the Mediterranean Sea. After functioning out the differences in scale, he'd overlaid the Modern Wonders over the Ancient Wonders, parsed the data into a visual image—and nearly knocked himself right out of his chair.

Most of the two images appeared to be enantiomers of each other—three-dimensional mirror images, matching up in the way someone's left and right hand might match up. But they weren't just near mirror images. They were *perfect* enantiomers. Six of the Ancient Seven Wonders matched six of the Modern Wonders, creating a swooping pattern that, if anything, resembled two interlocking snakes—a double helix, in mathematical terms—with one tail ending at the Great Wall of China, the other at the ancient Statue of Zeus at Olympia.

Jeremy knew that what he was seeing was impossible. According to Jack's lecture, the original Seven Wonders of the Ancient World had been chosen by ancient Greek historians. But the new Seven Wonders of the World had been chosen by a popular vote. The only way for the new Seven Wonders of the World to have ended up in a pattern geographically linked to the ancient seven would have been if that vote had been manipulated; for some reason, someone had wanted those specific monuments chosen— monuments that had been built on the exact mirror image geographic locations as the Wonders from the ancient world.

Jeremy noticed, as his mind continued to whir forward, that his right hand was in the air, his finger tracing the pattern on the screen in the empty space in front of him. Objectively, the double helix was such a beautiful shape; the fact that it was also the easily recognizable form of DNA—the chemical building block of all life—added even more weight to its palpable splendor. As he traced the shape again, moving across the brightly colored pinpoints that marked the geographic center of each Wonder, Modern and Ancient, he found himself focusing on what wasn't there: the two Wonders that didn't match up. On the Ancient map, the Hanging Gardens of Babylon, which made sense, since the Gardens might very well have been myth. But the missing Modern Wonder—Christ the Redeemer, the magnificent Art Deco statue in Rio, and the most recently built of all the Wonders—why didn't it fit the pattern?

Jeremy approached the desk again, this time turning to his laptop. Hitting keys with both hands, he quickly pulled up his satellite data on Christ the Redeemer, looking again through the topographical imagery, running through the equations that he'd used to calculate the Wonder's geographic center. As the numbers blinked across his laptop's screen, he paused, his fingers hanging above his keyboard.

He wasn't surprised he had missed it before; it was so small, barely a rounding error in the scheme of things. But certainly, given the image on the bigger computer screen, it now seemed very intriguing.

There was something off about that Wonder of the World—an anomaly in its topography. Something that wouldn't have been visible at all, without the sophisticated satellite equipment. The sort of thing that his brother, Jack, would want to check out in person; another adventure he could dive headlong into, halfway around the world. Jeremy would have to be content to study it via the safety of electronic packets of information, from a basement laboratory five thousand miles away.

He quickly transferred the information onto the thumb drive attached to the laptop. Then his eyes returned to the larger screen—to the vivid pair of snakes cavorting in the perfect shape of the double helix. *And what would Jack make of this?* he wondered. He grinned, thinking about his brother digging through the dirt in Turkey, probably looking for a couple of scuffed coins or rotting bones—while Jeremy, locked up in a basement lab, had just made the discovery of a lifetime. *Hell, maybe the discovery of a thousand lifetimes.*

He yanked the thumb drive out of the laptop—the gold-plated scarab keychain attached to the drive clinking with the motion—and snapped it into a USB port on the side of the enormous flat-screen. Three swipes of a mouse against the glass desk, and the packets of data were on their way from the security lab's computer system onto the drive. As Jeremy waited for the transfer, he turned back to the glowing double helix, swooping up and down through the filtered air. He was so enrapt by the brightly colored pixels, he didn't notice the figure closing in behind him—until a shadow flickered across the screen.

Jeremy turned just in time to see a flash of motion, and then something jagged and long was knifing through the air in front of him. There was a sickening sound, like a butcher's blade going through a block of raw meat, and Jeremy looked down. His eyes went wide.

Something long and almost impossibly white was sticking out of the center of his chest.

Jeremy crashed back against the glass desk, sending his laptop clattering to the floor. The figure in front of him was moving forward now, closing the distance between them. Jeremy felt himself sliding to the floor. As his knees touched the vinyl panels, he realized there was something in the palm of his hand. The thumb drive, hanging from the scarab key ring. He must have yanked it from the flat-screen on his way down. He had no idea if the data transfer was complete, but it hardly seemed to matter, because now the pain was starting to work through the shock in searing, gut-wrenching waves, emanating from the thing embedded in his chest. And then he realized that the pain wasn't the worst part. The worst part was that he could no longer breathe.

As his body crumpled forward, he used his last burst of strength to shove the thumb drive deep into the hollow scarab, hiding it inside the key-chain. A second later, his cheek touched vinyl, his eyes rolled up, and all that remained was the afterglow on his dying retinas of a pair of glowing snakes, intertwining in a sea of black.

CHAPTER TWO

Okay, Jack. It's not like this is the stupidest thing you've ever done. . . .

Jack Grady slid one gloved hand over the high-tensile aluminum rope, rechecking the iron clasps where it connected to his suspension harness. His other hand was straight out in front of him, his wrist working back and forth to steady his body in midair.

But hell, it's got to be in the top five. . . .

He tried not to look straight down, where his work boots were dangling above a blackness that was both thick and palpable. Likewise, he did his best not to dwell on the fact that the only thing between him and a plunge that would end in certain death was that taut, seemingly floss-thin aluminum rope.

"Everything okay down there, Doc?"

The speaker in Jack's fiberglass crash helmet was the size of a doll's eye, and still the voice was like a gunshot in his ears, amplified by the sheer rock walls of the pit. Jack fought to keep his body still, but even the slightest tremble was enough to put him into a gentle spin, the yellow cone of light from the flashlight attached to his open visor dancing across the three-hundred-and-sixty-degree circle of stone that surrounded him.

"Like a piece of bait on a hook, kid," he responded.

There was a laugh on the other end of the speaker. Then the aluminum rope gave a slight jerk, and Jack was inching downward again, into the soupy black.

He kept his breathing normal as he went, noting that the air had turned markedly cooler since he'd passed the hundred-foot depth marker they'd clipped to the rope. He also noticed that there was a new, musty scent, perhaps some sort of microscopic vegetation or bacteria living in the crags and seams of the nearly sheer rock walls. It didn't seem likely that anything substantial could live down there, although the pit itself appeared to be naturally occurring—Jack's best guess, the result of a meteor strike that, according to the local oral tradition and held up by the geological dating, had struck the area around thirteen thousand years ago.

About time someone came down here to kick the tires and check the oil. . . .

Jack gave it another ten minutes, inching downward, his body still revolving in a nearly silent spin, before he reached up and tapped the side of his helmet.

"Okay, hold up. I'm going to do a splat check."

The rope jerked to a stop. He was a good hundred and fifty feet down now, and still the pit appeared exactly the same as it had when they first broke through the limestone mantle beneath the dig site and peered down into the black drop from above.

Just getting to that moment had been heroic enough. First the plane from Boston, then a connecting flight from Istanbul to Izmir, then a bus ride to the nearby village of Selçuk, where he'd been met by his two grad students for a middle of the night bike ride into the Greek-era ruins of Ephesus.

Andy, by far the more talkative of his two charges, had grumbled the whole ride over that they should have waited until daylight and that he felt like some sort of grave robber sneaking into an archaeological dig at two in the morning. Dashia, for her part, had pedaled along in silence, trying to stay right behind Jack as they wound beneath the arched Greek ruins and around the Doric columns.

Along the way, Jack hadn't even bothered to try and respond to his lead student's whines; Andy Chen was a wise-ass, but he was one of the smartest students Jack had ever met. He'd graduated at the top of his class at Princeton at sixteen, completed a Fulbright at Oxford before deciding to letter in anthropology, and since then, he'd become indispensable to Jack's operation.

At the moment, Jack was certain Andy's complaining was more for Dashia's benefit than for his. Though his second grad student had proved over the past six months that she could hold her own in the brains department—a transplant from Harvard, a triple major in biology, anthropology, and computer science—Dashia Lynwood was surprisingly straight-laced.

To be sure, Andy knew full well why they couldn't wait until morning, and it wasn't just the oppressive heat that would swelter through the swampy field around the Temple of Artemis dig site, now a hundred and fifty feet directly above him. The truth was, Jack and his students were interlopers here. That they'd even managed to get permission from the Turkish Board of Antiquities for a late night survey of the area was a testament to Jack's persuasiveness and his department's prestige. This was an archaeological dig site; an anthropology fellow and his two precocious grad students shouldn't have been let within a hundred yards of the place.

Of course, if the Antiquities Board or the team from the British Museum who were running the dig had realized what Jack was *really* up to, he might have been on his way to a stay in a Turkish prison rather than lowering himself into an ancient abyss.

"Ignition in three, two, one!" Jack said, yanking one of the chemical flares from a compartment in his harness.

He pulled the cord on the end of the flare, and a burst of bright orange flame cut through the blackness. Jack leaned forward until he was parallel with the empty drop beneath him, the aluminum rope stringing out above him like a spider's web. He let the flare go, and counted quietly to himself as he watched the flame pinwheeling downward, spinning end over end.

He was still counting more than twenty seconds later, when the speaker croaked in his ears.

"Dashia wants to know why we call it the splat test."

Jack grimaced, certain that Andy would find the most inelegant way to explain it to her. It was mildly unsettling to think they'd been in enough situations like this over the past couple of years to have come up with a term for the test. Basically, if Jack's harness broke, they now had some idea how long it would take before Andy heard a splat. In this case, as far as Jack could tell, the torch was still spinning through the darkness.

But Jack wasn't thinking about the bottom of the pit anymore; in that first few seconds after the flare had gone off, he'd noticed something extremely interesting about thirty yards down from where he was hanging, along one curve of the circular pit walls. It might have been nothing—a trick of shadows, a discoloration in the stone—but Jack thought he'd seen an opening, at least the size of a six-foot-tall anthropologist.

"Andy, bring me down another three clicks."

Jack used his legs and arms to keep himself steady as Andy complied; he was still hanging parallel to the drop, a floating starfish, the flashlight on his helmet focused in the direction he'd seen the opening. The seconds passed in silence, broken only by the soft creak of the leather straps of the harness.

"Christ," Jack whispered as the opening suddenly came into view. "Stop!"

The aluminum rope jerked tight. Jack trained the flashlight directly ahead of him.

He'd been right. There was an opening in the rock, and it was even bigger than he'd thought. Arched, taller than him at its peak, with a floor that looked like it was sloping downward. It appeared to be the entrance to some sort of cave. Even more fascinating, it looked man-made. Not only were the edges smooth and the dimensions precise and symmetrical, in each corner of the opening, standing about a foot and a half tall, was a matching carved statue.

"You're not going to believe what I'm looking at," Jack said.

"Is it Artemis?" Andy joked. "She down there waiting to take you up to Mt. Olympus, introduce you to the family?"

Not a bad guess, Jack thought to himself as he shined the flashlight over the twin statues. They were both decidedly female. But where the Greek goddess Artemis, the goddess of the hunt, was usually depicted holding a spear or bow and arrow, sometimes on a horse, these statues were themati cally different. The two carved women were naked from the waist up and appeared to be covered in dozens of chiseled stone eggs. Furthermore, both of the statues had only a single breast; it appeared that on each one, the right breast had been removed.

"You're off by about three thousand years," Jack said, half to himself. His heart was beating hard, and there was a familiar feeling moving up through his spine.

It was the feeling he got when he was about to do something *really* stupid.

He began shifting his weight back and forth against the harness, causing his body to swing forward and back—inches at first, but steadily gaining in speed, his body arcing through the air like the metal weight at the end of a pendulum.

"It's a natural assumption," he said, reflexively shifting into teaching mode as he swung, rocking himself faster and faster, "that the Temple of Artemis at Ephesus was built by the Greeks to worship Artemis. And at least three of the iterations of the great Wonder—which was destroyed four times—were indeed built for the goddess of the hunt."

Certainly the version of the Temple described in most textbooks was dedicated to Artemis. It had once been twice as long as the Parthenon, the first building ever constructed entirely of marble, and had taken a hundred and twenty years to build. If the Goths hadn't burned most of it down in 268 AD, it might very well have remained one of the most impressive buildings in the world.

"The Temple before that was nearly as grand," Jack continued, breathing hard now as he rocked through the air, tilting his body so that he was facing the opening dead on, "but was much better known for how it had been destroyed. A local narcissist named Herostratus wanted to be famous and figured the way to fame was to burn the building to the ground. For his efforts, he was tortured to death; then the town leaders made a law that anyone who even mentioned his name would also be put to death."

It was that iteration of the Temple that the British Museum team had been studying when they had discovered the limestone mantle thirty feet beneath the base of the column that had been built from fragments of all four sets of ancient ruins—a memorial to the incredible feat of architecture that had once stood in this place.

"And even before that, the Temple was decidedly a Greek monument; there are writings from all over the Ionic empire lauding the people of Ephesus, who were diligent in their Artemis worship. But go back another few thousand years and that's where this place gets really interesting."

Jack took a deep breath of the cool, musty air that was now whipping against his cheeks. This seemingly bottomless pit, the dark opening in front of him—if he was right, the team from the British Museum had stumbled onto something much more ancient than the Greek monument they had been searching for.

"Uh, Doc," Andy's voice cracked through his helmet. ""What are you doing? The rope seems to be swinging kind of crazy."

Jack focused on the opening as he swung through the darkness. He couldn't be certain, but at the end of the arc on his pendulum path, he guessed he was about ten feet away. There seemed to be ample space between the two statues although he didn't know how steep the pitch was on the other side.

Not that it mattered; Jack's mind was already made up.

"Andy, that's because I'm about to do something a little foolish."

There was a pause on the other end of the speaker.

"Chief Jack foolish?"

Jack grinned. It was shorthand that Jack was sure Andy was proudly in the process of explaining to Dashia. It dated back three years before, when the two of them had spent four months living with the Yanomami, the legendary Fierce People who lived deep in the jungle on the Venezuelan-Brazilian border. During a hunting expedition, Jack had somehow insulted a minor chieftain, and the man had challenged him to a duel. Jack had foolishly accepted, and they had fought using ritual long spears tipped with scorpion stingers. Thankfully, the scorpions in that region weren't deadly— but the sting was immensely painful and caused debilitating hallucinations that could last up to thirty-six hours.

Jack had lost the fight, but both men had been pricked in the process. When they'd finally come out of their delirium, everyone in the village was calling him Chief Jack. To this day, Jack wore a pouch filled with the scorpion stingers on a leather necklace beneath his shirt to remind him where his bravado had gotten him.

"At the very least. When I give the signal, I want you to give me slack. Ten yards should do it."

"Doc—"

"Ten yards, kid. On my mark."

Andy knew better than to argue. Over the past few years, he had accompanied Jack on field expeditions all over the world. Before the Yanomami, there had been the Swat Pukhtun, the sometimes-violent nomads of the remote valley of Northern Pakistan. Before that, a tribe of mountain people in Tibet who lived so high up the rear face of Everest, their skin had turned a permanent shade of blue.

In Jack's mind, the best field anthropologists didn't ply their trade sitting in stuffy classrooms; they went out and took risks, submerging themselves in cultures that often seemed utterly alien.

Jack tightened his jaw, making his body straight like an arrow as he approached the height of the pendulum arc, aiming his arms out toward the opening—

"Now!"

And he was sailing forward, the slack aluminum rope trailing out behind him. For a brief second he was weightless, his legs windmilling in the darkness, and then he was angling down, right between the two statues. His boots touched dirt and a plume of dust erupted around him, momentarily blinding him. Then he was skidding down a forty-five-degree angle, dirt and gravel sliding with him. He was about to topple forward when the rope behind him went taut and he gasped, the harness digging into his chest and shoulders. He coughed, hard, and the dust finally began to settle around him, the orange cone from his helmet light painting the scene in shifting, momentary glimpses.

As he'd suspected, he was now in some sort of chamber, carved right out of the limestone. The sloping ramp he was on led down to a semicircular cave that appeared to be about fifteen feet high at its peak and maybe ten feet deep. The walls and ceiling were smooth, but when he looked more carefully, he could see hair-thin seams between carefully chiseled segments of stone.

Nothing primitive about the craftsmanship here, Jack thought to himself. He turned carefully on his heels, trying not to dislodge too much gravel as he shifted back toward the two statues at the lip of the cavern.

Up close, the statues were even more incredible. The details on the women's faces were precise, the features carefully crafted; both women were quite beautiful, with vaguely African features and braided hair. Looking at them—at the eggs that speckled their bodies, at the missing breast on each of their chests—Jack's heart rate began to quicken.

"I'm not hearing any screaming," Andy's voice broke the silence. "So I'm gonna assume you made it."

Jack turned away from the statues, back toward the descending slope. He was about to answer when his helmet light flashed on something directly across from him—something that seemed to flash right back.

"I'm going to need ten more yards," he said.

He made his way down the slope carefully, not wanting to upset more of the gravel. The cavern felt stable, but he was pretty certain now that he was in a man-made place that was much, much older than the marshy ruins high above.

As he made it to the bottom of the slope, he found he was walking on more limestone, similar to the mantle the team from the British Museum had uncovered. The museum team had thought they were looking at a slab from a massive roof that had stood for nearly two hundred years before Herostratus burned it down. But Jack had suspected something much different, because of a single piece of pottery that had been sent to him by a colleague in the antiquities department at the University of London who had accompanied the original British Museum team.

The image on the pottery had been very similar to the statues behind Jack—women with vaguely African features, covered in symbols of fertility. They were evidence that fit Jack's thesis: that the original Temple of Artemis predated the Greeks by thousands of years. And now, in front of him, was something even more definitive. *Something quite incredible.*

"It's beautiful," he whispered, his voice echoing through the chamber.

The painting took up most of the far wall of the cavern—five feet high, maybe twice as long, painted in lavish strokes of color with a true artist's skill.

"It's a mural," Jack said as he took his digital camera out of a pocket in his harness and began taking photos. "A tribe of women warriors leaving what looks to be a lush forest paradise. The women are similar to the ones pictured on the pottery and the statues. Each of them is missing a right breast. But instead of eggs, they're carrying what look to be war javelins. And the forest—it's hard to describe. So many greens, it's really quite amazing."

Then his eyes shifted to the glow that had caught his attention from across the cavern. One of the female warriors in the mural was carrying a large, flat stone, on which was carved the image of a golden snake, cut into seven equal segments. The segments were plated in some sort of metallic material, flashing in the glare of his helmet light.

Jack wasn't surprised to see a snake; he knew that the snake was one of the most common images in the ancient writings and drawings of nearly every culture on earth: from the Judeo-Christian Bible—in the very first chapter, a snake tricks Adam and Eve out of the Garden of Eden—to various Hindu texts dealing with Kundalini, the coiled Serpent, to the Egyptian Book of the Dead, where various spells dealt with snakes, to Chinese texts rife with snake demons, dragons, and gods. Jack himself had seen the snake carvings in the Pyramid at Giza that guarded the metaphoric entrance to the watery underworld.

The ancient Greeks seemed especially obsessed with snakes. In Greek mythology, nearly every Greek god had at one point turned into, killed, or had sex with some sort of serpent. It was no surprise that perhaps the most well-known symbol from ancient Greece in the modern world involved a snake. The Hippocratic symbol of health and life, used in hospitals and doctor's offices worldwide, was a snake wrapped around the rod of Asclepius, the god of healing, although in America, the image was just as often—and erroneously—a Caduceus, the staff of the god Mercury, which had two snakes wrapped together in the shape of a double helix. The confusion dated back to 1902, when a US Army officer adopted the Caduceus instead of the rod of Asclepius as the symbol of the Army Medical Core because he thought it looked cooler as a patch on his uniform. Jack guessed that the officer hadn't realized the irony of his act; the Caduceus was actually the symbol of the Greek and Roman god of thieves, deceivers, and murderers.

Still, no matter how popular the snake was as a symbol in the ancient world, the image in the mural was intriguing, like nothing Jack had ever seen before. Female warriors carrying a stone tablet with a seven-segmented golden snake out of a vibrant forest—it was the sort of picture that an archaeologist could spend years, perhaps a lifetime, studying.

Jack didn't need a lifetime to know that the mural—as mysterious as its details may have been—was further evidence that the Temple of Artemis wasn't built by Greeks to worship a goddess. And with that, he was one step closer to proving that the culture he had become obsessed with—the culture most historians, archaeologists, and anthropologists believed was more myth than real—had actually once existed.

"Amazons," Jack said, shooting picture after picture with the digital camera. "The women in this mural are Amazons."

The weight of what he was saying reverberated through his chest. The Amazons, a fierce tribe of women warriors dating all the way back to the beginnings of mythology and history, had been the subject of Jack's research for nearly half a decade. He had written a dozen papers about various relics and ancient documents that pointed to an incredibly advanced culture. Though nobody was certain who the Amazons were, where they had come from, or why they had eventually disappeared, there was much evidence, in Jack's opinion, that they had once built themselves into a powerful civilization. The individual warriors themselves were so fierce that, according to legend, each woman would cut off her own right breast to better enable her to throw a javelin. With a religion dedicated to serving an all-powerful female goddess—referred to as Diana, Artemis, and even Eve, the original first woman, borrowed by Judeo-Christian theology—Amazons featured in stories that crossed cultural and geographical boundaries. They seemed to be everywhere, from the Bronze Age to Alexander the Great through the Romans and Greeks all the way into Medieval times.

When Jack had learned of a possible connection to one of the Seven Wonders of the World and heard about the discovery of the mantle beneath the dig site, he had quickly used his connections at Princeton to insert his team into the archaeology project. All they'd needed was the help of three of the sites' local workers to unload the equipment Jack had sent ahead of their arrival, assist in cutting through the mantle with a rock drill, and set up the winch and pulley for Jack's harness.

Jack had known he was pushing the boundaries of academic ethics by taking advantage of the Brits, but he wasn't going to wait for the archaeologists; archaeology moved at a snail's pace, with brushes and combs. Field anthropologists dove in head first.

And now Jack had made what might very well be the discovery of his career. A mural depicting Amazons carrying some sort of golden snake out of a forest, painted deep within one of the Seven Wonders of the Ancient World.

He was still taking photos, his head swimming with images of female warriors and war javelins, when he heard Dashia's voice crackling over the speaker in his helmet.

"Dr. Grady."

"What is it?" Jack responded, leaning closer to a spot on the mural to get a good picture of one of the warrior's armor.

"It's your cell phone. I wasn't going to answer, but they kept calling."

Jack could hear the sudden tremor in her voice.

"Your brother. He's—Dr. Grady, you need to come back up here."

Jack paused. *His brother?* He couldn't imagine that anything involving Jeremy could be more important than what he was looking at, but he'd never heard Dashia sound so emotional before. He glanced at his watch—four a.m. With any luck, he'd still have a couple of hours before the Brits took over the site and kicked his group out. He could deal with whatever Dashia was so worked up about and still get back down for a second look.

"Okay, on my way."

With enormous effort, he tore himself away from the warriors, the forest, and the gold, segmented snake, and started back up the gravely slope, dragging the aluminum rope behind him.

CHAPTER THREE

Sloane Costa dug her fingernails into the stone wall as she shuffled her feet a few steps forward along the six-inch ledge. Her calves felt like they were on fire from the effort, the heels of her field boots hanging out over the four-foot-deep ditch. An hour a day on the elliptical back in the gym at Michigan State had not prepared her for whatever the hell this was, but then again, nothing in her precise, organized life could have prepared her for what she had stumbled into over the past three hours.

She took a deep breath, then glanced down past her heels. It was hard to see clearly in the dim morning light seeping through the spiderweb of cracks in the curved tunnel's ceiling, but she guessed she still had about five yards to go. The ditch appeared to end just as it had begun; a sudden, eight-yard gash in the cobbled floor of the tunnel, bordered on each side by just the tiniest of ledges.

When she'd first come upon the ditch, she'd considered climbing down instead of trying to shuffle across. Four feet wasn't that far; she'd already clambered down a rotted-out stairwell to get into the tunnel in the first place.

But then she'd looked closer, using the light from her miniature flashlight to illuminate the tangle of vegetation that filled the bottom of the ditch like twisting rolls of barbed wire. It had taken her almost two minutes to

25

identify the long, ovate leaves and the bell-shaped, dark brown flowers: *Letalis belladonna*, from the family *Solanaceae*, a distant cousin to the more well-known *Atropa belladonna*. Even though she couldn't see the vine's miniscule thorns hidden beneath its curled leaves, she knew what would happen if she took one step into that ditch. A single scratch, and her bloodstream would be coursing with the toxins scopolamine and hyoscyamine. A few minutes after that, she'd have the dubious distinction of being the first botanical geneticist to be killed by a plant.

She put her cheek flush with the stone wall and shuffled another few inches along the ledge. She considered herself in pretty good shape for a twenty-six-year-old scientist; she'd run two half marathons since completing her master's and tried her best to get to the gym every morning before locking herself in the lab. On the two days a week she was forced to teach undergrads to maintain her assistant professorship at Michigan State, she jogged the entire five miles to campus from her studio apartment at the edge of East Lansing.

But she was learning that there was a big difference between sweating your way through a training session in a state-of-the-art gym and being out in the field, dragging yourself deep through the bowels of one of the greatest structures in Europe, if not the world.

She took another careful step, then paused to listen for any Italian voices that might signal that the pair of Polizia who had first escorted her through the locked front entrance to the Colosseum—one of the oldest amphitheaters on Earth, the pride of the city of Rome, and one of the Seven Wonders of the Modern World—had noticed she had disappeared. Just a few minutes past five in the morning on a hazy Saturday at the end of August, the middle-aged Italian officers had been easy to slip; once they'd led her down the refurbished stairway that led into the vast, two-level hypogeum—the underground labyrinth of narrow alleys, sloped tunnels, and dead-end cubbyholes that had once run underneath the arena floor—they had been content to sit next to one another on the bottom step, sharing a pack of cigarettes. The Polizia had-n't spoken two words to her since she'd gotten Professor Lindhom, who'd spent three years as a visiting lecturer at the prestigious University of Roma, to call in a favor with the officer in charge of their garrison, getting them to bring her to the tourist attraction four hours before its opening time. Which was a good thing, since Sloane's Italian was more than a little rusty, to the embarrassment of her grandmother, who still spoke with such a heavy accent she might as well have just stepped off the boat at Ellis Island.

Still, Sloane hadn't expected to have been gone from her two irritated keepers for anywhere near this long. She gritted her teeth and took the last few steps along the ledge, then leaped back onto solid ground. She was relieved to hear the scrape of firm cobblestones against her boots. The tunnel was narrower here, the light from above even more obscured by the levels of hypogeum above. As she started forward again, carefully navigating along the cobblestones, she wished she'd packed a better flashlight along with the handful of tools she'd loaded into her backpack. She wasn't experienced at fieldwork; she'd made her bones in the lab, analyzing botanical specimens collected by others. Of course, she'd had to accompany Professor Lindhom on a handful of expeditions during her training, but she'd always deferred the dirty work to the more eager doctoral students, the ones who seemed to get off on backpacking across the Sichuan-Hubei region of China, climbing a thirty-foot *Metasequoia glyptostroboides* to collect a single leaf, or scaling a three-hundred-foot cliff in Patagonia to find the seeds of a *Fitzroya cupressoides*.

Sloane had never been built that way. She'd always been a bit of a geek growing up, burying herself in books and computers in her suburban bed-room not ten miles from where she now lived in Michigan, while her two older sisters shuttled from field hockey practice to ballet lessons. She'd hardly even dated in high school and college, telling herself that true scientists didn't have time for trivial distractions like men; she'd never even

27

owned a television set, and she'd been to maybe three movies since she'd turned eighteen.

Her oldest sister, Christine, had often joked that Sloane had chosen to dedicate her life to the study of plants because she was basically a plant herself. Sloane didn't take this entirely as an insult. There was something pure and logical about plant life, especially when you broke plants down to their internal elements. Not the pistols, stems, seeds, and leaves that kids learned about in grade school; deeper down, at the cellular level. Botanical DNA had a simplicity to it that filled Sloane with a sense of comfort and purpose. After receiving her master's, she had done her best to carve out a place in what was an obscure science: tracing the evolution of certain plant species by way of their DNA. It was painstaking, boring science involving test tubes and microscopes, but hopefully, important enough to lock down funding to keep Sloane's academic posting for enough years to earn herself a full professorship, and down the line, when Lindhom eventually retired, maybe even tenure.

Christine's jibes aside, the idea that you could trace a plant back to its historical origins through its cellular chemistry spoke to the order Sloane had always looked for in the world around her. She knew that human DNA worked along the same sense of logic. In fact, during her master's she was third author on an article outlining research that had led to the groundbreaking theory of Mitochondrial Eve—the evolutionary concept that all humanity could trace its origins to a single woman who lived around two hundred thousand years ago, somewhere in present-day Africa. Mitochondrial Eve was the Holy Grail of evolutionary science, one ancient woman whose DNA was the perfect, pure source of every generation that came after her.

Sloane wasn't tunneling through the Colosseum, her boots kicking up dust older than Christianity, expecting to find the equivalent to Mitochondrial Eve in the plant world; but to her, the mystery she was trying to unravel felt just as important. Christine might never understand, but even the greatest accomplishments of mankind—let alone some field hockey championship or ballet performance—seemed no more impressive to Sloane than the glory of a single, perfect *Leucobalanus* leaf that represented tens of thousands of years of evolutionary struggle, surviving fires, storms, pestilence, the rise and fall of civilization after civilization. And all Christine would ever see was the leaf of a common oak.

Sloane felt her way down the cobblestones, running the flashlight over the stone walls to her right and left, moving much more cautiously since she'd narrowly avoided the ditch and the poisonous vines. It wasn't oak leaves she'd ditched the two Polizia for, though she wouldn't have been surprised to find an oak sapling or two poking out from one of the numerous creases and gashes that she'd seen all over the hypogeum. From the very moment she'd set foot in the Modern Wonder, she'd been awed by vastness of the place, the scale of something built so goddamn long ago. But unlike other tourists who found their way into the Colosseum, it wasn't the architecture or the history that truly enthralled her. It was something that most tourists would hardly notice at all.

To Sloane, the subterranean tunnels were as fascinating as any imagined gladiator battle. Even without the help of a tour guide, she could make out the various notches and holes in the stone that were the remaining evidence of the machinery that had once functioned literally beneath the scenes: vertical shafts that had once held cages that could be lifted into the arena, depositing men, wild beasts, even scenery. Elevators, complex pulleys, hydraulics, most of it controlled by capstans—giant wheels pushed by slaves like enormous gears in the biggest watch ever constructed.

And even more incredible, as Sloane picked her way through the tunnels, pulling farther and farther from the Polizia, was the evidence of runoff canals she could see, often at waist level, dug right into the sides of the tunnels. She'd read in guide books that the entire arena could be flooded for the *naumachiae*, mock ocean battles that had involved small warships sailing through water as deep as nine feet.

But Sloane's fascination with the mechanics of the hypogeum was mainly academic; what truly thrilled her were the incredible wonders she was seeing within the cracks, seams, and cubbyholes dug into the ancient stone. She'd read about what she was seeing, but until she'd climbed under the rope and the bright red PERICOLO! sign—a warning she didn't need her grandmother to understand—and had started to observe the true diversity sprouting from every nook and gash in the elaborate tunnels of travertine stone, she didn't truly believe it could be real.

Sloane wasn't the first scientist to come to the Colosseum to study plants. According to the guidebooks, the Colosseum had one of the strangest botanical collections of any place on Earth. Vines, shrubs, and even trees had been found growing through the ancient ruins, a diversity that had yet to be adequately explained by modern science.

The first recorded study of the Colosseum's plants had been done way back in 1643 by a scientist named Domenico Panaroli who had listed over six hundred and eighty different species. Barely two turns in the first tunnel Sloane had crawled through, she wondered if old Domenico had undersold the place. She'd lost count after a hundred different species—some from as far away as China's South Sea, and some, like the deadly poisonous cousin of nightshade she'd almost stepped into, exceedingly rare. But it wasn't just the diversity of species that intrigued Sloane; she could imagine that many seeds had been inadvertently carried on the hooves and in the coats of the various animals brought into the arena, or that the millions of tourists and spectators who'd wandered through the place over the centuries had acted as human vectors, depositing seed specimens as they went. What surprised Sloane—and bothered her, as she began to think it through—was the diversity of *time periods* the various species represented. Plants with DNA ages hundreds to thousands of years apart growing right next to each other in seams in the tunnel walls, sometimes woven together in impossible tangles.

It was just this sort of mystery that had led her to the Colosseum in the first place. The envelope that was now sitting on the tiny desk in her hotel room had been sent to her by an Italian professor of botany she'd met online in a plant DNA chat room. (That such a place even existed would have given Christine a month's worth of material, but Sloane couldn't have cared less.) The envelope the man had sent her had contained a single seed he'd collected at the opening of one of the runoff drainage tunnels deep in the second level of the hypogeum—a single seed that Sloane had analyzed down to its DNA core.

A single seed that contained proteins much older than it should have, older than the Colosseum itself. In fact, that single seed had contained DNA fragments that—if Sloane's science was correct—predated the construction of the city of Rome.

So Sloane had immediately begun the process that had led her, three weeks later, to a narrowing tunnel in the depths of the hypogeum. She was certain that analyzing the DNA history of this bizarre seed, and the plant it must have come from, would be just the sort of research to secure continued funding for her work—and maybe jump her right to that full professorship.

Her calves still burning from the trip across the ditch, she came to another bend in the tunnel and another gradual slope downward. The roof seemed to be getting lower as well; she had to bend a few inches at the waist to keep the top of her high ponytail from touching the curved stone panels, or catching on what was left of the rusting iron clamps that held them in place. This was the fifth, maybe sixth turn in tunnel since she'd entered the runoff channel pictured on the back of the envelope, the place where her Italian colleague had found the strange seed. The fact that she'd entered the tunnel in the first place had surprised her; the Italian professor had been content with the single seed, rather than chancing what could very well have been an unexplored section of the hypogeum. But Sloane was determined; a seed was one thing, a living plant would be her own Holy Grail.

As she turned the corner and shined the miniature flashlight down into the narrowing space, she saw something that made her forget about the heat tearing through her calves.

The vine twisting and tangling across two connected slabs of stone was unlike anything she had ever seen before. Red-tinged, almost leafless, it was covered in thorns, many as big as her thumb. She racked her brain for any memories of anything even remotely similar as she quickly covered the distance. There was a vine she'd seen in a textbook, incredibly rare, something that had been discovered growing at some sort of religious shrine near an Egyptian village along the Nile, that had a similar red tinge to it. And another vine, with thorns of a similar shape, that she'd read about explorers documenting during a trip through Equatorial New Guinea.

But now that she was only a few feet away, reaching into her backpack to retrieve her latex gloves and her plastic specimen containers, she knew that what she was looking at had never been written about in any textbook. As she pulled the gloves on over her long fingers, holding the flashlight in her teeth, she could even make out a few of the vine's little seeds hanging beneath reddish bulbs between some of the thorns—the same shape, color, and texture as the seed her colleague had found at the entrance to the runoff.

Sloane was looking at something both new and very, very old. Still not daring to touch the plant, even gloved, she followed its structure with her eyes. Twisting and turning, she traced it up the stone to a seam at the very top, right against one of the iron clamps, where the vine seemed to disappear into the very structure of the tunnel wall.

Curiouser and curiouser. She glanced up toward the ceiling at the tiny fissures still letting wisps of early sunlight into the confines of the tunnel. Not much light, but certainly enough for the processes of photosynthesis. Plants grew in some of the deepest caves ever found, and thousands of feet below the surface of the oceans. Unlike humans, plants had found ways to survive in the harshest climates imaginable.

But as Sloane moved even closer to the vines—her face now just inches away from the angry-looking red thorns and leafless stems—she noticed something even more peculiar than the way the vine seemed to vanish into the stones.

She wasn't sure, but she thought she could make something out behind the tangle of vine, something carved right into the wall of the tunnel. She couldn't imagine that anything man-made would rival the botanical beauty she had just discovered, but she found herself intrigued enough to take a look.

With extreme care, doing everything she could to avoid the thorns, she gingerly began pulling the red vines apart. At first, it was difficult; the vines seemed to pull back against her, and twice her hands almost slipped, her gloved fingers almost touching one of the oversize thorns. But then the vine started to give way. A moment later, she'd gotten through the twists and tangles and found herself face-to-face with a visage carved directly into the ancient stone wall.

A woman's face. Vaguely African, wearing what appeared to be an Egyptian headdress. Beneath the face, also carved into the stone, were row after row of Roman letters and Egyptian hieroglyphs.

Christ. As a botanist, Sloane had studied a little Latin and Greek to better understand the various names of the plants beneath her microscopes, but apart from that, her grasp of ancient languages was pretty weak. The hieroglyphics were just pictures to her. But she could make out some of the Latin; specifically, halfway down the lettering, she recognized a single name: *Cleopatra*. Beyond that, her best guess was that the writing was some sort of dedication to the famed female pharaoh.

She paused, her gloved hands still holding back the vines. She wasn't certain, but she believed that Cleopatra would have been born right around the time of the construction of the Colosseum. She knew from the movies and television shows Christine had gabbed on about that Cleopatra had some sort of romantic involvement with a couple different Roman leaders:

Julius Caesar and Mark Antony. But other than that, she couldn't fathom why someone had carved a picture and dedication to Cleopatra into one of the greatest Roman constructions.

As she pondered the question, her gaze drifted back to the hieroglyphics. Most of it was strange squiggles and incomprehensible shapes; but then her eyes settled on an image that was strangely familiar:

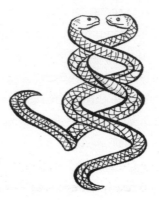

Two opposing snakes twisted together, intertwined in what appeared to be a double helix. At the very bottom, the tail of one of the snakes twisted off in the wrong direction—but other than the tail, the snakes seemed to be in a very close approximation to the shape of DNA.

Sloane smiled, chiding herself for letting her own mental character color what she was looking at; the double helix was a fairly common geometric image, and it wasn't always associated with DNA. In fact, double helixes had been popping up in artwork, archaeology, and mathematical modeling since well before the discovery of DNA. Sloane remembered reading somewhere that there were even ancient Sumerian tablets imprinted with double helixes, dating back more than eight thousand years.

Still, the image was incredibly compelling. As Sloane peered closer, she noticed that there were tiny scratch marks along both snakes, segmenting them into seven perfectly symmetrical pieces. Without even thinking about what she was doing, she reached forward with a finger and brushed it along the errant tail.

With a start, she realized that the tail wasn't simply carved into the wall; it was attached to the stone by some sort of internal mechanism—and it was movable. Even the slightest pressure of her gloved finger against the tail caused it to shift a few centimeters.

Almost by reflex, she used a second finger to push the errant tail back toward its symmetrical opposite, completing the perfect double helix. With a click, the tail locked into place.

There was a two second lag—and then suddenly, the sound of stone grinding against stone reverberated through the tunnel. The stone face of Cleopatra trembled—and then slid down, disappearing beneath the tangle of red vines.

In Cleopatra's place, Sloane found herself staring at a vivid, brightly colored painting. The painting was nearly twice as large as the face that had covered it, much of it hidden behind the vines that Sloane could only partially hold back. But she could clearly make out an incredible scene: a group of women carrying what looked to be white javelins, marching out of an incredibly detailed forest. The women were impressive; warriors, obviously, girded for war. But Sloane's attention was drawn to the forest. Some of the plant life she could recognize; ancient fronds from various palm families, cedars and fig trees from different parts of the Middle East, Baobabs and Mesquites from the Horn of Africa. Others were complete mysteries. And then she saw the red vines, curling around the warrior women's feet, nearly covering the ground where they were walking on their way out of the forest.

She realized it wasn't a forest, it was a garden. These disparate trees and plants wouldn't be found together, wouldn't survive together, unless they had been brought there, planted, and tended.

Sloane used one hand to reach into her backpack and retrieve a small scalpel and one of her plastic specimen containers. Carefully, she leaned forward and scraped a tiny portion of the painting into the plastic well. She wasn't certain, but bright paint like that, from an ancient origin, was most likely botanical in origin.

It wasn't until she had sealed the container with the paint chip and placed it into her backpack that she noticed what the tribe of female warriors was carrying on their way out of the garden.

A flat stone tile—and chiseled directly into the stone, a single, segmented gold snake.

When Sloane touched the object with her fingers, she realized that one of the segments was raised a few centimeters above the rest. As she pressed at the seams, the segment clicked out of the stone and into her gloved palm.

She stepped back, holding the snake segment in her open hand. It was heavy, like a paperweight, and when she turned it on one end, she could see that it was filled with what appeared to be mechanical gears. She also noticed that the gold coloring was just plate; the snake segment seemed to be made out of bronze.

Sloane stood there for what seemed like a very long time, trying to make sense of what she had found. Something mechanical and bronze, hidden behind vines that predated the Roman Colosseum by centuries. An object placed behind a dedication to the Egyptian pharaoh Cleopatra, one of the most powerful women in human history. An artifact found by solving a puzzle involving a double helix, the shape of the building block of life.

None of it made any sense—but there was no question that Sloane had stumbled into something much bigger than a strange little seed.

She placed the bronze snake segment in her backpack, next to the sealed flake of ancient paint. She took her cell phone out of her pocket and took a half dozen photos of the painting on the stone. Then she turned and started back through the labyrinthine tunnels of the hypogeum, toward the waiting Polizia.

CHAPTER FOUR

There is nothing more final than an autopsy table.

Jack tried his best to keep his attention focused on the stack of forms on the low counter ahead of him, but his gaze kept wandering across the harshly lit pathology lab to the pair of empty tables by the far wall. The corrugated aluminum frames, the eggshell-blue operating slabs, the shiny, stainless steel blood gutters that ran along each edge. Jack was thankful that both tables were empty, but he knew that at that very moment, in one of the half dozen other labs down the narrow hallway from where they'd sequestered him, his brother was on a table just like those.

Jack noticed that his fingers were trembling as he moved his pen across one of the forms. The woman with the bouffant of gunmetal gray hair standing next to him at the counter must have noticed too, because she put a hand on his shoulder.

"You don't have to do this right now. The paperwork can wait."

Jack hadn't realized there would be so many forms to fill out when your brother was murdered. Medical histories, insurance documents, autopsy permissions—and all this was in addition to what he'd gone through at the police station when he'd first arrived back in Boston. Three hours in a room with two detectives who had many more questions than answers.

"Is there anyone else we can call?" the woman asked, echoing the refrain from the police inquiry, after they'd realized that Jack knew very little about his brothers' day-to-day life.

In fact, in many ways, his twin brother was a stranger to Jack, going back deep into childhood. The only who who'd truly known his brother was their mother, and she had died almost a decade ago. Jack had already left a dozen messages for their father on the most recent voice-mail number he had stored in his phone, but he didn't expect to see the man stroll into the pathology wing of Mass General anytime soon. It had been over a year since Kyle Grady's last contact—a brief e-mail from a double blind server somewhere deep in Sub-Saharan Africa, where the elder Grady was about to embark on his latest adventure. Something about a lost tribe and a mythical Maasai warlord; Jack had long ago given up trying to keep track of their father's whereabouts. The last time the man had gone off on an exploration, he had been out of touch for more than four years. Then he'd shown up out of the blue, right in the middle of an Introduction to Anthropology seminar Jack had been giving to a group of incoming freshman at Princeton; just wandered right to the front of Jack's classroom, plopping his worn leather saddlebag down on Jack's desk, launching into a meandering tale about some epic jaunt up the tallest peak in the Andes, where he'd gone to live with a family of Sherpas for some book he was writing. Jack didn't even know if the voice-mail number was current—not that it mattered. By now, Kyle Grady was probably so deep in the bush, garbed in a grass skirt and covered in Maasai war paint, Jack wouldn't have recognized him if he'd walked through the door.

Which was just as well, because his brother, Jeremy, had always hated their father. Even before their parents had gotten divorced, Kyle Grady had no idea how to interact with a kid as introverted and troubled as Jeremy, and he'd pretty much ignored Jack's twin when he wasn't off in some foreign land, living with pygmies or shepherds or tribesmen. After the divorce, their mother had raised Jeremy exclusively. Jack had gone back and forth between both parents; at seventeen, for the last year before he shipped off to Princeton, he'd even moved in with his father full-time. It had been a learning experience. A dozen times over the year, his father had simply disappeared for weeks on end. No warning, no food left in the refrigerator, no money or car keys or even a checkbook to pay for electricity or heat.

"There's no one else," Jack said, steadying the pen against the top form.

"No friends? Colleagues?"

Jack knew that the woman was trying to be helpful. The hospital had assigned her to wait with him while the autopsy was taking place down the hall. She probably had a psychology degree, and spent most of her time gently patting the shoulders of people who'd just lost family members.

"I'm sure he has colleagues. I doubt he had any friends."

It was a terrible thought, but Jack knew it was true. Jeremy was different, or as their mother liked to put it, special. The smartest person Jack had ever met, a whiz with numbers and computers who couldn't carry on the most basic conversation with a stranger to save his life. As far as Jack knew, Jeremy had never gone to a party, gone on a date, or even had dinner with anyone who wasn't a blood relation. He was probably somewhere on the Autism-Asperger continuum, though their mother would never have allowed anyone to label him. She was the reason he'd been able to go so far; halfway through his PhD at MIT, a brilliant programmer who would have probably ended up in a backroom at Google or Facebook, making millions.

Except now, he was lying on an autopsy table, filling those stainless-steel gutters as a pathologist gathered evidence for the detectives who were still sifting their way through the crime scene.

Even twenty-four hours after a janitor had found the body and called the police, the detectives still had almost nothing to go on. According to the officers who had questioned Jack when he'd arrived off the plane, the high security laboratory where they'd found Jeremy's body had been scoured clean; no fingerprints, no shoeprints, no hair follicles, no DNA, and no murder weapon. No sign of forced entry; although from what Jack could gather, the underground lab wasn't exactly Fort Knox. Jeremy hadn't had clearance, but he'd had no trouble fooling his way in. The detectives were still trying to reconstruct Jeremy's last few days; nobody knew him well enough to have any idea what he was working on that would lead him to that particular lab. The head of his department, a Professor Earl Johnson, had described Jeremy as an "autonomous coding machine," meaning nobody really kept tabs on him. At MIT, that was par for the course: The merely smart had to follow the rules, but true genius roamed free.

"We weren't very close," Jack added.

The tinge of guilt that moved through him at the words was palpable. The distance between Jack and Jeremy was something that had bothered him since their teenage years. Many times, he'd tried to address it—a late night phone call, a long, emotional letter, an impromptu visit. None of his efforts had ever led anywhere. A phone call with Jeremy was like speaking into a tape recorder. Maybe you got a noise here and there when it was time to turn over the tape, but otherwise you were talking to yourself. Letters went unanswered, and visits invariably ended in an argument.

Like Jack's last and final visit just a few days ago, the tenth anniversary of their mother's death. Jack had started the tradition as yet another way to try and reach out to his twin; and over the years, there had been a few moments when it had seemed to be working: an emotional moment here and there, at the cemetery, on the drive from the airport, over dinner at one of the local burger joints near the MIT campus. But usually, those moments had quickly evaporated, replaced by pointless bickering.

Jack couldn't even remember much of what their last argument was concerning. He'd been excited to tell his brother about his upcoming expedition to Turkey, and then they'd gone off on some tangent about the Seven

Wonders of the World—and that was pretty much the end of his visit. They simply couldn't connect, they were just too damn different.

And now Jack would never have the chance to change that.

Jack's thoughts were interrupted by a whiff of antiseptic air as the glass door to the lab swung inward. Jack recognized the pathologist from his ring of wiry brown hair, now matted with sweat. He was wearing fresh scrubs and had ditched his latex gloves, but otherwise, he looked the same as he had earlier that morning, when Jack had been brought in to ID the body.

"Ms. Whitehead, if you could give us a moment."

The woman gave Jack's shoulder a carefully trained squeeze, then left the two of them alone in the lab. The pathologist pulled up a stool next to the counter where Jack was sitting and placed a plastic evidence bag on the surface between them.

"This isn't exactly protocol, but I've already checked with Detectives Murphy and Collins, and they've hit such a wall in their investigation, they were willing to give me a little leeway. Considering your area of expertise, I figured maybe you could help me out."

Jack glanced down at the plastic bag. Inside, he could make out something tiny—a sliver, or a splinter—of some sort of white material.

"My area of expertise?"

"I've read a few of your articles in *Science* and saw the documentary you did for Discovery a couple years back. I didn't make the connection when we first met, but while I was working on your brother, I realized there can't be many anthropologists who focus on ancient cultures."

Jack raised his eyebrows. It wasn't surprising that the pathologist had recognized his name; doctors subscribed to *Science* and watched the Discovery Channel, and a few of Jack's pieces had gotten a fair amount of attention. In particular, the video diary of the research journey he'd taken into Eskimo country in the Canadian Arctic had been one of the most downloaded series of anthropological pieces of the year—especially when on day thirty-seven, he'd nearly gotten himself buried in an ice flow and instead had uncovered evidence of an ancient Viking expedition to the area.

Andy had gotten great enjoyment out of reading aloud the fan mail that had come in after that excursion—including at least three proposals of marriage. Jack guessed the proposals had more to do with the fact that his shirt had been shredded as he'd climbed free of the ice, rather than the pair of rusted Viking swords and the wooden remains of the ship he had handed off to the nearest Canadian Royal Museum.

Jack could only imagine the sort of mail he would be getting after he published his work on the Temple of Artemis. If Vikings were sexy enough to get him interviewed on a handful of basic cable morning shows, Amazons would probably land him squarely in prime time.

"How can I help?" Jack asked.

"The autopsy confirms that your brother died from injuries sustained via sharp forced trauma; there was no tissue bridging, no signs of alternate lacerations. The wound edges remained well approximated, with very little differentiation between the entrance and exit. The projectile—for lack of a better word for it—entered the right hemithorax below the anterior aspect of the right sixth rib, and exited in the right infrascapular region below the posterior aspect of the sixth rib. These findings, along with the lack of trace evidence—hair, fibers, DNA on the victim's body—leads me to suspect that the projectile was thrown from a distance of between four and five feet."

Jack looked at the man.

"Thrown?"

"Yes. Furthermore, from the angle of entry and the form of the damage, I believe we're looking for a pointed object with a diameter of about three centimeters that is probably between two and four feet long."

"My brother was killed with a spear?"

The pathologist pointed to the plastic evidence bag on the counter between them.

"That isn't even the really strange part."

Jack looked more closely at the white sliver of material in the bag.

"This fragment was found lodged in a paraspinous muscle—the muscles surrounding the spine. From our spectrographic and chem analysis, we believe it's a fragment of pure ivory. Which is why I thought maybe you could help us figure out where it came from."

"Why me?"

"The chem analysis seems to indicate that this ivory is older than anything I've ever seen in my lab before. Too old for me to even date with anything available to me here. I'm going to send it out for analysis—but I was hoping you might have some idea where it came from."

"You're saying that my brother was killed by a spear made out of extremely old ivory."

The use of ivory dated back to prehistoric times; nearly every ancient culture had utilized the tusks of elephants in art, religious artifacts, and in weaponry. But the idea that some sort of ivory weapon had been used to kill his brother—it was beyond conception.

Jack shook his head.

"My brother was a computer scientist. I can't imagine why anyone would want to kill him—or where this ivory came from."

The doctor thanked him for his time and offered his condolences. Jack was barely listening as the man retrieved the evidence bag and headed back across the lab. A mixture of emotions was rising inside of Jack. Sadness at the loss of a brother, guilt that he'd never had the chance to fix their relationship—and most powerful of all, anger that Jeremy had died in such a violent, terrible way.

There was nothing Jack could do about the first two emotions—but the anger was something he intended to use.

CHAPTER FIVE

Clambering two stories down a steel-framed emergency ladder in an eleva-tor shaft on the MIT campus was a hell of a lot easier than rappelling down an aluminum thread in a nearly bottomless pit beneath a dig site in Turkey. For one thing, Jack didn't have to worry about Andy Chen braying in his ear. Instead of a crash helmet, Jack was fogging up the transparent plastic face shield of a Level B hazmat suit. And Andy was safely camped out in the utility closet in the Infinite Corridor with the floppy-haired sophomore who'd led them to the ventilation access point to the shaft and loaned Jack the biohazard suit.

Even in the cramped quarters of the elevator shaft, the suit was surpris-ingly comfortable. The thick white material covered his entire body, sealed at the wrists, neck, and ankles beneath his boots. The oxygen tank on his back, hanging from an oversize black backpack, was only a quarter full, but Jack wasn't worried about suffocating; he'd opened the valve on the suit's respirator. It was one thing to stay in character, but there was no need to go overboard.

The kid with the floppy hair hadn't had any trouble lifting the suit from the biology lab where he was working on a master's that had something to do with a modified form of smallpox—though Jack didn't really want to know anymore, since he was now breathing the guy's recycled air. Jack didn't love that they were relying on the help of a nineteen-year-old, no matter how smart he was, or how many proteins he'd named in just his second year at MIT. Like Andy, he was just a kid. But he'd also known about the utility closet that had shared a wall with the elevator shaft, and how to get through the ventilation panel that bypassed the elevator's security desk, which had been taken over by a pair of officers from the Boston Police Department.

Jack took the last three rungs on the ladder, then dropped to the cement floor, directly across the shaft from the interior of the doors that led to the basement hallway. Then he glanced up again to make sure the elevator was still fully perched on the top floor. He doubted anyone would be making the trip down to the underground security labs at four in the morning, but getting crushed by an elevator while attempting to commit a felony was not high on Jack's list of ways he wanted to die.

When Jack left the pathology lab, he had come to the sudden conclusion that getting into the crime scene was his necessary next step. The police had already given him the impression that they had very little to go on, and Jack didn't have the kind of personality where he could sit on the sidelines and wait for someone else to do the hard work.

Once he'd made the decision, it had seemed natural to involve Andy. Jack trusted his prized grad student with his life—had literally done so more times than he could count. But when Andy had first suggested they reach out to some of his contacts in the graduate community, Jack had balked at the idea. He was willing to take the risk, but he didn't want to involve a bunch of college kids in something that could them all arrested.

Eventually, Andy had convinced him that it was their best option, and besides, MIT had a tradition of flouting authority; campus pranks were legendary, like the time a group of seniors had taken the Dean of Students' car apart and rebuilt it on top of the big dome, a hundred feet above the student center. Or the time a group of engineering students had rewired the windows in the physics building to play an enormous game of Tetris that the entire city of Boston could watch.

Once he'd given the okay, Jack had been amazed at how fast Andy had been able to find what they were looking for. Although Andy had done his undergraduate work in Princeton, he had been a fixture at the Academic Decathlon championships that were held at MIT every fall. You didn't forget losing to a wiseass genius like Andy Chen every year.

The floppy-haired sophomore hadn't been the only undergrad on Andy's e-mail chain to respond to Andy's request for help, but he'd been the most creative. He'd known exactly where to go to get past the security at the elevator; and he'd also had access to the hazmat suit. Jack was a little terrified about a kid with such ready answers to the task at hand, but he certainly wasn't in the position to judge anyone. He'd been a bit creative as an undergrad at Princeton, too; the local police station had a cell unofficially dedicated to him when he'd graduated—only to see him return as a professor.

Confident that the elevator wasn't going to come down on him, Jack turned his attention to the double elevator doors. He crossed the shaft in three steps, then placed his gloved hands on the seam between the doors. On the second try, he managed to get the toe of one of his boots into the seam along with his fingers, and with a burst of effort, forced the doors wide enough to slide his body through.

The hallway was dark, the only light coming from a pair of pale blue emergency signals attached to police call boxes a few feet from the elevator, and Jack waited a few seconds for his eyes to adjust. Then he was moving forward.

He spotted the uniformed police officer the minute he took the first corner in the hallway; the man couldn't have looked more bored, leaning back as best he could in a metal folding chair, a school newspaper open on his lap. Directly behind him was a closed lab door, covered in bright yellow police tape.

Jack didn't even pause. He took the corner at full pace, then pulled a small Geiger counter out of the backpack that held his oxygen tank, flicked it on, and headed directly toward the officer.

The man didn't notice his approach until he was about two feet away. Then the cop looked up, saw the hazmat suit—and his eyes nearly bugged out of his head. He got up from the chair so fast the metal seat folded up into the frame, the entire thing clattering to the hallway floor.

"What the hell?"

Jack kept his attention on the Geiger counter, which was now chirping away, louder by the second as his finger shifted against the volume control.

"Nothing to worry about, officer. Just a little spill in one of the labs upstairs, happens all the time. They got me down here looking for runoff—whoops, that's odd."

Jack hit the volume again, causing the counter to chirp loud enough to send a piercing echo up and down the hall. Then he looked up toward the ceiling and held the Geiger in the air, just a few inches from the policeman's face.

"Getting a little reading here. You might want to move your chair to the other side of the hallway while I check this out."

The police officer was staring at the Geiger counter with eyes as wide as saucers. Then he looked at Jack's fogged up face mask. Jack could see the terror in the poor man's features.

"What kind of spill?"

Jack was running the Geiger counter along the wall, just to the left of the police tape, completely ignoring the officer.

"These damned hard elements, they get out of your controlled system, no telling where they're going to end up. Seep right on through the floor tiles, into the piping, get into the airflow—and then I'm up all night mopping up. Some freaking grad student overturns a beaker, we've got a radioactive incident on our hands, am I right?"

The officer nearly choked on his tongue. He took a step back.

"Radioactive?"

Jack glanced at him through the faceplate.

"Like I said, you probably want to move your chair over to the other side of the hallway. I'm going to have to get some scrubbers down here and deal with this."

The officer shook his head, backing away down the hallway, toward the elevators.

"Fuck that. I'll be upstairs by the security desk."

Jack shrugged.

"Suit yourself." Then he glanced down at the school newspaper, on the floor by the collapsed folding chair. "Probably going to have to burn the newspaper. Maybe the chair, too."

The man was almost jogging now. As he disappeared around the corner, Jack could hear the officer's radio coughing to life. Jack knew he would call it in to his superiors—but at four in the morning, Jack figured it would take some time for them to sort out what to do. This was a scientific institution, with plenty of labs and storage rooms filled with dangerous materials. And hazmat suits were like the modern-day version of medieval plague masks; you showed up in a hazmat suit, nobody stuck around very long to ask questions.

When he was sure the officer was far enough away, he exchanged the Geiger counter for a small pocketknife and turned to the lab door covered in police tape.

He made short work of the tape, then turned his attention to the door's magnetic lock, attached shoulder-high to the doorframe. It was a simple key-card system; Jack knew that Dashia and Andy would have been able to come up with a sophisticated hack to get through the lock, but Jack had never been one for subtleties. He jammed the sharp edge of the knife into the crease where the magnetic lock attached to the door, then pulled as hard as he could. There was a spray of sparks, and then the magnetic lock tore free. He stepped back and put his boot to the door, four inches from the doorknob.

The door crashed inward, the doorknob and part of the frame clattering to the floor. If the place was alarmed, Jack knew his "me" time was about to get much shorter. He quickly found the light switch, and two oversized fluorescent panels flickered across the low ceiling, illuminating a sophisticated, if somewhat sparse, computer lab. Corrugated steel shelves, counters filled with servers, routers, spaghetti curls of fiber-optic wires. Even some beakers and testtubes, though Jack had no idea what programmers needed with glassware.

Then his attention was drawn to the glass desk on the far side of the room—and the overturned leather chair beneath it, resting on the paneled floor beside a white chalk outline.

Jack's mouth went dry as he crossed toward the outline. He tried to control the thoughts jamming through his head. It was just chalk, a picture, nothing real, not flesh and blood and bones. Except as he got closer, he could see the dark stain emanating from the chest area of the outline, spreading out under the desk, lapping at the leather of the overturned chair. Jeremy's blood. Jeremy's life.

That outline was Jeremy, his last, brutal moment, as he collapsed onto the floor, some sort of ivory spear jutting from his chest. Jack could see from the drawing that he'd landed forward, angled slightly to the side, one arm outstretched, the other clutching at the thing between his ribs.

Jack dropped to one knee, just inches from the chalk. His face was cold, and he fought to stay in control. He only had a few minutes, and he needed all of his senses. The crime scene specialists had already gone through this lab a dozen times. He could see, glancing around the room, pieces of colored tape attached to various objects, some already tagged and wrapped in plastic evidence bags, logged and ready for transport to the CSI labs. Other pieces of tape near spots on the floor and the nearby wall marked areas of blood splatter. Jack couldn't be sure, but he guessed from the placement of the tags that the crime scene specialists had been working in a spiral pattern, starting at the door, ending at the chalk outline in front of him.

If the specialists had missed anything, it wasn't going to be something simple or obvious. Jack looked up toward the glass desk, just a few feet away. The desk was empty; the oversize computer flat-screen and the shattered remains of his brother's laptop had already been bagged, cataloged, and brought to the CSI labs. The detectives who'd questioned Jack had told him that both computers had been professionally erased before they'd gotten to them. A thorough job; both hard drives had been magnetically wiped, and then a virus had been implanted to make any sort of data recovery impossible.

Which begged the question: Was it possible that Jeremy had been working on something using the computers that had gotten him killed? Or did the computers somehow contain evidence that would lead to the killer— something as simple as an appointment calendar or a contacts list? The police had already gone through Jeremy's cell phone, and the only number that had come up over the past six months was Jack's. Four calls in total, all of them incoming.

The detectives had been shocked at the idea that Jeremy hadn't made a single outgoing call; Jack only felt embarrassment. Four calls in six months, and none of them lasting over ten minutes. Mostly just logistics surrounding his most recent visit to Boston.

Jack turned back to the chalk outline. He tried not to picture his brother lying there, gasping for air as the blood ran from his body. Reaching out for help, clawing at the floor, maybe trying to find some way to fight back, or to drag himself away from whoever had come to kill him.

And then Jack saw something glinting in the fluorescent light, about a foot beyond the chalk that designated his brother's extended right hand. A small item in a tagged plastic evidence bag, jammed right up against one of the brassy metal legs of the glass desk.

The item in the bag was almost the same color as the desk leg; even from a few feet away, one might easily have missed it, especially in the glare from the fluorescent lights. But the CSI specialists had dutifully marked, and probably fingerprinted and photographed, the object. Eventually, they'd bring it to an evidence locker, when they'd finished reconstructing the last minutes of Jeremy's life.

Jack crawled closer, then gingerly reached for the plastic evidence bag. Holding it in his hands, he was surprised to feel a brief smile moving across his lips. He hadn't known that his brother had kept the scarab that he'd given Jeremy after his first expedition. It was just like Jeremy, to turn something that was supposed to be sentimental into something useful—a keychain. Still, the very idea that his brother carried the gift with him—that he had it on him when he died—touched Jack deep inside.

He decided he would ask for the scarab back when the investigators were done with it; as little and insignificant as it might be, it was a memento of maybe one instance in their relationship that was almost something normal between brothers. Jack was about to place the bag back where he'd found it when his gloved finger felt something through the plastic—a hard edge, right where the scarab had been fitted with the key ring. Jack looked closer—and realized that Jeremy hadn't just glued the ring to the souvenir golden beetle; he'd drilled a hole in the thing, hollowed it out, then attached the ring through the scarab's core. And aside from the ring, it appeared that Jeremy had jammed something else into the hollow core, so deep that only the tiniest edge was still visible. Something hard and plastic, about the size of a thumb.

Jack unsealed the evidence bag and shook the scarab out into his palm. He turned it carefully on its side, and used two fingers to pull the plastic object loose.

A computer thumb drive.

Jack stared at the drive, his mind churning. He knew that the right thing to do would be to head straight to the police station and turn the drive over to the detectives working his brother's homicide. If Jeremy had been using the computers in the secure lab to do something that had led to his murder, the thumb drive might contain evidence that could point to the person who'd killed him.

Then Jack turned from the thumb drive to the golden scarab, still in his other palm. The thumb drive hadn't been in a coat pocket or in a wallet; it had been jammed inside a gift from his twin brother. Jack knew he might be reaching—but his brother was a logical person, to a fault. Like a computer trying to get by in a world full of people.

The thought struck him, like a mallet to his chest.

What if his brother had put the thumb drive in the scarab for a reason?

Jack exhaled, his hand closing over the drive. With his other hand, he carefully placed the empty scarab back into the evidence bag, resealed it, and placed it right where he had found it, against the leg of the desk.

Then he rose to his feet. He gave one last look at the outline on the floor, and then headed for the door. In his mind, it really was just chalk now, a drawing, nothing more. Jeremy was gone; but just maybe, he'd left something behind, in a place he knew his brother might look.

Maybe the detectives had been wrong. Maybe Jeremy had made one last, outgoing call.

• • •

"This is incredible."

Jack collapsed against the bench like a rag doll as Andy lowered himself to an inelegant squat on the grass in front of him, his laptop already open.

They'd been going through the contents of the thumb drive for the past hour—walking like zombies, tracing near circles around the MIT campus, Andy holding his laptop open in front of them like it was some sort of handheld GPS machine. Somewhere between the Infinite Corridor and Killian Court, the grass-covered area in front of Building Ten and the Great Dome where they now found themselves, the sky had gone from a deep, almost purple shade of black to a canopy of grays.

"It's pretty hard to accept," Jack said, rubbing his eyes. The manicured glade in front of them seemed to stretch out the length of a football field, bordered on either side by brick and stone buildings, and directly ahead, by the architecturally striking Building Ten with its façade dominated by ten Ionic columns, and topped by its Great Dome. The building—loosely modeled on the Parthenon in Greece—was geographically at the epicenter of the MIT campus, which was why most graduates knew it as The Center of the Universe. At the moment, sitting there, Jack felt the opposite; his universe had just lost its center, and everything seemed untethered, buffeted by a maddening wind.

"No," Andy said. "I mean this is incredibly fucking awesome. If this is true—but it can't be true, can it?"

Jack could see the screen's reflection flashing across Andy's high cheekbones. The glowing double helix that represented the two sets of six of the Seven Wonders of the World. If it hadn't been Jeremy—and if Jeremy wasn't lying open on an autopsy table at that very moment—he wouldn't have believed it. A link between the Ancient Wonders and the Modern Wonders? The Ancient Wonders of the World had been chosen by ancient Greek historians, but the Modern Wonders were the result of a worldwide vote. And besides, they spanned centuries—millennia, even. How could they possible be linked?

Jack exhaled, then looked past Andy, across the long glade of grass. Other than a lone figure, probably a student, sitting on a bench maybe fifty yards away in the shade of one of the many pin oaks that straddled the open courtyard, the place was deserted.

"I guess it's possible that the vote was manipulated," he finally said. "The contest was run by a Swiss corporation; the results were announced on July 7, 2007, in Lisbon. Over one hundred million people supposedly voted—but it wasn't like people were signing their names to a list."

"That's something we could look into," Andy said. "If someone manipulated the voting, there might be some way to hack into the data and find evidence."

Jack nodded. But that was only a small part of the bizarre mystery that Jeremy had uncovered. The rigged vote, though possible, didn't answer the much, much bigger question.

For what possible reason could six of the Seven Wonders of the World be linked? Built hundreds to thousands of years apart, by cultures vastly different, all over the world? And somehow, if Jeremy's numbers were correct—and Jeremy's numbers had always been correct—built in a pattern that mirrored six of the Ancient Wonders of the World?

"Why only six of them?" Andy asked. "Why not Christ the Redeemer?"

Jack pointed to a notation at the top corner of the computer screen, directly above the brilliant double helix.

"There's a second file. I think it might be some sort of answer."

In the ten minutes he'd had with Jeremy's thumb drive before Andy had taken the laptop from him, he'd gone from simply staring in awe at the glowing double helix, to reading the few notations that had gone along with it—basically, latitudes and longitudes of each of the Seven Wonders, and the basic methodology his brother had used to match up the enantiomers. That's when he had stumbled on the second file.

Andy clicked on the link, and the double helix disappeared, replaced by an instantly recognizable image: Christ the Redeemer, the enormous statue of Jesus Christ on the peak of a mountain overlooking Rio, Brazil, arms spread wide as if to embrace the entire skyline. Then beneath the image, something quite incredible.

"Am I looking at what I think I'm looking at?"

Jack nodded again. It was mostly a set of numerical notations, but also just enough information to tell the story behind the numbers. His brother had found something odd about Christ the Redeemer; something about the topography of the Wonder that Jack was certain he'd never heard about before.

"What does this mean?" Andy asked.

Jack reached past him and hit the computer's keyboard, shifting the screen back to the double helix. He wanted that image to sear itself into his brain; because if his growing suspicions were correct, that image was the reason his brother was lying on an autopsy table.

"It means we pack our bags," Jack said.

Until Jack understood how such an image could exist—and who had been willing to kill Jeremy because of it—he was going to do everything in his power to follow the leads Jeremy had left them. No matter how long it took, or how far they had to go.

For the moment, he only knew one thing for sure.

The first step was a thousand miles away—two thousand feet up the peak of a mountain, in Rio.

• • •

Fifty yards away, the figure on the bench watched as Jack Grady and his graduate student closed the laptop and headed slowly through the center of Killian Court. The figure knew exactly where they were going; Jack Grady's rental car, parked sixteen feet down an alley off of Memorial Drive, almost in the shadow of the Mass Avenue bridge. The figure waited until the two men reached the edge of the grassy court, their backs to her, before retrieving her cell phone from a pocket in her faded leather pants.

She sent a text, then sat back against the bench, waiting for the response. Her entire body was pulsing, her muscles taut, controlled, and eager. Like a coiled spring, waiting for release.

For most of the past day, since she had gotten her orders, she had been following and analyzing the two targets: Jack Grady, since he'd left the police station after his interrogation, and Andy Chen, the graduate student, since he'd checked into a nearby Marriott hotel. Phone records, bank accounts, credit cards—all of the usual information, which was now filed away for future use—but most importantly, their physical attributes and capabilities.

Unlike his twin brother, Jack was tall and lean, well muscled, a natural athlete. His arm span was slightly above average, and his hands had some weight to them, with boxer's knuckles. The other one was shorter, perhaps five-foot-six—no more than a hundred and fifty pounds. But of course, height and weight could be deceiving. She could not count the number of times she herself had been underestimated because of her angled form, because of her narrow hips. Because she was woman.

She liked it when they underestimated her.

She shifted her legs, feeling the blood heating within her coiled muscles.

As soon as she received the text, she would be across the glade in less than eighty seconds. Four seconds after that, she would snap the neck of the graduate student with her bare hands. Six seconds after that, with a single blow three inches above the sternum, she would puncture Jack Grady's aorta with his own shattered rib. Then she would retrieve the laptop computer, and whatever they had found in Jeremy Grady's lab.

She was still visualizing the mission in her head when the cell phone buzzed against her hand. As she read the words, her muscles uncoiled, the blood cooling in her veins.

Jack Grady and his graduate student would not die tonight. The order was still the same; follow, analyze, and report.

She closed the phone and slid it back into her pants. Her heart rate was now back to normal, and she reached behind her head, undid her tight ponytail, and let her jet-black hair cascade over her shoulders. Then she rose from the bench and began to stroll in the general direction of Memorial Drive and Jack Grady's rental car.

She was not disappointed. She knew that eventually, she would be given the order. And she would do exactly what she had been trained, from birth, to do. Like the seven ivory javelins in the quiver hanging down the center of her back, right up against her caramel-colored skin, she would strike with simplicity and speed—the living weapon that she was.

Silent, precise, and absolutely deadly.

CHAPTER SIX

"And they say diamonds are a girl's best friend."

Jendari Saphra feigned a smile as she slid her cell phone back into her Swarovski studded clutch, then took the last three steps that led from the mezzanine to the bottom floor of the grand, two-story hall. The ambient sound was near deafening here, just a few yards from the main clot of partygoers—four hundred of New York's most elegantly coiffed financiers, fashionistas, and favored families, gossiping and dancing beneath the ninety four-foot, twenty-one-thousand-pound blue whale suspended beneath the arched skylights. Even so Jendari had no trouble picking out the debonair, rotund octogenarian standing at the edge of the crowd, propped up between two twenty-three-year-old Ukrainian girls in matching silver Hervé Léger banded dresses, the material so tight around their serpentine curves they looked like something that had escaped from the Egyptian mummy exhibit on the third floor.

"Oh, I've got plenty of those too, Mr. Agastine," Jendari said, pausing for a brief moment as the phone beeped once from inside the crystal-lined purse—*text received*—then joined the trio in the shadow of the giant whale's tail. "Although tonight I thought pearls seemed more appropriate."

Agastine laughed, the buttons straining to contain his inflated abdomen beneath the flaps of his Armani tuxedo. The Ukrainian girls continued to look bored and hungry.

"It's your party, Ms. Saphra. You can wear whatever you'd like."

Jendari waved her hand as if banishing such hyperbole from her presence; then she ran her fingers down the three strands of natural, uncultured pearls that hung down the front of her Neptune-blue, Versace sheath. The pearls had been harvested from the volcanic atolls of the French Polynesian islands at considerable expense; at fifty-eight, she'd never be mistaken for a mummified supermodel, but she could certainly still turn heads. Especially here among her peers, the glittering fools sipping imported champagne as they danced among the life-size models of giant squids eating sperm whales, dolphins frolicking through choppy waves, and walrus clans battling across imitation ice floes that populated the Milstein Hall of Ocean Life.

Agastine wasn't wrong, of course; the invitations for the annual charity gala at the American Museum of Natural History might have listed a dozen corporate sponsors, and the RSVP insert might have been signed by the deputy mayor himself; but everyone in the room knew who had paid for the twenty-piece orchestra situated on the mezzanine, violinists lined up like so much krill, inches from the mouth of the great blue whale. Everyone knew who had draped the exterior of the monstrous museum—twenty-seven buildings in all, containing more than thirty-two million specimens, from one-of-a-kind dinosaur fossils, to meteors the size of compact cars, to ancient artifacts so rare and delicate they would never even be photographed, let alone displayed—with sparkling velvet tangles of blue that matched the whale, and more importantly, Jendari's dress, for all the city to see.

Last year, Jendari's Saphra Industries had spent four million dollars on the gala, and then led the annual donations with another four million, to help reconstruct a coral reef off the Japanese coast that had been severely damaged by a pair of tanker spills the year before. This year, Saphra Industries was adding another four million to the cause; at this pace, Jendari often thought to herself, they'd be paving half the Pacific Ocean in coral, just so a bunch of wealthy Manhattanites could eat caviar bathed in the glow spilling out of Plexiglas tanks filled with faux bioluminescent eels swimming through schools of computerized jellyfish.

Jendari had nothing against coral. In fact, she had a pair of magnificent chandeliers that had been carved out of endangered coral from the Great Barrier Reef hanging in one of her four homes in California, above a dining room table that she had never eaten off of, and probably never would. But she didn't give tens of millions of dollars to the American Museum of Natural History every year because she was concerned about some insignificant life form. A biological rounding error in the evolutionary equation had put mankind at the top of the food chain, and Jendari Saphra, with her billions in assets, her twenty homes in twelve countries on four continents, was at the top of the top. Her philanthropy had always served a purpose, ever since she had come into her own in her early thirties, and in this case, her millions hadn't gone simply to prop up a species that was essentially a rock that could breathe.

"We all do what we can," Jendari said. A waiter in white tails spun by, offering a tray of specialty cocktails. Jendari accepted a martini glass filled with something viscous and blue, while Agastine went for one of the fruitier concoctions, vodka with chunks of pineapple and lychee dodging ice cubes in an oversize highball. The girls were content sucking air through bee-stung lips. "It just so happens I *can* more than most," she continued. "Unfortunately, that means I'm usually a slave to my cell phone, even when I'm at a party."

She took a sip from the martini glass, noticing that a good portion of the nearby tuxedo- and designer dress–wearing crowd was watching her—some out of the corners of their eyes, some outright, over the shoulders of their dates or from where they were seated at the smattering of round hors d'oeuvre stations.

Jendari enjoyed the attention. When she'd strolled down Central Park West in the waning daylight hours before the gala began, in her Versace and pearls, the tourists in shorts, T-shirts, and sneakers had stared because they didn't know who such an elegantly dressed, handsome woman could be; here, the wealthy one percent of the one percent stared because they did.

Most of the faces, Jendari recognized. There was Arthur Lemmon, the timber magnate. Hansel Gelter, whose consulting firm worked with nearly every big bank on Wall Street. Francis Lopeman, whose hedge fund had just narrowly survived an SEC witch hunt, with most of its eight billion dollars in assets intact. Jerry Grossberg, Alex Feinstein, and Dormac Cooper, the CEOs of the three biggest insurance giants in the country. And then, of course, the men whose names were their introductions: two Rockefellers, a pair of Bloombergs, a gaggle of Guggenheims, three Kennedys, a handful of Rothschilds, and at least one Trump.

Almost all of the invitees were couples, captained by a tuxedoed man; Jendari counted an even distribution of first wives, second wives, mistresses, and expensive accessories. Years ago, Jendari had stopped inviting a date of her own. Not because she'd ever had any trouble finding an appropriate consort, but because what she had told Agastine was true. Her business was a constant pull, especially as of late.

She wasn't the wealthiest person in the room, or the only billionaire. But she believed her empire was unique in its scope—and had become even more unique over the past few years. *Unique in a way that will one day affect every single person in this room—and all of the tourists on the streets of this city and all the other cities around the world.*

A man on her arm would only have gotten in the way. And besides, no man, no matter how pretty, could compete with the dazzle of the Swarovski crystals on her clutch, or the pearls resting on her décolletage.

"Maybe you need a partner," Agastine tried, oblivious to the chunk of pineapple that had now lodged itself in one of his dentures. "Someone who could put a diamond on that lovely hand, big enough to make you forget about your cell phone for an evening."

Jendari looked at the two Ukrainians and tried to hide the distaste from her voice. "Unfortunately, I think I'm a few decades too late to join your traveling band, Mr. Agastine. Not that I don't appreciate the offer."

She knew that Agastine was at least a billion dollars richer than she, but she doubted he could give her anything she didn't already possess, except maybe some exotic venereal disease. Certainly she had enough diamonds. In fact, even tonight, despite the pearls, she was wearing one on a platinum chain, hanging down the center of her back. More than sixteen carats, a strange, smoky yellow color—and completely hidden from view. She'd worn it every year to the charity gala, and not just because she liked the way it felt against the hot, naked skin above her spine.

"I'd certainly make an exception," Agastine started, but he was interrupted as a short, stocky man with thinning hair the same color as his ill-fitting gray suit sidled up next to one of the Ukrainians, and bowed slightly in Jendari's direction.

"Excuse me, monsieur, madames—Ms. Saphra, if I could borrow you for a moment?"

Jendari felt no small sense of relief to see the stocky man in gray. Agastine, for his part, did not conceal his disgust at the poorly dressed interloper; the tiny metal pin affixed to the lapel of the man's suit, identifying him as a museum employee, only made the indignity of the interruption that much worse. Agastine gave the man a look, then put an arm around each of his Ukrainian girls' waists, and steered them toward the ice-buffet at the head of the room. When he was out of earshot, Jendari exhaled, depositing her drink onto the tray of a passing waiter.

"That's an image that's going to make me pray for early onset Alzheimer's, Mr. Grange."

Grange took her by the hand and began leading her through the crowd of tuxedos, toward an unmarked door beneath the dorsal fin of the hanging blue whale.

"In a moment, I'm going to show you something that will make you forget all about them."

Jendari felt the excitement rising as she let the stocky man pull her along, nodding at the guests she recognized as they ploughed forward, thankfully too fast to hear anything but the most cursory congratulations on the fabulousness of the party. She knew it looked strange, her being pulled along like a toddler in a tantrum by the only man in the room who wasn't wearing a tux. But she had known Henry Grange a very long time, and he wasn't the type to get this excited unnecessarily.

He reached the door, flashed a magnetic ID card against the plate by the doorframe, and then led her into an auxiliary hallway. The hallway was gloriously quiet, the noise from the gala swallowed up by the thick carpet beneath Jendari's red-soled Louboutins and the wood-paneled walls.

Grange didn't say a word as he continued to pull her forward. There were very few men Jendari would have let lead her along like this; but she had known Grange more than a decade, and she had never seen him this excited—which meant whatever he was about to show her was certainly going to overshadow the gala in the Hall of Ocean Life.

Two turns later, a near sprint through a pair of identical corridors, and they went through another locked door into a dimly lit exhibit hall that Jendari immediately recognized. To be fair, it would have been hard to miss the sixty-three-foot-long Indian canoe hanging from the ceiling. The canoe dated back to the nineteenth century, and had been carved from a single cedar tree. Covered in detailed aboriginal artwork, it was perhaps the most famous example of Northwest Coast Indian art, and along with the blue whale, was one of the museum's most iconic displays. During daytime hours, the room would have been so full of civilians gawking at the intricate woodwork, it would have been impossible to stroll at any pace more than a shuffle through the rectangular hall, let alone at a jog.

At the moment, Jendari would have happily used the canoe for kindling, if burning the damn thing would have gotten Grange to explain why he was dragging her through the desolate museum on high heels and at full speed in the middle of the night.

"Just a little farther, Ms. Saphra. I promise it will be worth it."

They were at a near sprint again, gliding past the canoe and out through the back of the exhibit, and into the Hall of Human Origins. Jendari felt her interest perk up as they moved past the three skeletons at the front of the hall—representing seven million years of human evolution, from apelike ancestors to modern Homo erectus. Jendari had spent many hundreds of hours wandering through this exhibit, which linked modern DNA research with fossil discoveries—tracing mankind through bones and chemistry back to where it all began.

She nearly pulled Grange to a stop as they sped past Peking Man, the partial skull discovered in China in the early 1930s that had allowed scientists to recreate the face of one of the earliest known examples of *Homo erectus* from more than four hundred thousand years ago. But Grange didn't let her pause, even as they moved from Peking Man to Lucy, the most complete skeleton of an early hominid, dating back a staggering four million years. Jendari had always felt it was fitting that the oldest skeleton of early mankind was actually the interior of a woman. Although Mitochondrial Eve—the mother of modern humanity, whose DNA lived inside each and every living person on earth—wouldn't exist until many millions years after the primitive Lucy, Jendari liked to think that some of Lucy's features would have carried over into the first woman, and through her, to every woman who has lived since.

But at the moment, there was no time to dwell on Lucy or Eve; Grange was moving them forward even faster as they burst from the Hall of Human Origins and bisected the circular Hall of Meteorites, dominated by the massive Cape York Meteorite, the thirty-four ton, mostly nickel piece of an asteroid so heavy that the steel support structure beneath the space rock plunged directly into the bedrock beneath the museum itself. And then they were in the Morgan Memorial Hall of Gems.

Jendari absentmindedly fingered the pearls on her chest as Grange slowed his pace, leading her past the glass display cases teeming with brightly colored baubles from all over the world. There was a time when Jendari had been obsessed by jewels like those around her now. In her early teens, after the death of her father had left her a millionaire and the largest stockholder in one of the Middle East's most profitable telecom companies, she had spent months aimlessly trotting the globe, buying everything and anything that turned her fancy. Even now, the dressing rooms of her various homes were cluttered with earrings, necklaces, bracelets, and rings that would have seemed appropriate in this exhibit; maybe nothing as grand as the Star of India, the prize possession of the Hall, standing in its own room, at five hundred and sixty-three carats, the largest blue star sapphire in the world, or the Patricia Emerald, the twelve-sided, six-hundred-and-thirty-two carat gemstone—but certainly she had one of the most expensive private collections of any of her teenage peers. It wasn't until her great-aunt, Milena Saphra, took her father's place—not just at the head of the company but as her mentor, her mother figure, her guiding influence—that she'd realized the insignificance of such gaudy material possessions.

Since that moment, more than forty years ago, Jendari had learned that possessions, like philanthropy, needed a purpose; they had to be useful. It was the purpose, the significance, that made a thing truly beautiful.

They were both breathing hard as Grange led her the last few steps past the Star of India, deep into the farthest reaches of the Hall of Gems. To Jendari, the most famous sapphire in the world was like a third presence in the room. The perfect dome-shaped gemstone, with its glowing six-pointed star created by the light bouncing off the crystal at its heart, wasn't beautiful simply because it was rare, or famous, or large. It was beautiful because it had a soul, a history.

Formed millions of years ago by natural forces, discovered almost four centuries ago in a riverbed in Sri Lanka, and donated to the American Museum by the banker J. P. Morgan, the Star had been a mainstay of the museum from its beginning. But as spectacular as it was, the Star of India's journey hadn't ended in the display room on the Upper West Side of Manhattan.

In 1964, the Star had been the centerpiece of a bizarre crime. A pair of beatnik beach bums, inspired by a Hollywood movie about jewel thieves, snuck through a bathroom window into the museum and stole two dozen irreplaceable gems, including the Star and the famous sixteen-carat Eagle Diamond, a rough, uncut gem found near the town of Eagle, Wisconsin, in the late 1800s.

Although the hapless thieves were quickly apprehended, the brazen theft would go down in history as one of the most audacious jewel heists ever conducted. After the Star of India was recovered from a locker in the Miami bus station, it attracted even larger crowds because of its infamy. The Eagle Diamond hadn't been so fortunate; to this day, its whereabouts remained a mystery, and most experts believed the rough mineral had been chopped up and sold off in pieces.

To Jendari, though the robbery had been primitive to the point of being comical, the disappearance and return of the Star had given it significance; it was a reminder of how quickly something that seemed so permanent could vanish, and how even a small-minded person could accomplish something well beyond his status, given the right opportunity.

But if Grange considered the Star of India anything beyond another gem in the museum's collection, he wasn't showing. In two seconds flat, he had passed the glowing gem and hurriedly unlocked another unmarked door. A moment later, they were both descending down a narrow stairway.

The stairs ended in front of a steel door. Instead of a wave of his magnetic ID card, this time Grange punched a series of numbers into an electronic keypad attached to the door's frame. There was a loud metallic click, and the door swung inward on automatic hinges.

Jendari found herself being led into a small, steel-walled chamber, almost devoid of furniture. In the middle of the room stood a single wooden crate about three feet tall, nearly as wide as it was long.

She realized immediately where they were. Grange had brought her to one of the numerous archival examination rooms set aside for receiving and documenting the literally millions of fossils, artifacts, and gemstones that arrived into the museum every year, from private collectors, archaeologists, other museums, and even foreign governments. The truth was, the vast majority of items that came through the museum never saw the light of a display cabinet. One could spend a lifetime crawling through the bowels of the museum, and still only see a fraction of what had been collected over the years.

Grange stood in silence as Jendari let the steel door seal shut behind them.

"I know you like to tease, Mr. Grange, but it's not good to keep a lady waiting. Especially this lady."

Grange grinned, trickles of sweat framing his cubic features. As one of the American Museum's most senior curators of antiquities, Henry Grange was an expert on many things—but pleasing women was likely not in his repertoire. Thankfully, Jendari hadn't spent the last decade funneling money into a private Swiss bank account she had set up for the curator because of his sexual prowess. To Jendari, the mysterious crate standing in the middle of this steel chamber was more exciting than anything any man could do for her.

"As you wish," Grange said.

With that, he nearly dove across the room, retrieving a heavy iron crowbar from behind the crate. He went to work on the wood, leveraging his considerable weight against the oversize steel nails that held the crate together.

"You can't imagine the difficulty we had in getting this here," Grange said as he struggled with the crowbar. "The paperwork involved in getting the permission to use the submersible in the first place was staggering. Then there were the payouts to the customs officers in Alexandria, at the stopover in Paris, and then again at JFK."

There was a loud crack as one of the wooden slats split down the middle. Grange jammed the crowbar into the opening and then twisted with both shoulders. The entire top of the crate cracked free, then clattered to the floor.

Jendari thought she caught a whiff of salt water, though it might have just been her imagination. She knew the items in the crate had been on quite a journey since they'd been pulled out of the cavern dug into the floor of Alexandria's Eastern Harbor—halfway between the isthmus where the Egyptian city had been built and the ruins of Pharos, a tiny, ancient island, sitting right where the Nile River drained into the Mediterranean Sea. The amount of bribes that she had funded to enable Grange's team to conduct the archaeological survey beneath the ruins of what was once known as one of the Ancient Seven Wonders of the World, the Lighthouse at Alexandria, were too numerous to count; when you added in the expense of all the red tape to get the artifacts Grange had found out of Egypt and onto American soil, it was well into the millions. But even so, Jendari had no regrets. When Grange had first informed her of the discovery of the cavern, she had been willing to pay far more to get her hands on what might be inside.

Her chest rising beneath her strings of pearls, Jendari crossed the room as Grange knelt by the open crate. She watched as he carefully lifted out two heavy objects, wrapped in plastic bubble wrap. He placed the objects side by side on the floor, then gently unrolled the wrap around the closest of the two.

Jendari gasped audibly as he pulled the statue free. It was two feet high, chiseled from what looked like polished limestone. A female warrior, holding an ivory javelin. Her right breast was missing, and there was a necklace of what appeared to be eggs hanging down around her shoulders.

From an archaeological perspective, it was an incredible discovery. The Lighthouse of Alexandria had been built in the third century BC, supposedly to honor Alexander the Great, who had died at age thirty-two. His successor, Ptolemy I, began construction shortly after Alexander's death, but it was his son, Ptolemy II, who had finished what the father had started: a magnificent lighthouse, four hundred and fifty feet tall, with a furnace at its peak that rotated three hundred sixty degrees, and could be seen as far away as twenty-nine miles. It was the model for all future lighthouses—all the way until the present day.

Although it was widely accepted that the lighthouse was a Greek construction, Jendari's own sources had led her to believe that Alexander's death was only one of the impetuses for the construction of the Wonder. A previously funded excursion to the island of Pharos had revealed a single stone inscription that had spoken of a much earlier temple at the location where the lighthouse had been built—one with a much older history. But until now, her only proof had been those etchings on stone.

Now she and Grange were looking at something much more concrete. Although Jendari had many similar statues in her private collection—most supplied by Grange and his teams over the past decade—she was certain that the statue in front of her outdated them all. It was, perhaps, the earliest representation of an Amazon anyone had ever found.

But the look on Grange's face told her that the statue was only the appetizer. With trembling hands, the stocky man reached forward and unrolled the wrapping from the second object.

Jendari's eyes widened and she immediately pushed Grange aside and dropped to her knees in his place. In front of her, flush with the floor, was a solid stone tablet, covered in ancient cuneiform. She knew from her studies of the last decade that the cuneiform was Sumerian. The age of the object in front of her had to be over eight thousand years: many millennia before the construction of the ruined lighthouse beneath which the table had been found. But it wasn't the Sumerian writing, or even the age of the stone, that sent spikes of adrenaline through Jendari's veins.

It was the single image in the center of the tablet. Vivid, indelible, and immediately recognizable:

"Two intertwined snakes," Grange whispered. "The double helix."

Jendari nodded.

"Somewhere near where your team uncovered this, there was a painting on the wall of the cavern."

It wasn't a question. Grange stared at her.

"Yes."

"A tribe of women warriors, leaving a jungle, carrying a stone."

"But—how could you know?"

Jendari didn't respond. Her head was swirling. The stone in front of her, the image in the center, of the two intertwined snakes, was more important than anything in Jendari's private collection. *Hell, it's more important, more significant, than anything in the entire museum.*

"Crate them both back up, and have them delivered to my plane imme-diately."

Grange nodded. Jendari rose back to her feet, her heels clicking against the steel-plated floor. She watched as the stocky curator began gingerly rolling the two objects in the bubble wrap.

Grange had no idea what his team had found. And even if Jendari had told him, he wouldn't have understood. The pictogram on the ancient stone was just a symbol to him. Even if she had explained what it really was—the oldest representation of the Order of Eve that had ever been uncovered, evi-dence of the greatest civilization that had ever existed—he would have seen it as just another object for the display cases upstairs.

He wouldn't have understood, any more than he'd have understood why, at that very moment, Jendari Saphra wore the priceless, stolen Eagle Diamond hanging down beneath her Versace sheath, the cold, unfinished gemstone nestled tight against the small of her back.

The truth was, it didn't matter what Henry Grange knew or understood. Despite what he may have thought, he wasn't a friend; he was just an object to her, like the diamond. As long as he had a purpose, he was significant and valuable.

When he no longer had a purpose, he would lose his value, and she would get rid of him. And when the time came, it would be as easy as tak-ing her phone out of her crystal-studded clutch and sending a text.

CHAPTER SEVEN

The jungle wasn't going to let them go.

Jack pressed his face against the window as the electric train surged beneath him, steel wheels struggling against the steep, winding track cut right into the Tijuca Forest. The scene on the other side of the glass was a thick blur of tropical green; ten minutes before, the train had pulled away from the crowded platform in Cosme Velho and was now halfway into its twenty-minute journey up the side of Corcovado Mountain. The small, picturesque village on the southern outskirts of the steamy, teeming metropolis of Rio had quickly given way to a smattering of poorly constructed wooden shanties, and then it was nothing but green as the train carved its way upward, the ascent so vertical, the rainforest so thick in some places, it felt as though it would take a miracle to keep the damn thing puttering up the track.

Then again, if you were looking for miracles, this was probably a good place to start.

He turned away from the window, toward his grad students, Andy and Dashia, who were seated next to him on a seat that would have felt crowded if he'd been sitting there by himself. Andy was hanging on to the edge closest

73

to the narrow aisle with both hands, a heavy duffel bag jammed against the floor beneath his legs. Dashia was between them, her oversize computer bag balanced precariously on her lap. Neither was saying anything—not that Jack would have been able to hear anything below a scream. The noise from the wheels against the aging track was only a small part of the cacophony assaulting his ears. Even though it was barely nine in the morning, the atmosphere in the car—one of two powered by twin overhead cables that ran the entire length of the twenty-three-hundred-foot ascent up the side of the mountain—was pure bedlam. Every seat was packed, and even the aisle was crowded, packed three deep in some places. It was an almost even mix of native Brazilians, many of them well-dressed Catholics making a religious pilgrimage to their country's most iconic symbol, and foreign tourists, in shorts and T-shirts, cell phones out and cameras clicking, fanny packs bulging with traveler's checks and credit cards.

In addition to the overwhelming crush of people, to add to the festive, earsplitting mood in the train car, there was a three-piece salsa band set up in the back row of seats, consisting of two steel drums and what appeared to be some sort of battery-powered xylophone. A pair of Danish girls with braided hair and clunky heels was dancing in front of the band, somehow managing to stay on their feet even as the train shifted into a near forty-five-degree angle, fighting through a twist of forest dense enough to block out most of the morning light.

It was hard to believe that the precipitous track had been built for steam engines by Emperor Dom Pedro II in 1884, and electrified over a century ago in 1910. Though in his professional work, Jack had seen feats of architecture and engineering dating back thousands of years that were truly mind-boggling, there was something about the contrast of technology and nature—the audacity of putting an electric train up the side of a goddamn mountain—that gave him pause. *And this was just the precursor to the main event.*

Jack glanced back toward the window, at the verdant swirl of vegetation whipping past as the train chugged upward. He was surprisingly alert, considering how far he and his team had traveled in such a short time. None of them had slept much on the fourteen-hour journey from Boston to Brazil, jammed together in conditions almost as harsh as those they found themselves in now, sharing a middle row in coach that made Jack pine for the relatively posh conditions of some of the most primitive tribes he'd lived with over the years.

Although he had been able to get enough funding from his department to bring his team to Brazil—no questions asked, since most of his work was so outside the box, his superiors had long ago decided to give him a fair amount of slack—they couldn't afford to travel in style. The hotel they'd checked into upon landing in Rio had a wireless connection, but no air-conditioning, and a bathroom that was shared by an entire floor. Andy had threatened to urinate out the window onto the cobbled alley that separated their building from what appeared to be a neon-lit disco; but Dashia, to her credit, had simply wrinkled her nose, then placed her efficiently packed suitcase on the chipped, redwood dresser, one of the few pieces of furniture in the room beside a pair of double beds.

A sharp turn in the track shifted Jack against the seat, and he watched as Dashia grabbed at her laptop bag, catching it before it slid off her lap. The fact that she had even volunteered to accompany them on the expedition was a testament to how much she had become a true part of Jack's team. She had listened intently as Jack had given her the rundown over the phone from Boston, on what he'd discovered on Jeremy's thumb drive—that there was some sort of link between the Seven Wonders of the Modern World; that six of them matched up with the ruins of six of the Seven Wonders of the Ancient World; and that there was something geographically intriguing about Christ the Redeemer that he needed to investigate. She hadn't asked any questions, she had simply told him that as long as she was still getting credit toward her PhD, she could be at the International Terminal at Logan in about four hours.

A part of Jack wondered if he was making a mistake involving his two grad students in something he didn't yet understand—something that might very well be connected to the violent way his brother had died—but the truth was, both of them had skills that were indispensable. Andy was almost as field ready as Jack himself; Jack knew he would need Andy's help if what Jeremy had uncovered about Christ the Redeemer was even partially true. And for Dashia's part, she had reached back into her former life as a computer wizard, and had already scripted a hacking program to look into the 2007 vote that had chosen the Seven Modern Wonders. Although she hadn't found much—just a few suspicious quirks that led her to believe that, indeed, the data had been massaged by an unknown party—it was enough to give more credence to the idea that someone, for some reason, had manipulated the hundred million votes toward a predetermined outcome.

Jack couldn't possibly imagine what they were getting themselves into; at the very least, the mystery they were trying to unravel was the last thing his brother had been working on when he was murdered. Jack believed he owed it to his brother to follow the clues he had left behind.

Jack's thoughts were interrupted as a sudden cheer erupted through the car, followed by the salsa band kicking into high gear, wooden sticks slamming repeatedly against steel drums. But despite the roar, Jack's attention was entirely captured by the scene on the other side of the window. One minute, everything was thick and green, and then suddenly, they were surrounded by swirling gray mist, churning across a steep vista of jagged stone. Then, just as suddenly, they were above the mist. Jack had a moment of vertigo as the train seemed to be going almost straight up, and then there was a lurch as the train pulled to a sudden stop.

They had reached the top of Corcovado.

There was a brief pause, then the crowd surged toward the open train doors.

CHAPTER EIGHT

"He certainly makes an impression, I'll give him that."

Andy was a half step ahead of Jack and Dashia, his neck craned upward as the steel-framed escalator deposited them, still crammed into the shoulder-to-shoulder crowd, onto the stone-paved viewing platform. Up close, the huge Art Deco statue loomed indescribably large, rising up out of the mist like something from ancient mythology. Though it had been constructed in France in the 1920s and shipped over to Brazil in pieces—white soapstone wrapped around a concrete and steel frame—the monument would have fit well in any Greek or Roman ruin: ninety-eight feet tall, perched atop a twenty-six-foot-high black granite pedestal, rising out of the peak of the twenty-two-hundred-foot-tall mountain, arms outstretched to embrace what looked like the entire world. Christ the Redeemer, perhaps the largest representation of the religious icon on Earth—and the most modern of the Seven Wonders of the World.

"View's not half bad, either," Dashia said, from Jack's left.

She was peering over the low wall that surrounded the platform as they shuffled forward with the crowd. Though most of the view was obscured by the rolling mist, which had followed them up as they'd made their way via a trio of elevators and a pair of escalators from the train depot, Jake caught glimpses of the incredible panorama down below. From a half a mile up, the urban sprawl of Rio was nearly postcard perfect, from its pincushion of gleaming skyscrapers, to its clustered apartment complexes, to its snow-white resort hotels, and of course, the legendary white sand beaches of Ipanema and Copacabana, bathed in the shadows of Corcovado and its slightly shorter twin, Sugar Loaf.

The crowd of tourists and pilgrims didn't seem to care that they were gazing down on Rio through breaks in the mist; to the contrary, the wisps of cottony white sweeping across the paved stones, so thick in some places Jack couldn't see his own feet, made it feel like they were walking on a canopy of clouds.

"I'm a little turned around," Andy said as they moved along the side of the black granite base. "You want to take the lead, Doc?"

Jack pointed at a woman two steps ahead of Andy, in a flowing white wedding dress, the train folded up beneath the arm of her tuxedo-clad groom.

"Follow her. She knows where we're going."

Somewhere between the elevators and the escalators, Jack and his team had found themselves intertwined with the wedding party. Besides the bride and groom, there were at least four bridesmaids in matching cream dresses jockeying through the crowd around them, escorted by groomsmen in dark suits. Jack knew that within the base of the great statue was a wedding chapel; even though the space was small, carved into the granite block whose main purpose was holding up the massive, seven-hundred-ton soap-stone monolith, the waiting list to hold weddings on Corcovado was months long. Jack supposed for a true believer, you couldn't do much better than getting married a few inches below Christ's toes.

As Jack had suspected, the wedding party was making a beeline toward the chapel, and Jack and his team fell into step right behind them, skirting

the granite base with the help of their pink-frilled escort as most of the surrounding crowd moved outward toward the front of the viewing platform,
which jutted out like a pirate's plank over the sprawling city.

A dozen yards from the entrance to the chapel, the bride and groom
exited the crowd and began their stroll down a red carpet that had been laid
out along the paved stones, bordered on both sides by a pair of photogra-
phers. Jack tapped Andy's shoulder, pointing him away from the carpet
toward a crook in the wall at the edge of the viewing platform. Andy nodded, and the three of them slipped out from between the bridesmaids and
regrouped right up next to the wall. Christ the Redeemer had his back
toward them now, his vast, soapstone hips disappearing into the soupy gray.

Jack glanced at the handful of tourists who were still nearby; almost all
were focused on the wedding party, still making its way down the red carpet
and into the chapel. Through the open doors, Jack could make out a handful of red velvet chairs lined up in two parallel rows and a small lectern,
manned by a priest in white robes. Then he turned his attention to the wall
to his right; it was a little more than waist high, topped by an iron railing.
Behind the railing, there was about a ten-foot drop, then a steep slope covered in chunks of rock ending in deep brush, the beginning of a thick twist
of the rainforest that ran up and down most of the mountainside. Three feet
into the brush, rising up on a black metal frame, was a bank of spotlights
aimed at the statue behind him. Jack knew that the lights were part of the
massive LED and spot system that had been added to the monument in
2011, giving the Wonder an entirely new dimension; at night, the intelligent
lighting system could bathe the Redeemer in full Technicolor, which could
be seen from every corner of the city below.

But at the moment, Jack wasn't interested in the technology or artistry
of the lighting panel; he was more concerned about its tensile strength. He
had spent many hours during the trip to Brazil studying the information
Jeremy had put on the thumb drive, coordinating it with geographic maps

and architectural blueprints Dashia had pulled off the Internet from local government servers. He had committed all of the data to memory, and as he scanned past the bank of lights, he counted another three yards of thick bush before the mountaintop gave way to what appeared to be a sheer twenty-foot drop into even thicker rainforest.

He put one hand on the railing, then nodded to Andy.

"This is where I go over."

Andy dropped the heavy duffel to the paved stone and went after the zipper, while Dashia unloaded her laptop bag. Jack kept an eye on a pair of nearby tourists who had their cell phones out, peering straight up through the screens, trying to catch a glimpse of Christ's outstretched arms above the clouds. Jack wasn't really concerned about anyone seeing what they were up to. Although he'd counted a handful of security guards at the train depot and another half a dozen scattered around the viewing platform, most seemed more concerned about making sure visitors had paid the twenty-five-dollar fee to visit the site; if anything, they were worried about people sneaking over the wall *into* the Wonder of the World, not out. Then again, looking up at a small break in the mist, up the steep, white curve of Christ's spine to the base of his vast, slightly bent head—Jack couldn't have asked for a better distraction.

Even so, Andy looked nervous as he retrieved a heavy coil of climbing rope from the duffel, placing it next to Jack's feet. When he carefully lifted a second object—a miniature dish wrapped in aluminum, similar in shape and size to the sort of dish one might install on a roof to get satellite television—out of the bag, he looked guilty enough to need a visit to the nearby chapel.

"Relax, kid," Jack said as he took the dish from Andy and attached it by a Velcro strap to a hook on the side of his tan safari jacket. Then he grabbed the coil of rope and shifted it over his right shoulder. If anything, in faded jeans and a safari jacket, with the dish hanging from the strap and the rope coiled around his deltoid, he looked like a high-tech repairman. Certainly not an anthropologist. Although as usual, he did have a couple tools of his trade hidden under his clothes.

"I'll hit you up when I'm in position. If anyone gives you any trouble, we'll meet at the base of the mountain. Should be about a two-hour hike down, if I move fast."

Andy was peering over the railing at the cliff behind the bank of spotlights.

"More like an eight-minute fall," he said. "I sure hope we brought enough rope, Doc."

"When have we ever brought enough rope?" Jack grinned.

And then he put both hands on the railing, gave one last look behind him to make sure none of the tourists were watching, and hoisted himself over the wall.

· · ·

The brush was thick, but no worse than he'd experienced in Venezuela with the Yanomami, or, for that matter, with the Penan tribe in Borneo during his first year of graduate study, or in the Visayan Islands where he'd spent a month with his dad when he was just nineteen, living with a group of Aboriginal Pinoy while still a college sophomore. It was on that early trip that his father had given him the first of his indispensable tools of the trade, which he now unsheathed from the concealed holster strapped down the small of his back.

The muscles in his forearm tightened as his palm felt the familiar grip, made of perfectly carved guava wood. It took almost no effort to swing the two-foot blade in a wide arc, cutting into the brush with each expert stroke. The *iták*—or bolo, as it was more widely known—had been designed specifically for work like this; the metal blade curved slightly outward and widened at the tip, putting most of the momentum at the end of each arc. Jack barely broke a sweat as he worked his way closer to the high iron frame of the platform of spotlights. In some places, he could crawl beneath the gnarled tree limbs or hanging vine, but where it became impassable, a few strokes of the iták gave him enough room to angle through. In a pinch, he also knew from experience that the weighted blade also made a hell of a weapon; a longer version, known as a *Pinuti*, was a standard armament of the natives of the Visayan Islands. Of course, when the tribal natives went to war, they usually tipped the end of the blade in snake or spider venom. Which was one of the many reasons that Jack's father had taught him to always keep a packet of antivenom vials in another pocket in his safari jacket, next to the chemical flares he brought with him everywhere as well, which he restocked before every trip.

As Jack reached the bank of spotlights, then cut a narrow path through the brush beyond the metal frame, he was much less concerned about venom than he was about the length of the coiled rope around his shoulder. Reaching the edge of the drop a dozen yards past the spotlights, he got down on his hands and knees, peering downward. The rock was nearly sheer for about ten feet, then became more jagged and crooked, disappearing into more of the thick underbrush.

Jack couldn't tell how much farther down it went after everything turned green. He knew from Jeremy's satellite data that somewhere down there, the cliff ended in a sort of valley, a ledge of more granite that ran thirty yards along the mountain, covered in forest even more dense than he'd just cut through. The ledge was bordered on all sides by an even steeper cliff face—hundreds of feet high, covered in more vegetation—and was a part of the mountain that was off the grid as far as Jack could tell, untouched by the hikers that regularly scaled the opposite side of Corcovado, which led down into one of the most picturesque parks on the outskirt of Rio. Although Jeremy's satellite data was precise in most areas, it hadn't given Jack an accurate read on how far the cliff in front of him went once it was swallowed by the rainforest. Infrared telemetry could only take him so far; hopefully, rope could take him the rest of the way.

He took the coil off his shoulder and quickly found one end, which was capped by a sophisticated steel clasp. Then he reached an arm into his jacket, all the way to another sewn pocket, right up against his side. He retrieved the next vital item he always carried with him; this time, something of his own design.

A little bigger than his palm, at first glance the item looked like some sort of metal spider, dead and curled up into a ball, legs twisted together. Then Jack hit a lever on the side of the device, the sharply clawed legs clicked free, and the thing opened into a compact, sturdy grapple similar to the grappling hooks one could find in any climbing equipment store.

One of the many pieces of advice his father had given him—besides the importance of antivenom and the need for a good, sturdy blade—was that field anthropology was ninety percent preparation, and ten percent trying desperately to recover when you didn't prepare properly. To that end, the portable grapple had gotten Jack out of more jams than he could count.

With three quick twists, he attached the open grapple to the clasp on the end of the rope. Then he backtracked the few yards to the platform of lights and used the itak to cut away an area of vegetation until he could reach the steel frame at the base of the construct. He saw a pair of cables running up toward the statue and around the back of the viewing platform; power cords, he assumed, leading to a generator somewhere back around by the train depot. Jack took care to avoid the cables, and found a place on the steel frame that seemed perfect for the grapple. He swung the rope carefully, then tossed the grapple over the frame, letting it twist around twice, the sharp claws grasping into place. He gave the rope a good tug, making sure it was going to hold his weight. Then he hiked back to the edge of the cliff.

Back on his knees, he reached for the Velcro strap and unhitched the aluminum-wrapped dish. He took a headset out of a pocket and put the earpiece in his right ear, the mouthpiece in front of his lips. Then he lay down against the mossy rock, flicked a switch on the side of the dish, and held his arms as far as he could over the ledge, aiming the dish straight down.

"Okay, talk to me," he said into the mouthpiece. There was a short pause, followed by some static. Then Andy was whispering in his ear.

"Lit up the second you engaged the dish. Christ, Doc, it's bright as a Christmas tree."

Jack felt heat rising in his chest. He knew exactly what Andy and Dashia were looking at on her laptop screen—because he'd seen the image on Jeremy's thumb drive. Jeremy had made his discovery by accident; he had been using the satellite images to try and pinpoint the exact geographic center of Christ the Redeemer, using different satellite spectrum data—infrared, radar, ultrasound—to function out the topographical specifics of the location. Jeremy probably hadn't realized it, but archaeologists and anthropologists had been using satellite surveys to look at ruins hidden beneath deserts and jungles for years; you could see things from thousands of miles up that you'd never find with a shovel and flashlight. Certainly, Jeremy hadn't been expecting to see something buried deep beneath the tropical brush; but when he'd seen it, he'd known immediately that he was looking at something bizarre—something that shouldn't have been there at all.

The dish in Jack's hand—which they'd borrowed from an MIT engineering lab with the help of one of Andy's fawning contacts—was a pinpoint method of double-checking what Jeremy had found in the satellite data. The engineering student had assured them the device would get an accurate reading on multiple spectrums like a satellite, and it was easily adapted to work with the Bluetooth chip in Dashia's laptop. Now Andy and Dashia had a bird's-eye view of the enigma to go along with Jeremy's space-eyed view.

And from the change in Andy's voice, Jack knew he had placed himself in the correct position.

"A cross," Andy whispered. "About fifty-five feet long, another thirty-five feet at the arms. Imbedded right in the granite, hidden beneath what looks to be a ten-foot-high unbroken canopy of flora. From the spectrum analysis, looks to be made of some sort of metal."

Jack whistled low to himself. A huge metal cross, dug right into the mountain, hidden beneath the rainforest. The thick canopy of forest explained why nobody else had stumbled over it in recent years—but how long had it been there? And who had put it there? Was it another religious icon, to go with the Redeemer?

There was nothing Art Deco about a metal cross hidden beneath the tropical forest.

"How far down is it?" Jack asked, bringing his arms back from over the ledge and trading the dish for the rope.

"At least forty feet," Andy said.

"And how much rope do I have?"

Andy paused on the other end of the headset.

"Thirty-five, minus whatever you're using to reach the light fixture."

Jack did the calculations in his head. He was going to be about twenty feet short. Not insurmountable; twenty feet down through thick forest probably wouldn't kill him. But it wasn't the way down he was worried about. It was the way back up. The valley below, where the strange cross was situated, was bordered by a cliff much steeper than the one in front of him.

One potentially fatal obstacle at a time, Jack thought to himself. And then he tossed the rope over the edge and let it unspool foot by foot down the sheer cliff face.

• • •

"I'm not going to say it," Jack hissed, breathing heavy as he rappelled the last few feet, kicking his way around a jagged outcropping of granite to position himself right above the thick canopy of gnarled trees. "But you can guess where I am."

The end of his rope, and still a good five feet from the trees, and another fifteen feet beneath the canopy, to the granite valley floor. Peering down, he saw nothing but chaotic gnarls of leaf, vine, and intermittent bark. The tropical canopy was twisted so tightly together, it was impossible to make out individual branches or trunks. He knew that the Tijuca was one of the most diverse rainforests—there could be more than four hundred different species of tree interlocked together beneath him—but he would have given anything for just one good climbing trunk. Instead, he was going to have to take his chances.

"Looks like I'm taking the express route the rest of the way," he said.

With one hand, he took the headset off and placed it back in his jacket. Then he lowered himself as far as he could with his arms, and let go.

There was a brief moment of weightlessness, and then his boots hit the top of the canopy, and the tangle bent inward. For a moment he thought it might hold—and then there were a series of cracks, and he was tumbling through, leaves and vines whipping at his skin. He covered his face with his arms, curling his body into a ball. He felt something hard catch him under his right rib, and a branch hit him behind his knees, pitching him forward. Then, suddenly, he was through the canopy and falling. He uncovered his face just in time to see the ground hurtling toward him. He twisted his body to the side, and then he hit, shoulder first. The impact knocked the breath out of his lungs, and shots of pain rocketed through his shoulder. He rolled onto his back, looking up at the rays of light that shined down through the small hole he had created in the canopy above. He could just barely make out the end of the rope dangling along the cliff face more than twenty feet above.

Hell, he'd probably been wrong—if it hadn't been for the canopy breaking much of his fall, the drop might very well have killed him. He was going to have to add this little stunt to his growing list of stupid decisions.

After another moment lying still, mentally checking himself out for any injuries he couldn't walk off, he rolled to a sitting position. The ground beneath him was covered in soft moss—another reason he wasn't damaged beyond a bruised shoulder—and the air was thick with spores, dust, and mist. Even with the light coming through the hole above, it was hard to see beyond a few feet; the canopy was thick enough to turn day into night, and the light streamed down through the hole like rays through a prism, reflecting oddly through the humid air, breaking off into miniature rainbows as it reached the ground, painting the moss in bands of color.

Jack shook the last effects of the impact away and rose to his feet. Squinting through the darkness, he saw that he was in a sort of cavern, formed by the granite below and the forest above. It stretched out fifty yards to his right and left. Ahead, he could make out the wall of the cliff, rising up into the canopy; it was as sheer as above, and would be difficult, but maybe not impossible, to climb. Behind him, he knew that somewhere there would be a ledge and another cliff, hidden behind more of the thick green brush. Jack had no intention of digging far in that direction—that would be a fall no amount of tree cover would be able to cushion.

Instead, he started carefully forward. He had made it a few yards before he stopped suddenly, making out a large shape stretching out across the floor of the canopied area ahead of him.

He reached into his jacket and found the headset. To his pleasant surprise, it looked intact, and he placed it back on over his ears and mouth.

"Hey, kid, up and running, no worse for wear. How's it going topside?"

"Damn, Doc, good to hear from you. One of the security guards came by to ask about the laptop, but we told him we're working on a high school paper on the statue. One of the benefits of being Asian, everyone thinks you're fourteen until you're fifty. You made the leap of faith, I assume?"

"Almost landed on my feet. And I think I've found something."

"Is it a cross?"

Jack exhaled into the darkness.

"We're about to find out."

Then he pulled one of the flares from his jacket, held it out in front of him, and yanked the cord.

• • •

It wasn't a cross, exactly. But the dimensions were right, and it was made of metal.

"It's an airplane," Jack said. "Twin propeller. Pretty old, from the looks of it. The fuselage and cockpit appear to be mostly intact, though the landing gear is gone. Most of the frame has dug itself into the granite floor."

"An airplane? You're shitting me. How did it get down there?"

Jack felt frozen in place, staring at the plane through the flame and sparks fizzing out of the top of the flare. It was like something out of an old movie or antique air show. Curved, knoblike nose, oblong wings extending out against the solid cavern floor, propellers attached to cylindrical engines. The tail was almost entirely intact, reaching within a few feet of the vegetation above. He looked past the tail at the canopy of green, and then back at the stone floor. He noticed a dark stain beginning near the center of the fuselage, spreading out to cover much of the floor from tail to cockpit. *Dried fuel.* He took a step back, making sure the sparks from the flare didn't land anywhere near the stain.

"I assume it landed here. Well, crash-landed, though from the relative lack of damage it appears to have been a controlled ditch. I'm far less bothered by how it got here than when."

"What do you mean?"

Jack squinted at the side of the plane. Though the metal was covered in rust, pockmarked by holes and jagged tears, he could see numbers imprinted along one wing. He couldn't make out all of them, but at least a few were still clear enough to read.

"Kid, I need Dashia to look something up for me."

He read the numbers that he could see out loud, and waited for Dashia to get the information via her laptop.

"I think it's a Lockheed Electra 10, but I can't get much more specific than that from what you've given me," Dashia said a few seconds later. "From the design you've described, and the numbers, it's circa 1930s, at the latest."

Jack whistled, low. The airplane in front of him was over eighty years old. From the trees that had overgrown the valley, he guessed that it had been there almost that long. Which would have placed this crash landing right about the time when Christ the Redeemer had been completed.

Jack let the flare burn down, then tossed it far behind him, away from the stain of dried fuel. Then he took a small flashlight out of his jeans pocket, and started forward.

"I'm going to see what's inside," he said.

Getting to the door of the cockpit proved more difficult than it looked. He had to climb over two sets of rock outcroppings to get to the closest wing, and as he put his boot against the metal, he nearly stepped right through; because of the heavy humidity in the air, the alloy had rusted through to the point of near collapse, and there was a good chance that if he wasn't careful, the whole thing would crumble beneath him.

But he wasn't going to turn back now. Using his hands, he slid himself onto the wing and pulled himself along the rusted surface, careful to keep his weight as balanced across his body as possible. By the time he made it to the cockpit door, he was breathing hard.

The door came open easily, two of the hinges snapping off and clanging to the cavern floor. When the first hinge hit, Jack noticed a strange echo—a sort of skittering sound that lasted long after the hinge had stopped bouncing against the granite. But he was too busy clambering inside the aging cockpit to give it much thought.

The interior of the cockpit was cramped and full of what felt like cobwebs; there was a thick, oily smell in the air, and the ceiling was peeling, strips of rubbery material hanging down so close it brushed against his hair. The control console looked ancient—two steering columns, lots of dials and switches. Most of the buttons and knobs had rotted away, and the glass windshield was shattered, a web of cracks extending from nose to roof.

Jack was about to climb back out of the cockpit when he caught site of something on the floor beneath the pilot's seat, jammed right up beneath the control console. He immediately dropped to his knees, aiming the flashlight.

In front of him was an iron crate, about the size and shape of a small briefcase. And on top of the crate, a leather-bound flight manual.

Jack crawled forward, grabbing the crate and flight manual, and dragged the objects back to the center of the cockpit. He flipped through the manual, glancing at the pages of notations, flight maps, longitudes and latitudes, and placed it on the floor. Then he turned his attention to the crate.

There was a lock on one side, covered in rust. Jack quickly retrieved his iták from the long holster in his jacket. The first swing only nicked at the rusted metal, but the second swing made a noticeable groove. Jack began swinging harder, the sound of the blade against the lock ringing in his ears.

As he worked, he again noticed the strange echo—a skittering, clacking sound that seemed to be reverberating all around him—lasting well after he stopped swinging the iták. And the sound seemed to be growing louder. Jack was about to take a look out the cockpit door, see what the hell was making the noise, when the lock suddenly came apart.

Jack forgot about the sound, slid the bolo back into the holster, and then opened the iron crate.

"My god," he whispered.

He reached into the crate, digging through a bed of straw to an object wrapped loosely in cloth. He tore the cloth away to reveal a stone tablet, about the size of a hardcover book, which he instantly recognized. It was remarkably similar to the tablet he had seen in the pit beneath the Temple of Artemis: the tablet in the painting, though apparently a smaller version of the one the Amazonian warriors were carrying out of the forest. Flat, with an image of a seven-segmented snake carved into its center. But on this tablet, Jack saw what appeared to be a tiny pictogram next to the first of the seven segments.

Jack looked even closer, holding the flashlight in two fingers, his face only inches from the stone.

The pictogram appeared to have been added to the stone; the rock itself appeared to be much, much older than the colored carving next to the snake segment. Though he wasn't sure what it meant, the image was clear: a drawing of a human head, bearded, with long, flowing hair. Even stranger, one of the eyes on the head had been painted metallic gold.

Jack stared at the pictogram, his heart pounding in his chest. Then he coughed.

"I think I know what this is," he said, aloud. "I think this is a clue—"

"Doc," Andy's voice burst through his ear. "Do you hear that? Is it interference? Because it seems to be getting a lot louder."

Jack blinked. He could hear it too, now—the scratching, clicking, skittering sound was bouncing through the canopied area, so loud the entire cockpit felt like it was trembling. Jack leaned forward and stuck his head a few inches out the cockpit door, extending the flashlight out in front of him.

Then he froze.

The ground around the airplane seemed to be shifting. He shined his flashlight farther back, but it was hard to see through the humid air. He made a quick decision, placing the flashlight back in his pocket and reaching for a second flare. He pulled the cord and then held the flare over his head.

"Shit," he gasped. "It's moving."

"Doc? What's moving?"

"Everything."

The floor, the vegetation running up the sides of the cavern, the wall, the canopy above—all of it was pulsating, moving. *Alive.*

"Spiders," Jack said.

Brazilian whiteknee tarantulas—Jack could instantly recognize them from their size, and from the bands of white across their long, pointed legs. He'd seen a few before, in previous visits to the rainforest, but never anything like this. There were thousands of them, covering nearly every inch of the cavern, and as he watched through the orange light of the flare, he saw hundreds more bubbling up through holes in the granite floor, climbing over each other until the entire floor was ankle deep.

And then Jack felt something touch his shoulder. He looked to his left and saw a tarantula clinging to his jacket. He swiped it away with the flare, sending it spinning toward the surging floor. Then something whizzed by his face, missing him by inches. He looked up and saw them dropping from the canopy, dozens of them, like a squirming rain.

Jack leaped back into the cockpit, slamming what was left of the door behind him. He was breathing hard, trying to think. Brazilian whiteknees weren't particularly poisonous, but they were damn big, with ridiculously large fangs. The puncture size of one whiteknee bite could cause serious problems. A thousand bites? Jack didn't want to find out.

He felt a sting against his wrist and nearly shrieked—and realized it was just a spark from the now dying flare. Watching the flame as it shrank to a bare, dull glow, he had a sudden, crazy, stupid thought.

He let the flare die and then leaped forward, grabbing the stone tablet and leather flight diary, tucking both objects into his jacket. Then he climbed on top of what was left of the pilot's chair and pressed his hands against the cockpit roof.

The rusted metal gave way on the second push. He used the metal as a shield against the spiders still raining from the ceiling and climbed up out onto the top of the plane. His first step went right through—his boot disappearing for a perilous moment before he yanked it back up—but then the roof held as he carefully stepped forward, kicking spiders out of the way as he went.

He focused his attention on the airplane's tail, extended about fifteen feet in front of him. Then he looked past the tip of the tail, into the hanging vines and twisted tree limbs. It was going to be close—but he didn't see another choice.

Still holding the metal above his head, he reached into his jacket and pulled out a third flare. He yanked the cord with his teeth and watched as the flame spit upward, again filling the cavern with orange light. Then he leaned a few inches over the side of the airplane, looking at the cavern floor.

The spiders were knee deep now, a churning carpet of fur, legs, and fangs. Hundreds were now working their way up the side of the plane, toward Jack's feet.

Now or never.

He searched the floor for a spot where the spiders were packed a little less deep—where he could see glimpses of floor, and the dark stain against the granite. Then he took aim and tossed the lit flare at the spot.

By the time it hit, he was already running forward at full speed. He heard the dried fuel ignite just as his boots hit the tail and then he was hurling himself upward, buoyed by the blast beneath him, his arms outstretched. He caught the bottom of the vegetation with his fingers, one hand grasping a stretch of vine, the other a rough twist of bark. And then he was lifting himself upward with all of his strength.

The heat hit him just as he was clawing through the first level of the canopy, a burst so hot he feared his jeans were going to go up in flames. There was a strange screeching sound—a thousand spiders burning simultaneously—and then, just as suddenly, the heat started to dissipate as the layer of fuel burned off and the thick humidity controlled the conflagration.

By the time Jack had reached the top of the canopy, delicately balancing himself against limbs that seemed big enough to support him, all he saw beneath him were wisps of dark smoke, working through gaps in the green.

He took a moment to make sure the stone tablet and the leather flight diary were still against his body, and then he began to make his way to the edge of the canopy and the short five-foot free climb up the cliff to where his rope was waiting. As difficult a climb as that would be, Jack knew that it was only the beginning. The stone tablet—and the strange pictogram next to the head of the snake—had told him exactly where he needed to go next.

In his mind, he was already on his way there: far above the canopy of green and the burning remains of the twin propeller plane.

CHAPTER NINE

Jack was fighting a battle against gravity. Hand over hand, fingers clenched white against the soapstone, he was nearly blind in the pitch black darkness, wind ripping like talons across his back, tearing at his jacket, threatening to pull him away from the statue and toss him, spinning like a rag doll, toward the city a half mile below. The rope tied tight around his waist dangled like a tail that was now limp and useless, leading back into the narrow access tunnel twelve feet below, halfway up the Wonder's chest. If he fell, the rope would catch him; but he was not at all certain that his grapple would hold against the floor of the tunnel that had let out to the exterior of the monument. Still, there hadn't been anywhere else to place it—unless he had been willing to dig the claws right into the soapstone exterior itself, and he was pretty sure he'd committed enough blasphemic acts already, without digging a grapple into Christ the Redeemer's flesh.

Getting inside the statue had actually been easier than Jack had expected. By the time he'd made the arduous climb back up Corcovado and scaled the wall in front of the light panel up to the viewing platform, it had been well after dark; the tourists and worshippers and wedding parties had been sent home. Andy had stayed behind, hiding in the brush right where

Jack had first made his descent; but after Jack had handed him the stone tablet and the leather flight manual, he had eventually gone as well, accompanying Dashia back to their hotel. This was something Jack had to do on his own.

Now a hundred feet up, so high the lights of the city were like Technicolored pinpoints, Jack clenched his jaw against the wind and worked one leg over the statue's collarbone, one hand beneath the bearded chin. Jack's biceps cried out as he pulled himself the last few feet, placing his body flush with the iconic face. Though most of Christ's features had been blasted away by the elements over the past near century, Jack had no trouble recognizing the symbol from the pictogram. The nose, lips, eyebrows, and ears were mostly gone, but the long hair, the beard, the high cheekbones—Jack believed the image in front of him was built to last a thousand years, not just a hundred.

It hadn't taken him long to decipher the pictogram. He'd considered waiting until he'd time to digest what he'd found, to try and understand how a version of the stone tablet, which he had seen depicted beneath the Temple of Artemis had ended up in a crate beneath Christ the Redeemer—but he'd quickly realized that the late hour, and the fact that he was already on site, were opportunities he couldn't pass up.

Before he'd begun his own trek down the tourist-friendly side of the mountain, Andy had helped Jack find the access panel to the interior of the hollow statue, a small door directly above a corner of the black granite pedestal, carved into Christ's right heel. Although there hadn't been any security guards on the viewing platform, they could hear Portuguese drifting up from nearby the escalators; they decided against taking the time to break into the chapel to find a ladder and had instead used a combination of Andy's shoulders and a judicial toss of the grappling hook over a crook in the black granite to hoist Jack up the twenty-five feet between the platform and the heel.

It hadn't been hard to pry the door open with his iták. Andy was gone before Jack shut the door behind him, leaving him alone in the vast interior of the Wonder, staring up at the huge framework of concrete and reinforced iron that held the separate pieces of the great statue in place. Jack knew the construct had been refurbished a number of times since it had been delivered by the French engineers in the late 1920s; at some point, thankfully, the workers had added a metal staircase leading up the interior to about Christ's chest level, maybe seventy-five feet above.

Jack had taken the stairs fast, careful not to make too much noise as he went. The stairs ended in what first appeared to be a sheer wall of soapstone and concrete; but as Jack got closer, he saw the seams to another small door, which led into a tight, narrow tunnel, three feet tall and barely as wide. Down on his hands and knees, he'd crawled the last few yards to another opening—and leaned out into blackness, the wind nearly pushing him back onto his heels.

Jack knew he wasn't the first person to climb outside the access tunnel and make his way up to the shoulders of Christ. In December 1999, an Austrian named Felix Baumgartner had leaped off the right arm of the statue wearing a low-altitude parachute, breaking the world record for the lowest BASE jump. And in 2010, vandals had used scaffolding that had been put up to repair some of the exteriors of the statue to ascend to the head and spray graffiti all over Christ's face.

But he was fairly certain he was the first person to scale the statue for a single, simple purpose: to look Christ right in the eye.

Holding tight to the bearded chin, Jack used his knees to lift himself until he was standing almost straight; his face came to about the statue's wind-damaged nose. He realized he was going to have to work a little harder, climb a little farther up the Wonder's twelve-foot tall head. With a burst of strength, he pulled himself up with the fingers of his right hand, until he was hanging from a groove where an eyebrow used to be.

Right in front of him was the statue's left eye, about the size of a small manhole cover. Up close, it seemed as smooth as the rest of the statue, a glade of soapstone on a concrete base. But Jack was certain there was something hidden behind that blank stare.

He got his iták free from the holster along his back and carefully ran the edge around the eye. It took a good minute before he felt the groove, right up where the iris would have been, had the statue been real. It was almost imperceptible, covered in a brush of soapstone, but once the iták dug through the outer layer, Jack was able to get a centimeter of the blade into the seam. Using his free hand, he twisted the iták—and a small section of the soapstone came loose on nearly microscopic hinges, about the size of a package of cigarettes, revealing a hollow cubbyhole.

Oblivious to the wind and the ache in his fingers where he gripped the statue, Jack reholstered the iták and jammed his free hand into the cubby. About a foot in, his palm touched what felt like parchment, wrapped around something small and solid. He pulled the item free, closing the soapstone cover behind it. Then he lowered himself back below the statue's chin and onto the shoulder. Straddling the vast deltoid with his legs, he unwrapped the parchment and lifted the object free.

Heavy, though it fit in the palm of his hand, plated in bronze that shone even in the near darkness, crafted with sophisticated precision, down to the carved, beady eyes and the hint of a forked tongue, the snake-head—the first segment from the stone tablet that Andy had taken back to the Rio hotel—was staggeringly beautiful. In all his expeditions, Jack had never seen anything quite like it. And then he carefully turned the segment over and saw something that shocked him even further. The segment was filled with mechanical bronze gears.

Jack's mind whirled. Just looking at the segment, he couldn't tell how old it was; but something about the artistry on the exterior of the object, the thin grooves that Jack recognized as having been made by bronze and stone tools, he had a suspicion that the thing was extremely old indeed. Certainly, if the ditched plane beneath the overgrown canopy of vegetation told him anything, it was that the segment had been placed in the statue nearly a century ago, maybe even before the Wonder of the World was finished being built. But the craftsmanship of the snake's head made him think in millennia, not centuries.

Certainly, there was plenty of evidence that complicated mechanical gear-work had existed for at least two thousand years. The famous Antikythera mechanism—gears designed to make astronomical calculations—had been found in a Greek shipwreck back in the early 1900s, and dated back to at least 100 BC. The Bronze Age itself, beginning 3300 BC, was defined by humankind's discovery of the processes of mining and smelting copper which, when combined with the alloy tin, could be made into bronze weapons, armor, and tools. There was plenty of evidence that certain Bronze Age civilizations had taken metallurgy further than that.

Even so, the snake segment's gear-work looked extremely complex; Jack had no idea what it was for, or what it could do. He realized he wasn't going to figure the mystery out there, hanging from the shoulder of Christ the Redeemer.

He began to rewrap the segment in the parchment when a stiff wind whipped across the statue's vast chest, nearly pulling the papery material out of his grip. He caught it just before it blew off into oblivion and noticed, with a start, that the backside of the parchment wasn't blank like the front.

Imprinted across the papery substance was the same symbol of the segmented snake from the stone tablet. Except this time, there was a new pictogram, flush with the second segment—one down from the snake's head:

The picture was strange, and at first Jack didn't recognize the symbol: a humanoid figure, half-man, half-woman, holding what appeared to be a sharply pointed trident. Jack immediately began to sift through his memory banks, guided by the familiar ancient weapon, trying to figure out which

Greek or Roman god might fit the iconography. And then it dawned on him.

He was off by three thousand miles, and more than two thousand years.

He began carefully rolling the segment back into the parchment, and was placing both into his jacket when a brilliant blue light exploded around him, briefly blinding him. For a moment, despite his scientific background, his thoughts raced to the supernatural—that he'd inadvertently triggered the rapture, and considering where he was at that moment, he was pretty sure he wasn't heading anywhere good.

But then the blue shifted to purple, and then burgundy red. Jack squinted down past his feet and saw the banks of LEDs bursting to life along the top of the statue's granite base. The light show had begun.

Rapture or not, it was time for Jack to get out of there, before someone noticed him hanging a few feet below Christ's head. He began the climb back down the chest of the great Wonder, his thoughts still captivated by the bronze snake's head wrapped in parchment, and the strange new pictogram.

Half man, half woman, with a trident in its hand.

CHAPTER TEN

The image was still fresh in Jack's mind as he leaped up the last flight of stairs leading to his team's hotel room, on the second floor of a flamingo-pink building at the end of a cobbled alley. The neon light from the disco across the street was even visible here, in a cinderblock stairwell with inch-wide slits instead of windows; garish orange and red and blue, flashing across his face as he reached for the doorknob.

He was already talking as he threw open the door, reaching into his jacket to retrieve the parchment and the snake-head.

"Get ready to have your minds blown," he started—and then he froze, the two items still hidden beneath his arm.

The hotel room was Spartan and compact; a dresser by the door, with a black-and-white television set. A pair of double beds by the window. And a little two-seater couch in front of a knee-high coffee table. Andy was sitting on one of the beds, a little plastic specimen container in his hands. Dashia was on the other bed, her laptop open on the pillow in front of her. But Jack's attention was immediately drawn to the couch.

"And who the hell are you?" he asked. He hadn't meant it to come out like that, but after the events of the past two days, he was beginning to run low on tolerance for surprises. And certainly, the woman was a surprise.

Angular face, with a nose a little too small to be perfect but not unpleasant; cheekbones that could have rivaled the statue he had just climbed down; long reddish-brown hair held back behind her ears, and gray-blue eyes. She was wearing a suit, which was strange, considering that it was Rio and well after midnight. And she had the leather flight diary that Jack had taken from the plane open on her lap.

"Relax, Doc," Andy said. "She's not here to repossess your car, although that was my first guess when she showed up at the door. She's a Doc, like you. Although she's a real scientist."

The woman attempted a smile, but it was obvious she wasn't used to the gesture.

"Botanical geneticist, actually. Michigan State. Sloane Costa. I'm sorry to barge in on you like this, but my flight got in a couple hours ago, and I was hoping you might be up."

Jack didn't move, his hand still cupping the parchment-wrapped snake-head.

"Do I know you?"

She shook her head, her hair barely moving with the motion.

"Although I'm a recent fan of your work. I've been reading your papers nonstop for the past twenty-four hours. In particular, your work on the mythological Amazonian culture intrigues me—well, enough that I tracked you down through your department head at Princeton and caught the earliest flight I could find to Brazil."

Normally, Jack would have been happy to shoot the breeze with a fellow scientist, but he had much more important work to do. Then his gaze went again to the leather-bound flight diary, and he felt a tinge of possessiveness.

"Do you have any idea what I went through to get that?"

"It's pretty amazing," Sloane said. "I mean, I'm sure it's some sort of hoax—it has to be some sort of hoax. But I think I've figured out what it's meant to make us believe. I think I know whose flight diary this is supposed to have been."

Jack was barely listening to her. He wanted to grab the leather diary off of her lap and toss her out into the alley.

"Dr. Costa, I'm sure whatever you came here for is important, but we're kind of in the middle of something."

Sloane looked at him for a full beat.

"I'm kind of in the middle of something too, Dr. Grady. I came here directly from Rome. The Colosseum, actually. Because I found something strange."

Andy held up the plastic specimen container. Jack could see a fleck of something inside.

"It's a paint chip," Andy said. "Dr. Costa says it was made from a pressed vine."

"A very unique vine," Sloane chimed in. "Of which I've also collected a very unique seed. That's how I found you."

"You found me because of a vine?"

"A very old vine. Dating back to the Bronze Age, to my surprise. After I left the Colosseum, I did some research. Turns out this particular red vine has been mentioned exactly three times in historical documents. A travelogue by the Greek historian Herodotus describing the Hanging Gardens of Babylon; a war record by an aide to Alexander the Great, describing the conquest of a small village defended by a tribe of women warriors; and a poem by a papal scholar from the first days of the Vatican, about a cult of female warriors he called the Order of Eve."

Jack blinked. The woman was watching him carefully now, and he found the experience a bit intimidating. She was sharp, that was for sure— but there was something a little terrifying about her stiffness, the way she perched on the edge of the couch, her fingers clasped above the open-flight diary.

"You can see how I got to you," she continued. "At least two of those documents had some relationship to mythical stories about the Amazons. And the Hanging Gardens of Babylon might very well have implied a connection as well. From what I understand, as the legend goes, King Nebuchadnezzar II built them to please his homesick wife—a former female warrior captured by the Babylonians."

Jack nodded. He wasn't sure he liked the way she was bandying about the term "mythical" with each mention of the civilization he had dedicated the past few years to studying. But he couldn't fault the logic that had led her to him. Still, it seemed a little crazy, traveling all that way because of a paint chip.

"That's all pretty fascinating," Jack started. "But I'm not sure how I can help. I don't know the first thing about vines—"

"Actually, the vine isn't the reason I'm here, Dr. Grady."

And then she unclasped her fingers and pointed with a short, unmanicured nail.

Sitting on the coffee table in front of her knees was a shiny bronze snake segment, filled with mechanical gears.

CHAPTER ELEVEN

The blade was incredibly sharp—a near microscopic sliver of titanium, mounted with fragments of pure obsidian, fractured down to the width of a single molecule. So sharp, in fact, that Jendari Saphra couldn't pinpoint the moment when it flicked across the palm of her hand.

It took less than an eighth of a second for the blade to remove the half-dozen skin cells the DNA lock needed to run the protein scan—and only twice as long again before the bright red light above the vault door blinked green, indicating that Jendari's DNA matched with the retina scan she'd already endured on the way into the mahogany-lined anteroom.

She took her hand off the scanning pad and instinctively brushed it against her pressed silk slacks. Of course, the scan had been completely painless. Jendari, who'd minored in electrical engineering at Yale nearly forty years ago and had endowed assistant professorships in biogenetics at no less than four Ivy League schools since then, had overseen the development process of the DNA scanner herself, and the device was considered one of the most reliable state-of-the-art security systems on the market. Electronic codes could be broken. Fingerprints could be faked. Even retinas could be counterfeited. But living DNA, literally the essence of life itself, was a pure and perfect signature.

In fact, over the past twenty-five years, Jendari had built an entire empire around the exploitation of those microscopic twists of DNA. The scanner was just one of a hundred such advances that had come out of Saphra Industries' dozen genetics-focused laboratories spread across Europe and Southeast Asia—everything from at-home tests for various diseases, to instant paternity assays, to prenatal scanners, to security identification platforms now used by the majority of commercial banks and government offices in the developed world. In the past year, even the Pentagon had installed a number of the DNA scanners, replacing outdated infrared readers that had a tendency to malfunction when the lower-floors' air-conditioning systems went out. Jendari had no idea how much the military contract had been worth to her company's bottom line; she'd long ago stopped thinking of her business in terms as petty and imperfect as revenue and profits. After the first billion, money lost its significance. There were much more palpable measures of continued success.

Jendari listened as the electronic locks that circumnavigated the vault's circular, reinforced titanium door began to click off, one by one. At around the halfway point, her attention was interrupted by a voice breaking out of an intercom panel on the ceiling above her head.

"Ms. Saphra, we're beginning our descent to ten thousand feet, in preparation for landing. We should be on the ground in less than twenty minutes."

Jendari felt the floor beneath her feet dip slightly, but she didn't reach for any of the polished chrome handles embedded in the leather-padded walls. As usual there was almost no turbulence. She'd had the Boeing 767 fitted with the most modern available dampeners—not because she was bothered by something as trivial as turbulence, but because lately, she'd spent more time on the plane than she had in any of her homes.

The 767 was almost as comfortable as many of them; she'd customized the thing with two bedrooms, three marble bathrooms, a small gym, and of course her traveling office, which was really more of a command center, outfitted with an electronic communication system that rivaled any of the airborne facilities she'd ever seen, except maybe the array on Air Force One.

Then again, she was quite certain that Air Force One did not have a built-in vault.

A soft buzz echoed through the anteroom as the final set of electronic locks disengaged. Slowly, the door swung inward on ultra-smooth magnetic hinges. The door was eight inches thick, both bulletproof and bombproof. Similarly, this entire section of the Boeing 767 had been crafted out of the nearly impervious material, and was designed to separate from the rest of the fuselage in the event of a crash. Of course, Jendari didn't expect to survive a thirty-thousand-foot plummet by sealing herself in a titanium can. But the vault wasn't a panic room; it hadn't been designed to keep *her* intact.

She stepped through the open doorway into complete blackness, shivering slightly as the cool air splashed against her cheeks. The windowless vault was kept at a brisk forty-three degrees Fahrenheit at all times. Likewise, twin dehumidifiers built into the self-enclosed ventilation system scrubbed most of the moisture from the air. The combined effect often made Jendari feel like she was stepping out of one of the most expensive private airplanes in the world and into some sort of ancient desert tomb.

As the door sealed shut behind her and the lights automatically rose to a level slightly dimmer than twilight, the shapes that appeared around her only added to the feeling. From free-standing stone, bronze, and ivory statues that rose up from the titanium floor to the hermetically sealed Plexiglas shelves filled with smaller items—gold coins, stone tablets, ancient carvings, bronze devices—that lined the walls, it was a setting that rivaled any museum exhibit dedicated to ancient cultures in the world. But from the moment she stepped deeper into the vault, her eyes trained on the ceiling, she knew she was in a place far beyond the reach of any museum curator's most frenzied dreams.

She didn't stop moving until she was directly under the great bronze wheel, which was suspended from the curved ceiling on an articulated, pneumatic arm. With the press of a button hidden next to a nearby shelf, she could lower the six-hundred-pound wheel almost to the floor; but for the moment, she was content to stand in silence beneath the polished bronze, marveling at the sophistication of its design.

To describe it as a wheel wasn't entirely accurate, though Jendari struggled to find a better word. The object was a perfect circle, and indeed, carved directly into its face were exactly ten thousand perfectly symmetrical spokes. Though impossible to see from that distance, especially in the dim light of the vault, Jendari knew that between the spokes were hundreds of thousands of pictograms—some as small as a pin's head, others the size of a finger or a thumb—that would take many, many lifetimes to completely decipher. Twice a week for nearly a decade, Henry Grange and his most trusted archaeological colleagues had been meticulously working their way from spoke to spoke, cataloging the pictograms, and in all that time, they had barely made it through five degrees of the wheel. Even so, what they had deciphered was nothing short of spectacular.

According to Grange and his scientists, the pictograms—a favorite early linguistic tool of many ancient human cultures, from hunter-gatherer tribes in Africa, the Americas, and Asia to early Sumerians, Egyptians, Greeks, and even Romans—were aligned in a rudimentary chronology, dating far back into the early Bronze Age, nearly eight thousand years ago. Though it was impossible to corroborate any of the details or events that were being chronicled—recorded history didn't go back anywhere near that far—the pictograms seemed to be charting the history of one particular civilization, from its inception in what appeared to be an idyllic garden, through various nomadic travels throughout the known world of the time period, via ship, foot, and carriage, on into a stationary culture, through the development of towns and even cities. Along the way, there were images of wars, natural tragedies, and technological developments—everything from primitive timekeepers and astronomy aids to irrigation aqueducts.

Grange's team had filled hundreds of notebooks, interpreting the tiny percent of the wheel they had gone through; stacked along one shelf on the far wall of the vault, the notebooks represented less than the first three centuries charted by the pictograms on the wheel. Jendari could only imagine how many books it would take to describe the civilization's history encompassed in all ten thousand spokes.

The detailed face of the wheel itself and the pictograms between the spokes would have been a find worthy of an entire museum, let alone any self-respecting billionaire's private vault. But the pictograms were not the most impressive feature of the wheel suspended above Jendari's head. The object's most impressive feature was something that she couldn't even see.

Jendari shivered again, though this time it had nothing to do with the temperature in the vault. Staring up at the huge circle of bronze, so many years since she'd gazed upon it for the first time, she could still hardly believe what she knew to be true. Only when she closed her eyes and thought back to the moment when she had first been led down into the basement of the nondescript cabin deep in the woods of her great-aunt's estate in Upstate New York and shown the wheel for that very first time— only then could she see what couldn't be seen, the secret that had opened the doors to so many more secrets, a rushing, violent river of secrets that had changed her world and guided her life ever since.

Imperceptible to the naked eye, the wheel was turning.

More accurately, the spokes along the face of the wheel were shifting around the center, like the interior of a roulette wheel—but at a pace so slow that it could only be properly measured in nanoseconds.

Jendari remembered what her fourteen-year-old self had thought when her great-aunt Milena, the woman who had raised her since the death of her father, had first told her the secret of the wheel. Even then, she had been skeptical that such a thing was possible. A bronze device older than the cabin they had been standing in, older than the towering fir trees in the forest around them, older than the bedrock beneath the cabin's basement floor—a device built with such sophisticated inner gear-work—it didn't seem possible. It wasn't until many years later, when Jendari had the wheel placed in a high-powered X-ray machine developed specifically for the task, that she had finally been convinced that it was true.

By then, of course, her aunt had given her many more revelations to be skeptical about. But at fourteen, the great bronze wheel had been enough to make her think her aunt had gone insane. When Milena had explained the purpose of the wheel—that it was, in fact, a cyclical calendar, not unlike the infamous calendar of the ancient Mayans, set on a vast, ten-thousand-year cycle—Jendari had known for certain: Her aunt had let a fairy tale corrode her brain.

Jendari smiled to herself as she reopened her eyes and strode out from under the wheel, toward the glass shelves that ran along the back of the vault. If only her aunt had lived a little longer, how shocked she would have been to see how far her skeptical charge had dove into that fairy tale, and how much truth she had found at the core of what had once seemed like so much fantasy.

A few feet beyond the wheel, Jendari passed between the two newest items in her vault's collection: the statue of the female warrior, now affixed to a clear, crystal pedestal, and the Sumerian tablet with the intertwined snakes—the double helix—etched across its center. The two new items fit perfectly with the other statues and artifacts strewn through the vault. A half-dozen similar female warriors, most of them smaller and in poorer condition, were scattered around the floor leading up to the glass shelves. Pottery shards, water-damaged coins, and even the odd breastplate and dagger, all imprinted with the snake-born double helix, filled many of the glass shelves. Jendari had spent a lifetime acquiring the items, spending tens of millions of dollars inserting Grange and his operatives into archaeological digs all over the world. And what she had achieved was nothing less than spectacular: the most complete collection of Amazonian artifacts in the world, arranged as chronologically as possible.

Beginning with the undatable, ancient wheel; moving on to the Sumerian tablet and the warrior statue; then on into the Minoan period in Crete, through a pair of ivory war javelins; and on into the Mycenaean period, the era of Greek mythology from 1600 BC to 1100 BC, with numerous pottery shards retrieved from the ruins of various *tholoi*, the large, hivelike tombs of the period; and beyond that, to the Dorian invasion, various coins harvested from shipwrecks along the Ionic coast; and then into the classical period, the age of Alexander the Great, where the collection grew necessarily sparse. Alexander was the first of the true ancient skeptics, the first to call the Amazons myths, even as his own generals claimed in historical documents of the time to have fought against them, and that, in fact, Alexander himself had captured and impregnated the Amazon queen Thalestris. Alexander's famous retort: "And where was I, then?" was recorded in a tract by Plutarch—an original copy of which Jendari had placed above a bronze breastplate, etched with the serpentine double helix, that Grange had found in a tomb dedicated to Thalestris that had been found via satellite telemetry, not eight miles from the ruins of the Library of Alexandria itself.

From the classic period, the collection shifted to Hellenic Greece, and then into Roman and Egyptian artifacts, ending with an entire area dedicated to the most famous of the female pharaohs, Cleopatra, who had called herself a descendent of the Amazons, and had been often portrayed in modern romantic literature as such. Two glass shelves filled with bronze and gold jewelry—wrist cuffs, necklaces, and a dozen gem-bearing rings—were Jendari's evidence that Cleopatra's claims were only a fragment of the truth.

Each piece of jewelry was imprinted somewhere on the band or base with the double helix—proof to Jendari that Cleopatra hadn't simply been a descendent of the Amazons.

She had also, almost certainly, been a member of the Order of Eve.

Jendari was engulfed in a surge of adrenaline as she passed by the shelves containing Cleopatra's jewelry, heading for the two glass units that held the most modern artifacts in the vault's collection. She always felt this way by the time she'd reached the last few items in the vault: thrilled, alive, but also tinged by something that could only be described as guilt.

She knew that her aunt's shock would have shifted into something more akin to horror had she lived long enough to see what happened when Jendari's skepticism gave way to something else: *curiosity*.

Jendari stopped in front of the final shelving unit and pressed her palm against another DNA scanner. As she waited for the shelf's lock to disengage, she thought back again to that cabin in the woods, that basement, when she had stood in front of the bronze wheel and heard the fairy tale for the very first time: that Jendari Saphra, a fourteen-year-old orphan and heir to her dead parent's multimillion dollar telecom, pharmaceutical, and biotech empire, was related by blood to a group that dated back longer than she could possibly imagine. A group that was supposedly a force of good in the world, tasked with protecting a secret that would eventually benefit all mankind. Guided by a cyclical calendar akin to the Mayans', measured in millennia by a huge bronze wheel.

Jendari had immediately begun to ask questions—but Milena had offered only blind faith. Even the highest level members of the group—wealthy, powerful women like Milena—did not know much beyond the barest details. Her only contact with the group had occurred once a year, when she would return to that same cabin, that same basement, to stand in front of the bronze wheel. If the group needed something from her, Milena would find a rolled parchment in an ornate iron box that sat on a stone bench her mother's mother had placed beneath the wheel.

At first, mostly for amusement's sake, Jendari had accompanied her aunt on the visits to the cabin; it wasn't until three years later, when Jendari turned seventeen, that she had witnessed Milena receiving a task—something mundane, involving the movement of money from one of her aunt's corporate accounts into a Manhattan-run hedge fund.

At the time, Jendari had assumed that at best, her aunt was stupid enough to have been the victim of some sort of scam. At worst, she had gone insane and dedicated her life to a bizarre cult. It wasn't until years later that she had realized her aunt wasn't stupid or insane. *She was something worse.*

The glass cabinet slid open, and Jendari reached into the shelf to retrieve two black-and-white photographs, sealed in transparent acrylic. Her adrenaline continued to rise as she held the photographs close, squinting through the dim light to make out the details.

The first photograph had been taken in front of what appeared to be the remains of a church. The church was badly damaged; the steeple had been entirely destroyed, and much of the rest of the building had collapsed in on itself, stone, chunks of mortar, and shattered bricks strewn haphazardly around what appeared to be a smoldering crater. Likewise, the area around the church was similarly ruined; buildings blasted down to their frames, sidewalks and narrow streets pockmarked with craters and holes. Though the image was black and white and grainy, any European history buff could have easily have identified what remained of the buildings and streets as pre-war Spanish in style; but no history expert could have explained what was going on in the forefront of the picture, directly in front of the church, where a group of workers were carrying what appeared to be a small iron crate out of the rubble, while in the background, three women stood watch. Two of the women were unrecognizable, but the third, younger than the rest, in a leather jacket, with short cropped hair, would have raised eyebrows the world over. Especially when one noticed the date in the corner of the photo, right beneath Jendari's thumb: September 16, 1937.

Two months after the woman in the picture supposedly had vanished at sea.

Jendari traced a finger over the iron crate in the picture, pausing on the tiny, serpentine double helix carved into the bottom corner on the far left side, then over to the faces of the three women standing watch over the workmen. She wondered, had the women in the photo spent their lives like Milena, blindly believing, blindly following orders? Had they their own cabins, their own similar drop boxes, which they dutifully visited year after year, waiting for those mysterious twists of parchment? Was it just such a parchment that had led them to that burned out church, to oversee a task they couldn't possibly understand, acting out of a pure sense of faith that left no room for questions?

To Jendari, those women, like Milena, were far worse than stupid or insane. They were followers. Naive, weak, nothing but cogs—as thoughtless as ancient bronze gears. Taking orders from an authority they knew nothing about, carrying out tasks for reasons that were never explained. Milena couldn't even answer the most simple questions about the Order to which she'd dedicated her wealth and her life—who they were, where they came from, what secret they were trying to protect—and yet she had expected Jendari to follow her down the rabbit hole of blind belief.

Jendari had not been born to be a gear. Though she had followed her aunt to the cabin and the drop box year after year, her skepticism had grown into something fiery: a passion to know more. As she had reached adulthood, she had built her own private surveillance team, using profits from her burgeoning biotech empire. Behind Milena's back, she had staked out the cabin.

It had taken years, but eventually, she had documented the arrival of a courier, who she had traced to a corporate account at a New York consulting company. She had then tracked the financiers of the consulting house to a multinational conglomerate run out of Dubai. A private company, the Euphrates Conglomerate, which, on the surface, had been almost as mysterious as the fairy tale her aunt had told her. Euphrates had no listed board of directors, no CEO—just a number of employees who worked out of an office complex in the desert capital's mercantile district. It was impossible to tell exactly what sort of business Euphrates was involved with; all Jendari's surveillance team was able to uncover for sure was that the company had endowed more than a dozen museums around the world, creating departments dedicated to unearthing and procuring artifacts from a number of significant eras in ancient history. And secondly, that Euphrates had spent a considerable amount of money on a mystery project in South America, in a remote section of Brazil, two hundred miles through dense jungle from the interior city of Manaus.

Jendari had known that her aunt would be angry at her efforts to learn more about the mysterious group behind the drop box. Milena had often told her that her own mother had passed down strict rules against digging deeper into what they were supposed to take on faith, and faith alone. But Jendari didn't care about pseudoreligious mythology. She cared about the truth.

Still, out of respect, she had waited until her aunt was on her deathbed, in the cancer wing of New York Hospital that Saphra Industries had endowed, to tell her what she had found. Jendari would never forget the look of betrayal and shock on her aunt's face and the last words she had ever spoken to Jendari before she had passed away.

You are unworthy.

Jendari felt her smile stiffen as she was overcome by resolve. She turned to the second photo encased in protective acrylic.

In the center of the photo was the same iron crate, being carried by a different set of faceless workers, in another part of the world.

A mountainous forest, beneath a recently finished monument at the southern edge of Rio that would one day become one of the Seven Wonders of the World. And there, in the background again, three women. The two older women were different than in the first photo, yet still unrecognizable; but the third woman was the same. According to the date on the corner of the picture, she had traveled nearly around the world at a speed that only a few people of her era could.

Jendari slid the photographs under her arm and headed back through the vault toward the circular titanium door.

It was those two photographs that had been the first real evidence that Jendari had uncovered—three years after Milena Saphra's death—that had led her to believe that the elder Saphra's fairy tale had been built on a basis of truth. That her fairy tale did, in fact, revolve around a secret that went far beyond any sort of financial scam or religious cult.

As Jendari crossed beneath the giant bronze wheel, the pilot's voice once again reverberated out of the PA system:

"We've reached ten thousand feet, and should be on the ground in seven minutes. The clouds have broken nicely, and there's a great view of the rainforest on either side."

Jendari could picture the undulating sea of green as she touched another scanner and waited for the vault door to reopen, so she could return to her office and prepare herself for the next phase of her journey.

It had been a long road, but she knew she was closer now than she had ever been. She could never have predicted the shift that had occurred in the past few days; like the spokes on the great bronze wheel, a part of her had always expected her journey to continue to move imperceptibly forward.

She could not have foreseen that the twin brother of a murdered MIT scientist would have been the key to unlocking the true secret behind the Order of Eve.

Milena Saphra would never have understood: Jendari was more than *worthy.* But she would never be content to be a gear, like her aunt, like the women in the photo, like the woman in the leather flight jacket who had traveled thousands of miles to deliver an iron crate.

Jendari wasn't a gear, and she didn't believe in fairy tales. If the Order of Eve had truly been built around a secret—protected and hidden for nearly ten thousand years—Jendari wasn't going to stop until she held that secret in her hand.

CHAPTER TWELVE

"I don't remember James Bond ever flying coach," Andy said as he worked himself and his oversized duffel bag through the narrow passage between Jack and Sloane, who were seated in two aisle seats across from each other. "It's hard enough getting all this spy shit through airport security—now I have to figure out a way to fit it in an overhead compartment?"

Jack laughed, then noticed that Sloane hadn't even cracked a smile. She had already unpacked her own carry-on, placing the items carefully across her lap and in the seat pocket in front of her. Jack saw an electronic reading device, a pair of boring-looking scientific journals, and the leather flight diary, which she'd held on to since they'd left the hotel room in Rio. The middle seat next to her was empty, and the heavyset guy in the window seat to her far left already had his head in a pillow, Xanaxed out for the long flight ahead.

"James Bond wasn't a doctoral student on a budget," Jack said, but Andy was already two rows back, rushing to catch up to Dashia, who had already found their seats. It was unfortunate that all four of them couldn't sit together, but booking internationally last minute was never optimal; add to that their shoe-string finances, and they were lucky they were only making a single stop as they nearly circumnavigated the globe.

Not just a doctoral student on a budget, Jack corrected himself—two doctoral students, a botanist, and a field anthropologist, who was now working so far outside the box, he was flirting in the realm of fantasy. He hadn't even tried to explain what he'd found at Christ the Redeemer to his department head—he'd just gone with a simple request for time and funds to continue the research that had started at the Temple of Artemis and led him down to Brazil. It wasn't a complete lie; as impossible as it seemed, there appeared to be a firm connection between the Ancient Wonder of the World and the most modern of the new Seven Wonders, though Jack still had no idea why or how. He was just lucky that he'd earned enough credit with his superiors at Princeton that they were willing to give him a little leeway.

Certainly, he was in a lot better political shape than Sloane; he'd heard part of her conversation with her supervising professor at Michigan through the cardboard-thin wall of the Rio hotel room. She'd practically had to beg the man for an expense account that would cover the coach ticket, and it was pretty obvious that she was taking a pretty big gamble attaching herself to Jack's team without any real support from her academic superiors. It seemed obvious to Jack that the paint chip and the red vine she'd found in the Colosseum were her version of a Hail Mary; the continuance of her career at Michigan might very well depend on where those clues led.

Jack had no illusions about why Sloane had followed him to Rio, or what had motivated her to join his team on this next leg of their journey. Despite what she'd said, it wasn't to pick his brain about the Amazons—a civilization which Sloane had noted again and again, she firmly believed was little more than a well-detailed myth—or to try and help him understand why they were now in the possession of two bronze snake segments, found in two separate Wonders of the Modern World. She was there to find just enough information to get her byline into one of the prestigious journals of her discipline. She was there because of a plant—something she considered a scientific riddle—and she was searching for a scientific answer that she could take back to her laboratory to study and deconstruct.

Jack, for his part, had spent the better part of his career trying to get beyond the science and to stay far away from the laboratory. As his father had always said, the laboratory was where you ended up when you could no longer hack it in the field. Kyle Grady was pushing sixty-four, and he hadn't set foot in a lab for as long as Jack had been alive.

Jack was still picturing his father, deep in the African bush, probably covered in face paint and dancing around a fresh kill with whatever new tribal family had adopted him, when the 747 began to pull away from the gate, taxiing across the tarmac. Jack glanced over at Sloane again, who was flipping between two pages in the flight diary, tracing a series of jagged lines with her finger. Her concentration was impressive; she didn't even glance up from the diary when the airplane made its tight final turn onto the runway and the giant turbine engines roared to life. It wasn't until the plane was arcing upward into the air, pressing Jack back into his seat, that she brushed an errant lock of red-brown hair out of her eyes.

"June 1, 1937," she said, barely loud enough to be heard across the aisle over the growl of the engines. "She takes off from Miami, Florida, making stops across South America, Africa, India, Southeast Asia, and ends up in Lae, New Guinea, on June 29."

It was an abrupt way to launch a conversation, but Jack had already begun to grow used to Sloane's clipped mannerisms; she didn't like to waste words, and he'd yet to see a real emotion spread across her tight, nearly porcelain white features. It was obvious she was a woman who put a lot of walls between herself and the people around her. She didn't seem at all displeased that there was an aisle between them, even as she continued the conversation that had started in the hotel room, when she'd first told him her incredible theory about the flight diary—and whose airplane Jack had found beneath the statue of Christ the Redeemer.

"And a few days later," Sloane continued, placing her glasses back over her gray-blue eyes. "She vanishes. Never to be seen again."

Jack nodded. The 747 was banking hard to the left as it cut through the cloud cover on its way to a cruising altitude.

"I think there was a book. And a movie. And a couple of documentaries."

"There have been a number of theories," Sloane said, ignoring him. "The most likely was that she'd miscalculated the distance, run out of fuel, and crashed during a mid-Pacific hop to Howland Island. Another possibility is that she'd turned back for some reason and had crashed on a nearby desolate atoll. The most outlandish theory was that she was a spy working for either the US government or the Germans, and she'd intentionally ditched the plane, then been secretly picked up by a naval ship, given a new identity, and had lived out the rest of her life, hiding in plain view."

As the 747 leveled out, Jack could see the flight attendants at the end of the aisle unstrapping themselves from their jump seats, getting ready to begin the first of their countless rituals. Soon they'd be pushing carts full of miniature beverages up and down the narrow aisles, checking seat belts, lowering window shades, and generally trying to make an eternity trapped in a flying tin can seem almost bearable. Jack figured he and Sloane had about ten more minutes to get to some sort of understanding of what the hell they were getting themselves into before the distractions became too many.

"Any of those theories have her heading to Brazil, then ditching her plane beneath Christ the Redeemer?" he asked.

He didn't expect a smile—hell, if Andy couldn't get her to crack her façade, he'd never had a chance. Still, he at least hoped for some acknowledgment that he was trying.

"According to this flight diary, she didn't go straight to Brazil," Sloane said, her voice as steady as ever. "She took off from New Guinea on July 2 at midnight, then headed into the Pacific, toward Howland Island, as she was supposed to; instead of reaching Howland, she touched down on Gard-ner Island, a little known spot in the Phoenix Island group nearby. From there, the plane doubled back toward Asia, and on into Europe, ending in an airfield near a village called Cuarzon, in the South of Spain. Two days later, she left Spain and flew back again across the Atlantic, finally heading toward Rio, Brazil."

Jack looked past Sloane's finger, toward the lines and numbers that spread out across the pages of the flight diary. He was impressed that she'd been able to interpret the notations so quickly. She was stiff and way too logical for his liking, but she wasn't going to be completely useless.

"That's quite a flight plan," Jack said. "Pretty incredible evidence that we're diving into something extraordinary."

"Actually, like I said before, I believe it's nothing more than an elaborate hoax. I don't know who set this up, and I don't know why—I'm just telling you what we're supposed to believe, based on this diary."

Jack touched the backpack he'd stored snuggly beneath the seat in front of him.

"These artifacts seem pretty real to me," he said quietly. He could feel the bulge of the stone tablet beneath the vinyl of the bag, and beneath that, the two snake segments, which he'd wrapped separately in hand towels from the Rio hotel. They'd attempted to place them gently together in the hotel, but the pieces hadn't fit; they hadn't wanted to risk damaging them by forc-ing the matter.

Even worse, Jack had been forced to take both segments out of the bag while going through security at the Rio airport; when the Brazilian equivalent to a TSA agent had tried to poke a gloved finger at the mechanical gears within one of the segments, he'd nearly decked the guy. Luckily, Sloane had stepped in, telling the man that the snake pieces were fragile antique toys she had bought for her cousin. The Brazilian TSA agent had shrugged, obviously more interested in the bottle of shampoo Andy had tried sneaking through in his duffel bag beneath the infrared dish and the climbing rope—both of which had garnered surprisingly little attention.

Sloane shrugged. There was no way she could explain away the segments or the stone tablet. Especially since she'd seen the exact same picture on the wall in the hypogeum of the Colosseum and after Jack had explained to her that he'd also seen and photographed the same painting in the pit beneath the Temple of Artemis.

For the moment, whatever Sloane believed, they needed to treat what they were diving into as more than a hoax.

"I've never heard of Cuarzon," he said, going back to the narrative she'd just given him. "But Spain in the late thirties was caught up in a pretty intense civil war. Towns and villages were getting bombed and burned into oblivion, and almost six hundred thousand people died."

"The Spanish Civil War. A devastating time—but what does it have to do with what we've found?"

"Maybe the destruction going on during the Spanish Civil War had something to do with the transportation of these artifacts halfway around the world. Christ the Redeemer had just finished construction, and though it wasn't yet a Wonder of the World, it was as impressive as anything that had ever been built in modern times."

A war was going on in Spain, towns were burning to the ground all over the country, and according to the flight diary, that's where the plane he'd found beneath Corcovado had made a stop after the pilot had faked her own disappearance. Jack wondered, *Is it possible that the stone tile and the snake segment were moved to a place that seemed safer than where they had been stored before? Had they been intentionally hidden beneath a Wonder of the World?*

The line of thought pricked at Jack's mind. He'd been studying one of the Seven Wonders of the Ancient World for some time because of what he believed to be a connection to the ancient Amazons. Along the way, he'd gained a broader knowledge of the other Ancient Wonders, and he knew that six of the seven had been destroyed over the years by natural disasters and wars. Even so, most of them had lasted hundreds, if not thousands of years.

The Seven Wonders of the Modern World, by the very nature of their worldwide designation, would probably last almost as long. *Didn't that make the Seven Wonders the perfect hiding places for something that was supposed to stay hidden for hundreds, if not thousands of years?*

"Supposing any of this is true," Sloane said. "What could be so important about the tablet, and the segments, that you'd need to hide them at all? And the time frame we're talking about it's hard to even fathom."

Jack had to agree with her. The object he'd recovered from the statue in Brazil had presumably been there as long as the ditched airplane—more than eighty years. The segment Sloane had recovered at the Colosseum had been sealed into an aqueduct perhaps as many as two thousand years ago. It was almost incomprehensible that the two objects could be related over such a long period of time, but there they were, wrapped in cheap, dirty hand towels in the backpack beneath his feet.

"A pair of snake segments," he said, mostly to himself. "Connected to a picture of women warriors carrying a tablet out of a forest—"

"A garden," Sloane corrected.

"What do you mean?"

Sloane's voice sped up a notch as Jack saw that the flight attendants had one of the beverage carts unlocked and moving already—still a good fifteen rows away, but making its way toward them, one miniature bottle of booze at a time.

"It's not a forest in the picture, it's a garden. The variety of plants and vines, and the way they are planted—grouped by species, carefully intertwined so that the more aggressive genuses don't overwhelm the more placid—implies that they were cultivated and controlled. It's not haphazard or random growth. Hence, it's a garden—not a forest."

Jack's mind started to churn. His first thought went right to his wheel-house.

"Like the Hanging Gardens of Babylon."

Sloane shook her head.

"I thought so too, at first. But then I looked up the Ancient Wonder and saw that every image of the Hanging Gardens, and every description—from Herodotus on up—describes a terraced palace, with sophisticated vertical irrigation. The garden on our tablet isn't terraced. And it doesn't appear to be mechanically irrigated."

Jack had another thought. The cart was eight rows away now.

"The Garden of Eden? I didn't spend much time in Sunday School, but if I remember my Genesis correctly, it was a natural garden, wasn't it?"

"It makes sense that you'd go there," Sloane said. "Considering where you just were. But garden imagery is common to almost every culture, and nearly every religion on Earth, past and present, begins with flora: a garden, a vine, a Tree of Life. Pick any god you'd like, the first thing he does is make a plant. Only then, he starts thinking about people."

Jack raised an eyebrow. That had almost qualified as a joke.

"You know a lot about religion?"

"I know a lot about gardens. Being a botanical geneticist."

She was definitely warming up—but then she shrugged again and closed the leather flight diary against her lap.

"But I still can't see how any of this is really relevant. The facts we're dealing with don't have anything to do with religious gardens or any other sort of superstition. What we know—and all that we know—is that some-one hid the tablet next to a ditched airplane beneath Christ the Redeemer and hid a snake segment at the statue's peak. They hid another segment beneath the Colosseum. Whether either of these events happened a hun-dred years ago, a couple thousand years ago, or last week, the fact remains that these items were hidden in two of the most famous architectural achievements in the world. Which leads me to believe they were hidden, but also meant to one day be found."

Cold, scientific logic. Jack wasn't certain that such an approach meant anything, in the face of what they had found—but he was willing to go along.

"Meant to be found by whom?"

"Presumably not us," Sloane said.

And presumably not my brother, Jack thought to himself.

The flight attendants were so close now, he could hear them chatting to the nearby passengers about the breakfast options. He looked around, at the people in the seats in the rows in front of him, at the strangers—men, women, a few children—that filled almost every other seat on the partially booked flight.

If his brother had truly been murdered because of what he'd found, Jack and Sloane were potentially in danger as well. Jack didn't care so much about his own safety; hell, he could handle himself, and he'd faced some pretty hairy situations over the years. But when he thought about Andy and Dashia, near the back of the plane, probably going over the same set of mysteries, he became extremely uncomfortable. Then he glanced back at Sloane, who had traded the flight diary for one of her scientific journals. The title of the article she was reading had something to do with dandelions and allergens. Not the sort of thing Jack would choose to begin twenty-two hours of traveling from Brazil to India by way of Frankfurt, but then again, he'd just learned the difference between a forest and garden.

He reminded himself: Sloane Costa was there on her own accord. Not because of his brother, not even because she truly believed there was a connection between the Seven Wonders of the World. Sloane was there because she was desperate, and trying to keep her job.

Even so, watching her sitting there, with her perfect posture, her hair combed so tightly against her head that he could see every strand, Jack knew that if what they were diving into was truly dangerous, if people were willing to kill to keep whatever it was a secret . . .

It would be up to him to keep Sloane, and the rest of his team, safe. Which meant somehow, he needed to figure out what the hell that were getting themselves into—as fast as he could.

CHAPTER THIRTEEN

The rat was huge.

At least eighteen inches tail to snout, but it seemed almost twice as big, lunging through the air at almost supernatural speed, front claws outstretched, oversized jaws wide open, fangs bared and dripping fetid teardrops of saliva toward the steaming sidewalk.

The thing was moving so damn fast, Jack didn't have time to think; his reflexes took over, and suddenly he was diving forward, catching Sloane around the waist with one arm and lifting her a full foot off the ground. Sloane screamed in shock, grabbing at him with her hands, but he ignored her, spinning on his heels away from the rabid creature.

He was halfway around when he realized he had miscalculated Sloane's weight; her body was a good deal tighter and toned beneath the thin material of her pantsuit than he had expected, and the added momentum sent them teetering across the crowded sidewalk, right over the low stone curb. Only a last-second adjustment—a dip in his knees, a twist of his waist, putting her halfway over his right shoulder—kept them from toppling beneath the motorcycle rickshaw that was blasting past them, going the wrong way through the surging, traffic-laden street.

And then Jack heard the laughter, which seemed to be coming from everywhere at once. Still holding Sloane over one shoulder, he whirled back toward the rat—and that's when he noticed the collar, studded with what appeared to be rhinestones, tight around the hissing creature's throat. A metal linked chain ran from the collar to a steel post set in front of a narrow glass storefront. Above the rat, a web of cracks spread across most of the glass, but in between the jagged shards, Jack could see shelves lining three walls of a space barely larger than an airplane lavatory. The shelves were cluttered with cheap-looking souvenirs: wood-carved Buddhas, brassy statuettes of various Hindu gods, ornate, painted festival masks with wide eyes, beards, and toothy grins beneath headdresses made of peacock feathers and dried flowers.

"Unless you want to go for an encore," Sloane hissed in his ear, "I think you can put me down now."

Jack glanced sheepishly at the small throng that had gathered around them on the crowded sidewalk. Nobody else seemed bothered by the snapping mutant rodent, still hurling itself repeatedly into the air toward every errant calf that seemed within a fang's length of the end of the creature's chain.

Then again, Jack shouldn't have been surprised. After all, this wasn't his first time in Delhi.

"Sorry," he said, gently returning Sloane to her feet. Then he pointed past the rat, at the storefront. "Heck of a marketing gimmick. Nothing like a little rabies to make you feel right at home."

Sloane brushed dust from the street off of her slacks. The crowd around them had returned to its normal pace, which meant it was like trying to stand still in torrential floodwaters. Arms and knees and elbows everywhere as a continuous stream of humanity buffeted by, taking up nearly every inch of the cobbled sidewalk. The street was no better. They had been lucky that it was just one rickshaw going the wrong way that had almost decapitated them. The crumbling pavement was so thick with traffic, it was impossible to know where one lane ended and another began.

"This is the place?" Sloane asked, straightening up. She looked at the broken window, and then at the rat. "You've got to be kidding me."

Jack grinned. Despite the look on her face, Sloane had actually been taking things in stride since they'd landed at New Delhi International, which was really the only way to face India. The country in general, and Delhi in particular, was a place of such violent extremes, you either went with the flow, or you went crazy trying to swim against it. From the minute they'd stepped out of the modern airport into that thick blanket of oppressive heat and fought their way past a sea of beggars, street salesmen, and taxi drivers to the pair of three-wheeled vehicles Andy had hired to squire them about town, it had been like diving into a sea of perpetual motion. The deeper they'd gone into the old city nestled in the heart of the throbbing Eastern metropolis, the more frenetic the pace had become. Everything in Old Delhi *moved*; winding spaghetti twists of streets pulsing past slums built right in the shadows of fancy condominiums, outdoor markets teeming with salesman selling anything and everything, seedy alleys crawling with beggars, pickpockets, and packs of wild children. The place was alive, beautiful and horrible and terrifying and thrilling, all at once.

Jack had been to India a half a dozen times before he'd learned to just breathe—no matter how thick and pungent the air seemed. But Sloane hadn't seemed fazed at all. There were no cracks in her cool façade, no matter how hot it had gotten around them.

"A souvenir shop?" she said.

"Something like that," Jack said, leading her to the door on the other side of the broken glass, keeping a healthy distance away from the leaping rat.

As he opened the door, he took one last glance down the street behind them, not sure what he was looking for in a mob of strangers, most in traditional Indian garb, flowing white, brown, and gray shirts and pants tied at the waist. But since leaving Brazil, his paranoia had continued to grow. It was part of the reason he'd decided to split his team up upon landing in Delhi, and had sent Andy and Dashia out on their own to make arrangements for the next leg of their journey. Truth be told, he'd rather have been alone at the moment. And it wasn't just the thought of what had happened to Jeremy that had him on edge.

"Just follow my lead," he whispered to Sloane as he stepped into the shop. "And let me do the talking."

"I thought this guy was supposed to be a friend of your father's," Sloane whispered back. "I thought that's why we were coming to him for information."

"I didn't say he was a friend, just that he and my father spent time together out in the field."

"What sort of field?"

Jack didn't answer, instead shutting the door behind him, effectively cutting off the sound from the street outside. The shop was deserted, the cluttered shelves around them much more towering up close, some of them seeming to be on the verge of collapsing under the weight of so many wares. Jack counted at least thirty Buddhas to his right, of assorted sizes and poses. The shelves, filled with statues depicting various other gods, were almost twice as crowded, the diversity of shapes, creatures, and stances almost mind-numbing.

"So many gods," Sloane said, her voice echoing off the bare cement ceiling and floor.

"So many religions," Jack said. "Most people think of India as divided between Hindus and Muslims, but there are actually over a hundred different religions here. As well as eighty-five indigenous languages—eleven of them official. People say that America is a melting pot, but we've got nothing on this place."

"Melting's the appropriate word. I think it's hotter in here than it was outside. Is this place even open? I don't think anybody's home."

Jack looked past the farthest shelving unit, which was only about five feet in front of him, to a small desk and cash register stuffed into a corner beneath a poster of some famous Bollywood star decked out in bright red robes. Sloane was right, there didn't seem to be anyone manning the place. Jack was about to suggest that they return later when he noticed a discoloration in the wall behind the register—and realized he was looking at a door. Well, half a door; it couldn't have been more than two feet wide, and there was no knob.

"Stay here," Jack said. "I'm going to check something out."

He hadn't taken more than two steps toward the cash register when a buzzer went off somewhere above his head, and suddenly, the half door swung open and a man with wild eyes came barreling out of the opening toward him. The man looked disheveled and unshaven, except for his head, which was as shiny as blown glass. The man was average size, a little smaller than Jack; but there was a gun in his right hand, aimed directly at Jack's chest. The gun looked like a museum piece—a German Luger with a pencil-neck tip and an ink-black grip—but it was coming toward Jack faster than the rat outside on the sidewalk.

Again, Jack let his reflexes take over. He stepped into the attack with his left foot, putting himself out of line with the gun barrel, while in the same motion his right hand slid around beneath his jacket and withdrew his iták. Before the man's wild eyes even saw what was happening, Jack had the blade out, caught the man by the wrist, and slammed the iták's hilt down on the back of the man's extended hand.

The man screamed, his fingers opening as the gun clattered harmlessly to the floor. He yanked his wrist free, then stepped back and looked wildly from Jack to Sloane. Jack lowered the iták, holding up his free palm.

"We're not here to cause any trouble."

BEN MEZRICH

"I got nothing worth stealing," the man spat back in a heavy, down-market English accent. "And if you're with Interpol, I ain't the man on the posters. It's a goddamn case of mistaken identity, it is."

"We're not thieves and we're not cops. This is Sloane Costa, and my name is Jack Grady."

The man's eyes got a little less wild.

"Grady?"

"Kyle Grady is my father."

A wide smile broke across the man's unshaven face. There was a tooth or two missing, but overall, it made him look almost friendly.

"Little Jacky. I remember you when you were just a tow-headed shit. Why the hell didn't you say something?"

"Didn't really get a chance."

"Sorry about that," the man said, still grinning as he rubbed the growing bruise on the back of his hand. "You've got your dad's reflexes, that's for sure. Can't tell you how many scars I've got from wrestling with your old man, back when we were hopping freights along the Trans-Siberian."

The man pointed at the iták that was still hanging from Jack's grip.

"Visayan Islands. I'd say Kalip Tribe, up the Northern Shore. You looking to sell? The grip alone'd probably get you three grand."

Jack shook his head, both impressed and unnerved by how accurate the man's guess had been. Then again, from what his father had told him, Gordon Unger had an eye for antiquities. Especially objects from Southeast Asia, although his focus had primarily shifted to the Indian subcontinent in recent years. Kyle Grady had referenced Unger a number of times, back when Jack had been spending time with him; he was supposedly the man you went to when you needed information that involved Southeast Asia. Jack's father had also warned him that information from Unger often came with a price—but Jack needed an expert, and he didn't have time to go touring museums.

"We're not here to sell anything. We're here to ask you a few questions about the Taj Mahal."

Unger laughed, then saw that Jack was serious. He waved his unbruised hand toward one of the nearby shelves, which was loaded with miniature plastic and wooden models of the great Indian Wonder of the World.

"You came to the right place. I've also got posters and some tourist maps, if you're keen."

He shifted his gaze from Jack to Sloane. His eyes lingered a little too long as he looked her over, then he pointed his finger back at Jack.

"But something tells me you're not here for a poster or a map."

He grinned, and suddenly bent forward to retrieve the gun from the floor. He jammed it into his belt, then turned and headed to the half door behind the cash register.

"Follow me, Little Jacky. We'll see if I've got something in the back that can help you out."

• • •

"Quite simply, it's the greatest love story ever told."

The teeth weren't quite as bad seen through the neck of a bottle of Jack Daniel's, but there was still something unsettling about that grin, halfway between wolf and weasel, which were two of the words Jack's father had often used to describe Unger, his former expedition partner. Kyle Grady had never been clear about where, or for how long, he had traveled with the Brit; but it was clear the two had spent some quality time living in the wilderness of at least two former Soviet republics before Unger had turned his focus toward Southeast Asia.

The minute they'd entered the back room of the souvenir shop, Unger had begun to regale Jack with stories about his father, most of which involved drinking, women, and violence; from the time they'd nearly been beheaded because Unger had made a pass at the daughter of a Kyrgyzstani warlord, to the moment Kyle and he had parted ways, due to a "misunderstanding" involving a pair of emerald daggers they'd liberated from a Mongol tomb. According to Unger, they'd remained friends—even though both bore matching inch-long dagger scars hidden somewhere under their clothes.

But Jack wasn't in Delhi to reminisce about his father. It wasn't until Unger led him and Sloane through a second door—this one much more substantial than the first, thick redwood lined in what appeared to be plates of iron—and shifted his dialogue to the great mausoleum, the subject of "the greatest love story ever told," that Jack's focus snapped tight.

The change from the front of the shop to the back was night and day; all pretense of the place being a common souvenir market disappeared the moment Unger flicked on the fluorescent ceiling lights, revealing a windowless, rectangular room lined with pristine glass shelves and oversize, backlit onyx cabinets. The fixtures alone looked like they'd cost a fortune, but it was the items on the shelves that immediately drew Jack's attention. In just the first few shelves, he counted three Buddhas carved from pure jade, a pair of gold statues of Ganesh, the Hindu elephant god—each of her eight hands holding what appeared to be a perfectly formed opal, sparkling ocean-blue in the harsh light—and an Indo-themed Fabergé egg, lodged in a Plexiglas cube.

The collection only grew more exceptional the farther Unger led them into what could only be described as a warehouse for precious antiquities. A second shelving unit displayed more gold statues of a dozen different Hindu gods, spaced between cabinets filled with glistening antique jewelry—necklaces, bangles, anklets, rings. Next to that, a cabinet was filled with a variety of swords, daggers, and other ancient weapons of war—spiked maces, halberds, and spears, as well as various antique torture devices, including brass thumbscrews, steel-tipped flails, even a miniature iron maiden in perfect condition. Another cabinet contained more of the traditional masks that Jack had seen out front, but these masks weren't made of cheap plaster. They had been carved from the finest bronze, gold, and silver, their features accented with semiprecious gemstones.

Jack knew, from the first item to the last, that none of these objects had been acquired legally; you didn't store a legally acquired Fabergé egg in a backroom in a slum in Old Delhi. This wasn't a souvenir store, it was a one-stop shopping mart for black-market antiquities. No wonder Unger had come at Jack with the gun; just one of the golden elephant gods, no doubt pilfered from a local tomb, could land Unger in an Indian prison for the rest of his life.

But Jack kept his thoughts to himself as Unger showed him and Sloane to a small circular table at the back of the room, right in front of the glass cabinet of weapons and torture devices, and directed them to a trio of metal folding chairs. While they took their seats, he rummaged through a large crate tucked behind the cabinet; when he returned to the table, his grin had doubled in size, revealing a few more missing teeth—and in his hands was a long cardboard canister about the size of a poster mailer, sealed on both ends with plastic knobs.

"Like you said," Jack started as Unger yanked at one of the knobs. "Love story or no, a poster of the Taj isn't exactly what we're looking for."

Unger laughed, then pulled a rolled-up sheet of aging paper out of the canister and slammed it down against the table.

"Impatience runs in your family, Little Jacky. Feast your eyes on this."

It wasn't a poster, it was an architectural blueprint of the entire Taj Mahal complex, and it was quite unlike anything Jack had ever seen before. The level of detail was incredible, from the three-dimensional cutaways of the famous white marble tomb that topped the mausoleum, to the four paneled gardens that led past the reflecting pool, to the building's arched entrance.

It was as if almost every blade of grass was accounted for, every inch of marble and stone. Much of the written notations along all four sides of the blueprint were in Hindi and Sanskrit, languages that Jack had never mastered; but there were also measurements in easily decipherable numbers, along with longitudes and latitudes.

"So the story goes," Unger said as Jack and Sloane leaned over the blueprint. "The Taj was built between 1632 and 1652 by the most powerful Mughal king, Shah Jahan, as a mausoleum for the beloved third wife of his harem, Mumtaz Mahal. Architecturally, it's an Indo-Persian blend of style, technology, and artistry that set the bar for all Muslim constructs that came afterward."

"The third wife of his harem," Sloane said. "Not exactly an auspicious beginning for a love story."

"Harem or no, it was a special relationship," Unger winked. "Especially for the time period. Mumtaz Mahal had been given to Jahan in childhood, and he had grown up with her as his best friend. He called her 'the chosen one of the palace,' and considered her not only his wife, but also his most important advisor. Together, they built his empire into one of the most powerful and enlightened of the time; its breadth and scale rivaled that of his forefather, Genghis Khan."

Jack had heard the story before, at some point in his undergraduate work at Princeton. He'd even visited the Taj twice with his father, but he'd been too young to appreciate the magnificence of the architecture, which was surprisingly even more pronounced in the perfectly balanced lines and symmetrical curves spread across the antique blueprint.

"When Mumtaz passed away giving birth to her fourteenth child," Unger continued, "Shah Jahan went into a fit of mourning. He fasted for eight days, and spent the next two years alone in the dark basement halls of the Red Fort, his castle in nearby Agra. When he came out of the basement, he set to work building the ultimate memorial to his perfect love—the Taj Mahal."

Jack's father had given Jack the same monologue as they'd toured the pristine gardens, then gazed at the shimmering reflection of the marble Wonder in the still water of the reflecting pool at the garden's exact center.

"On her deathbed," Jack said, remembering, "Mumtaz had asked Jahan to build her a resting place that rivaled anything that had ever been built before. She asked for nothing less than the most beautiful building in the world, something that would be eternal, like their love."

"Women, right?" Unger grunted, giving a sideways glance to Sloane, and again, lingering a little too long over the soft glade of pale skin above the collar of her buttoned shirt. Then he turned back to Jack.

"When you think of the Taj, what do you think of first?"

Jack didn't have to pause.

"The dome."

"Of course. White marble, perfectly, mathematically symmetrical. One hundred and fifteen feet tall, one hundred and eighty feet in diameter, situated on a cylindrical base that's about twenty-five feet long. Shaped like an onion, a true wonder of architecture."

Jack nodded. It was all there in the blueprint. No mortar or support struts; the dome had been built by laying concentric circles of stone on top of each other, and it was actually the weight of the construct itself that kept it together. The main dome was surrounded by four smaller onion domes, which in turn were placed between four working minarets, each a hundred and thirty feet tall. The minarets were perfectly symmetrical with each other—but instead of being built at a ninety-degree angle with their base, the minarets stood at ninety-two-degree angles, bowed slightly outward, away from the central dome. Jack remembered his father telling him that this had been done for two reasons. First, it created a highly sophisticated optical illusion when you stared at the complex from directly ahead. The minarets appeared perfectly straight, rather than bowed inward, as they would had they been built at the proper ninety degrees. Secondly, and more importantly, in the event of an earthquake, the minarets would fall outward, instead of crashing inward, destroying the perfect main dome.

"But see," Unger said, pointing with a thick finger. "The dome is really just an ornament. It draws the attention, gets all the press. But it really is an onion—peel away the circles of stone, you've got nothing but air. It's the base of the building that's truly magnificent—more than that, it's the base that's *significant*."

He ran his hand above the central portion of the blueprint, careful not to touch the yellowing paper. Jack couldn't begin to guess how old the blueprint was; for all he knew, it dated all the way back to Jahan's day, which made it insanely valuable. It should have been in a museum behind glass, not in a cardboard canister in the backroom of a store guarded by a drooling rat. Jack was reminded again of what his father had told him about Unger, after a phone call from the Brit that had interrupted one of Jack and Kyle's rare dinners together. *If you truly need something that nobody else can deliver, Unger's your man. Otherwise, avoid him like rabies.* And then he'd added: *Sharp as a weasel, hungry as a wolf.*

"The base is essentially an enormous cube cut into many chambers, with arched doorways at each entrance. In the center, on a raised platform, is a gilded, gem-encrusted sarcophagus."

"Mumtaz's coffin," Sloane said. She seemed surprisingly captivated by the blueprint, and didn't seem to mind Unger ogling her as he spoke. Or maybe she was just oblivious. She didn't strike Jack as a woman who was aware of how she looked. The way she kept her hair, the stiff way she moved, the beige of her clothing—this wasn't a woman who knew, or cared, that she was pretty enough to affect the men around her.

"That's what you're meant to think, my dear. And most of the two million visitors who wander through the gardens, gazing at the mausoleum every year, believe it to be so. But Mumtaz isn't in the sarcophagus. It's actually a cenotaph, an empty tomb."

Jack took Unger's lead, nodding toward the blueprint.

"There's a second, identical chamber below the domed mausoleum, built entirely of marble, that contains the actual sarcophagus of Mumtaz."

"Secrets within secrets," Unger said. "The second chamber is only the beginning. The interior itself is a goddamn labyrinth, full of hundreds of secret rooms, chambers, and even faux domes. And much of the building has been inaccessible for years. Hell, there are rumors that the subground floors haven't been entered in centuries. The entire complex is built on the edge of the Yamuna River. Like an iceberg, most of it is underground, many feet below the river. Nobody has been down there in years, maybe centuries."

Sloane looked at him.

"Why? It's one of the Seven Wonders of the World, and the most famous building in India—maybe the world. I'd expect daily tour groups, if not periodic scientific surveys."

Unger shrugged.

"Since 2007, the official reason is terrorism, the threat from militants within India, or from neighboring Pakistan. But in truth, the interior of the Taj has been closed for decades, and much of the complex has been forbidden ground dating all the way back to the beginning. Shah Jahan was one of time's great lovers, but he was also an Emperor, and a man of many dark secrets."

"How dark?" Jack asked.

"When the complex was finished, the story goes, Shah Jahan invited all of the workers who had been involved in the construction to a grand party. As many as twenty thousand skilled engineers, architects, and manual laborers partied the night away under massive outdoor tents, imbibing from Jahan's personal wine collection, dancing to the music from his royal musicians."

Unger's grin shifted slightly, more wolf than weasel.

"At first light, Jahan gathered the drunken workers beneath the main tent, all twenty thousand of them—and then he had all of their hands cut off, so that they could never build anything as beautiful as his love's tomb again. Supposedly, the hands are buried somewhere beneath the Taj, in one of those many secret chambers."

Jack saw a tremble move through Sloane's shoulders. If Unger saw it, too, he didn't seem to mind. In fact, he seemed more than a little pleased with himself, for getting some form of emotion out of her. Jack took the heavy moment as a cue to shift the focus to the real reason he had sought out Unger among all the shady contacts his father had collected over four decades of living primarily off the grid.

Jack reached into an inner pocket in his jacket and retrieved the folded parchment from beneath Christ the Redeemer, spreading it out on the table in front of him next to the yellowing blueprint. He tried his best to cover much of the snake image with his hand and wrist, but he made sure Unger could clearly see the tiny pictogram—the half man–half woman holding the trident aloft—next to the second segment.

For a brief moment, Unger's grin seemed to freeze in place, his eyes growing a fraction larger. Then he quickly tried to cover up his reaction, leaning closer to the pictogram.

"Ardhanarishvara," he said, and Jack nodded.

Jack had recognized the Hindu god shortly after he'd first seen the pictograph, which was why he knew they'd needed to head to the next most recent of the Seven Wonders: the Taj Mahal. Though a slightly lesser known deity than many of the other major idols of the ancient Indian religion, Ardhanarishvara was the composite, androgynous form of the main Hindu god Shiva, blended with his consort Parvati. As such, Ardhanarishvara was depicted as half-male and half-female, split down the middle. There weren't many temples in India—or anywhere, for that matter—dedicated to the androgynous deity, but it was clearly an image that pointed toward India. Jack just didn't know what a Hindu god had to do with a Muslim mausoleum built by a lovesick, seventeenth-century Mughal emperor.

Unger rose away from the parchment, and then pointed toward a shelving unit nearer to the front of the room.

"I've got a few of the she-hes behind the one with the elephant snout, the too many hands, and the bit of the weight problem. One of 'em is top condition, gold and inlaid pearl, from a tomb up north. A steal at twenty thousand, and I'll even include a paper that might get you through customs."

Jack shook his head.

"Again, just looking for information." He nodded toward the blueprint, still open on the table. "Specifically, anything you might know about a connection between Ardhanarishvara and the Taj Mahal."

Unger paused, drumming his fingers against his jaw, then spun on his heels and dove back into the crate where he'd first gotten the blueprint. When he returned to the table, he was holding a stack of black-and-white photographs held together by a pair of rubber bands, and there was a new, almost manic energy flowing through him.

"Well, now, that's interesting. Because everything I've just told you about the Taj, the great love story, the dark and brooding Shah Jahan—take all of that and shove it right in a fucking dumpster."

He tore the rubber bands away and spread the photographs out next to the blueprint. Most of the pictures had been taken in extremely low light, and had faded so badly, it was hard to make out anything beyond shapes and shadows. But a few were a little more clear: Jack could see old stone statues, similar to the cheap ones in the souvenir shop out front, and the expensive, gilded ones in the glass shelves. Hindu gods, hidden within the shadows of some sort of underground chamber.

"There's a growing movement pushing a pretty remarkable theory about the Taj," Unger said. "That, in fact, its origins predate the Mughals and Shah

Jahan, perhaps by hundreds of years. That Jahan had usurped the location for his architectural love story, and that originally, it was the site of a major Hindu shrine. Supposedly, some say, in those subground levels beneath the mausoleum, there are numerous sealed floors with hundreds of rooms, bricked over and never opened, containing evidence of the site's original purpose."

Sloane picked one of the photographs up, peering at one of the statues, a creature with a lion's head and a woman's body.

"These were taken inside the Taj? In one of the forbidden chambers?"

Unger held his hands out, palms up.

"I buy things and I sell things. Beyond that, I don't ask a lot of questions. But I've heard stories. About an anteroom, six floors below the empty sarcophagus. An anteroom filled with statues. And at the end of that anteroom, a red brick door sealed for a very, very long time. And in front of that door, a particular statue of a particular Hindu god."

Unger dug through the photographs until he'd found what he was looking for. He held the black-and-white picture up so both Jack and Sloane could see. The lighting was bad, the shadows so extensive that most of the photo was indecipherable, but near the very back corner, almost as much shadow as form, a small statue—half-man, half-woman, with a trident in its hand.

"Christ," Jack whispered. Unger laughed.

"Off by a few thousand years, Jacky."

Then Unger jabbed a finger toward the parchment and the pictogram.

"You'll notice the she-he in my photo isn't wearing the necklace."

Jack looked down at the pictogram and noticed that indeed, Ardhanarishvara appeared to be wearing a tiny pendant.

"Ardhanarishvara isn't usually depicted that way?"

Unger shook his head.

"May I?"

Jack didn't like handing over the parchment, but he didn't see what choice he had. Unger held it by the upper corners as gingerly as his thick fingers would allow. He put his face so close to the pictogram, the material of the parchment fluttered with each of his breaths.

"Well, look at this. It's not a necklace at all. It's a moondial."

"A what?" Sloane asked.

Then Unger was up out of his seat, still holding the parchment. He rushed over to a shelving unit on the other side of the one holding the bejeweled masks and worked quickly at a combination lock. The shelves came open, and he retrieved a small stone object on a linked necklace chain, then hurried back to where Jack and Sloane were waiting.

"A moondial. A fourteenth century design, similar to a sundial, but designed to be accurate only during the full moon."

He handed the stone moondial to Jack. It looked very much like a miniature sundial, with a raised lever that would cast a shadow toward a series of etched lines and circles that circumnavigated the rim of the device. It was pretty obvious how the dial would work; held beneath a full moon, the shadow would aim like an arrow toward one of the etchings.

Jack didn't know why the god in the pictogram was wearing a moondial around its neck, but he assumed it was significant.

"We can't pay much," Jack started, but Unger waved him off.

"It's my gift to an old family friend. Perhaps you'll find a way to return the favor, whenever you find whatever it is you're looking for—beneath the Taj."

Jack didn't respond as Unger watched him place the moondial in one of his many pockets. Then Jack held out a hand for the parchment. Unger was much slower to hand it back than the dial, but eventually he gave it over, still grinning.

"That's it, right? You're going inside the Taj, hoping to find your androgynous god?"

Again, Jack didn't answer. But Sloane didn't seem to notice the growing tension in the room.

"If we did want to find this antechamber—this red door," she said, beckoning toward the blueprint, "how would you suggest we proceed? Do we just walk right up and ring a doorbell?"

Unger was still watching Jack while he folded the parchment and put it back in his jacket.

"Not exactly."

Then he cocked his head toward Sloane.

"How well can you swim?"

• • •

Unger stayed glued to the metal folding chair, his feet bouncing up and down beneath the circular table, his hands hovering over the unrolled blueprint, his body alive, electric, on fire—until he heard the buzzer signal that Jack and the girl, that goddamn pretty, pretty, girl, had passed through the souvenir shop and out toward the front entrance. He gave it another two minutes, listening for the glass door to shut behind them, followed by the hiss of Henry the Ravenous Rat, his official mascot, watch rodent, and early warning system. Eight years, he'd gone without a single proper bust, and for the past two of them, he had that rat to thank. The closest he'd come to getting nicked was a good eight months ago, when a pair of local constables had made it as far as the cash register before he'd seen them on the CCTV screen hidden behind one of the fat elephant gods. He'd had plenty of time to seal the iron-plated door and make a hasty exit up through the escape hatch he'd built above the backroom's ceiling panels.

But at the moment, he was damn thankful that his ravenous rat hadn't discouraged his latest pair of interlopers. When he'd recognized Little Jacky, Crazy Kyle's spawn right in his own shop, spitting image of the wild bastard, and judging from the way he'd disarmed Unger without breaking a sweat, just as fast with his hands, he'd never expected the kid would leave him so excited. Kyle Grady was a rogue and a bastard, but he was also a goddamn moral prince who still considered himself an anthropologist, a scientist, no matter how deep into the shit he let himself go. He'd never accepted that Unger was simply a businessman with a very specific set of business skills. It was the main reason they had grown apart and eventually gone their separate ways. Kyle had thought of him as no better than a grave robber—and yet, here was his prized son, chip off the old cock, wandering into Unger's shop with a plan to rob the greatest grave of all.

Hell, Unger himself had thought about putting together an excursion into the Taj many times over the years, ever since he'd bought the stack of photographs from a notorious antiquities thief, right before the poor fucker had been sent to jail for two decades for an unrelated heist. Unger had no idea if the photos were real or not; but just looking at them always got his saliva flowing. Still, based on photos alone, such an expedition seemed much too risky. You didn't break into the Taj to steal some fucking stone statues. And anyway, whatever you found there would be too hot to fence. No museum, no matter how shady or third-world, and no collector, no matter how rich and unencumbered by morality, was going to shell out top dollar for something stolen from the most famous tomb on earth.

But then there came Jack Grady, his pretty, pretty sidekick—and that incredible parchment.

Unger shivered, the excitement rising inside of him.

It wasn't the pictogram of the half man–half woman god that had set his veins on fire. It was the image next to the pictogram, the image that Jack had first tried to cover up with his hand when he'd placed the parchment on the table.

It wasn't the first time Unger had seen the snake figure. The serpent was usually part of a double helix, and carved into something stone or ivory, something very, very old.

Hell, there was nothing uncommon about a snake. Snakes were one of the most overused images of the ancient world. It was a snake who had coaxed Eve and Adam out of the goddamn Garden of Eden. Snakes crawled around the base of the Mayan Tree of Life. Snakes were everywhere.

But it was *that* particular snake, in that particular curved shape—segmented or whole—that mattered to Unger. For the past decade, he'd seen objects imprinted with similar snakes floating through all his regular stomping grounds, the various, shady underground trade outposts that defined the black market for antiquities.

Rumor was, there was a billionaire collector driving the sudden influx, a billionaire with incredibly deep pockets who would pay top dollar for ancient items imprinted with that snake.

Unger wondered, *What would a billionaire pay for a parchment like the one Jack was holding? And how much more would a billionaire pay for whatever Jack was seeking beneath the Taj Mahal?*

Unger bounced his feet against the floor, unconsciously running the fingers of his bruised hand against the bulge of the Luger semiautomatic strapped to his outer thigh.

Next time, he wasn't going to let his old, moral prince of a friend's spawn get the jump on him.

Little Jacky was fast—but he wasn't faster than a goddamn bullet.

CHAPTER FOURTEEN

The great silver bird plunged out of the low cloud cover, wings spread wide, banking steeply toward the blanket of green rainforest that ran down the valley, descending toward the scar of brown dirt at the valley's base. The bird's silver beak glimmered even in the tropical haze of a mostly overcast morning, while its sharp tale cut a swath through the humid air, trailing swirls of condensation and melting wisps of ice, which it had carried down from altitudes even higher than the tree-covered mountain peaks that bordered the valley on all four sides.

For the briefest of seconds, it seemed as though the enormous bird might dive right into the rainforest; at the last moment, the vast wings shuddered, and bladelike flaps shifted upward to catch the air just right. The bird leveled off, skimming the tops of the trees. Then it made its final approach in near silence, lowering foot by foot toward the bottom of the valley.

Vika watched as the clouds of dust and dirt plumed upward, the rubber tires of the Boeing 767 skidding across the barely paved jungle runway. Although Vika was a good thirty feet away, sitting behind the wheel of her camouflage-green military Jeep which was parked at the edge of a rocky path leading back up through the rainforest, she could smell the sharp odor of jet fuel mixed with burning rubber. Even more overwhelming, she could feel the way the forest around her seemed to contract and go dead silent as the roar of the engines finally hit, so brutally alien, so intrinsically wrong. Only after the plane had pulled to a stop, the dust settling back around its landing gear, did the rhythm of the forest return. Once again, she was engulfed in the near-deafening caw of macaws and parrots, the caterwauling of the tiny rhesus monkeys and the red-furred uakari, the incessant creaking of a dozen types of miniature frogs and a thousand different species of insect.

Even behind the bulletproof windshield of the Jeep, her long, lithe body garbed in an off-white, near-skin-tight special ops uniform, she felt herself relax, soothed by the cacophony of the rainforest. This wasn't simply her home, the place of her family, the world where she had grown up; she was a part of this forest, and it lived in her blood. Generation after generation, her family had sworn to protect it, and anything that threatened her forest, threatened her personally. She had been born, bred, and trained to respond to such a threat.

If she had not recognized the call letters on the private 767 as it had broken from the clouds, she would not have remained behind the windshield of the Jeep. She would have retrieved the shoulder-ready stinger missile launcher from the trunk of the vehicle and positioned herself on the Jeep's front hood. She would have quickly let the launcher's guidance system lock onto the 767's superheated twin engines. She would have taken the great silver bird out of the sky before it had gotten within fifty yards of the runway.

Instead, she sat patiently in the Jeep, watching the silver bird taxi down the runway. When it finally came to a stop, she watched until the oval door near the front of the main cabin unsealed itself and fell forward, revealing a carpeted stairway. Only when the figure of a well-dressed woman with frosted hair piled atop her head appeared in the doorway holding a small briefcase in one hand did Vika reach for the ignition.

As the Jeep sputtered to life, Vika kept her gaze pinned to the woman, who was surveying the jungle around her like it was her own, private domain. And in truth, much of it was; her company, Saphra Industries, had purchased the entire valley from the Brazilian government—the trees, the mountains, the dirt runway, even the small village where Vika had grown up, tucked in front of the mouth of an underground river, one of the many tributaries of the legendary Amazon, the life giver. Supposedly the company was to research curative chemicals harvested from the skin of the local amphibian population.

But even so, no matter how much money had changed hands, no matter what sort of documents had been signed or official stamps tendered, the woman would never be anything but a stranger here. As brutally alien and inherently wrong as her great silver bird.

As Vika watched, the woman searched the forest around the runway, an irritated look spreading across her face. It took her a full three minutes to spot Vika's Jeep, and then the woman waved her free hand in a sharp gesture—a command.

Vika dutifully put the Jeep into drive, and began to carefully navigate the vehicle over the rocks and thick mud toward the runway and the plane.

In the end, it didn't matter to Vika who the woman was, or how alien and wrong she might be. Just as Vika had been born, bred, and trained to protect the forest around her, she had been born, bred, and trained to follow orders. That was her own internal rhythm.

It wasn't a matter of thought, or choice; it was a matter of nature.

• • •

The javelins were little more than flashes of white tearing through the air in parallel arcs toward the row of canvas targets. The hurtling weapons made almost no sound—just the slightest hiss of razor-sharp ivory moving at speeds in excess of eighty miles per hour—until they found their marks, exactly fifty yards across the mud-paved central square. All twelve struck the direct centers of the torso-shaped canvas bags filled with thick straw; two were thrown with such force that they went right through, emerging out the other side and traveling another ten yards to the wooden wall of the nearby armory and imbedding, point first, into the thick Brazilian wood.

"Impressive," Jendari mused, watching through the open window in the Main House overlooking the central square. "It's certainly an elegant weapon—if perhaps a little conspicuous, don't you think?"

As usual, Vika remained stone-faced and still, coiled like a snake against the hard stone bench on the other side of the long "family" table that dominated the center of the Main House. For as long as Jendari had known the woman, she had been this way: silent, statuesque, unemotional. It was incredibly unnerving, and yet Jendari accepted it, because Vika was an invaluable asset. If some of her choices seemed a bit, well, *eccentric*—such as the javelins, or the matching white uniforms the dozen trainees wore as they continued their exercise—who was Jendari to criticize? In terms of a silent ballistic weapon, perhaps a javelin wasn't the worst of choices; Jendari had access to plenty of ancient ivory, and it was very hard to trace a weapon that hadn't been used for thousands of years.

Still, truth be told, she was much more impressed by the high-tech shooting range on the other side of the armory, where the other dozen or so of Vika's current batch of trainees were currently going through their rotations; every now and then, Jendari could hear the rapid patter of light ballistics echoing through the village, the signature cough of automatic M-16s and Israeli-built NG-7s. In previous visits, she had toured the armory and the range and had been impressed by the array of weapons her money had bought: from the machine guns to much larger, shoulder-held missile launchers, to grenade throwers and light mortars. There was even a fair collection of experimental nonlethals, such as handheld sound cannons and time-release blast grenades. Since Saphra Industries had purchased the village and the surrounding area from the Brazilian government, Jendari had spared no expense in upgrading the village's main indigenous industry—and despite what the Brazilian officials might have believed, it had nothing to do with curative frog sweat.

Jendari turned away from the window and crossed to the long table, retrieving her briefcase from the bench opposite where Vika was sitting. She could still remember the first time she'd met with Vika in this main house, nearly ten years ago—shortly after her surveillance team had traced the Euphrates Conglomerate's holdings to this remote part of Brazil. According to her team, Euphrates had owned and protected this jungle paradise for decades, if not centuries; once Jendari herself had investigated the area, she had understood why.

The Main House and armory were just two of sixteen unmarked wooden buildings that made up the bulk of the village grounds; from the air, there was nothing remarkable about the architecture or the placement of the buildings—a concentric circle of living spaces, animal confines, and multi-use sheds that was consistent with other tribal towns that speckled the vast rainforest.

But like the nearby rock quarry that hid the entrance to the vast underground river network that had given the village its name, Fluindo Aldeia, the ordinary appearance of the place was a carefully crafted lie.

Jendari opened her briefcase and carefully removed the two photographs from her vault, placing them gently on the table between herself and the stone-faced operative. If Vika was surprised by anything in the images, she didn't show it. Jendari wondered what it would take to rattle a woman such as her—a woman who had been born in a place like this.

When Jendari had first discovered what Euphrates had been up to in this isolated corner of Brazil, she had immediately dispatched Grange and a team of handpicked experts to compile a history of Fluindo Aldeia, because the idea that such a place could exist seemed almost unthinkable. An entire community, hidden deep in the Amazonian rainforest, that had essentially been transformed into a sophisticated mercenary training camp. Even more confounding, nearly eighty percent of the town's population had been female.

After weeks of digging, Grange's report only added to the mysteries. According to his findings, Vika's village was over two hundred years old, settled by an offshoot of a much larger tribal community that had traveled down one of the Amazon River's tributaries, ending up at the mouth of the underground river that had given the village its name. These tribal settlers were more than simple nomads; they were a legendary group who a hundred years earlier, had given the entire rainforest, and the river that ran through it, its name.

As the story went, midway through the sixteenth century, the Spanish explorers who made the first journey down the rushing, exotic waters of the great river were attacked by a tribe of female warriors—the *Icamiabas*, roughly translated as "women without husbands." Franciscode Orellana, the lead Spanish explorer, named the river after these women, whom he likened to the mythical Amazons. To this day, nobody knew for sure where the Icamiabas had come from, or what had happened to them after the Spanish exploration and eventual invasion.

Based on writings found in caves near the underground river, Grange and his experts were convinced that Vika's forest home was the only known remnant of the legendary tribe.

Euphrates's interest in the village had been more than historical; when Jendari visited the village for the first time, she had found more than a piece of Mesoamerican history. She had found an incredible group of female warriors who had been trained since birth to fight and kill. Euphrates had taken what these women did naturally and turned it into a business.

Jendari had used her own money and connections to make contact with the middlemen who assigned the various missions to the mercenary group, and eventually hired them to work for her. She'd effectively closed out the Euphrates control of the mercenaries—whom she'd redubbed the Vipers—and for more than a decade now, Vika and her team had worked exclusively for Saphra Industries.

For the first few years after Jendari had made her move, she'd expected Euphrates to respond. Yet all she had gotten from the mysterious, faceless corporation was silence. Either Euphrates was as toothless as she had begun to suspect, and the Order that her great-aunt had worshipped so completely was nothing beyond some shadow bureaucracy, a cult long since faded into obsolescence, or they'd already accepted Jendari as the true heir to their organization. *Their modern Cleopatra, leader of the new Order of Eve.*

"So tell me," Jendari said, after Vika raised her eyes from the pair of photographs. "Did he find the crate?"

The clatter of a half-dozen submachine guns going off in concert on the far side of the village echoed through the open window as Vika considered the question. Finally, she shrugged her taut shoulders.

"We were unable to get close enough to know for sure," she said, her words tinged with an accent that was very difficult to place. A hint of Portuguese, a hint of Spanish, but also something else that Jendari had never heard anywhere else. "We couldn't risk exposure. However, we believe he found something hidden in the canopy beneath the statue, which led him to a second item—hidden in Christ the Redeemer's face."

Jendari raised her eyebrows. It wasn't at all what she had expected to hear—but the fact that at least one of the two items he had found had been hidden *inside* the Wonder of the World set her heart racing. Real, solid evidence had eluded her for so long: The very nature of the Wonders made them impossible to excavate, even for a woman as rich and powerful as she. The best she could do was station Vika's people at safe distances at each Wonder, keeping an eye out for anything unusual.

Such as an anthropologist scaling the chest and shoulders of a one-hundred-foot-tall statue of Christ, half a mile above the city of Rio.

"Unfortunately," Vika continued, "we were unable to survey the cave after he left, because it was destroyed. We can't be sure what he found was contained within a crate. After retrieving both items, he returned to his hotel and immediately booked a flight to India."

Jendari nodded, her excitement growing. Whether or not Jack Grady had retrieved the crate the workers were carrying in Jendari's photographs, he had obviously found something that had led him to the top of Christ the Redeemer. Whatever the second item was that he had found, it had led him to India—and assuredly, the next Wonder of the World.

"One more thing," Vika said, no inflexion beyond the accent. "He was joined at his hotel by a woman named Sloane Costa, a scientist. We're in the midst of compiling her dossier, so far mostly unremarkable—except for one notable exception. She recently conducted research at the Colosseum, in Rome."

"Is she connected to the twins?"

"I don't believe so. But she joined Jack and his two graduate students on the flight to India."

So the woman was involved, now. Which meant she'd found something at the Colosseum that had led her to Jack Grady.

There was no doubt in Jendari's mind: She had been right to let this anthropologist run with whatever his brother had found. It appeared that Jack Grady was succeeding in days at what she and her operatives had been working on for a decade.

The question was, how much farther should she let him go? Certainly, Vika could take him out now and retrieve whatever it was he had found at Christ the Redeemer.

With Jeremy Grady, there had been no doubt. He had simply been a threat that needed to be removed. But Jack was different: He was useful. She had seen it the minute Vika had given her his dossier; he was an explorer, an adventurer, a problem solver. Exactly what she needed.

Whatever he'd found in Brazil was leading him to India; no doubt he was interpreting clues, finding his way through to the Order's hidden secret. If Jendari took what he had and eliminated him, would she be able to continue what he had started? There was no way to know for sure.

Which meant that Jack Grady was still useful—for the moment.

"Continue your surveillance," she said, still listening to the staccato report of the submachine guns from across the village. "Find out what he's got, and where it's leading him. But keep whatever distance you can."

As usual, Vika remained still and unresponsive. Even so, Jendari knew she would obey, perfectly and precisely. For the time being, Jendari would let Jack continue doing the hard work for them.

As legend had it, the Amazons had always employed men to do the dirty work that they found beneath them; in fact, the legend went, Amazon warriors would maim the men whom they captured—as it was thought that invalids made better workers, and more loyal lovers.

In a way, Jendari had already maimed Jack by killing his twin, his other half. Now he would find the secret of the Order of Eve for her, and then she would have Vika finish the job.

CHAPTER FIFTEEN

If Christine could see me now . . .

Sloane almost cracked a smile, imagining the expression on her older sister's face—if only Christine could have somehow magically materialized next to her on the floor of the bobbing wooden skiff. Just seeing Sloane crouching there, so low that her face was almost touching the damp, rancid floorboards of the barely river-worthy craft, hands furiously working the zipper of her rented rubber wetsuit, which had caught halfway up her cleavage, would have left her sister speechless. Seeing Jack Grady crouched next to her—his rugged features halfway covered in a silk Indian scarf, his muscled body perfectly filling out his matching wetsuit beneath a loose, gray smock he'd bought off the fisherman who'd rented them the boat, his deep blue eyes barely visible, scanning the Yamuna River as he piloted the skiff against the current—would have knocked Christine right overboard in shock.

"I think we're clear," Jack whispered, his voice barely carrying over the sound of the skiff's motor and the lapping of the murky water. "Another ten yards, and we should be at the right spot."

Sloane shivered, still fighting with the zipper. She was amazed at how calm Jack sounded, considering what they were about to attempt. A moment ago, they'd passed right by a security cutter heading the other direction along the river, carrying three uniformed Indian officers, and Sloane had nearly hyperventilated. If the officers had decided to check out their skiff—and had seen Sloane in her wetsuit—God only knew what would have happened. But Jack had simply nodded at the men, grinning amiably beneath his scarf, and they'd gone right on by.

So much confidence, so much bravado, so much eagerness to dive right into things, no matter how risky or insane—Jack certainly wasn't like any scientist she'd ever met before. He was so damn sure of himself. He was just the sort of man she'd always done her best to avoid; a self-styled adventurer, a rogue who'd somehow gotten himself a PhD. Still, he wasn't stupid; there was a natural intelligence in him that she couldn't deny. The works she'd read by him on the mythical Amazons, though completely fanciful, were well written, and he was obviously respected in his profession. Field anthropology, sure, and a strain of the discipline that seemed to involve safari jackets, grappling hooks, and one mean-looking Filipino sword—but still, he wasn't *all* show.

Even so, he had to be feeling a tiny fraction of what she was going through—if not the fear, at least the sheer disbelief that a tiny clue found at the top of Christ the Redeemer could somehow have led them *here*. The truth was, when she had first tracked Jack down in Brazil through his work on the Amazons, she hadn't expected more than an expert opinion on the red vine and the painting she had photographed beneath the Colosseum. She couldn't have guessed that he'd have found a second snake segment—or that the two of them had somehow independently stumbled into a mystery that connected at least two of the Modern Wonders.

She didn't really believe that it could possibly go any farther than that; Jack's insistence that the pictogram on his parchment was a clear link to the Taj Mahal didn't exactly seem scientific to her. It was based on a fantastical—and thus unscientific—premise: that his murdered brother had uncovered an overarching link between the Ancient and Modern Wonders. But even so, she found herself unable to walk away. It wasn't just the paper she hoped to write about the seed and the vine or the fact that she was trying to save her job at Michigan, it was the need to find a scientific answer to all of this, because without one she was going to end up just like Jack Grady, chasing fantasies.

"How can you be sure we're there?" she asked, trying to keep the tremble out of her voice. For some reason, she didn't want him to know how scared she actually was.

"I'm counting the windows," he said.

She raised her head, looking over the edge of the skiff toward the shore, about thirty yards away. Though it was twenty minutes to midnight, and a thick fog had just begun to settle in over the water around them, there was no missing the spectacular Wonder, rising up in the darkness—the huge, curved onion of a dome with its golden finial spiking out of its peak, the vast arch at the center, the matching, smaller arches that signaled doors, windows, and apertures across the glimmering white marble façade, and of course, the four immense minarets, daggers reaching right up into the cloudless sky.

Even in the darkness, it was enough to make Sloane gasp. When she noticed Jack looking at her, she quickly shook the awe away. She wasn't sure what it was, exactly, about him—aside from the obvious—that pushed her buttons, but she found herself even more guarded than usual in his presence.

"You're serious?" she asked.

He smiled, then turned his right palm over, showing her his smartphone, running a GPS app. She blushed, feeling foolish. Of course a field anthropologist would know how to use GPS. That disgusting grave robber, Unger, had gotten a precise location off of his blueprint after he'd told them the only viable way into the historic monument. If he was right, and Jack's phone wasn't misleading them, all that was left was the hard part.

"Here we are," Jack said, cutting the skiff's engines.

The air around them went near silent, except for the water against the wood. The bobbing increased, and Sloane felt a surge of nausea in her stomach, which she quickly pushed back down. Jack reached behind himself and retrieved a pair of oxygen tanks attached to regulators, along with matching clear plastic masks. It took him less than a minute to expertly slip his tank over his shoulder, letting his mask hang down around his neck. Then he glanced at Sloane.

"Ah, you need a little help?"

"I took scuba in high school. I know how to put on an oxygen tank."

"I mean with the zipper," Jack said.

Sloane looked down and saw that the damn thing had receded almost to the bottom of her rib cage. She blushed, then yanked the zipper upward as hard as she could, until it clicked into its proper place, flush with her throat. Then she took the oxygen tank out of his hands and with some difficulty angled it over her shoulders. She was still working on the mask and regulator when Jack propped himself up onto the edge of the skiff, his back to the sparkling Taj Mahal. To his left, Sloane could just make out the beginning of the thousand-foot-long, carefully cultivated greenery that stretched out beyond the marble tomb, divided into its four quarters by the cross work of raised paths.

It was not lost on Sloane that here in front of them was yet another spiritually significant garden—supposedly, a representation of the green Paradise written about in the Koran, *Jannah,* the Islamic version of heaven—described as a garden of infinite abundance fed by four rivers, much as the Garden of Eden in Genesis was fed by four rushing tributaries. And considering what Unger had told them about the Taj perhaps having an even older history lodged in Hinduism, the garden could also be seen as an interpretation of the four-fold garden described in the Vedas, the Sanskrit text dating back to 1500 BC—considered the original scripture of Hinduism.

Sloane wasn't sure what it all meant, but somehow, it felt significant. The painting she'd seen at the Colosseum, the tablet Jack had found beneath Christ the Redeemer, the same image he'd reported seeing beneath the Temple of Artemis—they all revolved around garden imagery. And here they were, in front of the Taj Mahal, facing yet another garden with ancient, historical significance.

What could it possibly mean? Sloane knew that Jack believed his brother had uncovered a link between the Seven Wonders of the Modern World— something important enough that he had been murdered because of it. Could that link have something to do with the garden imagery in the paintings? The garden that seemed to pop up in so many different religions, in so many vastly different cultures around the world?

Sloane didn't have time to ponder the question any longer as Jack gave her a thumbs-up, then flicked on a waterproof flashlight he'd attached to his left wrist.

"Stick close, it's going to get very thick down there. And watch out for alligators."

Sloane stared at him.

"Another joke?" she said, stiffly.

Jack laughed, then yanked his mask over his eyes.

"Yes. There aren't any alligators in India."

Right before he put the regulator in his mouth, he gave her a wink from behind the transparent plastic.

"Around here, they call them crocodiles."

And with that, he kicked himself over the edge.

CHAPTER SIXTEEN

Breathe in. Breathe out.

Ten feet below the surface of the river, Jack kicked against the current, chasing the eerie yellow cone from his flashlight through the murky water. He couldn't see Sloane next to him, but he could feel her presence, the way the bubbles from her regulator swirled around her elongated body, mingling with his own, spiraling upward toward the chop above their heads. Every now and then he felt her hand against his wetsuit, but overall he was relieved to see she had no trouble keeping up with his pace; she was in much better shape than he would have expected from a botanist. Still, it was obvious from the moment she'd followed him into the room-temperature water and hung there in the murk, kicking furiously until she'd caught sight of his light and relaxed, that she was far out of her comfort zone.

Jack slowed for a brief moment to check their progress on his waterproof phone, tucked into a pocket next to the flashlight. Though he'd lost satellite reception the minute he'd broken the surface, the electronic compass was still operational, and he could see that they were more than halfway to their target. That is, if Unger had been telling them the truth—and if his sources had been selling more than some faked photographs and a bullshit story. Jack didn't trust Unger any more than he trusted the rat outside of Unger's shop. The fact that Unger had offered to meet them on the other side of the river to escort them back to their hotel when they'd returned from their expedition wasn't exactly comforting. But Jack figured he could handle the antiquities smuggler. He was more concerned about returning empty-handed.

After a slight adjustment in direction, he kicked off again, Sloane's flippers parallel with his own. Another ten minutes piloting through the murk, and he began to see a shape take form ahead, a cliff-like slope of rocks and mud rising up from the bottom of the river, a sign that they were getting close to the shore. Jack knew from Unger's blueprints that they were now swimming in the shadow of the backside of the Taj, to the right of the center of the building and the massive onion dome, which would be looming a hundred and fifteen feet above the river, set a dozen yards back from a low breakwall. Though most of the mausoleum complex was bordered by a red stone fence, the architects who had built the Wonder had used the river itself as a natural fourth wall. No doubt, scuba gear had not been on their minds.

Jack slowed his kicking as they approached the slope, reaching out to gently grab Sloane's wrist. He held his other arm straight out, using the flashlight to scan the rocks and mud, first horizontally, and then vertically. An errant fish flashed through the cone of yellow, but otherwise it was all thick mud and jagged stone, leading down God only knew how far. Jack was beginning to get concerned, when Sloane jerked her wrist free of his grip and jabbed a finger at a downward angle to the very bottom corner of the cone of light.

Jack's eyes widened behind his mask. There it was, almost invisible between two jutting edges of rock: a circular opening, two feet across, bordered in chipped marble. Jack kicked twice with his flippers, exhaling as he pushed himself the last few feet downward until he was flush with the marble lip of the opening. Sloane floated down next to him, then began tracing the dark stains of moss and river algae that ran down from the edges of the marble. No doubt she could identify every strain of flora that had exploited whatever drainage the ancient inhabitants of the immense mausoleum had generated. If exploiting what was essentially a three-hundred-and-fifty-year-old drainpipe was good enough for moss and algae, Jack figured it was good enough for him.

Grinning, he put his hands on the base of the opening and started to pull himself inside when a dull clang reverberated through the water around him. He jerked back—and saw that Sloane was pointing at his oxygen tank. He looked back at the opening and realized she was right; there was barely enough room for his shoulders, let alone the breathing contraption on his back.

He leaned forward, holding the flashlight inside the opening, following the light with his eyes as far as it went. The marble-lined drainpipe seemed to be sloping gently upward, maybe five or ten degrees from the horizontal, but it also appeared to be full of water for as far as he could see—not far in the murky water. From Unger's blueprints, Jack doubted the cylindrical marble pipe was much longer than fifteen yards—but then again, there was no way to know how much might have changed in more than three centuries.

Still, Jack didn't see any other choice. He swam a few feet over from the opening and found a ledge along the muddy slope that he figured was big enough to hold his gear. Then he beckoned to Sloane, using his hands to try and communicate what he was going to do. When she began reaching for the clasps of her own tank, he grabbed her wrist and shook his head, hard. She had more than enough air to wait for him down here. But she shook her head right back, her eyes fierce behind her mask. He didn't know if it was her fear of staying alone in the dark water or her determination to stick with him, but she wasn't going to be left behind.

Finally, Jack nodded. He tapped his fingers against his cheeks, miming a blowing motion to remind her to exhale on the way up. Then he unhooked the clasp of his own oxygen tank, pulled the straps off of his shoulders, and watched as Sloane did the same. He rested the equipment on the ledge, still breathing through the attached regulator, and faced the opening. When Sloane was ready next to him, he gave her hand a quick squeeze. Then he yanked the regulator out of his mouth, switched off his air, and pushed off with all of his strength, thrusting himself headfirst into the opening of the marble drainpipe, Sloane one kick behind, exhaling bubbles as she went.

• • •

Thirty seconds that felt like a lifetime later, Jack was still tearing upward through the tight, claustrophobia-inducing marble drainpipe, his lungs beginning to burn, his shoulders, arms, and chest aching from the half crawl, half swim up the too-gentle incline. The water was still just as thick and murky as it had been in the river, and even with the flashlight, he could only see a few feet ahead: more drainpipe, more water. He could feel Sloane pushing herself forward just behind his flippers. When he glanced back, he could see that she was having a slightly easier time than he was, because of her narrower form. But the look in her eyes through her mask mirrored his own growing sense of panic. Another few seconds, and they were going to have to try and turn back—hopefully, they'd make it to the tanks before either of them blacked out and drowned.

Jack cursed to himself, his fingers clawing at the marble. He couldn't be sure, but they had to have gone fifteen yards by now. Either the blueprints were wrong, or there had been some construction since they were drafted; if those photographs that Unger had shown them had really come via this route, then the men who had taken them were small enough to get through a drainpipe wearing scuba gear, or they had lungs like goddamn dolphins.

Jack nearly choked as the top of his head suddenly touched metal. He whirled upward, his mask inches from a circular metal grate. In front of him, the drainage tube ended in a chipped marble wall.

Jack reached up and gripped the metal with his fingers. No time to pray, he thought to himself. And then he pulled with all of his strength.

Nothing happened. He was about to give it another shot when Sloane reached past him and pointed to a latch at the top of the circle. Jack was thankful it was too dark for her to see him blush as he flicked the latch with his finger, then used his entire weight against the metal.

There was an audible creak, and then the grate swung downward on rusted hinges. Jack crouched low, then lunged upward through the opening, exhaling the last of his air as he went.

· · ·

"Not exactly pine fresh," Jack gasped as he pulled Sloane up out of the water, "but it beats drowning."

She collapsed next to him on the marble floor, her chest heaving beneath her wetsuit. He could see her blinking hard behind her mask, and he understood her disorientation. If anything, it should have been even darker in the underground chamber than in the drainage tunnel, considering they were at least six stories underground. But somehow, the small chamber was lit by a soft, greenish glow that seemed to be coming right through the walls. Not that there was much to see; other than the grated hatch they had just come through, the chamber was a perfect cube, seemingly made of sheer marble—the same type of marble that had been used to build the onion dome, now many stories above their heads.

Jack took off his flippers and mask and stretched his cramping shoulders, trying to breathe shallow breaths as he reoxygenated his lungs. The smell in the small chamber was unlike anything he had ever experienced before; musty and acrid at the same time, with a hint of something noxiously floral. As he rose to his feet and took a couple steps away from the hatch, he noticed that the smell got even stronger, making his eyes start to water.

"We're not going to want to breathe this in for very long," Sloane said as she rose next to him, kicking off her own flippers. "I suggest we get out of this room as soon as possible."

Jack looked around them at the four glowing green walls.

"I'm open to suggestions. It's like some sort of twisted children's riddle in here. An anthropologist and a botanist have to get out of a room with no windows and doors. Maybe if we could figure out where the light is coming from—some sort of hidden skylight, maybe? Reflecting moonlight down from the higher floors?"

He scanned the ceiling, but nothing jumped out at him. Then he noticed that Sloane had taken a step to their left and was focused on the nearest glowing wall.

"It's not coming from the ceiling," she said. "And it isn't moonlight."

"How do you know?"

"The smell. It's coming from the walls. And I think it's going to help us find our way out of this place."

She ran a tongue along her bottom lip, tasting the air.

"*Omphalotus olearius*. A species of bioluminescent fungi that grows in rotting wood."

"Glowing fungus?"

"Fungi. The cells of the olearius genus emit luciferase, an enzyme that reacts with a second chemical called luciferin; even the slightest stimulation—a change in temperature, a light breeze—causes it to emit light. It's a pretty fascinating adaptation, actually."

Jack peered toward the nearest wall; when he looked more closely, he noticed that what had previously appeared to be an evenly distributed glow was actually stronger in some areas, weaker in others.

"So there's fungus running inside these walls? How does that help us?"

"Fungi. As I said, *Omphalotus olearius* grows in rotting wood—not marble. So although there are spores cultivating all around us, the source has to be something made out of wood."

"Like a door," Jack said. "How do we find the source?"

"We follow the smell," she said, starting forward. Jack followed a step behind, watching her with no small sense of awe as she walked them toward the far corner of the chamber, pausing only once to whiff the rapidly thickening air. When they'd reached the corner, she pointed to a spot halfway up the sheer marble. Now that they were up close, it was clear that one section of the wall was glowing a much deeper green than the rest.

Jack moved next to her and placed his hand against the marble. He ran his fingers up and down, but didn't feel a seam. He shrugged, then moved Sloane out of the way and lowered his right shoulder.

"Is this really the best way—" Sloane started, but Jack was already moving forward.

He hit the wall shoulder first. Almost the moment he came in contact with the marble, a thin, perfectly straight horizontal crack appeared a foot above his head, lining up with two vertical cracks rising up from the floor. Jack stepped back, then placed his hands on the marble and carefully removed what he now realized was a three-inch thin sheet of the polished stone, placing it on the floor next to them. As Sloane had predicted, behind the marble was a rotted-through wooden door, covered in glowing green fungi. The stench was overwhelming, but Jack was too excited to give in to a sudden bout of nausea.

There wasn't a knob, but a simple push of his foot against the damp wood caused the door to swing inward. A blast of slightly fresher air swept into the chamber, and Jack moved quickly through the doorway and found himself in another chamber—this one much larger than the first, and rectangular in shape. Again, the walls glowed green, but the expanded space made the smell much less overpowering.

"This looks like the right place," Sloane said, stepping into the room next to him. She pointed at the first line of statues standing just a few feet ahead of them on black marble pedestals. "From the photos, I couldn't tell that there would be so many."

Jack didn't respond; even though he'd already seen the photographs, seeing the statues up close, in person, was instantly humbling. Six floors beneath the most iconic, famous mausoleum in the world, he was now standing in a hidden chamber filled with stone representations of many of the most important idols of an ancient religion—a chamber that had been literally hidden from history for centuries. Right in front of them, not three feet away, Jack recognized Ganesh, the elephant god; and behind him, Hanuman, a Vanara—a human with a monkey-like face. Beyond these were a dozen more statues, many of which Jack didn't recognize; but then again, there were so many deities in the Hindu religion, it could take a lifetime to learn them all.

"The Vedas mention thirty-three gods, but the common conception is that the Hindu religion contains as many as three hundred and thirty million lesser deities."

"I count about fifty in here," Sloane said, looking over the rows of statues. "Maybe the other three hundred odd million are behind the red door."

She was nodding toward the far side of the room—and then Jack saw it too, the same red brick door from Unger's photographs. And right in front of the door, there it was: the half-man, half-woman deity resting on a pedestal that seemed twice as high as the pedestals holding the other stone gods. Jack started forward, winding his way through the other statues, careful not to touch anything as he went.

He didn't stop until he was just a foot away from the pedestal, so close he could see every detail etched into Ardhanarishvara's face: the symmetry of his-her cheeks, the thickness of his-her eyebrows, the third eye, in the direct center, below a partial crown. And of course, in one of the god's four hands, the tall trident, pointing right up toward the ceiling of the chamber.

Sloane had passed to the other side of the statue and was running her hands over the red brick door.

"I don't think you're getting through this one with your shoulder," she said. "There doesn't appear to be any way inside."

"There's always a way inside," Jack said. "You just have to know where to look."

Without another word, he unzipped the top of his wetsuit and retrieved Unger's moondial. Carefully, he rose to his tiptoes and hung the chain around Ardhanarishvara's neck. Then he carefully positioned the dial at the exact center of the god's chest, right where it was hanging in the pictogram. He leaned close, focusing on the small jut of stone in the middle of the dial.

The shadow was almost imperceptible, the ambient light so low that Jack had to get within inches to barely make it out, but there it was, a thin line of gray pointing down across the moondial at a slight angle. Jack followed the shadow down the legs of the statue, all the way to the pedestal— and right where it would have hit the black marble, he saw what appeared to be the head of a small, black stone nail—almost flush with the pedestal. Without knowing where to look, it would have been impossible to find.

Jack knelt down and held his hand over the nail, breathing hard. He glanced up at Sloane, then slammed his hand down, palm first.

The nail sunk into the pedestal, and for a moment, nothing happened.

Then there was a deep rumble beneath the floor of the chamber, followed by the grating sound of stone against stone, growing louder by the second. Both Jack and Sloane whirled away from the statue just in time to watch the red brick door collapse inward.

• • •

Jack's heart was on full throttle as he picked his way over the pile of bricks and through the billowing cloud of reddish dust and glowing green fungi spores, one hand on Sloane's arm to keep her steady as she followed close behind. She was covering her mouth as she went, probably to avoid breathing too much of the bioluminescent material, but at the moment, Jack didn't care about a little bit of fungi.

As the cloud settled down around their feet, Jack saw that they'd moved into a much larger chamber—a cubic space at least fifty feet across, with walls rising more than twenty feet on all four sides. Unlike the last two chambers they had gone through, these walls weren't sheer, and they weren't covered with fungi; the glistening white marble was covered in meticulous carvings. Stepping closer to the nearest wall, Jack followed the carvings with his eyes and saw incredibly detailed pictures of plant life—vines, flowers, bushes, even trees. A chiseled garden that seemed to repeat itself every few feet, mimicking the symmetrical precision that he knew characterized the magnificent complex six stories above their heads.

Around the plants, Jack saw geometric patterns inlaid with precious and semiprecious stones, in shapes such as hexagons, ellipticals, and swirling nautiluses that ran down the walls between the faux plant life and across the floor, even beneath their feet. He was about to ask Sloane if she could identify any of the flora on the walls, when he noticed the lack of color in her cheeks.

"My god, is that what I think it is?" she gasped, her words suddenly echoing around them.

She wasn't pointing at the walls or the floor. She was pointing above them, toward the ceiling of the center of the enormous room.

Ten feet above Jack's head, the plant-covered marble walls bowed outward, traveling another ten yards into a generous curve; then back again, folding slowly together, narrowing toward a perfect, cylindrical point.

Jack knew exactly what they were looking at. The roof of the underground chamber was a smaller replica of the interior of the great onion dome that topped the architectural Wonder more than six stories above. The room they were in, with its detailed walls—and, Jack noted, as he shifted his attention ahead and saw the raised platform in the exact center of the room, containing a single sarcophagus—was at least the second such replica of the infamous tomb. The main floor, containing Shah Jahan and Mumtaz's empty coffins—their cenotaphs—was all that most tourists knew about. Beneath that stood a second tomb, with the real bodies of the emperor and his beloved bride. And here, six floors down, yet another tomb, this one with a single coffin. But if Jack was right, this coffin might very well contain something much more precious than the remains of a star-crossed lover.

Jack started forward. As he crossed the room, he again noticed the echo he had heard when Sloane had pointed out the domed ceiling. The sound of each of his steps reverberated off the curved dome and the detailed walls, and as he went, he counted down the seconds—then smiled, realizing it was exactly right.

"Twenty-eight," he said as Sloane caught up with him, five yards from the base of the coffin.

"Sorry?"

"Something my dad told me when I visited the real dome upstairs when I was a kid. The interior of the onion is one of the most unique acoustic settings found in architecture. The shape of the marble creates an unbroken echo that lasts for twenty-eight seconds. Every noise we make, every step—it echoes for exactly twenty-eight seconds before the sound waves dissipate past being audible."

"I guess the phenomenon carries just as well down here in the basement," Sloane said, the last syllable bouncing around them as they reached the marble base. "Hopefully, we won't wake any sleeping mummies with our racket."

Jack didn't expect to see any mummies, though out of reflex he found himself touching the hilt of his iták, which was still strapped to his back beneath the partially unzipped wetsuit. The coffin was almost at eye level on top of the five-foot-tall base and appeared to be made out of solid gold. The sarcophagus was decorated with jewels; Jack counted dozens of diamonds, rubies and emeralds, some as big as his fist. He could only imagine how Unger would have reacted, seeing such treasure. Even Sloane's breath had gone rapid.

"It's beautiful," she said, and Jack wasn't sure if she meant one of the gems, or the coffin itself.

Apart from the stones, the cenotaph was also covered in elaborate calligraphy; Jack recognized Sanskrit, but also a few words of Ancient Greek, as well as multiple lines of Sumerian cuneiform and an entire section in Egyptian hieroglyphics. Given time, he knew he could have translated some of the passages, but at the moment, he was much more interested in what was inside.

He put his hands on the marble base and carefully pulled himself up until he was kneeling next to the coffin. The lid was adorned with what appeared to be flower petals, so he guessed it was supposed to mimic the cenotaph of Mumtaz, the emperor's beloved bride. He knew that if he were in the real tomb—not the one the tourists saw—but the real burial place of the emperor and his bride, when he opened that lid, he would see the decayed remains of Mumtaz Mahal, wrapped in silk, facing to the right toward Mecca. But deep in the depths of the Taj Mahal, he guessed that this sarcophagus contained something completely different.

He ran his fingers along the edge of the lid and then glanced back at Sloane.

"One thing I neglected to mention," he said, letting his words echo for the full twenty-eight seconds. "You might want to be ready, okay?"

"For what?"

"The thing is, guys like Unger have been around for a long, long time. As long as people have been building tombs and treasuries, other people have been robbing them. And they didn't have cell phones, or alarm systems, or police call boxes back then. You wanted to protect something from grave robbers, you came up with your own methods. Some of the things I've seen—well, just do me a favor, and be ready."

"You're talking about booby traps."

He shrugged as her last syllable echoed through the chamber. Finally, she nodded. Jack turned his attention back to the sarcophagus and gripped the lid tightly in both hands.

With a burst of strength, he yanked the lid upward. There was a loud hiss, and a cloud of greenish dust floated upward. Jack jerked his head back, holding his breath. When the cloud cleared, he peered down into the coffin.

It took less than a second for him to find the object, dead center, right where Mumtaz's heart would have been. Just as in the eye of Christ the Redeemer, it was wrapped in parchment.

Jack's fingers trembled as he lifted the object free and carefully unwrapped the parchment. The snake segment shined in the green glow of the bioluminescent fungi. It was about the same size as the other two they had recovered—the head from Christ the Redeemer, and the section Sloane had found in the Colosseum—this time curving slightly to the right. Jack could see the same strange bronze gears inside, clearly visible from both openings. Then he turned his attention to the parchment, spreading it out against the open sarcophagus lid.

Once again, he was looking at an image of the segmented snake. But this time, there was a pictograph next to the third segment:

Three trapezoidal shapes that could have been windows or stones above another geometrical shape—a stepped cross, symmetrical rectangular arms around a circular center. Jack instantly recognized the Incan Chakana, one of the most holy symbols of the lost Peruvian civilization. He knew from his time spent in the nearby jungles with the Yanomami what the Chakana was supposed to represent: the Tree of Life, similar in form and context to the Tree from the Judeo-Christian Garden of Eden. But he'd never seen a version of the Chakana that had looked quite like this. The edges of the stepped cross seemed to be on fire—metallic wisps of flame leaped from every corner. Even without understanding the details, he knew what the pictograph was trying to tell him—and where they needed to go next.

"Machu Picchu," he said. "The sacred, lost city of the Incans."

It made chronological sense. Machu Picchu had been built sometime in the middle of the fifteenth century, two hundred years before the Taj Mahal, and was the next of the Modern Seven Wonders in terms of age. If this snake segment had been hidden here when the Taj Mahal was built, then it would have been possible—as crazy as it sounded—to reference an architectural wonder that had been built before *it* was. Though from what Jack remembered from his South American history, Machu Picchu had been lost for centuries, only rediscovered by an explorer in 1911. Then again, that didn't mean the ruins were lost to *everyone.*

"Jack," Sloane said—but he was still running through it all in his head.

"One segment beneath Christ the Redeemer, the next at the Taj Mahal. A third somewhere in Machu Picchu. Where is this leading us?"

"Jack. Shut up for a second and listen."

Jack looked up, surprised by her tone. Then he noticed it, too.

"The echo," he said. "It's gone."

He could only think of one reason why the echo would have disappeared. He looked up toward the ceiling and saw that a panel had suddenly opened in the curved marble, maybe twenty feet above. There was something shifting behind the opening.

"Move!" he shouted, shoving the segment and the parchment into his wetsuit.

He leaped off the base and grabbed Sloane by the wrist.

"What the hell—"

"Go, go, go!" he yelled, tearing across the detailed floor, dragging Sloane behind him.

They had made it halfway to the collapsed brick door when he heard the first crash; despite himself, he glanced back over his shoulder—and saw the open coffin disappear in a crush of white and gray objects falling from the opening in the dome. As he watched, another panel opened in the marble, and more of the objects began raining down into the tomb, plunging straight into the floor and shattering against the hard stone.

"Faster!" he screamed.

They were almost at the pile of bricks when one of the objects sailed right by Jack's shoulder. He caught a glimpse of what it was out of the corner of his eye—and yanked Sloane even harder, pulling her up the pile and nearly hurling her through the opening. He dove right after her; just as he crossed out of the tomb and into the chamber full of statues, one of the objects glanced off of his extended calf, tearing a three-inch gash in his wetsuit. He

179

hit the ground next to Sloane, then rolled over, staring down at his leg.

The object was still caught in the rubber of his suit by one of its five razor sharp points. Thankfully, the point hadn't gone all the way through to his skin, and he didn't appear to be bleeding.

He kicked the object off of him and watched as it clattered against the floor, landing at the base of the androgynous statue that still wore Unger's moondial. Sloane's jaw dropped open, shock evident in her eyes as she stared at the object.

A dismembered, skeletal hand, fingers outstretched, yellowed nails as sharp as daggers. Still aghast, Sloane turned back toward the opening to the tomb. Jack followed her terrified gaze. Beyond the pile of bricks, he could see the fountains of similar skeletal hands still pouring from the ceiling, piling up in the center of the room. The sarcophagus was already buried, the base where he had been kneeling, just moments ago lost beneath a growing sea of razor-sharp skeletal fingers.

Jack wondered how long it would take for twenty thousand pairs of severed hands to fill the entire marble tomb.

He didn't intend to stick around and find out. He let Sloane help him to his feet, and then the two of them started back past the statues and toward the waiting drainpipe.

CHAPTER SEVENTEEN

It looks like Christmas is coming early this year, Gordon Unger thought to himself as he tucked his cell phone back into his pants, right up next to the leather holster of his vintage, but fully functional, Luger semiautomatic. The Luger wasn't the most accurate sidearm Unger owned; in fact, he had a fairly sizable armory tucked into a safe behind one of the glass display cabinets in the storage room not ten feet from the reinforced door that led to the souvenir shop outside. But the Luger was *authentic*, not just functional, and a man in Unger's line of work knew the value of authenticity. His Luger had once been carried by a Sturmbannführer in the Waffen-SS; Unger had received the gun as part of a payment for a pair of rare jade Buddhas he'd liberated from a jungle tomb near the Indian-Bangladesh border, and he'd carried it with him ever since. Something about the long thin barrel gave him an extra edge of confidence, because it was a killer's gun, not for show, not for decoration. It was a gun that had killed before, and would happily kill again.

Unger grinned his wolfish grin as he reached the reinforced door and made short work of the lock. As he pulled the door open, he imagined the look on Little Jacky's face when the poor sod saw the gun again—this time,

Unger would make sure he was out of Jack's reach when he fired. Maybe the first bullet wouldn't kill the boy, but it would certainly slow him down. Since the anthropologist and his lady friend had left Unger's shop, he'd gotten a little nostalgic for the boy's pop, his former friend; if Little Jacky handed over whatever he'd gotten from the Taj, maybe Unger would even let him go with that single bullet as a souvenir. Then again, the boy's pretty friend might kick up a fuss, and then he'd have no choice but to do away with them both. Business was business, after all.

He'd gone two steps into the front section of his store, passing the shelves cluttered with cheap souvenirs, still thinking about Jack's sidekick, when he noticed something strange. Normally, the minute he opened the reinforced door, he could hear Henry the Ravenous Rat hissing and scratching at the sidewalk outside—but for some reason, there was nothing but the normal cacophony of passersby, the errant honk of a triwheeled cycle, and the creak of a wooden rickshaw. He began to wonder if Henry had finally succumbed to his perpetual state of near starvation—and then he saw the woman, standing in the open doorway, her hand on the cracked glass. She was tall and lithe, with sharp, angled features and jet-black hair pulled back tightly behind her head in a thick ponytail.

"Sorry, love," he said. "We're closed. You'll have to come back later."

The woman ignored him, stepping fully into the store, carefully shutting the glass door behind her. He opened his mouth to say something else, then paused, confused. She wasn't Indian, and she didn't look like a tourist. Despite the heat, she was wearing black leather pants and a dark top made out of some sort of stretchy material; it might have been a bodysuit with a zipper that ran all the way up to her tan, toned throat. She had a matching satchel over her left shoulder, hanging down next to her thin, tight waist.

Whoever she was, she was beautiful, from her brown eyes to her long, muscled legs.

"Christmas and New Years," he said, "All rolled into one."

And then her eyes narrowed, and the skin of her face seemed to tighten, her chin and cheekbones suddenly sharp enough to cut glass. Despite himself, his eyes instinctively roamed downward—he couldn't help noting that she was particularly flat-chested—but the way she was carrying herself, it didn't seem natural. For some reason, he realized, she had tied her breasts down against her rib cage, beneath her bodysuit.

Unger could only think of one reason a woman would want to do that.

He drew the Luger out from its leather holster and held it out in front of him.

"I think you better turn right around, pretty lady. Or this isn't going to end well."

She looked at the gun, then back into his eyes.

"You're right about that," she said, in a strange, heavy accent.

And suddenly she was moving forward. Jack Grady had been fast, but this woman moved like lighting. He aimed the Luger and tried to depress his finger—but before he could finish the act, her hand had whipped forward and her own finger had caught just beneath his, keeping him from getting the shot off. In the same instant, her other hand shot out, fingers extended, and she jabbed him hard in the throat, right below his jaw.

He staggered backward, gasping, as she wrested the gun from his hand and tossed it to the floor. Then her right foot came up, and her steel-toed leather boot caught him directly in his abdomen. He crashed backward through the open reinforced door, landing on his back on the floor, still clutching his throat as shards of pain erupted in his stomach.

She moved with him, still fast as a snake, slamming the reinforced door behind her. While he tried to push himself to his knees, still desperately fighting to catch his breath, she expertly engaged the door's lock and reset the alarm.

He spat out a glob of bright red blood, then finally found his voice.

"Who the fuck are you?"

She stepped forward and grabbed him by his hair, then half dragged, half carried him over to one of the metal folding chairs. He tried his best to resist—until she brought a solid knee up into his groin. For a moment, all he could see were bright flashes of light. By the time he'd regained his senses, he was slumped against the metal chair, his arms wrenched back behind him. She was tying his wrists together with tight plastic cuffs.

Three seconds later, she was standing in front of him, and her face had relaxed, an almost indifferent look in her dark eyes.

Unger pulled at the plastic cuffs, and only felt them get tighter against his skin. In a moment, they'd be cutting off his circulation. He tried to kick at her with his right foot, but she simply stepped back, watching him, that damn indifference spreading to her full red lips. He even thought he saw a hint of a smile at the edges.

Who the fuck is this woman? Unger had been robbed before, numerous times; once, he'd even gotten shot in the process, taking a bullet in his left thigh, which had led to an infection that had nearly killed him. But this woman—Christ, she was something different. Something terrifying.

"What do you want?" he said, his eyes wild. He jerked his head toward the glass shelves and cabinets that surrounded them, toward the jeweled statues, antique weapons, and ceremonial masks. "Take whatever you'd like. I won't be calling the police."

She turned, looking over the shelves. Then she paused, focusing on one of the closer cabinets: the one containing row after row of ceremonial Indian masks. Unger knew that many of the masks were nearly priceless; one that he had acquired from a tomb in the Northern mountains had eleven matching rubies inlaid above the eyes. He had guessed he might sell it for twenty thousand in the markets across the border in Pakistan. Still, at the moment he'd have considered it a bargain if that mask would get this woman out of his store. Once she was gone, he'd try to find out who the hell she was— and then goddamn it, he would go after her.

"You want a mask? Go ahead, whatever you'd like."

She crossed to the cabinet. Then she pulled her right sleeve over her hand—and smashed her fist, heel first, into the glass. The glass shattered, shards clattering to the floor. She reached into the shelves and retrieved a mask from behind a pair of elephant faces. Then she turned and held it in front of Unger.

He saw that it was metal, oversize, almost big enough to be a helmet, with a snout like a jaguar. He assumed it was one of the lesser Hindu deities; shit, who could remember them all? Then the woman turned the mask around and showed him that there was a small panel on the back of the mask, held shut by a single screw. She reached up with her other hand and slowly undid the screw, and the panel swung open.

"Mr. Unger, it looks like you've filed this one away in the wrong cabinet."

Unger coughed, tasting blood. His wrists were burning where the plastic cuffs were beginning to cut into his skin.

"What do you mean?"

She pointed to the cabinet off to her left—the one full of antique torture devices.

"This isn't a ceremonial mask. Although it is quite antique, and I'm sure immensely valuable. It's from the mid-sixteenth century, a Mughal design. Quite effective, I'm sure. It was used primarily on traitors and thieves. I believe the proper term for it was Chuha Pinjare. Am I saying that right? Hindi was never my best subject."

Unger felt his eyes widening. *Chuha Pinjare*. He made the translation in his head. *The Rat Cage*. She couldn't be serious. Jesus Christ, she couldn't be.

And then he saw her draw the rat out of her satchel. She'd somehow gotten a makeshift muzzle over Henry's snout, and there were plastic cuffs around both sets of claws, but otherwise he looked as energetic as ever, twisting his rangy body back and forth as she held the rat in the air between them.

185

Then she was moving forward.

"Hold on," he said. "I already said you can take whatever you want."

She placed a leather boot-heel on one of his knees, holding him in place, and with a sudden motion, jammed the mask over his head. The metal felt cold and hard against his skin.

"What the hell are you doing?" he screamed, his own voice strange from within the confines of the heavy mask.

Her boot was still hard against his knee. He couldn't see the rat, but he could suddenly hear it hissing and spitting, because now she had obviously removed the muzzle.

"I'm going to ask you a few questions, Mr. Unger. About a pair of visitors you had recently. I want to know why they were here and what, exactly, they were looking for."

"Please," Unger hissed as he heard the rat's hiss getting closer "I'll tell you anything."

"No," the woman said. "You're going to tell me *everything*."

Suddenly, her boot was off his knee and she had crossed around behind him. He felt a brush of cold air as she opened the little panel on the back of the metal mask.

"You crazy bitch!" he screamed, trying to lurch out of the chair, but her free hand was like a vise on his shoulder.

"Mr. Unger," she said, leaning close to his left ear. "You have no idea."

And then he felt something claw at the back of his skull as she pushed the screeching rat into the mask.

• • •

Twenty minutes later, Vika leaned against the edge of the round table in the backroom of the souvenir shop as she typed her report into the keyboard of her cell phone. In the background, she could still hear the rat clawing around within the mask, but the grave robber had long since stopped twitching. His body was slumped against the metal chair in her peripheral vision, but he barely rated notice anymore. Gordon Unger wasn't simply dead, he was no longer relevant.

In the end, the grave robber had told her everything he could, and she had shown him some level of mercy. The mottled blue spots that covered his throat, where she had pressed her fingers for the four minutes necessary to fully end all brain function, would only add to the unique circumstances of his death; but the wonderful thing about the developing world—and specifically, these particularly rough and tumble slums of Old Delhi—was that you didn't need to worry so much about the details. Another dead black-marketeer in this part of the world wasn't going to raise any alarms.

Vika finished with her text, then hit the Send button and waited for her new orders. The interrogation had gone well; in her line of work, it was often the improvisational performances that rendered the best results. But Unger's knowledge was far from complete. She was quite sure he had told her everything he knew. But he hadn't known much.

As she'd just informed her employer, Jack Grady had indeed retrieved at least one significant item from Christ the Redeemer: an ancient parchment, imprinted with a picture of a segmented golden snake. Next to one of the segments, there had been a pictogram that had led them to the Taj Mahal. Supposedly, they had managed to get inside an underground chamber in the Taj and had retrieved another item—perhaps another parchment and another pictogram—but beyond that, Unger couldn't say.

Vika had to admit, as she patiently watched the blank screen of her phone, that the anthropologist and his female companion were showing great resourcefulness; her surveillance team outside the Taj hadn't seen him enter or leave the complex, so if Unger was correct, and Jack truly had retrieved something from inside via a water entry, he had evaded some of her best operatives.

Still, she wasn't concerned. She knew that given the order, she could take Jack out with as much ease as she'd handled Unger. Unger, at least, had been armed. And of course he'd had his pet rat.

Vika listened to what sounded like claws against bone as her phone finally blinked back to life. She read the text twice, then returned the phone to her pocket.

The order was clear: They were still primarily in surveillance mode, but if an opportunity presented itself to get a hold of whatever Jack Grady was carrying, her people had been given the go-ahead to make their move.

Vika rose off the table and casually headed for the locked, reinforced door. She didn't need to rush—and she didn't need a parchment to follow the anthropologist and the botanist, wherever they were headed next. She had operatives stationed at every nearby airport, bus depot, and train station who would quickly pick up his tail. And besides, her people were already scouting all of the remaining Wonders, as they had been for nearly a decade.

No matter where he went, he was going to be within her reach. And even if she wasn't there to deal with him personally, she trusted her operatives like they were family—because, indeed, every one of them carried the same blood in her veins.

The blood of the warrior.

The blood of the Icamiaba.

CHAPTER EIGHTEEN

"Are you sure there's somebody up there driving this thing? Because I'm pretty certain we're about to die."

Andy was leaning over the vinyl seat in front of Jack, holding on for dear life as the bus sped into another hairpin turn, jerking so far to the left, it felt like the damn thing was actually up on two wheels. There was a screech of rubber against pavement, a roar of diesel engines, and then they were through the turn and continuing up the steep, narrow road, tree branches scratching at the open windows on either side.

Jack pointed to the seat next to Andy, where Dashia was quietly reading her tablet computer, oblivious to the winding ascent up the four-thousand-foot mountain. If the nauseating turns, four-hundred-foot cliffs on either side of the snake-thin road, or shallow oxygen were bothering her, she wasn't showing it. She'd had her head in the tablet since they'd left Cusco, by way of the mountain train ride down to the valley city of Aguas Calientes, the last stop before the ascent to the base of Machu Picchu. Jack knew that before the twenty-two hour flight from Delhi to Lima, Dashia had downloaded enough data on the Peruvian Wonder of the World to write her own guidebook; but somewhere between the flight and the harrowing bus ride up to the site, she'd switched gears and was now sifting through the various symbols of Incan mythology.

"Why can't you be more like your sister?" Jack asked. "See how she stays in her seat and doesn't bother the other passengers?"

"She doesn't know any better. She's never seen a bus topple over the edge of a mountain cliff. And there's only about six other people stupid enough to take this death ride at five thirty in the morning—and five of them look like they've got one foot in the grave already."

Andy waved toward the front of the bus, where a group of elderly ladies were chatting away in the front two rows. One of the women was actually knitting as the bus corkscrewed up the mountain road, her shiny metal needles flashing whenever the rising sun peeked in through breaks in the trees and cliffs around them.

Aside from the gray-haired women, who had been right ahead of them in line when they'd boarded the bus at the station in Aguas Calientes, there were only a smattering of tourists and Peruvian locals taking the journey at this hour, just as Jack had hoped. He knew that by midday, the Wonder would be crowded with tourists—camera phones flashing, video cameras churning—which would only make their task that much more difficult.

Jack glanced at Sloane, who was seated next to him on the two-seater, right up against the open window. She'd spent the first ten minutes of the ride gaping at the view: the rising mountain peaks that flashed between the gaps in the trees, and the four-hundred-foot sheer drops toward the valleys below that appeared at random intervals along the serpentine road. There were metal guard rails set up around the most jagged of the turns, but for the most part, they were relying on the reflexes of the driver, a middle-aged Peruvian with a Yankees cap pulled down low over his eyes and a cigarillo hanging from his pursed, chapped lips.

About midway into the ride, Sloane had obviously had enough of the stomach churning panorama and had asked for the parchment again, which

Jack dutifully retrieved from the zippered pocket of his backpack, now propped against the floor beneath his feet. Since leaving the Taj Mahal, they had both taken turns going over the pictogram; Jack was pretty sure he had at least the basics of the riddle figured out, but he was still waiting for Sloane's input. They had spoken very little since leaving India, and he was beginning to think that she might be suffering from a bit of shock. After all, it wasn't every day that you're almost buried beneath twenty thousand severed hands.

When Unger failed to meet them at the rendezvous point, they had been picked up by Andy and Dashia and had headed directly to the Delhi airport. Jack didn't think anyone had seen them enter or exit the Taj, but they'd just infiltrated the most celebrated building in the world and had caused a fairly seismic change in the deepest subfloor of India's most famous national treasure. Then again, Jack was pretty certain that the snake segment and the parchment had been beneath the Taj long before Shah Jahan had constructed the upper levels of his marble love story.

"Trust me," Jack said, still watching Sloane with the parchment. "The ride up is way better than the ride down."

"You've been here before?" Sloane asked.

"Once. I was fourteen, so I don't remember much. I kind of ran through the site."

"You were with your father?"

Jack nodded, though that wasn't completely accurate. He had traveled to Peru with his father, and they had checked into a hotel in Cusco together, but that was the last he'd seen of the man for the entire eight-day trip. Jack had been entirely on his own—no money, no credit cards—selling off items from both of their suitcases to buy food from the local markets. He'd taken a few day trips on his own to the famous hot springs in Aguas Calientes and up to Machu Picchu, but he'd spent most of his time at the hotel, sitting by the oversize bathtub they called a pool, waiting for his father to return.

Twice, he had called home to check in with his mother, but she'd been too busy dealing with Jeremy's issues—shuttling him home from school early because he'd locked himself in a janitor's closet to get out of gym, disassembling a moped engine he'd connected to the vacuum cleaner to see how fast he could get it to move across the living room—to understand his predicament.

Eventually, Kyle Grady had returned carrying an Incan Chakana, the stepped cross of the Incas, made entirely of gold, with stories of a tribe of Peruvian jungle dwellers who had incorporated a stash of Incan antiquities buried beneath their main house into their own animistic religion. He hadn't even understood why Jack was furious with him. By fourteen, Kyle Grady had been living with Pygmies in Borneo, while his own parents— Jack's grandparents—went on monthlong safaris across the Horn of Africa.

"You're lucky," Sloane said. "My parents never took us anywhere. Well, we did go to Disney once, but the trip got cut short when my oldest sister tried to run off with the monorail driver. Christine was very advanced for fifteen."

Jack and Andy both stared at her.

"Was that a joke?" Andy said.

Sloane shrugged, the expression on her face as cool as ever. Then she pointed to the parchment.

"So you've been to this Temple of Three Windows? And you're sure that's what this pictogram is guiding us toward?"

Jack noticed that her voice had gone down an octave as she switched con- versational gears, and out of reflex he touched the heavy backpack on the floor in front of him with one of his feet; he had one strap around his ankle, just to keep it from sliding out into the aisle every time the bus took a partic- ularly winding curve. He'd made that adjustment five minutes into their ride up the side of the mountain, when the bus had made its first hairpin turn— sliding so close to the metal guard rail that separated them from a two-hundred-foot drop that he thought he saw sparks—and both he and the back-pack had nearly toppled across the aisle and into the lap of the poor young woman who was sitting across from him.

Then again, the way the no more than eighteen-year-old girl had smiled at Jack when he'd apologized for almost crushing her, Jack wasn't sure she would have truly minded. Her dark brown eyes had flashed at him from beneath razor-sharp bangs, and Andy, who had noticed the exchange from one row up, had rolled his eyes, then whispered something about Jack getting arrested for robbing the Mesoamerican cradle.

"It's a best guess," Jack responded, comforted by the bulge of the three snake segments through the material of the pack that he felt with his foot. "The three trapezoids represent the Three Windows. They overlook the Sacred Plaza, a stone perch which is one of the highest areas of the ancient city. The Plaza is surrounded by the ruins of a number of sacred buildings, including the Principle Temple, with its sacrificial altar; it's also close to the Intihuatana Stone, the hitching post of the sun. You get up there via a staircase that goes up from the terraced Main Plaza."

He could tell that much of what he'd said were just words to Sloane; she hadn't had much time with Dashia's notes, and to her, Machu Picchu was little more than an exotic destination she might have noticed in passing on a travel show, or seen on the back of someone's postcard. Even the four hundred thousand tourists who made the difficult trek to the high altitude ruins every year knew little beyond the barest details about the site: a six-hundred-year-old, fifteenth-century Incan ruin sitting seven thousand feet above sea level, tucked into the Andean mountain range, consisting of stone buildings, terraced greenery, and elaborate fountains and aqueducts. The fact that it was so remote and little understood was part of Machu Picchu's charm—and the main reason it existed at all. Most experts believed the city had only survived the Spanish genocide of the Incan culture because it was so damn hard to find—and before planes, trains, and buses, almost impossible to reach.

"These three windows had some sort of religious function?"

"Like most of Machu Picchu," Dashia said, over her seat back, "nobody's really sure. There's certainly a religious aspect to many of the hundred and fifty buildings that make up the site; some experts believe the entire place was some sort of sacred zone, built for worship. But others contend that it was a fort, or a royal palace, or even an astronomical research center. The Incans were obsessed with astronomy, and many of the buildings stand at precise astronomical points, corresponding to different positions of the sun."

"And the Chakana," Sloane asked. "Is there one in the Temple of the Three Windows?"

"There are Chakanas everywhere." Jack shrugged.

"But I assume if there is, it isn't on fire," Andy said.

"Probably not. But it's not an entirely surprising image. The Incas loved fire. Theirs was essentially a heliocentric religion. I'm sure you've seen pictures of the Incan god, Inti. He's often portrayed as a flaming sphere with a face in the middle."

"The original emoticon," Andy said.

"And the Incan story of creation involves both the sun, the Chakana, and fire. Dashia?"

She turned halfway in her seat, showing Sloane her tablet. On the screen was a picture of Inti, and below that, two flame-covered people, a man and a woman. The man was holding what appeared to be a golden staff, wedge-shaped, narrowing where it reached the ground.

"Like most cultures, the Incan civilization started with a flood. The Creator, dissatisfied with the way primitive people were behaving, unleashed the 'waters of the sun' to extinguish mankind. When this flood of fire cleared, Inti, feeling bad for the few humans who had survived, sent his favorite son and daughter down from the heavens on a mission. He gave them a golden wedge, which they were to plunge into the ground. If they were able to penetrate all the way to the hilt with a single stroke, that was supposed to be the spot for mankind to build a new, pure civilization, to last forever. The Incas."

"Forever," Andy said. "Or until a bunch of Spaniards inadvertently infected them with smallpox, then went about destroying all evidence of their existence."

"Okay," Sloane said, ignoring Andy, "so we've got the Three Windows, and the cross, but it probably isn't burning—"

"Yet," Jack said, and again he touched his backpack. He'd made a couple of stops in Cusco before they'd left for Aguas Calientes, and he'd put together a plan. Judging from their experience with the moondial and the red brick door, he had a feeling the pictograms were more than geographic clues. They were steps to be followed, a riddle that was meant to be solved.

It was obvious from Sloane's expression that she didn't share his optimism as she re-rolled the parchment and handed it back to Jack. Maybe his methods weren't scientific, but even so he was amazed that she could remain skeptical, with all that they'd discovered so far. Whatever mystery they had gotten themselves into, this was far outside the laboratory and the rules of science.

He leaned forward, unzipping the top pocket of his backpack, and carefully placed the parchment back inside. Just as he was rezipping the pocket, the bus went into another turn, and the pack slid a few inches into the aisle. Jack reached for it, and nearly bumped heads with the pretty brunette teenager from across the aisle, who had also leaned down, probably to help him out.

"Thanks," he said as her hand reached out toward the strap. "Appreciate the help, but I've got it—"

And then something flashed by the corner of his vision, followed by the hiss of steel against vinyl. Suddenly, the strap in his hand split down the middle—and the backpack was yanked out of his grip and across the aisle.

Jack looked at the girl. She was half out of her seat, his backpack in her left hand. In her right hand was a knife. The eight-inch blade was shiny, serrated, and steel.

"Hey," Jack started, shocked—but the girl was moving quickly up the aisle, toward the front of the bus.

Jack didn't have time to think. He leaped after her, ignoring Sloane's surprised yell from behind. The bus was still halfway into its turn, and Jack nearly lost his footing, but then he was moving forward, his hand outstretched toward the girl.

She spun around, catching him with the hilt of the serrated blade in the dead center of his forehead. He felt a sharp pain explode through his temples, and he fell back, hitting the floor of the aisle spine first.

He could hear Andy shouting something through the ringing in his ears, but the words were quickly drowned out by a rush of adrenaline and anger. He pushed himself back to his feet. The girl was now ten feet ahead, halfway to the front of the bus. The few other passengers were staring at her, but nobody was moving to help, which was unsurprising, considering the knife.

Jack started after her, his anger continuing to rise.

"Where the hell do you think you're going?" he shouted.

The girl paused, then turned to face him. His backpack was hanging from her left hand, the eight-inch serrated knife from the right.

Jack slowly drew his two-foot-long iták out from behind his back. The girl looked at his machete and smiled.

Suddenly, she lunged, the knife moving almost too fast to see. Jack barely parried her first blow, but in an instant her hand lunged the other way, and she caught the back of his grip with the hilt of her blade. The iták whirled out of his hand, spiraled through the air, and landed with a thud, point first, in the center of a nearby empty seat.

The girl lunged again, the blade heading straight for Jack's chest. At that very moment, the bus came out of the turn, and Jack used the momentum to sidestep her blow by mere centimeters. As she went by, he stuck out a foot, and she stumbled forward, losing her footing. She tumbled into the aisle, but even before she hit the floor, her legs were underneath her, readying for a catlike spring back toward him—

And just then, Andy brought Dashia's tablet down against the back of the girl's head. Her body went limp, and she collapsed to the floor of the aisle.

There was a screech of brakes; Jack nearly tumbled over himself as the bus came to a sudden stop. He whirled around, looked out through the front windshield, and saw canvas tents, stone steps leading up to a wooden gate, and a smattering of tourists heading into a group of metal turnstiles. They'd arrived at Machu Picchu.

Jack looked back at the girl. She'd just started to move against the floor, and he came to a quick decision.

"Move!" he shouted toward Andy and the rest of his team.

He grabbed his iták and yanked it out of the vinyl seat, then quickly retrieved his backpack. He let Andy, Dashia, and Sloane pass by, then followed them toward the front of the bus, keeping one eye on the girl, who had made it to a knee. Then he was out the door and racing after his team, all of them running as fast as they could toward the turnstiles.

"Who the hell was that?" Sloane gasped as they pushed their way to the front of the handful of tourists.

Jack had no idea; but he didn't intend to stick around to find out. Andy's quick move had saved him from the girl and bought them some time. But Jack was pretty sure a computer tablet wasn't going to keep someone like that down for very long—no matter how much data it contained.

CHAPTER NINETEEN

Jack took the last set of stone steps two at a time, half pushing Sloane ahead of him. The terraced grass of the Main Plaza had receded into the mist coming off of the mountains behind them, and Jack could no longer see Andy and Dashia, who they'd left camped out below by the entrances to the Royal Tomb and the Temple of the Sun. The tomb and the temple were two of the most popular locations in the ruins, which meant there would be plenty of people around, and maybe even a security guard or two. Andy had pretended to put up a fight when Jack had insisted that his grad students stay behind as he and Sloane continued to the peak of the mountain by themselves, but Jack could tell that the incident with the tablet had shaken the kid pretty good.

As Jack followed Sloane out into the open stone glade of the Sacred Plaza, his mind was still trying to deconstruct what had happened. Obviously, Sloane was doing the same, because as soon as they slowed their pace, both of them gasping from the high altitude exertion, she grabbed him by the wrist.

"Shouldn't we tell someone? Call the police?"

Jack didn't shake her loose, but he continued moving forward, picking his way past the few clusters of tourists who were milling about, using their phones to take photos of the various buildings that ringed the stone clearing.

"Jack, do you hear me?" Sloane said, her fingers tightening. "We need to call the police. That woman tried to rob us."

Jack pushed through a group of German tourists gathered around a Peruvian guide who was using broken English and hand gestures in a futile attempt to give them details about the highest, most sacred level of the Incan ruin. In front of him, he finally spotted the entrance to the Temple of the Three Windows—basically a path that wound around a loose pile of stones. As he led Sloane toward the path, he lowered his voice.

"I don't think it's as simple as that."

As much as he'd have liked to have believed that the incident on the bus had been a robbery attempt, there were too many things that bothered him about what had happened—starting with that damn serrated blade. He'd been robbed before, twice in the Philippines, once in Eastern Europe, and he'd also been threatened by assailants wielding knives on at least three occasions. But the blade that girl had been carrying wasn't the sort of thing you picked up in a Peruvian pawn shop; it was a survival knife, military grade.

Even more troubling, the woman—girl, really—had moved fast. Exceedingly fast. She had disarmed him of the iták with such ease, hell, he had been little more than a nuisance to her. Jack was certain that if the bus hadn't come out of that turn at just the right moment, the situation would have ended differently. The way she moved, the precision in her actions— that girl had had combat training.

Jack had learned to fight in the bush, and before that, he'd trained with his father at a makeshift gym his dad had built in the basement of his home in California. But even with fairly adequate skills, he'd barely gotten the better of her—with Andy's help, and more than a little luck. If that girl had been a bandit, well, she was the most dangerous bandit Jack had ever encountered.

"So you think she was after us," Sloane said as they reached the entrance to the Temple of the Three Windows.

"I don't know. But I think we need to start taking better precautions."

If someone had tracked them all the way to Peru, then whoever they were up against had impressive resources. If it was the same person or people who had murdered his brother—well, it was a terrifying thought. Calling the police wasn't really an option; the evidence they had would confuse the situation more than edify it, and besides, what police force would they even try to explain it to? The Boston cops investigating Jeremy's death would have no jurisdiction in Peru. And once they started down that road, they'd have to explain their expedition into the Taj Mahal, the climb up Christ the Redeemer, and why they were now charging up to the top of Machu Picchu. Jack couldn't foresee such a conversation going well for any of them.

He only hoped Andy and Dashia had enough sense to stay out in the open, surrounded by people. It would be just like Andy to go snooping on his own, especially into the Royal Tomb. The tomb was fascinating for a number of reasons—but especially significant considering his and Andy's most recent research. According to the latest studies, more than eighty percent of the mummified remains buried there happened to be female.

When Andy had first heard the statistic, he had suggested the peculiarity had something to do with virgin sacrifices—a practice of which the Incas were supposedly quite fond. Another possibility, Dashia had pointed out, was that perhaps the area was a fort built specifically to keep the royal princesses safe from the ravaging Spaniards.

But Jack couldn't discard the thought that there might be a different reason. Many times in his research, he'd come across stories about the legendary Brazilian Icamiabas: the South American version of Amazon warriors. He had never heard of an Incan link to the tribe of warrior women, but then again, he'd never before heard of anything linking the Amazons to the Taj Mahal, Christ the Redeemer, or the Colosseum—and yet in his backpack there were now three snake segments and two parchments, all connected to the painting he had photographed beneath the ancient Temple of Artemis.

Unlike the Temple of Artemis, as far as he knew, Amazons hadn't built Christ the Redeemer, the Taj Mahal, the Colosseum, or, for that matter, Machu Picchu. But it was seeming more and more likely that at one time or another, Amazons had visited all of those sites and left something behind.

Sloane finally let Jack's wrist go, and he slowed his pace as they entered the Temple of the Three Windows. It was essentially an open-air rectangle of stone, thirty-five feet long and fourteen feet wide, bordered on three sides by walls of stacked granite. The main focus of the temple was the main wall, containing the three matching trapezoidal windows, each about four feet in height, offering incredible views of the tree-covered mountain peaks that surrounded Machu Picchu on all sides. Jack knew from Dashia's notes that the Incan viewing windows—alternatively thought to have religious, astronomic, and military uses—were the largest of their kind still in existence.

"Just like the pictogram," Sloane said quietly because two of the German tourists had now followed them into the temple and were taking turns sticking their heads through one of the trapezoidal openings. "And the view is staggering. It's like being on top of the world."

But Jack was no longer looking at the windows, or the view, or, for that matter, the Germans. He had turned his attention toward the center of the temple. In the middle of the open-air space were a number of large stones, beginning with a tall monolith, easily equal to Jack's height, and around its base, a pile of lesser cubes of granite; but it was the stone in between the monolith and the cubes that had caught his attention. He touched Sloane's shoulder, and she followed his gaze.

"A Chakana," she whispered.

Chiseled from what appeared to be a single block of granite, the Chakana was large—probably a few hundred pounds, if not more—and it seemed to be positioned exactly across from the center of the three trape-zoidal windows. Seen from below, the Incan stepped cross would have appeared exactly as in the pictogram, with three windows above the cross.

Jack looked around and noted that aside from the pair of Germans, they still had the temple to themselves. It was as good an opportunity as they were going to get.

"Give me some cover," he said to Sloane as he unzipped one of the pock-ets of his backpack.

"How am I supposed to do that?"

"Improvise."

Sloane glared at him, but he was already pulling a small, sealed paper bag out of the pocket. Realizing she had no choice, Sloane walked over to the pair of Germans, and nervously held out her cell phone.

"Could you please take my picture?" she said. "By the windows? I really want to show my boyfriend the view."

Jack was pretty sure the only thing the Germans understood was the extended phone, but nowadays that was a pretty good universal language. Sloane positioned herself next to one of the open trapezoids, so that the Germans had their backs to Jack and the Chakana.

Jack quickly unsealed the paper bag, and held it carefully over the stone cross. He tipped the bag over, and let a thick, sparkly powder rain down over the granite, covering as much of the stone as he could.

Making sure the Germans were still occupied with Sloane, who was going through a series of dramatic poses in front of the window, he pulled a box of matches out from one of his pockets.

He waited for a lull in the breeze coming in off the nearby mountains, then struck one of the matches and tossed it at the granite cross. There was a sharp hiss—and suddenly a bright red flame leaped across the stone, the blast of heat knocking Jack back on his heels. Almost instantly, the flames began spreading outward, creeping from one leg of the cross to the next until the entire thing was engulfed. The color shifted from bright red to blinding orange, and plumes of sparks began spraying into the air, caught by the gusts of wind coming through the three windows.

And then, just as suddenly as it had started, the flames began to dissipate, the brilliant orange shifting once more to something close to purple. Jack felt the heat disperse, and he took a step forward, squinting through the lessening flame at the sizzling granite beneath.

Even though Jack had mixed the powder himself, he was amazed at how well it had worked. Strontium salts harvested from four of his emergency flares, cut with powdered sugar to control the resonance, and mixed with methanol, an accelerant. Chemistry 101—the perfect concoction to light a stone on fire. The entire process had lasted less than three seconds; the Germans were still snapping photos, though Jack was sure if they'd looked carefully, they would have seen quite a startling reflection in the curves of Sloane's eyes.

Another few seconds, and the flames had entirely disappeared. Jack moved even closer, noting that the surface of the granite looked exactly the same as before. He ran his eyes over the staggered arms of the cross, then shifted his attention to the center—

And that's when he noticed the crack, directly in the middle of the Chakana, right at the heart of the Incan cross.

Jack took a deep breath, the acrid hint of burnt methanol stinging the tip of his tongue. He peered even closer and watched as the crack began to grow larger, spreading outward from the center, widening in concentric circles like a fracturing pane of glass.

"Christ," Jack whispered to himself.

And suddenly, the Chakana trembled—and the entire stone cross collapsed with a groan, spewing up plumes of thick, gray dust.

Jack heard one of the Germans shout, but he didn't care. He was already diving forward into the clouds of dust, dropping to his knees, his hands sifting through the rubble. A moment later, he felt Sloane's hand on his shoulder, trying to pull him back to his feet; there were more shouts from somewhere outside the temple, but Jack kept on digging, his hands scraped and bleeding from the broken stones—

And then his fingers touched parchment, and an almost electric thrill moved through his arms.

"Got it," he hissed, using both hands to dig the object free.

He tucked the object into his jacket and sprang back, nearly knocking Sloane over. The two Germans were still standing in front of the windows, pointing at the pile of rubble, shocked looks on their faces.

"I guess that's why they call them ruins," Jack said.

Then he grabbed Sloane by the hand and took off toward the exit.

CHAPTER TWENTY

"I assume this is where you keep the dinosaurs," Jendari said as she followed the squat, spark plug–shaped man in the white lab coat out through a cylindrical air lock and into a painfully bright, windowless lab.

The man looked at her from beneath the few wisps of graying hair that still clung to his shining scalp. His thin lips were pressed tightly together, his pinpoint eyes dancing over dark rings of skin. From the expression on his face, his brilliant pedigree had not included pointers on developing a sense of humor.

"Dinosaurs? We don't have any of those. Although I think Dr. Jenkins in lab C-33 is working on a mammoth sample that one of the research teams brought back from Antarctica."

Jendari sighed, stepping past the fool and into the front area of the state-of-the-art lab. As genetics facilities went, it was near the top of the food chain; she was pleased to see that the tens of millions of dollars she had poured into this complex, housed in a series of nondescript, single-story cement-walled buildings in a dingy North London warehouse district thirty kilometers away from Heathrow International Airport were worth it. From the outside, the complex was boxy, gray, and purposefully unremarkable;

the only external evidence that it was more than just another collection of warehouses filled with cargo designated for the airport was the twelve-foot-high electric fence and the dozen armed guards stationed at the single entrance gate.

The interior of the complex was another story, especially the main laboratory building, which consisted of over a dozen air-lock secured labs similar to the one Jendari had just entered. Even though her background was in engineering, she could appreciate the detail that had gone into designing what had to be one of the premier genetics labs in Europe, if not the world. From the pristine, black granite counters filled with assay stations, pewter sinks, and rack after rack of glassware, to the pair of centrifuges in the far corner, to the fully functional MRI machine on the other side of a Plexiglas wall to her right, the lab was shiny, new, and fully stocked with every modern toy in the field. Although Dr. Benson, the head of the biogenetics wing of her empire—and her glorified tour guide—had made sure the lab was off-limits during her visit, she knew that the place was usually pulsing with people; at least a dozen top scientists she had culled from the best university programs all over the world, eager to be part of her incredibly well-funded research and development initiative.

Over the past decade, Jendari's cadre of eggheads had made unbelievable advances—many of which had led to commercial successes, such as the DNA security panels and the various disease therapies and testing kits. But recently, she'd pushed Dr. Benson and his minions in a different direction. The regular updates she'd received over the past few months had hinted at spectacular possibilities, but this was her first visit to see the progress for herself.

As Benson took position next to her at the front of the room, she felt her attention drawn to a glass tank in front of the closest of the centrifuges. The tank was huge, about the size of a small automobile, with a chain-link cover. The floor of the tank was covered in what appeared to be yellow straw, and

Jendari also noticed a small water bowl in one corner. In the direct center of the tank stood a white calf.

The animal was no more than two feet tall, and just about as long from tail to snout; there were tiny black spots along its spindly legs and hindquarters and a bright orange tag was pinned to one of its pointy pink ears. Jendari stared at the calf for a full beat, then turned to Benson.

"Impressive. You've invented veal."

"Um—" Benson started, confused, but Jendari cut him off.

"Just get on with it."

Benson coughed, then quickly reached for the nearby light switch. There was a loud metallic click, and then the fluorescent lights flickered off, bathing the windowless lab in darkness. Almost immediately, a dull blue light rose from within the glass tank. Jendari realized, with a start, that the glow was coming from the calf.

"Veal that glows in the dark," Jendari whispered.

"SCNT subject A23," Benson said. "Our twenty-third generation clone, approximately three months old. Perfectly healthy—and, of course, an exact match to the other twenty-two generations, as well as the source material."

Jendari took a step closer to the tank, letting the blue glow splash across her cheeks. The creature was much more beautiful in the dark. She didn't need Benson to explain the process by which the calf had earned his designation; she was quite clear on the advanced cloning process, somatic-cell nuclear transfer, that had first been perfected by South Korean geneticists a half decade ago. Basically, the nucleus of an organism's—in this case, a cow's—somatic cell was harvested, then placed within a deprogrammed embryonic casing. Electroshocks caused the nucleus to begin to divide, mimicking the mitochondrial division that occurred naturally during cellular gestation. Eventually, the process formed a blastocyst—a group of living embryonic cells—that contained exactly the same DNA as the original organism.

At the end of the process, you got a clone of the original. Or, for that matter, twenty-three clones.

"And the glow?" Jendari asked.

"We spliced in a fragment of DNA from a deepwater jellyfish with photoelectric properties. It took a few tries, but we've managed to perfect the process."

Jendari stopped right in front of the glass, so close she could see her own reflection in the eerie bluish glow.

"Beautiful," she said.

"We can also make him in red."

Jendari looked back at Benson, but his face was still devoid of any hint of humor. Still, he did look pleased with himself, and Jendari didn't blame him. She understood the significance of the glowing lamb. Not only was the creature a living, healthy clone, grown in this laboratory in a petri dish from a single cell, but Benson and his scientists had also managed to enhance the animal at the genetic level, changing its DNA, the very essence of what it was, forever.

When Jendari closed her eyes, face inches from the glass, she didn't see a glowing calf. She saw a million microscopic double helixes, the very signature of the calf's soul, the history of its species, forever changed. All by men in white coats, men on her payroll—men under her command.

She immediately found herself reminded of the dossier she had been reading on the flight from South America to London, the pages prepared by Vika on the woman, Sloane Costa, who had joined Jack Grady in Rio and accompanied him to India and apparently back to South America. The botanist with the shaky professional standing and peculiar scientific curiosity that seemed to have inadvertently driven her into Jack Grady's sphere. An unimpressive woman, really, in terms of her accomplishments; had she submitted her résumé to Saphra's HR representatives, she would never have been granted an interview with Dr. Benson and his staff, let alone been offered any level of employment. Even so, one small undertaking had stood out. During her graduate studies in genetics, the woman had written a paper on the theoretical work behind the concept of Mitochondrial Eve.

Jendari didn't consider Sloane Costa's résumé-filler as any great coincidence; there was hardly a geneticist who had trained in the nineties who *hadn't* spent some time considering the theoretical discovery. It was quite a spectacular notion, focused on what many scientists called the Holy Grail of DNA studies: the idea that somewhere in the past, there was a single woman from which all living humans had evolved. Not a man, because mitochondria were inherited along matrilineal lines, but a woman, a single Eve containing perfect, essential DNA. Eve, mother of all who came after her; and every living soul on Earth could trace their own degraded, mutated DNA back to her.

According to the theory—and literally tens of thousands of historical genetic samples—this female ancestor had lived around two hundred thousand years ago in sub-Saharan Africa. Perhaps in a jungle, not a garden— but still, the religious, scientific, and cultural implications were staggering.

Mitochondrial Eve—the original woman—with her perfect DNA, her perfect double helix. And since then, a thousand, thousand generations had endowed that double helix with millions upon millions of mutations— defects, leading to nearly every disease that existed all the way to the cellular deterioration commonly known as aging, and through aging, to shortened life spans. Everything that mankind had become—perhaps even the mortality alluded to in the Judeo-Christian Bible, the result of a misuse of the wondrous Tree of Life—was due to transcription errors that had built up, generation to generation, over the ages.

Jendari opened her eyes and once again peered through the glass at the glowing calf in the tank.

Cloning a cow, adding a bit of jellyfish DNA to make it glow—it was a parlor trick compared to what Jendari knew was coming next.

She felt a chill move through her. To Sloane Costa, Mitochondrial Eve was a theoretical concept, a paper to be written in a prestigious journal, maybe something that could help her on her way up the pillars of academia. The poor fool—she had no idea what she and her anthropologist were chasing, no idea what they were nearing with every riddle they solved and every Wonder they conquered.

No idea that before they reached the final secret, Jendari would take it from them, and with it—she shivered again as she wondered, *What if Dr. Benson and his scientists had something much more powerful than a jellyfish to work with?*

Such science would change the world.

And whoever controlled that science would wield power beyond comprehension.

CHAPTER TWENTY-ONE

One short flight from Lima to Cancun, then a three-hour drive in a cheap rental car, nearly bottoming out against the damn speed bumps that seemed to litter every road in the Yucatán Peninsula, followed by a couple of stops for more equipment, picking among the many contacts Jack had made years ago on numerous expeditions to study the aboriginal tribes that had once dominated much of the area—and here they were, transported backward eight hundred more years into the past from the already ancient ruins of Machu Picchu.

Jack stood next to Sloane behind a waist-high rope, staring up the ninety-one stone steps that led to the top of the Temple of Kukulcan, the grand, ninety-eight-foot-tall centerpiece to the Mayan Wonder of the World known as Chichen Itza—and all Jack could think of was snakes.

"Right there," he said, nodding his head past Sloane. "Down from the top of the steps to that stone creature at the base. It's supposed to end up right at his head."

Sloane peered over the rope at the statue at the bottom of the pyramid: an enormous feathered snake, mouth wide open, almond eyes seeming to squint angrily in their direction.

"He's a nasty looking fellow, isn't he?"

"Kukulcan wasn't known for his kind temperament. Then again, despite popular conceptions, the Mayans themselves weren't the most gentle of people. The only things they loved more than calendars and astronomy were human sacrifices—and snakes."

Jack wasn't surprised he had snakes on his mind; he'd been staring at the pictogram on the parchment he'd retrieved from the burning cross at Machu Picchu for much of the trip to Mexico:

A tiny image of Kukulcan, the Mayan feathered snake deity, which he'd recognized at once, and a second snake rendered in black, curling across the parchment from above Kukulcan's head to a spot below his flickering tongue.

Like anyone who had ever Googled the Mayan Wonder of the World, Jack was aware of the ancient pyramid's most interesting feature: how twice a year, on exactly the spring and autumnal equinoxes, just as the sun began to set, a snakelike shadow appeared on the pyramid's steps. Riding downward from the northwest corner, the shadow-snake descended ninety-one steps until it hit the head of Kukulcan—then disappeared until the next equinox.

Jack knew that the optical phenomenon was an incredible feat of both astronomy and architecture; nearly fifteen hundred years ago, the Mayans had been advanced enough to chart the sun and the stars with near perfect mathematical precision.

And yet, Jack hadn't immediately understood how that phenomenon, so obviously referenced by the pictogram, could lead him to the next step.

It wasn't until Sloane had taken her turn with the pictogram—and then asked a simple question—that it had dawned on Jack. If the Mayans were known for being mathematically precise, then wouldn't it stand to reason that the pictogram associated with their greatest city might also be referencing that precision? Might precise mathematics be the solution he was looking for?

"If the snake shadow is supposed to connect with the snake god," Sloane had asked, "then why does it seem to be passing right over his head?"

Finding a protractor somewhere between Peru and Cancun hadn't been easy; but once Andy had located one in a drugstore inside the Mexican airport terminal, Jack had been able to look more closely at the pictogram from a mathematical perspective.

The shadow-serpent on the parchment didn't just miss Kukulcan; it missed the feathered snake god by exactly twenty-three degrees. Once Jack had done the measurement, he'd suddenly understood where the pictogram was leading him—and he'd begun to come up with a plan.

Leaving Andy and Dashia at a well-populated resort in Cancun had been the first step of that plan. Neither of them had complained about getting a day to lounge around a pool shaped like a kidney bean; Jack only wished

that he could have convinced Sloane to remain with them, though her company had made the three-hour drive through the jungle moderately bearable. Either she was starting to warm to him, or he was starting to see
through her walled-in façade. They'd even had a chance to talk a bit about
his brother—the reason Jack was so determined to see this mystery through.

Talking about Jeremy didn't come easy for Jack, and not simply because
of the guilt he felt for not working harder to be a part of his twin brother's
adult life. The wound left by Jeremy's passing went back much farther than
that.

Jack's earliest memories of his brother barely resembled the strange, brilliant, and obsessive introvert his twin had grown into; on the playgrounds
and backyards of their early childhood, they were just two little kids with
personalities that complemented each other. In fact, Jack's father had often
joked that in the right light, you could see how close together those two
perfect zygotes had been. Even as a child—five, six years old—Jack had
been the headstrong one, a wild kid, climbing trees that were too tall for
him, diving into lakes that were too deep, picking fights with bullies that
were twice his size. And it was Jeremy who had been there to pick Jack up
off the ground, drag him out of the water when it got too rough, and call for
the teacher when the bullies got the better of him.

Even when things began to change—somewhere between the ages of
nine and ten, when Jeremy's trouble with social situations became a full-
blown disability and he started to recede into the lonely world of his neu-
rosis—there were still moments that stood out in Jack's mind, flashes of a
bond that seemed deeper than mere brotherhood. He'd tried to describe one
of those moments to Sloane as the jungle flashed by on either side of the
winding road from Cancun.

"There was this tree house our dad had built in our backyard," he'd
started, keeping his gaze focused on the strip of road ahead of him. "Well,
it wasn't really much of a house. More like a wooden board hanging

between two branches that could just barely support our weight. But we'd sneak out there once in a while, after our mom would fall asleep. I'd bring an empty mayonnaise jar to try and catch fireflies; Jeremy would just lie on his back and count the stars. And I mean he'd really count them, sectoring up the sky using astronomical charts he'd memorized, making sure he didn't miss a single one. And I remember, I'd ask him: 'Why, Jeremy, what does it matter how many there are?' And he'd just look at me, sitting there next to him with my little jar filled with bugs. And then he'd go right on counting, all the way until morning. I didn't understand until years later. For Jeremy, it wasn't the number of stars that mattered, it was the counting. It was this ten year old kid in a world that was rapidly turning more and more terrifying, taking control of something so vast and incredible as the entire night sky."

Sloane hadn't said a word, but Jack could tell that she'd understood. From the outside, Jeremy might have seemed damaged and bizarre; but to Jack, he had always been that little kid in a tree house counting stars—all the way to the end. And Jack—the wild, adventurous half of that zygote out in the wilderness with his empty mayonnaise jar, chasing bugs—couldn't shake the feeling that he had failed his brother.

He didn't intend to fail Jeremy again.

He put a hand on the rope in front of them, then gave one more glance over his shoulder, making sure they were alone.

"Good to know American dollars still have value in some places," he said as he lifted the rope so Sloane could go under. "Although we'll be sharing a room from now on."

Altogether, it had cost two hundred dollars to get them alone at the edge of the pyramid. The first hundred had gotten them through the front entrance gate, even though it was an hour after the official closing time; Jack had read online that the site offered special "sundown" viewing for those willing to make the guards out front an offer, and once inside, Jack had been lucky enough to find a second guard who was happy to make sure they got some time by themselves at the pyramid itself. The man hadn't questioned why a couple would want to be alone at sundown at one of the great Wonders of the World. It wasn't exactly the Taj Mahal—not with the Cenotes, the ceremonial sinkholes where the Mayans used to toss their human sacrifices, within a stone's throw—but it had its charms.

When they'd first entered the site, they'd played the part of privileged American tourists, walking hand in hand in a clockwise circle around the central section of the site, hoping as they went that none of the guards would notice the oversized duffel bag Jack had brought with him from the rental car. From the visitors' entrance, they'd crossed by the Great Ball Court, a rectangular playing field with stone rings attached like sidewise basketball hoops on either end. Jack could only imagine the viciousness of the games that had been played there—especially considering that the entire losing team would usually be killed, their bodies tossed into one of the sinkholes. From the Ball Court, they passed by the Temple of the Jaguars, a smaller pyramid than the Temple of Kukulcan, as befitted a smaller form of deity, and skirted the Sacred Cenote, the largest of the great sinkholes, which was essentially an ancient well, thirty-eight feet deep, that acted as a natural source of irrigation to much of the old city. Then the Platform of Venus, the Temple of the Warriors, the Astronomical Observatory—and at last, the main event: the Temple of Kukulcan, where they'd arrived just minutes ago.

Jack wasn't wearing a watch, but he could tell by the way the sun was beginning to dip toward the top of the pyramid that they were pushing things very close. Sundown couldn't be more than a few minutes away, which meant they would have to move fast.

Once Sloane was on the other side of the rope, Jack grabbed his duffel and crawled under after her, then quickly started up the ninety-one steps. Although the pyramid had been off-limits to tourists since 2006, when an eighty-year-old woman had tripped and fallen down sixty of the steps to her death, Jack felt the architecture was much more impressive once you got up close and personal. Made up of nine limestone levels, the four-sided pyramid was perfectly symmetrical; ninety-one steps on each side, then one big step at the top, which added up to exactly three hundred and sixty-five steps, one for each day in the Mayan calendar.

Halfway up, Jack could already feel the sweat running down his back. The sun felt so low now that it seemed to be almost touching the top step.

"Faster," Jack said—then noticed that Sloane was actually two steps ahead of him, her firm legs pushing her upward with practiced ease.

By the time they made it to the top, Jack was already working the zipper of the duffel bag. Sloane had her hands on her knees, breathing hard as she took in the view. From the top of the pyramid, it was mostly jungle, though Jack could pick out a few of the stone temples and the ant-hill shaped mounds that surrounded the nearby sinkholes. Then he turned his attention to the duffel, from which he retrieved a large black pouch, a drawstring hanging from one side.

He rose back to his feet and yanked the drawstring. The pouch unfolded with a snap, canvas material stretching across a tentlike, circular frame. Jack shifted the saucer-shaped frame, and a sudden burst of bright, golden light flashed directly upward as the embossed interior of the Sunburst photography reflector caught the rays of the rapidly descending sun.

"Portable gold," Jack said.

He'd never been much of a photography buff, but his mother had dabbled at the art, and he was quite familiar with the various reflectors the professionals used to get the light just right. Once he'd figured out why the shadowy snake in the pictogram had been exactly twenty-three degrees off its expected mark, he'd known exactly what he needed. The Sunburst was the most powerful portable reflector on the market, and it hadn't taken long to find one for sale through his contacts outside of Cancun.

The Sunburst unfolded, Jack took the plastic protractor from the airport drugstore out of his pocket and handed it to Sloane.

"You're going to have to help me out," he said as the sweat beaded across his forehead. "We need to aim this exactly twenty-three degrees off of the angle of the pyramid."

Sloane raised her eyebrows. She looked over the edge of the pyramid, down the long flight of steps toward the base far below. Jack could see that she was working it through in her head—and she was beginning to understand.

"You're going to recreate the equinox phenomenon of the shadow-snake going down the pyramid's steps, but you're going to put the shadow in the wrong place—by twenty-three degrees, like in the pictogram."

"Actually, it's the pyramid that's in the wrong place, not the shadow."

Jack had realized what the pictogram was pointing him toward the minute he'd first read the protractor.

"The Mayans were amazing astronomers and mathematically gifted," he said as he positioned himself at the northwest edge of the top platform of the pyramid, then carefully lifted the reflector above his head. "But when they first set out to build this wondrous temple to their snake-headed god, they made one minor error. They began their calculations by presuming that the world was round."

Sloane got down on one knee next to him, steadying the protractor at an angle flush with the downward slope of the pyramid's steps. Then she carefully measured her way to twenty-three degrees off the slope—exactly as the shadow-snake image had appeared in the pictogram.

"But as anyone who remembers their eighth-grade Earth Science can tell you, it's actually not. The Earth bulges at the equator and flattens out at the poles. Because of this, as the Earth revolves around its axis—and in turn, around the sun—it has a slight wobble. Over time, this wobble shifts the sun's progress in the sky. Eventually, you get an error—of exactly twenty-three degrees."

"But I thought this temple was properly aligned with the sun," Sloane said, confused, as Jack shifted the reflector a few more inches to align it with her protractor.

"It is. But this isn't the first Temple of Kukulcan that the Mayans built in this spot. It turns out there was an earlier temple, built one century before this one; the Mayans eventually realized their error, and corrected it by simply building a new temple over the old one."

"So beneath us—"

"Is a temple that catches the sun exactly twenty-three degrees the wrong way. Like this."

He shifted the reflector a few more inches, then held it steady, catching the last rays of the setting sun in the exact center. The sun's reflection hit the northwest edge of the temple—and suddenly, a dark, serpentine shape slid down the first few steps. As the sun continued moving lower, the shadow grew, sliding step by step until it was more than halfway down.

"A few more seconds," Jack whispered as Sloane stared almost in disbelief.

The shadowy snake slithered the rest of the way down the steps, extending to a full one hundred feet, and passed directly over the head of the statue of Kukulcan at the bottom.

"Now let's see where this leads."

He ignored the rivulets of sweat running down the back of his neck and the heat of the low sun against his forehead as he held the disk steady for a few more seconds. The serpentine shadow continued past Kukulcan, wriggled across the tops of trees and over the low, tangled brush, then suddenly slithered up a low hill, above a stone wall—and over the lip into what appeared to be another one of the site's many sinkholes.

"The Xtoloc Cenote," Jack said, pulling the name from his memory. "The second largest well, after the Sacred Cenote. It would have been here at the time of the original temple. That's where we need to go."

"Into the sinkhole?"

Jack tried to think of something reassuring to say—but he was inter-rupted by a sound from behind, coming from the staircase that led back down to the front of the pyramid.

Footsteps, he realized. One of the guards must have decided to come after them—maybe looking for another bribe. Jack turned toward the noise, annoyed, just in time to see a flash of motion coming up off the last step and lunging in his direction. A woman with dark hair. In her right hand was a serrated knife.

Jack swung the reflector around and aimed the golden disk directly at her face. The last licks of the sun hit the disk and rebounded right into the woman's eyes, and she covered her face, stumbling back. Before Jack could move, Sloane stepped forward and kicked out a leg, hitting the woman dead in the stomach.

The woman toppled backward, then hit the stone steps, tumbling down head over heels.

Jack stared at Sloane, but she was already moving down the steps on the other side, toward the Xtoloc Cenote.

Jack grabbed the duffel and followed, just trying to keep up.

• • •

"I don't see her," Sloane whispered frantically as they crouched at the edge of the sinkhole. "Was she the same one from the bus? How could she have followed us here? That knife—"

Jack shook his head. He hadn't gotten a good look, but he thought this woman had looked a little older, and there had been streaks of brown in her black hair. A different woman, but with a similar military-grade knife. And again, he had gotten extremely lucky. A few more seconds, and the sun would have been too low for the reflector to do any damage. Already, the air around them had turned a dull gray color, accentuated by the thick, blanket-like mist coming up from the sinkhole. Jack looked down into the well, which was about thirty feet across, bordered on all sides by jungle fronds. The water was murky and brown.

"Either way, we need to move fast. We've gotten lucky twice. I don't want to try for a third time."

He began pulling off his jacket.

"I wish we had our scuba gear," Sloane said.

"It should be less than forty feet. I can free dive that far."

"In this?"

Jack looked at the brown surface of the water again. Jack knew that it was actually worse than Sloane realized. The Cenotes provided irrigation for the town, but they were also important religious locations. Sinkholes were considered portals to the underworld; many of the Mayan rituals began with live human sacrifices being thrown into them, weighted down by heavy stones. A few years back, the Mexican government had allowed divers to do a survey of the Sacred Cenote on the other side of the pyramid, and they had found numerous human skeletal remains.

"I'll keep my mouth closed," Jack said. "The shadow ended exactly two-thirds of the way across. I'm going to focus my search there."

He kicked off his shoes, then stood at the edge of the well.

Another addition to the list of stupid, he thought to himself.

And then he dove headfirst into the murky brown water.

• • •

Down Jack swam, arms straight out in front of him, legs kicking hard against the muddy water. The waterproof flashlight in his hand was almost useless, and he was going mostly by memory; he was pretty certain he was directly under the end point of the serpentine shadow, but after the first few feet into the Cenote, he'd lost all sense of direction. All he knew for sure was that he was going down.

As he swam, he tried to keep his mind from replaying the moment with the woman at the top of the pyramid. It had all happened so fast. Who was she? How had she found them? What would she have done if Jack hadn't blinded her with the reflective disk?

It dawned on him that perhaps Sloane was wrong. Perhaps the woman hadn't followed them from Peru. Perhaps she had already been at Chichen Itza, waiting for them.

If Jeremy had died because he'd found a connection between the Seven Wonders of the World, then it stood to reason that someone else already knew about that connection. Which meant that there was no need to follow them. Whoever had killed Jeremy already knew exactly where they were going.

Jack felt the water cool around him as he pushed deeper. He knew that in the Mayan perspective, diving into the pool was like entering a portal into the Underworld; he half expected to swim right into a tangle of heavy tree roots. According to the Mayan sacred book, the Popol Vuh, the first thing created by the Mayan gods was a World Tree—the Mayan version of the Tree of Life. The branches represented the heavens, the trunk the Earth, and the roots, the Underworld, a place of darkness, pain, and death. As Jack's extended hands finally hit bottom, upending a swirl of thick mud, he didn't feel any roots; just gravel, a few strands of silky plant life, and packed dirt. He kicked harder with his feet, digging his hands back and forth, his fingers sifting through the gravel.

Nothing. His lungs were beginning to throb, and the pressure from the water was sending shoots of pain through his ears. Still, he kept himself against the well floor, trying to use the flashlight to see through the heavy clouds of mud. As he searched the bottom, he noticed something interesting about the plant life; it all seemed to be congregated around one spot—right around where he'd traced the end of the shadowy serpent from the pyramid steps.

He reached down and started pulling at one of the stringy plants. Just as the plant started coming loose, something flashed by his peripheral vision a few feet to his right. He instinctively swung the flashlight toward the motion but whatever it was, it was moving too fast for him to see. Maybe some sort of fish? Or a piece of floating limestone?

He went back to the plant and gave the silky fronds one last yank. Immediately, a fountain of bubbles sprang up from where the plant had been, momentarily obscuring his already limited vision. When the bubbles cleared, he saw that the group of plants were clustered around a small opening, about the size of his fist. When he reached down with his fingers, he realized that the opening was the top of what appeared to be a clay pot, sunk deep into the mud.

Excited enough to forget that his lungs were ready to burst, he dug both hands into the mud and got a grip around the pot. He braced his bare feet against the mud, then pulled as hard as he could. For a brief second, nothing happened—and then the pot slid loose, amid another spray of bubbles. Jack was so thrilled, he almost didn't notice another flash of silver flickering above his bare right foot—

And then he felt two spikes of pain rip upward through his ankle.

He stared down at the long, slithering creature that was now attached to his skin, fangs first. He kicked his leg, but the damn thing held on, a little cloud of blood spreading from where it was digging deeper into him.

Still holding the vase, he bent at the waist and got one hand around the creature's throat. He put a thumb beneath its jaws and squeezed as hard as he could; finally the thing released its grip on his ankle, its mouth flipping open, revealing a pair of fangs around three centimeters long.

Jack lifted the long creature to eye level, noting its long, flattened tail, and the valves over its nostrils. He flipped it over and saw the yellow streak along its wriggling belly. *Pelamis platurus*. Venomous, of course, but that wasn't Jack's main concern. His main concern was that *Pelamis platurus* usually hunted in packs.

He looked up—and that's when he saw them. At least two dozen, churning up the muddy water near the bottom of the sinkhole, barely three feet away. Jack's eyes went wide, and he tossed the snake in his hand toward the pack, tucked the clay pot under one arm, and pushed off the ground, ignoring the shards of pain that ricocheted up his leg.

He swam as hard as he could, shooting upward so fast that his ears felt ready to explode. Something touched the bare skin at the bottom of his right foot, and he kicked out, hitting cold, slithering flesh. Then a flash of silver flickered right by his left cheek, and he realized the pack was all around him, diving and darting in concentric circles as he tore upward. Halfway to the surface, the first snake lunged at him, aiming for a flash of bare skin right above his jeans. He brought his knee upward, catching the thing right under its jaw, and it flittered past, harmless. Then a second snake aimed right for his face. Jack unhooked the clay vessel from under his arm and swung it in an upward arc. The pot connected with the snake's head with a dull crack, and the snake's entire body went limp, its long tail curling in on itself. A dozen of the other snakes descended on their wounded colleague, tearing into it with their fangs. Jack kicked twice more, and his head burst through the surface of the water.

Coughing and sputtering, he dragged himself the last few feet to the edge, and Sloane helped pull him out of the murk. He twisted onto his back, holding the clay pot against his chest. He could feel the blood trickling from the wound on his ankle, but he didn't care. All he could think about was how heavy the clay vessel felt now that he was out of the water.

He pushed himself to a sitting position, then held the pot up so Sloane could see. Any adornment or decoration had long since washed away, but from the craftsmanship and the style, Jack knew that it was old—at least as old as the pyramid behind them.

Without a word, Jack raised the pot over his head and brought it down hard against the stone lip of the sinkhole.

There was a loud crack as the pot fractured into three pieces—and a small, shiny bronze object tumbled to the ground. Sloane knelt, and lifted up the snake segment, shaking it dry.

"No parchment," she said. "Does that mean there are no more clues?"

Jack shook his head. He was looking past her at the pieces of clay on the ground. The exterior of the pot was unadorned, but the interior, it seemed, had flashes of color, twists of ancient ink.

"Maybe next time you'll find a better way to get something out of a fifteen-hundred-year-old vase," Sloane said.

Jack turned over the pieces, one at a time. There it was: the segmented snake, painted in stains of black, and next to the fifth segment another pictogram. This one was familiar: a red-tinged, leafless vine, covered in thorns, twisting through a Roman aqueduct, until it ended over a tiny portrait of an Egyptian queen.

Jack looked at Sloane.

"I think we're one riddle ahead," he said. And then he noticed the expression on her face. She wasn't looking at the clay shard, she was looking down toward his feet.

"It looks worse than it feels," Jack said. "But don't worry. I've got about twenty more minutes before the venom takes effect. After that, some muscle pain, some spasms in my jaw. Then blurred vision, my lungs will seize, and I'll start to suffocate."

Her expression only got worse.

"I'm kidding," he said. "I'll be fine. I've got my antivenom kit in the trunk of the car."

"Jack," she said, and he saw that she wasn't looking at his ankle, but the ground in front of his bare foot.

A two-foot-long, yellow-bellied water snake was wriggling across the mud toward his heel.

He reached down, grabbed it expertly below its head, and tossed it back over the lip of the cenote, where it landed with a mud-spattering splash.

CHAPTER TWENTY-TWO

Be it ever so humble, Jendari thought to herself as she raised the four-inch stiletto heel of her bright green Manolo Blahnik over the unfortunate, squirming dormouse. In truth, she was more curious than annoyed. The engineer in her wondered how the poor creature could have gotten itself trapped like that: long curl of a tale pinned between two of the wooden slats that ran along the base of her aunt's cabin's quaint front porch; while the genetic expert she had become wondered how such a mindless, irrelevant creature had made it into the twenty-first century, let alone onto the isolated grounds of her inherited, upstate New York country escape.

Then again, at this point, the dormouse had about as much claim to the desolate log cabin and the four hundred acres around it as anyone else. Even Jendari's late great-aunt, who had little to hide besides her own unre-searched and unwavering beliefs, had kept the location off the books and off the grid; out of habit, Jendari had continued the exercise, even going so far as to have the few weather satellites that crisscrossed the inner atmos-phere over this section of the continental US rerouted to pass an extra thou-sand miles out of photographic range. Not even the IRS knew of the cabin's existence, and aside from Jendari's annual visit, the place lay as fallow and uninhabited as the defunct copper mine tucked into the foothills eighty miles to the north.

Many times over the years since Milena Saphra's death, Jendari had thought about getting rid of the estate. The childhood recollections she carried of the place—from the moment her aunt had first revealed the bronze wheel in the basement to the week after her aunt died, when she'd had the wheel removed and brought to her waiting plane—had grayed and faded, and now, as she stood on the porch, watching the dormouse, she wasn't even sure why she bothered with the annual visit. Sentimentality? Tradition? Sense of habit?

Shackles of youth, she thought. She watched the dormouse for another moment, then lowered her heel, purposefully missing the pathetic creature by a shadow of an inch. Such an irrelevant failure of evolution didn't deserve the time it would take to scrub his blood off of her eight-hundred-dollar shoes.

She crossed the porch and unlocked the front door. No DNA scanner here; just a key and a padlock. She wasn't afraid of anyone breaking into the cabin, even if there was anyone other than her and maybe the pilot of her plane who could locate the damn thing. She'd long since emptied everything of value from the place.

Jendari entered the cabin and quickly moved through the Spartan living area. The dust on the three-seater leather couch by the empty fireplace was so thick, she could see tiny rodent footsteps crisscrossing the fading pillows. She passed two empty bookshelves, a low credenza containing empty picture frames—and arrived at the door leading down to the basement.

Another lock, another key from a ring she had brought with her from the plane. The steps were wooden and creaky, and she had to be extremely careful because of the shoes; boots might have been a better choice, but she'd always been the type of woman whose exterior matched the level of energy she was feeling inside. Today, her pantsuit was impeccable and bright, an almost electric green to match her shoes. Today, she was alive inside. Even though the last text she'd received from Vika hadn't been entirely the news she had been waiting for, her operative did get confirmation that Jack Grady was moving forward at an incredible pace. Two clumsy attempts to take whatever it was he had found without giving themselves away had failed; but both operatives had been able to report that Jack had found something in Machu Picchu, and in Chichen Itza. And Jendari had a very good idea where he was going next.

She reached the bottom step and slowed her pace as she crossed the basement. The rectangular room with low ceilings and poor lighting was the only room in the cabin with a floor that wasn't made out of wood. Her heels clicked against the smooth cement, which her aunt had once told her was over two feet thick, poured over a frame of solid steel. Milena had put the floor in the week she had inherited the great bronze wheel from her own mother to support the hefty mechanism's sizable weight.

Halfway across the basement, Jendari stepped into the shadow of the iron frame that had once held the artifact; it rose almost to her height, two triangular legs supporting a thick iron crossbar. As she moved closer, it was like traveling back in time: her fourteen-year-old self had actually trembled when Milena had shown her the thing and filled her head with the heady talk of the Order of Eve. A sermon of sorts, a speech of indoctrination. The shackles of a cult that Milena hadn't herself fully understood.

Jendari felt her lips twitch as her eyes drifted to the ornate iron and bronze drop box beneath where the wheel had once stood. It was the one true item of her aunt's that Jendari had left in the cabin—the thing she had returned to year after year like the dutiful cog in the Order of Eve that Milena had hoped she would become.

Jendari heard her own laughter echo off of the cement floor, disappearing into the low wooden rafters. Milena had died without ever really understanding the Order she had dedicated her life, and her wealth, to following. She had just been a simple, unthinking cog. Like dozens, perhaps hundreds of other powerful women around the world that had been recruited over the centuries—women like the ones in Jendari's precious black-and-white photographs, some of them powerful and famous and even historical, others forever unnamed and unknown—indoctrinated into a loose network of operatives held together by nothing more powerful than belief, performing the occasional task without ever asking why, or for whom.

Such was the power of faith. Milena had known nothing about Euphrates, the shell company that was actually sending her those parchments—a company that had built a mercenary training camp out of an Amazonian rain-forest village, and had, in 2007, hacked an international charity to massage a vote that had led to the modern list of the Seven Wonders of the World.

Milena had died knowing nothing about the secret that the Order she so fully believed in was keeping.

Smiling, Jendari bent to one knee over the decorated drop box. *Ritual, tradition, sentimentality, habit.* Once a year, she had knelt in exactly this spot, thinking of her foolish, dead aunt. And every year, she had opened that drop-box lid—and found nothing. More than a decade, year after year, and nothing.

Jendari had used the unknowing middlemen to take over Euphrates's jungle training camp and had co-opted Vika and her team for herself. She had collected an entire vault filled with ancient Amazonian artifacts, including her aunt's great bronze wheel.

And still, every time she'd opened the drop box—nothing. If the Order of Eve really did still exist—beyond her own empire, her own deeds—then it was either toothless or blind. Or, perhaps, they truly had recognized her as the natural new leader—their modern-day Cleopatra.

With supreme confidence, she opened the lid of the drop box, and stuck her hand inside.

Almost immediately, her fingers touched parchment. She froze, her smile instantly evaporating. Then she lifted the parchment out of the box, and still on one knee, unrolled it in front of her eyes.

The message written across the parchment took up only a single line, and the script was a form of ancient Greek that Jendari's aunt had forced her to learn as a child. Once she'd made the translation, the words drove right into the pit of her soul.

"Διακοπή. Είσαι υπηρεσίες που δεν χρειάζονται πλέον."

Stop. Your services are no longer needed.

Jendari felt a searing heat rising behind her eyes. *Your services are no longer needed.* Such disdain, like she was nothing, no more significant or important than the dormouse struggling its life away on the front porch.

Jendari's hand closed around the parchment, and she rose to her feet. The fury inside her was like a storm, tearing at her internal organs. She could barely feel her feet as she crossed the basement to a small shelf right below the stairs. On the center of the shelf was a stone incense jar, long since empty. Beneath the jar was a package of self-lighting matches, more than a decade old.

Jendari took one of the matches and scraped it against the side of the stone jar. A teardrop of flame flashed near her perfectly manicured fingertips. She touched the flame to the parchment and watched as it crawled across the aged paper. By the time the fire reached the Greek words, she could feel the heat splashing against her frozen cheeks.

She took the flaming parchment and held it high above her head, letting the fire lick at the dry, aging wooden rafters of the basement's low ceiling. It took less than a second for the rafters to light, raining sparks and flickers of flame like a halo around her frosted hair.

She turned and tossed the burning parchment into the open drop box. Then she headed for the stairs, seemingly oblivious to the fire that was now engulfing the ceiling above her. As she reached the steps, she removed her cell phone from her pocket and began typing a text message.

It was time to set the endgame in motion. If she was correct, Jack Grady would be heading to the final two Wonders. Which meant he was rapidly moving toward his own obsolescence. If he could have make it this far—through five Wonders, including the Colosseum, which it appeared the botanist had cracked—then Jendari and Grange could figure out the rest.

The time for surveillance had ended. Now she needed to take whatever it was Jack Grady had found, and eliminate him.

Jendari had sent the text by the time she'd reached the last step. Behind her, she could feel the flames leaping across every inch of wood, extending outward across the basement and beginning to eat through the rafters to the cabin above. Again, she smiled.

Sentiment, tradition, habit—cleansed in fire. Every last trace of the parchment, her aunt, and Jendari's childhood self was gone in a flash of devouring flame.

CHAPTER TWENTY-THREE

Jack clung to the saddle of his temperamental mount, his entire world reduced to a sliver of two blindingly bright inches as he tried to stay focused on the three camels loping across the stone path a few yards in front of him. Even at such a close distance, he could barely make out the men atop the camels, their long, white cotton Arabian thobes blending into the fierce eddies of white-hot sand that swirled up from the desert floor. It wasn't Jack's first time on a camel, but the conditions were more challenging than he'd ever experienced before—and growing steadily worse by the minute. He didn't dare try to adjust the kaffiyeh that hung down low over his forehead. Even one hand off the reins might tempt the camel to shift off the narrow path, and Jack wasn't certain he'd ever find his way back.

In retrospect, he'd probably let his machismo get in the way when Magda Al Muhammed, the leader of the small Bedouin troop, had offered to tether him to one of the lead camels for the forty-minute trek. Magda hadn't given Andy and Sloane a choice—and they were now clinging for dear life to a shared mount a few feet to Jack's right, guided along by Magda's cousin, who couldn't have been older than fourteen.

It had taken Jack the first kilometer to get used to the jerky, bouncing motion of the ride as the camel picked its way across the sand-swept stone path on long, spindly legs. Both Sloane and Andy had turned green by the time they'd passed the outer tombs—mostly outcroppings of rock, polished smooth by two thousand years of dry desert wind—but only Andy had kept up a steady cadence of complaints, which had eventually prompted Magda to offer him a roll of chewable Dramamine pills from a pouch hanging next to the curved sheath of his ceremonial Bedouin scimitar. Magda's brother-in-law, who was riding point for the brief crossing, had laughed so hard he'd nearly fallen out of his saddle.

It wasn't until the wind had started to pick up and the sand had started to swirl that Jack's camel had begun to buck and tug against the leather reins every time he'd tried to correct the animal's direction. Jack had realized he was more passenger than driver, and now he was pretty much at the mercy of the one-ton beast. Thankfully, for the time being, the animal seemed content to follow the three Bedouin tribesmen, who had no trouble navigating the stone path by feel alone.

"The Siq is just ahead," Magda called back, his accented voice a hiss within the wind, "But we should move faster, *sadeke*. Another ten minutes and the storm will be upon us."

With that, the three lead camels quickened their pace, and Jack felt his own ride jerk forward into a mild trot. His fingers went white against the reins. He wished he'd had a few days to reacclimate himself to the desert before seeking out Magda and his clansmen, but after the events at Chichen Itza and Machu Picchu, he'd wanted to avoid any sort of delay. He might have been able to ignore a single robbery attempt; but two attempts in two days meant that they were being stalked. Sooner or later, whoever was after them was going to try again.

Which meant they needed to move quickly—and as unnoticed as possible.

Jack leaned forward into the saddle, his camel lurching over a pile of rocks that partially covered the path ahead. He could feel the wind yanking at his own long white thobe, similar in style to the light cotton robes worn by the three Bedouin. The kaffiyeh —checkered in red and white—covered everything but his eyes, and even if Jack hadn't been riding through the beginnings of what appeared to be an epic sandstorm, he was indistinguishable from the rest of Magda's clan. Andy was likewise covered, head to toe, in white; Sloane's thobe was a deep blue, as befitted a woman of the Bedul, Magda's tribe; instead of a kaffiyeh, her head was covered in a tassled veil, adorned with a single, polished blue stone above her eyes.

Magda's generosity in providing them with both transport and the clothing was admirable—and not unexpected. Nomads who had spent the past few thousand years traversing what was arguably the harshest environment on Earth, the Bedouins had developed a sophisticated culture that revolved around tenants of loyalty and hospitality. Even complete strangers were treated like members of the tribe—given food, water, clothing, whatever the Sheik and his family could spare.

And Jack wasn't a stranger to the Bedul, though Magda's use of the honorific *sadeke*—friend—was more evidence of the Sheik's generosity. Jack had only met Magda twice, when he had been studying a rival clan that shared water rights to the system of natural wells that ran along the base of this section of the Wadi Araba, a desert valley that stretched from the base of the mountain Jebel al-Madhbah to the shores of the Dead Sea. Even so, when Jack and his team had arrived twelve hours before at the Sheik's village—little more than a circle of large, black tents made of sewn goat hides, strung in front of the entrances to cave-like, deserted tombs—Magda had immediately agreed to provide everything Jack needed for the short journey. He'd even offered himself, his cousin, and his brother-in-law as personal guides, though he'd suggested that they wait until after the predicted sandstorm passed. But Jack had seen the sandstorm as another bit of luck. As long as they had reached their destination before the worst of the storm hit, it was only going to make what he was planning easier.

Once the pictogram on the broken pottery from Chichen Itza had pointed to the Colosseum, where Sloane had already recovered one of the snake segments, Jack had assumed that Petra, the next chronological Wonder among the seven, would be the penultimate stop on their journey. With that in mind, they'd begun scouring the photos Sloane had taken in the hypogeum, searching for the next pictogram. To assist them, Dashia had enlarged all the photos using a computer at the resort in Cancun's business center, then devised a simple image recognition program to seek out any snakelike markings.

After the program was engaged, it hadn't taken them long to locate what they were looking for: The seven-segmented snake had been carved directly into Cleopatra's headdress, right above the Egyptian queen's eyes. It had taken Dashia another few clicks on the computer to enhance the tiny image next to the sixth segment on the snake:

At first, Jack thought he was looking at some sort of oblong barrel, slightly off-kilter, covered in spots; but then he'd come to the conclusion that it wasn't a barrel at all, but a pockmarked urn, with two curved handles leaning slightly backward and to the left. That's when Jack had known for certain—their next stop was a two-thousand-year-old ancient city, built into the stone foothills of a historic mountain in the Eastern desert of Jordan: Petra, the Rose City, with its famous façades carved directly into the stone cliffs that had once been home to a lost and mysterious desert civilization, the Nabataeans.

"Up ahead!" Jack heard Magda shout. "Into the Siq!"

Jack squinted through the brightness and saw the base of the mountain looming up in front of them—and there, right down the center, a crack shaped like a lightning bolt, ripping right through the solid stone. The Siq—literally a shaft or gorge naturally occurring in the stone that ran for more than a kilometer through the mountain of Jebel al-Madhbah—was the main entrance to the Rose City, and could not have appeared ahead of them at a more opportune moment. The wind howled behind them, and Jack felt himself suddenly pelted and buffeted by sand on all sides. Magda and his camels surged forward, and Jack fell flat against his saddle, his legs tight against his animal's heaving sides. He felt spikes of pain move up from his ankle where the water snake had bit him. The antivenom he'd given himself in the parking lot at Chichen Itza had saved him from the worst effects of the bite, but he still had twin fang marks that he'd carry with him for the rest of his life. Then again, they were no worse than the check-shaped scar beneath his second rib from the scorpion tail-tipped fighting stick of a Yanomami chieftain. He ignored the pain, clinging to the animal, completely blind from the sweeping waves of sand, praying that Andy and Sloane were still on their camel—

And then suddenly, the wind died down to a steady breeze, and the camel slowed back to a trot. Jack lifted himself off the saddle and looked around; they were inside the Siq, the high, red-tinted sandstone rising on either side as far as he could see. The ground was loosely paved in well-worn cobblestones marked by hoof prints, thousands of years of sandals and shoes, and even the ancient scars of chariot wheels, and the sound of the camels' hooves echoed through the air. Jack could still hear the vicious winds whipping up the desert outside, but within the mountain, they were protected from the worst of the sandstorm.

"I think I swallowed an entire sandbox." Andy coughed as his and Sloane's camel drew close to Jack's. "Moses spent forty days out there? I barely lasted forty minutes."

Jack unwrapped the lower part of his kaffiyeh, now that his mount had settled into a controllable rhythm behind the three Bedouins. He noted the white streaks riding up the reddish sandstone of the walls, and the rough traces of erosion from two millennia of wind and the odd flash flood. The Siq was staggeringly beautiful, and Jack could imagine what sort of miracle it must have looked like to the ancient peoples who used it as a thoroughfare to the capital city of the Nabataeans—and to even earlier desert wanders, perhaps even Moses himself, as Andy had intimated. To this day, Jordanian guidebooks still referred to the area as the Valley of Moses; as the legend went, Moses had traveled this way when he'd left Egypt with the Israelites on his journey to his promised land.

The history of this place was even more overwhelming than its staggering beauty. Jack shifted his gaze to Magda and his tribesmen, still wrapped up in their kaffiyehs and thobes. To them, this place wasn't just history, it was home; the Bedul were one of the oldest Bedouin clans in Jordan, and the only people on Earth who actually still lived in one of the great Wonders of the World. In the eighties, the Jordanian government had taken great pains to try and relocated the nomadic inhabitants out of what was rapidly becoming the country's most popular tourist attraction—they'd even built an entire modern village, Um Seihoum, to house the thousand or so remaining Bedul—but Magda and his clan had resisted, and still resided in the outer tombs of Petra, raising their camels and tending their sheep as they had since Moses' time.

"Luckily for him," Jack said, "Moses didn't have to share a camel with you. With all the noise you've been making, I'd imagine he'd have turned right around and headed back to Egypt."

Usually, Dashia would have joined in to help tear Andy down a notch, but she was safely ensconced in one of the Bedul's black tents, using a satellite phone to begin making arrangements for their next journey after Petra, the last and final Wonder of the World. Sloane wasn't interested in the banter; she was looking at a row of carved niches that had now appeared on the red-and-white streaked walls of the narrow Siq. Most of the niches contained cubic stones, lined up in rows of three.

"The Nabataean gods," Jack told her, his voice echoing through the gorge. "Although most ancient and modern cultures have gods they represent in human or animal form, the Nabataeans used square and rectangular stones."

"Not very imaginative," Andy said.

"Quite the contrary. It takes a pretty sophisticated imagination to see a god in a block of stone."

The Siq took a hard turn to the left, narrowing to only a few meters across. Then another shift to the right. The wind was barely a whistle now, though Jack could only imagine the powerful storm tearing through the desert behind them. Usually, the Siq was crowded with tourists, making the journey to Petra on horseback, by carriage, or on foot. Because of the storm, the Jordanian guards who patrolled the site were turning people back. Of course, nobody told the Bedul where to go; this was their desert. Jack's timing couldn't have been more fortunate.

After the next turn, they passed another carving, this one more elaborate: an obelisk, standing on a large stone block. Again, faceless, but there were winding grooves around the obelisk's sides. At first glance, it looked like more erosion, but Jack had seen the image before.

"This is the main goddess of Petra—Al Uzza. She's the matron of power and fertility, and was supposedly a fierce defender of the nomadic people. Those grooves are supposed to represent vegetation, vines running down a single desert tree."

Sloane raised her eyebrows. Jack nodded.

"It doesn't matter where we go," he said. "We always seem to end up back where we started. The Nabataeans were desert nomads who left behind no literature or inscriptions of any kind. Their gods were featureless blocks of stone. And yet even they left references to a spiritual tree. But it gets even more interesting."

The Siq made one more turn, and Jack could see the opening at the other end of the narrow gorge, a vertical slice of brightness reflecting its way down the rose-colored walls. The wind around him had begun to pick up, even though the other side of the Siq was more protected by the mountain's cliffs.

"Al Uzza was often associated with Artemis, the Greek goddess of the hunt."

"Who was associated with Diana," Sloane said. She'd read Jack's articles thoroughly. "The goddess of your Amazons."

Jack smiled. *His* Amazons? They had come a long, long way from the Amazon culture he'd attempted to reconstruct from archaeological finds and assorted artifacts. *His* Amazons battled ancient Greeks and Alexander's armies; perhaps even fallen in love with Roman generals and populated Brazilian rainforests. But they didn't leave snake segments beneath Wonders of the World.

"Diana, or sometimes Eve. But the connection doesn't end there, as you'll see in a moment."

Jack pointed up ahead, where the three Bedouin had drawn their camels to a stop, right at the opening of the Siq. Magda made a noise with his lips, and Jack suddenly felt his camel lurching downward, into a controlled kneel. Andy gasped as his and Sloane's camel did the same, nearly pitching the two of them onto the cobbled stone floor.

"I think this the end of the ride," Jack said.

He slid off his saddle and stepped away from the camel, shaking his throbbing ankle as the blood moved back into his legs. Then he helped Sloane off of her ride, leaving Andy to pitch himself gracelessly to the ground. The three of them headed for the opening. As Jack passed next to Magda and his clansmen, Jack bowed his head, pressing his hands together.

"وستي‌م دادس ضيافـتكم," Jack said as Magda waved him on.

"The storm should last another thirty minutes. Then it will be safe to make your return. My cousin will stay with the camels at the entrance to the Siq. As-salaam-alaykum, *sadeke*."

With that, the three Bedouin turned and led their camels back through the Siq, the way they had come. When their hooves were only echoes against the walls, Jack turned back to the opening. He readjusted his kaffiyeh over most of his face and gestured for Andy to do the same. Sloane pushed her veil back over her eyes, and they stepped into the wind, sand, and light.

• • •

It didn't matter how many times Jack had stood in this very spot, staring up at the magnificent, multistoried façade of Al Khazneh—the Treasury, Petra's most iconic building—carved right into the red-and-white streaked stone. Every time was like the first, a breathtaking moment even without the fierce wind-whipping sand against his kaffiyeh. The scale of the thing was magnificent: from the thirty-foot-high Greek-style columns that held up the first story, to the carved statues standing in covered alcoves along the second floor, to the peak of the center citadel, rising right up into a ledge of the cliff face above. There was an open doorway on the first floor, leading into blackness. Jack knew from previous visits that the Treasury had actually been built as a crypt, and the bottom floor had once housed the coffins of various Nabataean royalty before ten generations of grave robbers left nothing but an empty cave filled with more elaborate carvings.

But at the moment, Jack wasn't interested in the crypt or the missing coffins. Instead, he pointed at the two human-size statues on the second floor, flanking the central citadel. He leaned close to Sloane, so that she could hear him through the veil.

"Tell me what you see," he said as she held one hand over the blue material above her eyes, holding it against the wind.

"Two women. I think they're holding something."

"Axes," Jack said. "The two women are Amazons. Elaborately detailed, carved two thousand years ago—by a people whose gods were nothing more than faceless cubes."

The two statues were the reason Jack had visited Petra numerous times over the years, especially when he was studying the nearby Bedouins. To him, the statues were some of the best evidence that the Amazons were more than myths; the Nabataeans left their myths to be detailed by the imagination. In Jack's view, these two sculptures were something else, something based in reality. Two axe-wielding Amazons to guard the Nabataean royalty on their way to the afterlife.

"Above them are the four winged eagles that were supposed to carry the dead souls up to whatever the Nabataeans viewed as heaven."

"I thought this was a Treasury."

"Actually, that's a misconception. It was originally a tomb, built around the time of Christ. Over the years, a number of legends of it being a storage house for hidden treasures sprang up, which led to it being renamed. The most famous of these legends was that Moses himself had stopped here on his journey to Israel; at Aaron's behest, he'd hidden some of the gold he'd taken from the Egyptians, then continued on his way."

Jack couldn't see Sloane's eyes, but he could tell that she was staring at him.

"Moses' gold, here?"

Jack pointed to the top of the citadel at the peak of the second floor of the façade almost eighty feet above his head.

"There," he said. "In that urn."

Even through the wind and sand, Jack could make out the stone sculpture: three feet high, oblong, with curved arms that almost looked like wings, standing atop a circular base. The rounded sides of the urn were covered in pockmarks.

"The pictogram."

"Exactly. The pockmarks are actually bullet holes. The Bedouin believe that some of Moses' gold is hidden inside that urn, and when they ride by on their camels, they often fire their rifles at the stone. But all indications are that the urn is solid, through and through."

It was almost too perfect, Jack thought to himself. A pair of axe-wielding Amazons guarding a stone urn that was supposedly full of gold. If he'd thought it through before, he wouldn't have even needed the pictogram to know where he was supposed to go next.

As he started forward toward the façade, he reached into his long white robes and retrieved his folded-up metal grappling hook. Andy was right behind him, but Sloane paused, still staring at the urn.

"You're going up there?"

"We're all going up there," Jack yelled, through the wind. "It's too dangerous for us to be separated. Right now, we've got the place all to ourselves, but that could change."

He hit the switch on the edge of the grapple, and the spiderlike claws flicked open. Andy was already pulling the heavy rope out from under his own robes. Jack approached the rock face and began scanning for a good place to make their ascent. As cliff climbs went, it wasn't going to be difficult to chart a path up to the story of the façade; there were many gaps and cracks in the red sandstone, and even with the wind, they shouldn't have much trouble pulling themselves up along the rope. He knew that Andy was up to the task, and from what he'd seen of Sloane so far, she could certainly keep up.

The truth was, Jack had wanted to climb Petra ever since he'd first come through that Siq, years ago. He had just been looking for the right excuse.

• • •

"I don't think I can make it," Sloane hissed as Jack held out his hand as far as he could, trying to reach to where she clung to the stone eagle, her long blue robes billowing around her like a typhoon's waves. "I can't reach."

The terror in her voice was palpable, but Jack tried his best to ignore it, extending his body from the ledge of the citadel roof. Andy was holding him by his legs, helping to keep him steady as he tried to grab Sloane's extended wrist. Again, he missed by inches.

"You're going to have to jump," he shouted, over the wind. "It's only a few feet. I'll catch you."

Sloane yelled something back, but her expletives were lost in the wind. Jack glanced down at the eighty-foot drop to the stone floor in front of the Treasury. A little higher up, he could barely make out Sloane's veil where it had caught on one of the Greek columns, a fleck of blue against the red-white stone.

"I promise I won't let you fall."

Sloane looked at him, her face pressed against the eagle's beak. Then she nodded. She took one last breath, her porcelain cheeks tight against the rock, and then she leaped toward him through the air. Jack reached out with both hands, nearly kicking Andy off the citadel roof behind him, and made a grab for her wrists. At the last second, his fingers touched skin, and he pulled her toward him, using her inertia to swing her onto the citadel roof behind him. Then he grabbed Andy by the back of his robes and yanked him back onto his knees.

Jack exhaled, tasting sand and sweat, then turned his attention to the urn, which was between the three of them at the peak of the sloped citadel roof. Up close, the bullet holes were like miniature craters in the stone. Jack could only guess at how heavy the thing might be—one hundred, two hundred pounds? From a few feet away, it appeared that the archaeologists were right, that it was solid through and through. But Jack hadn't climbed the façade to break into the urn.

"Thirty degrees to the back and left," Sloane said, a tremble in her voice. Jack could see that her eyes were red, but he didn't know if it was from the sand, or the fear.

Jack nodded. Dashia's enlarged version of the pictogram had been clear. It wasn't a broken urn that the image had shown, but a tilted one. Jack crawled closer and put a hand on either side of the sculpture. The stone felt cold against his skin, a single bullet-made crater digging against the base of his palm.

He pushed as hard as he could, using his shoulders and thighs, ignoring the pain in his ankle and the stinging sand against the back of his neck—and the urn started to move. Barely at first, centimeter by centimeter, but then more smoothly, as if on tiny ball bearings. Jack kept pushing until the thing was at the proper angle, back and to the left—and he felt a slow rumble beneath his legs. For a brief second, he feared that the citadel was about to collapse beneath them. He grabbed the rope, right up near where the grapple was still dug into the lip of the citadel's roof, but then Andy was jabbing his shoulder and pointing to a spot directly above the urn where the façade met the uncarved cliff.

A dark, oval opening had appeared in the solid rock. Grooves in the stone directly behind the urn led into the opening—where they disappeared into complete darkness.

Jack looked back at Sloane and Andy.

"It appears that Moses liked a good climb," he said, grinning.

And then he started up the grooves and into the darkness.

• • •

Jack held the lit flare high above his head as he pulled himself up the last groove and out onto a stone ledge that overlooked an interior cavern stretching a good fifty feet in every direction; the walls were rough and red, streaked with white like the exterior of the cliff and the cavern floor— another ten feet below the ledge, stretching out ahead of him like the semicircle of an amphitheater—was covered in thick sand. But it wasn't the floor or the sand that caught Jack's attention as he peered through the orange glow of the flare. It was the elaborate stone catwalk that ran up the far wall: three connected platforms, with more of the ladderlike grooves rising up along the wall between them, each no wider than the two-foot ledge on which he now stood. The platforms weren't attached to the wall; instead, they appeared to be held up by thin, cylindrical columns, two on each side, all of them approximately fifteen feet high. Unlike nearly every other surface of the cavern, the columns contained no red at all. Their curved surfaces were smooth and a much purer shade of white than the flecks and stripes within the sandstone.

Andy nodded toward the top platform of the catwalks.

"I think that's where we're supposed to go."

Jack saw it too; at the very end of the top platform stood another urn on top of a small, circular pedestal.

Without wasting any more time, he swung his legs over the ledge where they were standing and dropped the ten feet to the sand. He sunk into the sand almost to his calves, then started forward, using the flare to search the ground in front of him for any signs of traps or triggers. *Or snakes, or spi-*

ders. Jack pushed the thought away; when you couldn't see your feet, it was never good to imagine things with fangs.

He could hear Andy and Sloane plodding along behind him, but he didn't turn until he reached the grooves leading up to the first platform. By then, his flare had just started to die down, so he tossed it to the sand and lit a second one. The orange flame flashed against the closest cylindrical support columns, and he reached out with two fingers to touch the sheer white material.

Ivory. His mouth went dry as he remembered the sliver that the pathologist had removed from his brother's rib cage. The ivory columns brought him right back to that lab, yards away from Jeremy's autopsy table. He knew that ivory was a material used extensively by ancient cultures; no doubt the Amazons had a fascination for the hard, yet pliable material as well. He wondered, *If these columns are more evidence of an Amazon connection, does that extend to the ivory in my brother's chest?*

He thought back to the two robbery attempts. Both of his assailants had been women. *What if they were Amazons?* It was a preposterous thought. Even if the snake segments had been left by Amazons, the idea that remnants of a culture had survived in secret for so many millennia was unthinkable.

Jack took his hand off the column and moved to the first set of grooves leading upward. Then he began to climb.

By the time they reached the top catwalk, all three of them were breathing hard. Although Jack's first step off the grooves caused the entire catwalk to rock a few inches in either direction, the stone felt stable enough to hold their weight. Still, they moved forward carefully, keeping close together, all three holding onto the rope, which was grappled to a jut in the wall near the roof of the cavern, ten feet above.

"It's smaller than the one outside," Andy said. "Moses must have dropped some of his gold on the way up."

Jack approached the urn slowly, holding the flare out in front of him.

The urn was about half the size of the one on top of the Treasury, and its surface was devoid of any pockmarks or carvings. It still appeared to be made out of stone, but even from a few feet away, Jack could see flickers from his flare glancing inside the lip of the vessel; it seemed to be hollow. He also saw that a few feet above the urn, a pair of grooves led to another oval opening in the wall similar to the one they had come through from outside. Perhaps another way out, or maybe a dead end—it was hard to tell. Jack turned his attention back to the urn.

"Looks like it's hollow," Jack said.

He was about to reach for the urn with his free hand—when he noticed something about the circular base that the urn was sitting upon. It wasn't a single stone; it was a number of circular stones, each a few inches thick, piled one on top of another.

Jack felt a shiver move through him, and he quickly held up his free hand, stopping Sloane and Andy. Then he lowered himself to one knee, peering closer. At the very back edge of the stone circles, he saw it: a long sliver of ivory, almost thin enough to be invisible, leading from the bottom of the base to the top of one of the ivory support columns.

"An ενεργοποιούν," he said, using the ancient Greek. Andy exhaled— his Greek wasn't as good as Dashia's, but he obviously understood. Sloane touched Jack's arm.

"What is it? A trap?"

"A pressure scale. These stones are held down by the weight of the urn. The original design is ancient Greek, but there's evidence that the origins are much older. It's pretty sophisticated, actually—"

"What happens if you remove the urn?" Sloane interrupted.

Jack waved with the flare.

"Not sure, exactly." He bent forward again to take another look at the strip of ivory—and just then, something whizzed by his right ear and exploded against the rock wall to his right.

Flecks of sandstone rained down onto the catwalk, and Jack grabbed Sloane by her robes, pulling her down next to him. Andy was already flat on his stomach, peering over the edge.

"Three of them!" Andy said. "They just came through the tunnel from outside. Shit, Doc, I think they're armed—"

Another bullet cracked against the wall, inches above Sloane's head. Jack's jaw clenched. He grabbed Sloane's hand and pointed to the opening above the urn. She nodded as another bullet whizzed by.

Jack knew he had to move fast. He could already hear footsteps moving across the lowest of the three catwalks. He gripped the flare tight in his hand, then rolled to the edge and flung the flaming stick as far into the air as he could.

Gunfire erupted, and the flare jerked and twisted as it spiraled toward the sandy floor of the cavern. The catwalk around Jack descended into darkness, and Jack pulled Sloane over him, shoving her toward the urn.

"Jump!" he hissed.

She didn't even pause, hurling herself over the urn toward the grooves that led up to the opening. She hit the wall hard, gasping, but her hands found the grooves and she was moving upward. As she pulled herself into the opening, Jack grabbed Andy by the arm and yanked him forward.

"Your turn!" he yelled, pushing Andy as hard as he could.

Andy let out a yell as he leaped, just missing the top of the urn. For a brief moment it seemed like he was going to slide right down the wall, but then Sloane was reaching down, grabbing him by the collar of his robes and yanking him upward. He clawed at the grooves, and then it was just his legs dangling out of the opening as Sloane pulled him the rest of the way.

Jack was about to leap after them when he heard a noise directly behind him on the top catwalk. He turned as a yellow flare burst to life.

The woman stood still as a statue at the far edge of the catwalk, one hand nonchalantly holding a military-grade flare, the other caressing the grip of a semiautomatic handgun. She was dressed in desert camouflage-her long, lithe body hidden beneath flashes of gray and brown. Her long, dark hair was pulled back behind her head in a severe ponytail, and her face was the shape of a diamond, her eyes vaguely almond, narrowed to near slits.

"Dr. Grady," she said, in a thick, unplaceable accent. "You're much taller than your brother."

She said the words as if she were simply stating a fact, but Jack was suddenly hit with a burst of white-hot rage. His eyes drifted from the gun in her hand to his rope, which was now on the floor of the catwalk by his feet, still attached to the grapple that was hooked into the wall. While the woman watched, he slid the toe of his boot under the rope, then returned his attention to the woman's chiseled features.

She cocked an eyebrow, amused.

"You're very resourceful. But what do you think you're going to do with that? Climb out of here like a spider on a web?"

Jack could hear more footsteps below them on the second catwalk. Andy had counted three assailants, but there was no way to know how many more were on their way into the cavern.

"We've already done spiders," Jack said.

And then he smiled, slowly extending his right hand behind his back, his fingers reaching for the lip of the hollow urn, just a few feet away.

The woman followed his motion with her eyes, her gaze moving past his fingers to the urn, then down to the rounded stones—and then her expression froze.

Just as the gun shifted up, Jack lunged backward, grabbing the urn and lifting it off of the stone base. There was a sudden crack, and then the catwalk lurched inward as the ivory columns twisted free. The woman's gun went off, the bullet glancing across Jack's left shoulder, tearing through his robes and slicing an inch out of his skin—but then the woman was tumbling downward, toward the center of the lurching catwalk.

In the same moment, Jack's boot flipped upward, sending the rope flying into the air. He caught it with his free hand just as the entire catwalk disappeared beneath him, taking the woman, her flare, and her gun with her, hurtling toward the floor fifty feet below. He caught one last glimpse of her as she pirouetted through the air, her hands clawing at one of the falling ivory columns as she desperately tried to break her fall—and then she was gone, and Jack was swinging hard into the wall. Thankfully, the grapple held. The stone knocked Jack's breath away, but somehow he managed to hold on to the urn. He could feel that there was something inside, but he didn't have time to look.

He pulled himself up along the rope, then found a ledge large enough to support his weight. Then he detached the grapple and flung it toward the opening where Andy and Sloane had just disappeared. The grapple caught, and Jack was clambering after them, the urn tucked tightly under his arm. As he pulled himself into the opening, he cast one last look down toward the floor of the cavern.

The three stories of catwalks were nothing but a pile of stone and ivory, dark, jagged shapes rising up from the sand. He thought he heard a groan in the darkness, but he didn't see any movement. He felt his teeth touch the air.

That was for Jeremy.

Then he yanked himself the last few feet into the opening, leaving a small trail of blood from his shoulder along the stone wall.

CHAPTER TWENTY-FOUR

Sixteen hours later, the choppy waters of Bohai Bay flashed by beneath the bulbous Plexiglas windows of a Chinese-built private helicopter. Jack's shoulder throbbed along with the rhythmic beating of the helicopter's blades, his wound still fresh beneath a thick wrapping of gauze and medical tape. Jack had changed the bandages himself in the airplane lavatory minutes before they'd begun their descent into Beijing; no doubt, if he'd had the time to stop at an emergency room after his team had worked their way out of Petra, and—with Bedouin help—toward the international airport in Amman, the flesh wound would have earned him a handful of stitches. Instead, he'd had to get by on desert medicine, which had consisted of a foul-smelling salve mixed up by one of Magda's wives and a half a tube of Neosporin from Andy's first aid kit. After what they'd just been through— as close as they'd come to death at the hands of that terrifying woman—Jack counted himself lucky.

Jack tried to ignore the pain as he clung to his seat belt harness with both hands, forcing himself to concentrate on the woman's voice that was now echoing through the heavy headphones pressed against his ears. The roar of the chopper and the way the damn craft kept banking hard to the left to avoid sudden outcroppings from the clifflike shoreline made the task difficult—and the woman's thick Chinese accent certainly wasn't helping. Even though she was just a few feet away, seated directly across from him and Sloane in the passenger cabin of the aging machine—furnished in faded leather, from the harness digging into his chest and waist to the oversize seats, built-in minibar, and interior walls—they may as well have been miles apart, and not just because of the quality of the radio transmitters of their headsets or the language barrier. No matter how important Jack knew the information she was giving them was to their journey to the final Wonder of the World, Jack simply couldn't do the one thing that would have made the distance between them disappear. He couldn't look her in the eyes.

Jack could tell by the way Sloane was watching him that she sensed his discomfort. On the trip from the Beijing Capital International Airport to the airfield on the southeastern edge of the vast city, Jack had given Sloane only the barest details about Hinh Hu Li: that she was the lead curator of the People's Museum of Beijing and an expert in Chinese antiquities, specifically, anything having to do with the Ming dynasty that had ruled most of the country from the fourteenth century to the seventeenth century. When they had reached the fenced-in airfield and were led through a pair of security gates by uniformed Chinese soldiers to the waiting helicopter—fiberglass and steel frame glistening in the morning sun, rotors already beginning to spin—Sloane had begun to pepper him with questions. But when she'd seen the woman for the first time, standing on the bottom step leading up to the passenger cabin, the questions had frozen in the air between them, and Sloane had been content to stare in silence. Late thirties, dressed in a stiff gray pantsuit open at the collar, five-foot-ten in high leather boots— Hinh Hu Li had that effect.

Twenty minutes later, enclosed in the throbbing belly of the racing chopper, the woman's aura was no less palpable. Unlike Jack, Sloane could only briefly take her gaze off the high-ranking academic's dark, perfect features: lips like crimson clouds, eyes the shape of teardrops, pupils painted in pitch-black oil, cropped hair combed above brows drawn with the severity of cut glass. She was a beautiful woman—and that only made Jack even more uncomfortable, because it reminded him of how much he'd always hated her.

"You're definitely on the right track," she was saying as Jack watched the helicopter's shadow dancing over frosted waves through the thick glass to his right. "And I can understand why you thought of me. This pictogram seems to be referencing a particular section of the Great Wall with which I have an intimate familiarity. But I believe you've gotten two things wrong."

Still avoiding eye contact, Jack turned from the window to see her shift the curved fragment of stone that she held in her hands so that both he and Sloane could see the tiny picture imprinted next to the final segment of snake, the twisting serpent's tail:

"The image in the pictogram is not another snake," she said, pointing with a sharp, red nail. "And it's not an apple."

Jack felt Sloane shift in the seat next to him as she leaned forward to peer more closely at the piece of stone which they had carefully cut from the urn Jack had removed from the interior chamber at Petra. Unlike on the banks of the sinkhole in Chichen Itza, Jack had immediately searched the urn for the snake after he'd removed the sixth bronze segment from within the hollow vessel. When his flashlight flickered across the colored image on the inner wall, he'd had Andy run out and find him Magda's sharpest dagger to hack his way to the next pictogram.

Even before Jack had seen the image, he'd known where they were headed next. The problem was, he'd also known exactly who he'd needed to contact to help them decipher the final pictogram—and also give them access to the last Wonder of the World, the Great Wall. The tiny picture on the inside of the urn of a scaled, serpentine, fanged creature, wrapped around a spherical piece of fruit, had made Sloane think again of the Garden, and of Adam, Eve, and a snake bearing an apple. But Jack had known better. He'd let Sloane run with her theory, only because he hadn't wanted to tell her what he'd known the instant he'd seen the pictogram. The image hadn't only led him to a particularly intriguing section of the Great Wall of China. It had also led him straight to the woman he still blamed for shattering his parents' marriage fifteen years ago.

"You can see here," Hinh Li continued, "the creature has feet. There are three claws on each appendage, running around most of its elongated torso. And its head is equine, with pronounced nostrils, and teeth that are reminiscent of a crocodile. It's not a snake. It's a dragon."

Jack turned back to the window. He had been only sixteen when he'd met Hinh Li for the first time, in the apartment in LA that his father had rented for the two of them. She'd been one of Kyle's graduate students, only a handful of years older than Jack and Jeremy. Even at that young age, Jack had known that his anger toward her had been immature and unfair; Kyle Grady had checked out of his relationship with the twins' mother long before. But seeing his father like that, laughing and smiling with a woman half his age—even one who shared his passions, his sense of adventure, his love of the exotic—had filled Jack with difficult emotions.

Of course, that relationship had been as doomed as Jack's parents'; Hinh Li had lasted about as long as the apartment in L.A., which Kyle soon traded for a mud hut in a Kenyan village. Hinh Li had headed back to China, where she'd risen through a combination of brilliance, hard work, and impressive connections. Her father's brother was one of the top bureaucrats of an industrial province that included much of the country's rich copper processing plants, and her own brother was the founder of a Hong Kong–based, government backed social network that had made him a billionaire by his midtwenties. The helicopter they were traveling in was his; the two pilots in military uniforms in the front cockpit were courtesy of Hinh Li's uncle—and they came with a piece of paper from Beijing that would get them past any local security stations without any explanations necessary.

"The spherical fruit has slight cross-hatching," Hinh Li said, showing Sloane. "It's a common *gongbi* effect. It symbolizes a softness of surface. Like a peach."

"A dragon," Sloane said. "And a peach."

Jack nodded, understanding. "The peach tree is the Taoist version of the Tree of Life. According to legend, somewhere in the countryside stands a magical peach tree, and on this tree a single peach grows every three thousand years. Whoever eats the peach is granted immortality. It's cyclical symbolism, similar to the Mayan calendar; the peach is reborn every few millennia, offering mankind a shot at transcending his own mortality. And it's kind of an opposing story to the Judeo-Christian version, where the forbidden fruit growing on the tree makes man mortal, rather than immortal. But it's still a Tree of Eternal Life."

The pilot's voice broke over the headphones, speaking in clipped Chinese. Hinh Li responded, then shifted back to English as she pointed again to the pictogram.

"Right. In the Taoist legend, wrapped around the base of the tree sleeps a coiled dragon. The dragon acts as the tree's roots, lodging it to the Earth, while the tree's branches are protected by a phoenix, who guards the way to heaven."

"So the dragon is benevolent," Sloane said. "No fire breathing, eating knights, kidnapping maidens—"

"In the East, dragons aren't the mythical monsters that they are in your culture. Benevolent dragons are interwoven into our history—in fact, dragon worship dates back to the beginning of Chinese culture. The earliest dragon sculptures we've found go back to before 5000 BC. Dragons protected emperors, guided kingdoms, and are, to this day, considered the emblem of successful people. Chinese mothers want their children to grow up to be dragons."

Hinh Li was looking right at Jack as she said this, and he forced himself to finally match her gaze. Her full lips turned up at the corners. It wasn't the first time she had called him a dragon; the day his father had left them both alone in the apartment, off on one of his first journeys to Africa, she had used the complementary term as she'd packed her bags. At the time, Jack had shrugged it off, lost in his teenage anger. But as he'd gotten older, although he hadn't ever forgiven her, he'd understood that she was just another casualty of his father's adventuresome spirit.

"Some anthropologists believe that dragons have a real world basis," Jack said, trying not to dwell on the past. "Perhaps the concept of the dragon grew out of contact with prehistoric snakes, or maybe a fear and respect for *Crocodylus porosus*—an enormous species of crocodile that used to roam ancient China. Another theory is that unearthed dinosaur bones led early Chinese storytellers to imagine giant reptiles years before we discovered dinosaurs ourselves in the West. In fact, the Chinese word for dinosaur is *Konglong*—great dragon."

"So you do remember some of your Chinese," Hinh Li said. "Good to know our weekly lessons left some impression."

"You left an impression, all right, but I don't remember more than a handful of words."

"What we choose to forget is sometimes more important than what we choose to remember," she responded.

Then she pointed out the window to where the shoreline had suddenly changed from rock outcroppings and cliffs to a low, gravelly slope running parallel with a paved road.

"We're three miles south of the Shanhaiguan Pass, in Hebei Province. Up ahead is the eastern beginning point of the last portion of the Great Wall to be built by the Ming dynasty, somewhere in the mid-sixteenth century."

"The mid-sixteenth century?" Sloane asked. "I thought the wall was much older than that."

"Sections of the wall go back three thousand years. The oldest part was built somewhere around 700 BC, but much of the wall has been rebuilt many times, by the different dynasties who ruled China. Altogether, the Great Wall stretches almost thirteen thousand miles east to west, and in some places reaches as high as a hundred feet. It's mostly stone, brick, and mortar, a barrier meant to protect from Mongol invaders, but also to control the spice trade—and often, to keep the peasant class from emigrating when times were hard."

"Thirteen thousand miles," Sloane said. "That's quite a haystack to sift through."

Jack tapped the helicopter window with a finger, and Sloane leaned closer, just in time to see the paved road end, replaced by a stretch of beach-like sand. And then, rising up from the shore, a stone, almost medieval-looking section of wall jutting right out into Bohai Bay. Where the stone met the water rose a sturdy, castle-like tower with arched portals and small stone lookout. In front of the tower, the wall continued into the water for about sixty feet.

"My god," Sloane whispered. "It's shaped like a—"

"Like a dragon taking a drink from the bay," Hinh said. "This is Old Dragon's Head—it's the easternmost edge of the Great Wall. Built by the Ming dynasty in 1560, it was destroyed by Japanese warships in 1904, during the suppression of the Boxer Rebellion. In 1980, my government rebuilt the landmark, down to the very last stone."

The helicopter passed directly over the castle, and Jack could see that it was deserted, the stone path leading out over the water glistening from the spray of the waves that crashed against the high outer walls. He knew that usually, the place would be crawling with tourists from Beijing and the outer villages; but Hinh Li was more than just a glorified tour guide. The presence of the two military officers in the front of the helicopter were just one indication of the lengths she had gone to help him out. And all he had told her was that it had something to do with Jeremy's death.

He realized, as he turned back from the window and saw the pensive look on her exquisite features, that she wasn't simply trying to help, she was also attempting to make amends.

"It really does look like it's leaning out onto the water, drinking from the bay," Sloane said. "But if it was built in the midfifteen hundreds, then rebuilt in the 1980s—Jack, that piece of urn is two thousand years old."

Jack watched as Hinh Li held the shard more carefully, the pictogram still visible between her fingers.

"Like I said," she responded, "sections of the wall were rebuilt by each ruling dynasty, including the Ming. Old Dragon's Head was built on top of previous construction, then repaired numerous times over the centuries. There is a small alcove in the basement of the dragon's snout that still contains an original section of the Wall."

"And you've seen this image there?" Jack asked.

Hinh Li hadn't been surprised when he'd first described the pictogram to her, and asked about an association with the Chinese Wonder of the World. And she had simply taken it as a matter of course that he would trust her with such a seemingly important task, along with the bare bones of what had happened to Jeremy. As conflicted as he had been about her being in his father's life, he knew she had always loved Kyle Grady. Telling her hadn't been a great risk— Jack knew there was no more room for risks. After the attack at Petra, he'd even sent Andy and Dashia back to Princeton, and he would have packed Sloane along with them, had she not continued to insist that this was where she was supposed to be. That woman who had confronted him at the top of the catwalks—he had never seen anyone as cold and terrifying before. He had no doubt that she would have killed him without a second thought. He hadn't seen her body, but he assumed she was now lying in the rubble of many tons of two-thousand-year-old sandstone. But he didn't know how many more like her were still out there, waiting, watching, ready to try again.

"I can give you one hour alone at the site," Hinh Li said, in way of an answer. "After that, the guards stationed farther down the Wall will start making phone calls."

"Hinh Li," Jack said, "I don't really know how to thank you—"

She waved him off, then carefully handed over the shard of urn and watched as he returned it to the front pocket of his backpack. When he looked back at her, she was still watching him, a spark behind the darkness of her eyes.

"Your father would be—"

"Proud?" Jack heard himself interrupt, more emotion in his voice than he would have liked. "My father doesn't even know that my brother is gone. My father is off on another one of his adventures, and I haven't spoken to him in more than a year."

She reached across the cabin, touching his hand as the helicopter suddenly shifted downward, descending roughly toward the sandy beach.

"I was going to say, your father would be right here next to you, chasing dragons."

Jack felt a shiver move through him, and he found himself suddenly flashing back to one of the last times that he, his brother, and their father had all been together. The twins couldn't have been older than thirteen, and Kyle Grady had somehow convinced their mother to let him take his two kids camping for a night. For Jeremy, the entire week leading up to the endeavor had been sheer torture; just the thought of being out in the woods, away from his computer and the safety of his bedroom, had filled him with terror. When the day finally came, Jeremy didn't speak a word the entire ten-hour drive to the campground.

To both twin's utter surprise, when they arrived at the campsite, they discovered that Kyle Grady had exchanged the planned tent for a rented RV—and had turned the entire interior into a makeshift computer lab, complete with sat-link and all the latest gaming systems. He'd given Jeremy a hug, and then he'd handed Jack a flashlight, and the two of them had set off into the woods for the first of many outback excursions.

That day, Jack's father had shown how much he loved both his sons— those two complementary zygotes. And where Jeremy was a complex child Kyle Grady never truly understood, Jack was cut from a cloth that his father knew as well as his own skin.

Hinh Li was right; Jeremy wasn't the only reason Jack was in China, risking his life to chase a mystery that seemed to grow deeper with each clue he found. He was in China because like his father he was born to go into the bush.

• • •

The bright orange flames licked at the brick-ceiling work as Jack held the wooden torch in front of him, carefully navigating the last few steps of the corkscrew stairway that led down into the lowest section of the ancient stone Wall. He guessed they were at least thirty feet out into the bay; he could hear the waves crashing against the outer walls on both sides, and he could feel the pressure building in his ears, the dampness in the air increasing with each descending step.

Sloane followed him in silence, staying close enough to be able to see her footing in the flickering circle of light from his torch. He'd found the torch after they'd gone through the second set of locked doors that led from the touristy part of the tower complex into the older, interior halls that harkened back to this section of the Wall's Ming-era past. The key ring Hinh Li had provided before they'd disembarked from the helicopter had gotten them to the stairwell, but now they were on their own, working deeper into the base of the drinking dragon's head.

Jack slowed as he stepped off the last step and into a narrow, cramped passageway. The ceiling was so low he had to hold the torch at chest level, the heat from the flames stinging his cheeks and making his eyes tear. After another five yards straight ahead, the passageway curved to the left—and Jack found himself entering the alcove Hinh Li had described. The passageway widened by a few feet, and the ground shifted from packed mud to paved stones, each slab the size of a man's head. The walls on either side were lined with antique Ming-era suits of armor hanging from wooden hooks pounded directly into the stone. Shiny bronze breastplates, pewter helmets, and heavy wooden shields, as well as a handful of halberds, axes, and spears.

A few more feet, and Jack saw that the alcove was essentially a dead end; but as he got closer, he realized that the back wall was actually three separate stone panels, each reaching from floor to ceiling. Even from a distance, he could tell that the panels were much older than the rest of the alcove; the stone had a faded, charred appearance, with roughly hewn edges that had obviously not been worked by any modern cutting tool.

As Jack moved closer, he saw that the three panels were covered in Chinese calligraphic carvings, running down from about eye level to just above his knees. Jack only recognized a few of the characters, but one name stood out.

"It's the story of Wang Zhaojun," he said, running his gaze across the calligraphy as Sloane moved next to him. "Dates back to the Han dynasty, which ruled China from around 200 BC to the first few years of the new millennium. As the legend went, Wang Zhaojun was one of the four greatest beauties in all of Chinese history. Originally of low birth, she had been chosen to serve as one of the Han emperor's numerous concubines. But when the royal portrait artist came to paint her, she refused to bribe him, so he painted her portrait with a huge mole, distorting her ephemeral beauty. Because of this, the emperor never chose her for his bed. When a rival king asked for one of the concubines to solidify a treaty, the emperor offered up Wang Zhaojun. It was only at the rival's wedding banquet that the emperor finally saw Wang in person and realized the mistake he'd made. But by then it was too late."

Sloane ran her palm over the carvings, the elegant swishes of ancient black ink sunk into the even older stone.

"A little superficial, for a love story."

"I'm not sure it's supposed to be a love story. More of a political tale. The Emperor's rival is so taken with Wang's beauty, he pledges to make peace with his former enemy—"

Jack paused, his gaze frozen halfway through the writing on the third stone panel. He took a step closer, lowering the torch, and then Sloane saw it, too. Five lines of calligraphy from the bottom of the stone.

The serpentlike dragon, wrapped around a spherical peach, was carved directly between the two characters that symbolized Wang Zhaojun's name.

Sloane dropped to one knee, inspecting the image.

"Anything in the story about dragons and peach trees? Or is it all just beautiful concubines and sexually frustrated Emperors?"

Jack shook his head, still staring at the panel. There was something about the image that bothered him, but he couldn't quite place his finger on it.

"Any idea what we're supposed to do now that we've found it?" Sloane asked.

She touched the image with a finger, tracing the coils of the dragon's serpentine body.

"It's carved right into the stone, like the other characters—"

"Hold on," Jack said suddenly. "Do you notice anything wrong about the picture?"

Sloane lifted her finger, looked at it again, then shook her head.

Jack shifted his backpack off of his shoulder and reached into the front pocket, retrieving the shard from the stone urn. He held it next to the image on the wall.

"It's backward."

On the wall, the dragon's equine head was facing to the left—not the right, as it was on the shard from the urn. The creature's tail curved off in the opposite direction, tilting slightly toward the ground.

"It's a mirror image," Jack said. "An enantiomer to the pictogram."

"A mirror image," Sloane repeated. Then she looked at Jack. "Which came first?"

"What do you mean?"

"The pictogram, or this carving on the wall? Which is the mirror image?"

Jack wasn't sure what she was getting at.

"We found the pictogram at Petra, which was built at least a few hundred years after this section of the Great Wall."

"And we were led to Petra by a pictogram we found at the Colosseum, which was built fifty to a hundred years later. We were led to the Colosseum by the image we found at Chichen Itza, built six hundred years after that—"

"And Machu Picchu led us to Chichen Itza. The Taj led us to Machu Picchu. We've already established that we're moving back in time—"

"But don't you see, Jack—these pictograms, these clues, this road map leading us from Wonder to Wonder: It was all planned out ahead of time. Your brother, Jeremy, the link he found between the Modern Wonders and the Ancient Wonders, his mirror image—that's the only way it makes sense."

Sloane stood back from the stone panel, shaking her head.

"These segments that we keep finding, they weren't just placed in random monuments, which somehow became the Seven Wonders of the World. This was all planned from the beginning."

Jack realized what she was saying, because it had been in the back of his mind since he'd first seen Jeremy's program, the glowing double helix that had gotten his brother killed. He nodded.

"An architectural roadmap of human evolution."

"From the Great Wall to Petra to the Colosseum to Chichen Itza to Machu Picchu," Sloane said. "And on and on. All doubling as markers built to house, hide, and protect our seven bronze segments."

"You don't sound so skeptical anymore."

"I reserve the right to go right back to being skeptical until we find the last segment and see where it leads us. Because there has to be a pretty incredible reason that the greatest landmarks of human evolution were chosen to lead us here."

Instead of responding, Jack handed his torch to Sloane, then turned and crossed the alcove to one of the shiny breastplates hanging from the wall. Using both hands, he removed the piece of armor and carried it back to where she was standing.

"In ancient times, mirrors were more than simple objects we used to see how pretty we looked when we woke up in the morning. They were considered gateways to secret worlds, sometimes to the heavens, or the clouds where the gods resided."

He bent forward and shifted the shiny breastplate so it was directly in front of the image carved into the stone panel. Then he adjusted the angle, using the light from the torch in Sloane's hands until the image was reflected across the shiny bronze surface—a perfect mirror image, exactly the same as the original pictogram.

Almost immediately, there was a loud churning sound, like heavy water against a hidden stone wheel. Jack felt a cold, damp breeze against his cheeks, and then the third stone panel tumbled backward—revealing another stone stairway that led directly downward.

Jack tossed the armor to the floor. Then Sloane held the torch forward, trying to see past the first few steps.

"I kind of wish the stairs led up instead of down. What did she say, a phoenix in the branches?"

Jack took the torch from her and started down the steps.

"And a dragon down below."

• • •

"Look out, the last step is a doozy."

Jack held out his hand, stopping Sloane on the stairwell. He lowered the torch, letting the flames play across the surface of the murky water that stretched out across the long, rectangular basement, lapping at the walls and disappearing into the shadowy corners. The room was part cave, part chamber; in some places, the walls were made of the same stone panels they had just come through, in others, it was just mud and rock, chunks jutting out like knuckles over the fetid, liquid floor. The ceiling was too far above to see clearly, but Jack's attention had already shifted across the long room to a raised stone platform up against the far wall. In the center of the platform stood some sort of altar, about waist-high, in front of what appeared to be a sculpted diorama. Even from a distance, Jack could tell that the craftwork didn't appear to be from the Han era, or even Chinese. If anything, it looked

Greek—but Jack had a feeling it wasn't the ancient Greeks who had led him to this place.

Jack turned back to the water below his feet, then shifted his gaze to the nearest wall, searching for the sturdiest looking outcropping of rock. He moved his free hand into his jacket, reaching for his grapple.

"We should be able to make our way along the far wall, for at least the first ten yards. Then we'll cross back to the other side—"

Before he could finish his sentence, Sloane strolled past him and stepped boot first into the fetid water. There was a splash, and then she was standing in front of him, the water reaching to just above her upper thigh.

"Really, Jack, enough with the theatrics. It's not that goddamn deep."

Jack's eyes widened.

"How did you know?"

She pointed to the surface of the water, a few feet to her right. Jack saw a clump of thin, green strands, each about the width of a strand of hair, floating on the top of the murk.

"Filamentous algae. It only grows in shallow water. Are you coming?"

Jack placed his grapple back in his jacket and stepped off the last step. The water felt cold through the material of his jeans, but his boots easily found the floor—slick and flat, more packed mud than stone. He moved next to Sloane, and together they started forward across the rectangular room.

Each step took effort, and twice Jack almost lost his footing, but Sloane caught him both times, gripping his jacket tight enough to send jabs of pain into the flesh wound on his shoulder. When he grimaced, she apologized, but he waved her off with the torch; the pain was keeping him alert, reminding him that one wrong step, one inch to the left when he should be going right, and there was a good chance the blood was going to flow. Though they were solving riddles, this wasn't a game; they were in a chamber over twenty-two hundred years old beneath the last and oldest of the

Seven Wonders of the Modern World, searching for the final piece to a mystery that had already gotten his brother killed. A mystery millennia in the making—

"There it is. The last segment."

Sloane's voice was a whisper, nearly lost in the lapping of the murky water against the walls. Jack followed her gaze to the raised stone platform, now only a few feet in front of them. There on the waist-high stone altar sat the final bronze segment, the snake's tail curved and shiny in the torchlight.

"No parchment," Sloane said. "No protective vessel. It's just sitting there."

But Jack's gaze had already moved from the segment to the diorama behind it, which he suddenly realized wasn't made of stone like the walls and the rest of the section of Wall above them. The diorama was glistening white, with smooth lines and curved edges.

"Ivory," he said. "It's beautiful."

It was the same image from the mural he had seen over and over again—beginning in the pit beneath the Temple of Artemis, again on the stone tablet he'd found in the crate beneath Christ the Redeemer, and again in Sloane's photos from the hypogeum of the Colosseum. Except instead of paint against stone, this time the mural was carved in pure ivory, from the dense spectacle of the ancient garden to the group of armed women carrying the tablet of the segmented snake. And in this version of the mural, there was one marked difference. The women weren't simply leaving the garden. They were heading toward something. Something huge, intricately carved—and instantly recognizable.

Of course. It makes perfect sense.

Sloane leaned closer as Jack played the light from the torch over the statue, the flames flickering over its hunched lion's body to its chiseled human head, crowned in the Egyptian pharoanic tradition, rising up over a pair of great, resting paws.

"The Great Sphinx of Giza," Jack said. "It stands in front of the Pyramids of Khufu and Khafre."

Sloane squinted her eyes as she focused on the sculpture's face.

"But it doesn't look right. I've seen pictures of the Sphinx. In real life, the nose is missing, but more importantly, the Sphinx at Giza is male, isn't it?"

Jack smiled.

"Actually, no."

He shifted his feet against the slick floor so that he was right up against the altar, getting the torch as close to the diorama as he could. As he did so, he thought he heard a quiet splash coming from somewhere across the room—but when he looked over his shoulder, he saw nothing but shadows. He assumed the motion of his feet had churned up a little wake and turned back to Sloane.

"Up until just a few years ago, it was assumed that the Pharaoh Khufu built the Sphinx, along with his pyramid, in the year 2500 BC. But recent dating technology tells a different story. Most likely, Khufu *unearthed* the Sphinx when he was surveying the area—the Sphinx was already there, buried in the sand, and had been there for a very long time."

"How long?"

There was another quiet splash. This time Sloane heard it, too; she glanced back toward the stairs leading up the way they had come, but also saw nothing. She gave it a moment, waiting to see if the splash returned, then turned back to Jack.

"At least ten thousand years," Jack said. "Furthermore, the Sphinx that Khufu found looked very different than the one we see today. The original Sphinx was indeed a woman. Khufu had it altered to look more like him; he couldn't have a woman guarding the entrance to his pyramid, no matter how ancient she might be."

"A woman's face," Sloane said, "on a lion's body. Something an Amazon might carve."

Jack shrugged, inwardly pleased that Sloane was now breaking far beyond her scientific mold. He shifted his attention to the armed warrior women—and to the tablet they carried. He pointed at the last segment.

"Either way, I think it's pretty clear where we're supposed to bring our snake."

"Shouldn't we try to put it together here?"

"Sure," Jack said, "But if the Seven Wonders really are a road map of some sort, I think we can see where that map is supposed to lead. The Sphinx—maybe the oldest standing relic on Earth, perhaps the most significant physical link to the ancient Amazon civilization—"

And then he stopped, because the splashing noise had returned—only now it was much, much closer.

"Jack," Sloane started, but he was already turning.

Ten feet away, moving quickly across the surface of the water, each raised nostril the size of Jack's fist, the snout twice as long as his arm, and those eyes, slitted, yellow, with pitch-black pupils, each as big as a saucer, staring right at him—Jack couldn't see the body of the beast, but he knew it stretched back an ungodly distance, propelled by a tail strong enough to shatter stone.

Sloane screamed. Jack grabbed her by the shoulder and shoved her behind him. Then his right hand went into his jacket, while he waved the torch at the creature with his left, trying to scare it back; but the damn thing just kept coming, rippling across the water, moving faster and faster—

And then it lunged, its enormous head coming up out of the murk, jaws opening wide on hinges of muscle, eight-inch teeth tearing through the air toward Jack's face. Jack flung the torch at its head, where it glanced harmlessly off the plated scales. His other hand tore the grapple out of his jacket. Just as the creature's jaws were about to close on Jack's face, he jammed the grapple deep into its mouth, then hit the switch, releasing the metallic, spiderlike claws.

273

There was a horrible rending sound as two of the claws pierced upward through the top of the creature's upper jaw. The bottom claws tore downward into the reptile's tongue, spraying blood in an arc out both sides of the animal's mouth.

Jack dove backward onto the altar, nearly upending the ivory diorama as the creature whipped its head back and forth, its entire body thrashing across the shallow water. For a brief, agonizing moment, it seemed like the creature was staring right at him, its jaws pinned open by the grapple, its fetid breath splashing against his face.

And then, with a massive swish of its monstrous tail, the thing swung around and rocketed back the way it had come, disappearing beneath the murk, trailing a pool of dark red blood.

Jack heard coughing, and saw Sloane pull herself out of the water. He helped her up onto the altar next to him and noticed that she had the bronze segment gripped tightly in her hand. She'd obviously grabbed it on the way down. Jack was impressed. For a woman who'd spent most of her life in a laboratory, she'd come a long way.

"I think we just met the dragon," Jack said, wiping crocodile blood from his cheeks. Or more accurately, he thought to himself, perhaps the last remaining relative of *Crocodylus porosus.*

Sloane leaned against him, shaking water from her hair.

"One myth at a time, Jack."

And then she slid off the edge of the altar and began leading the way back toward the stairs.

CHAPTER TWENTY-FIVE

The leech was hungry. The scent of blood was everywhere, filling its micro-scopic pores, setting off neural sparks that overwhelmed the circuits of its primitive cerebellum, enacting muscular commands that instantly overrode all of its other limited senses.

The leech was hungry, and it was going to feed.

Vika clenched her teeth as she watched the bulbous black worm crawl across the flat skin of her naked stomach on an inexorable journey toward the two-inch, mud-covered wound that stretched along her flesh just below her bottom right rib. An involuntary cry erupted from her throat as the crea-ture reached the edge of the opening, its prickly, circular rows of teeth click-ing against the white shard of bone that stuck a full centimeter out through the mud. Then the leech clamped down, sucking on the blood that still oozed out through the palliative sludge—a recipe that had been handed down for a dozen generations. Vika closed her eyes, forcing the pain back behind mental walls that had taken a lifetime to build, brick by agonizing brick.

She was lying flat on her back on a woven reed mat, tucked into the corner of the mud and wood hut where she had grown up—a single-story, windowless shelter bathed in the shadows of the Great House where her team was hurriedly packing up their equipment for the fifteen-hour flight.

Her body felt shattered, her muscles and bones throbbing as if even gravity itself had become palpable. The broken rib was only her most visible injury. She was certain there was much worse damage inside, in her battered organs and connective tissue—places that mud patches and leeches couldn't reach. She should have been in a hospital, on an operating table, or in a grave. But somehow, she was alive, and she was here. The journey from the rubble-strewn inner chamber of the Treasury to her village in the rainforest a hundred miles south of Rio was a blur of helicopters, private jets, and a multitude of intravenous painkillers, most of which were now wearing off as she turned instead to the ritual medications of her people. Life, or death—it no longer mattered to her as much as the reason she had returned to her ancestral home.

Suddenly, she opened her eyes. The pain was still there, a dagger lodged between her rib and her diaphragm; but the pain didn't matter. Her life didn't matter. What mattered was that she could still function, and as long as she could still function, she had a job to do.

She reached down, grabbed the leech between two fingers, and gave it a good yank. The creature hung on as long as it could, pulling her skin up over the piece of visible bone before its teeth tore free. She clutched the leech in her palm and squeezed until the thing burst, her own blood pouring down her wrist, pooling in the crook of her arm.

Then she rose to a sitting position, ignoring the new shards of pain that exploded down the right side of her body. She took a length of gauze out off of the low table by her makeshift bed and tucked it around the mud patch, hooking the Velcro tabs behind her back. Then she reached for her long, white underwrap—still stained with her blood and pierced through in numerous places—and began to wind it around her chest, flattening her bruised breasts.

She had been wearing the underwrap for as long as she could remember; like most things in her brutal life, it had two functions, one ceremonial, the other practical. Underwrapping was a ritual handed down since the dawn of her people—a recognition that although there were differences between men and women, these differences were only as relevant as the individual chose to make them. And from a practical standpoint, the underwrap made it easier to throw a javelin—or fire an automatic rifle.

Once the underwrap was in place, she pulled on her camouflage shirt, making sure to tuck it in tight to her pants so that the bulge of the mudwrap barely showed. She knew from experience that an enemy could take advantage of any signs of weakness, physical or mental. Though she did not believe this particular enemy had the battle experience to use her wound against her, she never took chances. Even the most experienced foes got lucky. And Jack Grady, damn him, had been smart enough to use his luck like a weapon, again and again.

Vika rose from the mat and slowly crossed the stark interior of her hut. Each step sent more pain up her rib cage. As she moved, she also noticed that she still had a limp. When she had regained consciousness after the catwalk had collapsed beneath her, she had found herself lying facedown on a pile of stone; the first thing she'd noticed, even before the broken rib, was the two-inch piece of ivory sticking out of her ankle. She'd removed the ivory on the spot, fully aware of the irony of the moment. She'd killed Jack's brother with a length of ivory not much longer than the piece that had ruined her ankle. He had nearly killed her with the same ancient material via a booby trap even older than the javelins she carried on her back.

The fact that Vika was still alive was a minor miracle, though it had helped that she had been on the top level of the catwalks, facing Jack head-on, when he'd lifted the urn off the pressure trap. Vika's four operatives, who had all been working their way up the lower levels, had not been as fortunate. All four had been crushed beyond recognition by the falling stone. It had taken three hours for Vika to remove their corpses from the chamber and carry them back to her waiting helicopter. Unfortunately, she would not be at their burial ceremony; as soon as she'd landed in Brazil, she'd received the call from the surveillance team in Beijing.

Jack Grady had found what ought to have been the final clue beneath the last Wonder of the World—and once again, he had taken flight, on his way to what appeared to be a new, surprise destination. Vika's team hadn't been able to get inside the Old Dragon's Head until after Jack and the botanist were gone; it appeared the anthropologist had secured himself a private flight to his next stop, provided by the billionaire brother of one of Jack's father's many past lovers. Even so, an hour behind the explorer and his companion, Vika's team had found enough information in the underground chamber beneath the Wall to tell Vika exactly where Jack was heading.

He had a head start, but Vika was certain she would be able to catch him before he finished whatever it was his late brother had started. Already one of Jendari Saphra's planes was waiting for her on the jungle runway. And Jendari herself was already on her way to Egypt. She wanted to be there in person. Obviously Vika's employer believed that Jack was on the final leg of his journey, hours away from uncovering the secret she had been seeking for decades.

Vika should already have been on her way as well, but there was one more thing she needed to do before she boarded that plane. One more duty to perform, one more ritual that had to take place.

She reached the far corner of her hut, and with difficulty, dropped to one knee. Then she brushed her hand along the dirt floor, revealing the hooked metal handle of her buried drop box.

Vika felt a tremble move through her that had nothing to do with the opiates in her veins or the injuries to her body. The ritual had always affected her this way, even when she was just a child. Since the age of twelve, when her ailing mother had passed the duties over to her, she had made the annual pilgrimage back to her home, back to this hut, no matter where she was or what she was doing.

Over the years, the parchments had been scarce; for many years at a time, she'd found nothing inside the box. In 2004, she'd been asked to eliminate a minor politician in a small European country that she'd never even heard of before. In 2007, the parchment had asked her to retrieve and destroy a series of computer codes that had been used in the hacking of a Swiss Internet contest. In 2009, she had been asked to set up a surveillance team with access to Jendari Saphra's private plane—it had contained a vault that had been quite tricky to access—until Vika had given a sample of Jendari's hair to the scientists at Euphrates, who had then provided her with a special, and quite unique, skin-colored glove.

Since then, there hadn't been a single parchment. And yet still, Vika had returned every year. Now, because of the events of the past week, for the first time in her life, she was two days late to the box—but she was here, and she was going to do her duty.

She pulled on the hooked handle, and the lid came open. Vika reached inside, and her fingers touched a roll of aged paper.

Vika paused, then lifted the parchment out of the drop box and broke the seal.

She read the words twice, then a third time to be sure.

And she understood.

Without a word, she placed the parchment back in the box, clenched her teeth against the pain, and deliberately rose to her feet.

CHAPTER TWENTY-SIX

"Ten minutes," Jack whispered as he pulled Sloane by the wrist, dragging her away from the back of the crowd of Egyptian students gathered in the shadow of the Pyramid of the Pharaoh Khafre, with a final nod toward the two archaeologists from the British Museum who were leading the small educational tour around the most famous site in all of Egypt. "After that, they're going to send someone looking for us. It was the best I could do."

Given what Jack had pulled off at the Temple of Artemis right under the noses of the two archaeologists' colleagues, it was more than he had expected from the two visiting experts, both on loan to the University of Cairo as part of a museum exchange. Jack had made the deal via the phone in Hinh Li's brother's private jet while they were somewhere over the Pacific Ocean. The archaeologists would let him wander free from their tour group for a brief amount of time, in exchange for his notes on whatever he'd found beneath their colleagues' dig site in Turkey. When the time came to deliver, Jack felt certain the men from the British Museum would think he'd gone completely mad—at least until they'd journeyed into the pit themselves. Then, God only knew what they would think.

And if they had any idea what Jack was now carrying in his backpack as he rushed Sloane across the rapidly cooling sand beneath the early evening

sun, they would never have let him leave their sight. The seven bronze segments had to be the greatest archaeological treasure in history, but to Jack,
at the moment, they were just another riddle, one he felt certain he was
about to solve.

"Jack," Sloane said, pointing as she ran after him. "Christ, it's enormous."

Even in the shadows of the three towering pyramids of Giza, the Great
Sphinx took one's breath away. Over sixty feet tall, more than two hundred
and sixteen feet long, made of solid, quarried limestone, the Sphinx rose up
out of a depression in the sand, bordered on two sides by a high stone wall,
with two small temples to its East, one resting almost between the sculpted
creature's extended paws. The facial features, though worn down by wind,
sun, and time—and perhaps purposefully mutilated by one pharaoh or
another—were still distinct enough to power even the most sedate imagination. A human face, beneath what remained of a pharaoh's headdress, on
top of a ferocious lion's body. Jack knew that historically, the Sphinx could
also be portrayed with a hawk's wings; but even without the power of flight,
the creature was terrifying, down to its macabre name.

"The strangler," Jack said as they crossed the last few dunes that led past
the low wall, toward the statue's enormous haunches. "Derived from the
Greek, it either refers to the way a lioness strangles its prey—biting down
on an animal's throat until it suffocates—or the way the demonic mythical
creature put down those who answer its riddle incorrectly."

Interesting that so many riddles embedded in pictograms had finally led
them to the ultimate riddler, who had supposedly crafted the first riddle
that mankind had ever encountered. The original Sphinx, guarding the
entrance to Thebes, had asked every passerby: *What walks with four legs in
the morning, two legs in the day, and three legs at night?* Only those who
answered correctly—*a person*—were allowed within the city's walls. Those
who got it wrong were strangled and left in the sand to rot.

"And this angry, violent creature—it was originally a woman?"

Jack slowed as they approached the Sphinx from behind. They were alone, but Jack had no idea how long their isolation would last. Any minute and another registered tour group could come by, or an Egyptian army officer, or a security guard. If they were found wandering unattended, they'd probably be arrested.

"According to the ancient Greeks. It only became male when the Egyptian Pharaohs began using the creature to guard their pyramids and tombs. Recent scientific studies of our friend here's facial structure seems to agree with the Greeks; there's internal evidence of stonework indicating fuller, female lips, higher cheekbones, and a more feminine brow than what you see today. The fact that there appears to be a vaguely African nature to the facial structure is more open to debate, but other Sphinxes across Egypt have similar features."

"Like the Amazonian women in our mural."

Jack shrugged, then dropped to his hands and knees, crawling the last few feet to the base of the great statue—exactly in front of the spot where the woman in the ivory diorama beneath the Great Wall seemed to have been heading.

"What are you looking for?" Sloane said, lowering next to him.

"I'm not sure," he said. "But these riddles were meant to be solved. I'm hoping whoever has led us on this journey doesn't want to leave us strangled in the desert."

He paused as his eyes settled on a group of scratch marks near the very bottom of the Sphinx's left haunch, right above a sweep of glittery sand. He reached forward and brushed the sand away. In front of him were three rows of hieroglyphics, mostly words he didn't recognize. But right in the center, a single glyph he could see even when he closed his eyes:

Two snakes, intertwined, in a perfect double helix.

Jack glanced over his shoulder, making sure they were still alone. Then he opened his backpack and carefully began removing the seven bronze snake segments. He placed them in order on top of the sand, head to tail.

Almost immediately, the segments began to tremble. He could hear the sound of gears turning, and caught a whiff of something that smelled like burning metal.

"My god," Sloane said, "how is this possible?"

Jack shook his head.

"There's a lot we don't know about Bronze Age science. Even though ancient cultures were primitive in many areas, they were also advanced in ways we're still trying to understand. The Mayan and Incan facility with astronomy, the Egyptian and Greek abilities in architecture, the Chinese developments in math and language, the Indian's spiritual depths—there was so much more going on than most people realize. Sophisticated gearwork, the science of magnets—these were things that we know have ancient, ancient pasts. . . ."

Jack went silent as the segments began moving to seal together, one after another: first the head they'd found at Christ the Redeemer, then the neck they'd found at the Taj Mahal, next the four body segments from Machu Picchu, Chichen Itza, the Colosseum, and Petra, and finally the tail they'd found in the base of the Great Wall of China. And then, as Jack and Sloane stared, the connected, mechanical bronze snake began to wriggle along the sand, slithering toward the base of the Sphinx. The head touched directly below the etched double helix, and suddenly the snake burrowed through, disappearing right into the solid stone.

The ground beneath Jack's feet began to move.

Sloane grabbed his arm and yanked him backward. He fell on top of her in the sand, and together they watched as a trapdoor slid back, revealing a cubic opening three feet across. Instead of steps, they saw a stone ramp leading down into the darkness.

Jack looked at Sloane, his mouth as dry as the desert around them. Before he could say anything, she had already risen to her feet. This time, he let her lead as they headed through the trap door, and began the descent down the stone ramp.

• • •

They had only been standing at the edge of the rushing waters for a few minutes, but if felt like much, much longer, both of them caught in the spray from the underground river, listening to the echo of the fierce current as it reverberated off the high, curved walls of the vast cavern. The river was at least thirty yards across, God only knew how deep, cutting directly down the center of the cave and heading for about a hundred yards beyond the cone of light from Jack's flashlight before surging left, out of sight.

"A river flowed out of Eden," Jack whispered, "to water the Garden, and there it divided. . . ."

"Genesis, Jack? Really? The statue we just crawled through to get here is five thousand years older than the Bible."

"The Bible, yes, but not the story. The Sumerians had the same garden, and the same rivers, nearly eight thousand years ago. The Veda of the Hindus had it even earlier than that. And, of course, when we get to the Tree of Life, we've also got the Koran, the Mayans, the Inca, the Chinese—"

"I don't see a garden or any trees. I just see a river. A goddamn big underground river."

Jack nodded, but his attention had suddenly moved from the water to the trio of large objects leaning against the wall behind them; he'd first noted the sarcophagi when they'd left the bottom of the ramp, a few yards to their left, but if Sloane had seen them, she'd been too busy staring at the rushing water to make any mention of it. Jack crossed to the closest of the three, playing the flashlight over its vaguely trapezoidal form. It was about a foot taller than he was, and twice as wide as his shoulders, shaped like a coffin with an ornately carved front showing the visage of an Egyptian pharaoh in full royal regalia, bound foot to neck in the burial fashion of the time. He reached forward and tapped his fist against the lid—and to his surprise, found that it was heavy rosewood, not stone. From the sound, it appeared to be empty.

Sloane turned at the noise and saw what Jack was doing.

"You're not thinking—"

"You know that I am," Jack said. "Come over here and give me some help."

Sloane shook her head.

"I'm not getting in that thing. Hell, I don't want to even open it. What if there's something inside?"

"And you're supposed to be the science-minded of the two of us? It's empty, and even if it's not, whoever was inside is long since dead."

Jack gripped the edge of the sarcophagus and gave Sloane a nod. Finally, she crossed to the other side. Together, they managed to drag the thing down from the wall and slide it across to the edge of the underground river.

Before Sloane could protest, Jack grabbed the lid and yanked it open. As he'd suspected, the oversize coffin was empty. The space inside was more than enough for the two of them. The only question that remained was how well it was going to float.

"You first," he said.

"You've got to be kidding."

"You want to push me into the water and jump in before I float away? Look, I don't see that we have much choice. Unless you expect Tom Sawyer to come floating by in a raft, this is our best option."

"Even if this works," Sloane said, "how do we get back?"

Jack paused. Then he shook his head.

"That's the kind of question we ask when we get where we're going."

"Jack—"

"We'll find a way," he said. "Are you going to get in this coffin, or am I going to have to go the rest of the way on my own?"

Sloane exhaled, but then stepped past him and lowered herself into the front of the wooden sarcophagus.

Jack bent low, pushing with his thighs, and slowly slid the heavy vessel to the very edge of the river. The front tipped forward, and Sloane grabbed at the sides, emitting a terrified shriek—and then the base touched water, and the current began to push it forward. Jack hurled himself over the rear ledge, landing a few feet behind Sloane, and the momentum pushed them the rest of the way in; the front end dipped a few feet down with the motion, then the entire coffin twisted to the right, nearly toppling over. Thankfully, it righted itself, bobbing upward under their weight, and suddenly they were moving with the current, cutting across the top of the water like a spear. Jack carefully handed Sloane the flashlight, then leaned back against the rear of the sarcophagus.

Of all the stupid things he'd ever done, he felt for certain that this topped them all.

He grinned in the darkness and leaned back to enjoy the ride.

CHAPTER TWENTY-SEVEN

Jendari blinked back tears as the enormous spotlight flashed alive, turning night into day, bathing the enormous, underground cavern in an almost apocalyptic glare. Instinctively, she took a step closer to the rushing underground river, staring down toward the curve a hundred yards away where the water disappeared around a near hairpin turn. Then she shifted back on her boot heels toward the base of the ramp they had just come down, to where Vika knelt next to the portable spotlight, her hands still holding the long extension cable that ran up to the surface, where they'd installed the generator, right up against the base of the Great, and in Jendari's mind, hideously ugly, Sphinx.

"How far ahead do you think they are?" Jendari asked as Vika let the cord fall to the sand and slowly raised herself to her feet.

For a moment, a flash of visible agony flashed behind the assassin's normally stoic features, but then she regained control, shifting her eyes toward the pair of sarcophagi that still stood against the nearby cavern wall.

"By the depth of the tracks leading to the water's edge," she said, her voice more clipped than normal, "and the erosion of the tracks up on the surface, I'd estimate they went into the water at least thirty minutes ago."

Jendari nodded, her gaze playing over the closest of the two sarcophagi. *Ballsy of Jack, putting his trust in a coffin that's been standing there for thousands of years*. But then again, she'd learned not to be surprised by anything the anthropologist seemed willing to do. The fact that the untrained man had bested Vika's operatives twice, and nearly killed Vika herself, was evidence that he was more than he seemed. Determined, certainly, but also a little crazy—or stupid enough to make decisions that were impossible to predict.

Still, no matter how he'd done it, Jack Grady had found his way through all Seven Wonders of the World—and led Jendari to what she now believed was the final resting place of the secret that the Order of Eve had spent ten thousand years protecting. The river behind her was evidence enough; nearly every culture and religion that spoke of a Garden or a Tree of Life also spoke of the river that led there. In many of the stories, it was that same river that humankind was supposed to use to get back to the floral paradise—either through death, as in Islamic, Hindu, Sumerian, and Jewish ancient lore, or at the end of a preordained length of time, as in Mayan, Incan, Chinese, and countless other religious traditions.

To Jendari, it was still just a river. And if Vika was right, unless he'd drowned or floundered somewhere along the way, Jack had already been riding the current for thirty minutes or more, which meant Jendari had no more time to waste. She opened her mouth to give the command, but Vika had already taken out her cell phone and was speaking in Portuguese.

Jendari understood most of the words; Vika had told her operatives stationed aboveground by the generator to retrieve the inflatable skiff from the jeep. She'd ordered one of her operatives—a woman named Villia, her eldest cousin—to bring the skiff down the ramp. And then she had told the rest to fan out and take defensive positions around the statue above.

When Vika had hung up the phone, Jendari caught her attention.

"Why only one skiff?" she asked. "And why only one additional operative? We should bring the entire team with us. We can't risk him getting away again."

"There are only two of them, and we have the element of surprise. And you were very clear—we don't want to endanger the artifact."

Jendari watched as Vika moved toward her, noticing the assassin's slight limp, and the way the woman seemed to be dragging the entire right side of her body. Still, she didn't seem any less deadly than usual. And Jendari knew that the other operative, Villia, was one of her best people.

Besides, she realized, the fewer operatives who accompanied them down the river, the fewer loose ends Jendari would eventually have to deal with.

Vika was the ultimate tool—but she wasn't going to be necessary for much longer.

"Okay," Jendari said. "And no firearms. As you say, we don't want to risk the collateral damage."

Jendari still couldn't be certain what they were going to find at the end of the river, but she had a pretty good idea. It bothered her that Jack Grady was going to get there first. Still, the anthropologist's mode of transportation was more than fitting.

She was going to make damn sure he returned the same way he went in—in a coffin.

CHAPTER TWENTY-EIGHT

Thirty minutes of near silence, apart from the rushing of the water and the creak of the sarcophagus beneath their bodies. Thirty minutes lost in the maddening thoughts swirling through Jack's mind—of Seven Wonders built to hide a road map, of an underground river beneath the oldest sculpture on Earth, of a civilization that wasn't really supposed to have ever existed, leaving evidence behind in cultures all over the globe—and then, suddenly, they took another hairpin turn, buffeted nearly sidewise by the fierce current, and Jack's entire world became engulfed in a paradise of verdant green.

It was the mural come to life, stretching for a hundred yards across an island in the middle of the widening river, an incredibly thick assemblage of plant life, from low brushes to twisting, serpentine vines to towering trees, reaching higher and higher, so incredibly high. That's when Jack realized that the roof of the cavern had risen hundreds of feet above them, and that his flashlight had suddenly become useless—because from above, a strange, yet natural glow filled the air, wisps of colored light reflecting through the very stone roof of the indescribably massive chamber.

"We must have been traveling downward the entire time," Jack whispered. "Deeper beneath the desert. The light—it's like rays reflected through quartz."

"Or sand," Sloane said. "Jack, this garden—the diversity—I can't believe what I'm seeing. Birches, a dozen different palms. *Iriartea deltoidea, Chamaecypari thyoides, Fagus diospyros, Ilex opaca, Fagus grandifolia*, and that's just right by the shore. Some of these other plants—they've been extinct for thousands of years. And most of them are growing bigger and healthier than they would in their natural environments."

Jack could still hear her voice, but her words were just sound against his ears, because his attention had suddenly focused on one particular tree, rising up near the center of the florid island. An oak, at least forty feet tall, and halfway up its trunk, suspended between two immense branches, he saw a glistening white platform. *Ivory*, he thought, his heart racing. Matching white steps led up from the ground, rising over what appeared to be a deep moat that had been dug around the tree's vast base. And up on top of the platform between the branches, twenty feet in the air, another sarcophagus not of wood, but of brightly polished bronze.

Sloane finally saw the oak as well, because she went silent. Jack finally shifted his gaze back to the river. He looked past the island, and to his surprise, saw a sheer stone wall. It appeared that the river went underground again; out of the corner of his eyes, he noticed a slight break in the sheer stone. It was the opening of some sort of tunnel—perhaps a natural channel, perhaps something that had been purposefully dug. *Might be another way out*, he thought to himself.

He leaned over the edge of the sarcophagus and began paddling against the current, trying to steer them toward the shoreline of the island. Sloane saw what he was doing and joined him in the effort.

It took a good ten minutes, but eventually, they'd managed to get close enough for Jack to reach out and grasp a section of tree root that was visible along the surface of the water. He hooked one arm around the rough wood and pulled until their vessel slid onto the sandy shore.

Sloane didn't wait for him to give her the signal; before he'd even finished beaching their sarcophagus, she was up and over the ledge. She took a few steps along the shore, then stopped as she reached the beginning of the low brush.

"Do you see the way these *Acalypha deamii* are spaced? And these *Olearia*? These aren't random growth patterns. These were planned. Cultivated."

Jack climbed out of the sarcophagus and joined her at the edge of the bushes. His eyes moved over the low brush and settled on a familiar red vine, strung along the tops of the greenery. He followed the vine backward and saw that it led to the base of the giant oak and up the backside of the trunk. He reached forward, gingerly avoiding the enormous thorns, and plucked one of the bright red leaves.

He showed it to Sloane.

"A lot bigger, and probably a lot older, than the leaves you photographed at the Colosseum," he said.

Then he started forward, letting the vine guide him through the thick brush, deeper into the garden.

By the time he and Sloane had reached the stone steps leading up to the platform in the oak, they were both breathing hard. Working their way through the flora had been difficult; though the plants had been spaced carefully, there were plenty of exposed roots and dozens of species of vines ready to trip them up at every step. Even so, Jack felt his adrenaline rise as he moved toward the bottom step. But before his foot left the ground, Sloane grabbed his shoulder.

She pointed at the moat that that had been dug around the base of the tree not ten feet in front of them, part of it lost in the shadow cast by the rising stairs.

Jack squinted down into the darkness—and saw that the ground at the bottom of the moat appeared to be moving. As his eyes adjusted to the change in light, he made out individual twists of motion, and that's when he saw the scales and the flickering tongues.

"Snakes," Sloane said. "A whole lot of snakes."

"Asps," Jack said. "Extremely poisonous. I'm counting at least a dozen different species. There isn't an antivenom in the world that could cure you if you fell in there. Once they sink their fangs into you, you've got about five minutes—and then you're on your way to becoming a corpse."

Jack involuntarily inched back from the bottom step, surveying the walk up to the platform that hung between the branches and the waiting sarcophagus. He felt something brush his back and saw that he was standing beneath a variety of birch maybe a dozen feet taller than the top of his head.

"Then I guess you'd better be careful," Sloane said.

"You're not going up there with me?"

"I think this time I'll stay behind. Whatever's up there, in that coffin . . . I think I'd rather you saw it first."

Jack understood. They were so close to the end now that it was almost difficult to breathe. But snakes or no, Jack had no intention of stopping. They had come too far.

He started forward, his boot lifting toward the first ivory step, when something blindingly white flashed by his peripheral vision, catching his right sleeve and spinning him around on his heels. He slammed backward into the birch tree, his arm suddenly pinned to the wood. He looked down and saw it—a two-foot-long ivory javelin sticking out from the birch trunk, piercing right through his sleeve, inches from his wrist.

He looked up to see two dark-haired women rushing toward him through the garden. Behind them was a third woman, moving much more deliberately through the underbrush. An older woman with frosted hair and a vaguely recognizable face.

Jack turned to Sloane.

"Go!" he screamed. "Into the bush! Find someplace to hide!"

"Jack—" she gasped.

"Now!"

And then she dove between the plants to his right, cutting a path deeper into the greenery. Jack turned back toward the two dark-haired women, who were now only a few yards away. He immediately recognized the woman in front from the catwalk in Petra; those dark, soulless eyes, those chiseled, tan features. As he watched, the woman pulled another javelin out from a sheath strapped to her back and took aim.

The javelin whizzed past his head, disappearing into the garden the way Sloane had just run. For a nauseating second his heart stopped in his chest—but then he heard the thwack of ivory hitting wood.

The woman cursed, then turned to the second woman, who Jack also recognized from the brownish streaks in her dark hair. It was the woman from the Temple of Kukulcan at Chichen Itza. The first woman said something in stilted, accented Portuguese, and the second woman ran past Jack, diving into the brush after Sloane.

"Hold on," Jack said. "I think we got off on the wrong foot."

The dark-haired woman stopped a few feet in front of him and waited for the older woman with the frosted hair to finally work her way the last few feet through the garden.

"Dr. Grady," the older woman said, after she'd caught her breath. "I have to thank you. You've done excellent work."

Something about her face pricked at Jack's memory.

"Do I know you?"

"I certainly know you," the woman responded. "You and your brother saved me years, perhaps decades. Certainly millions of dollars."

And then Jack realized where he had seen the woman before: on television. A biotech billionaire, Jendari Saphra. What could she possibly have to do with any of this? Jack was about to ask, when Jendari suddenly looked past him toward the giant oak, and the stairway leading upward.

"The Tree of Life," she whispered.

Jack followed her eyes and realized she wasn't actually looking at the oak, she was looking at the bronze sarcophagus.

"What is it?" he said. "You had my brother killed—for what?"

The woman ignored him, heading for the bottom step. As her foot touched ivory, she glanced back at the dark-haired woman, still standing a few feet in front of where Jack was pinned to the tree.

"Vika," she said as if it were merely an afterthought. "He's of no use to us anymore."

Then she started up the steps. Jack turned his eyes forward, just in time to watch Vika pull a third ivory javelin out from behind her back.

CHAPTER TWENTY-NINE

Sloane's lungs burned as she dove through the underbrush, fronds and thorny vines whipping at her arms and shoulders, pollen clinging to her hair. She could still see the first javelin tearing through Jack's sleeve, and the second javelin, which had missed her by mere inches, plunging into the trunk of a mature cyprus.

Even with a head start, she could hear her pursuer closing in. No matter how many hours she'd spent on StairMasters and ellipticals, there was no way she was going to be able to outrun a trained killer. She began to frantically search the plants around her for something she could use as a weapon. Maybe an oversize thorn? A broken tree limb? But she knew she was just being foolish; she wasn't going to beat the woman in a fight, and she wasn't going to get away. Which meant unless she came up with something brilliant, and something fast—she was going to die.

Sloane leaped over a high fir root. *No, damn it.* She wasn't going to let it end like this. Not here, of all places. She had dedicated her life to the study of plants. Hell, she was in this garden because of her obsession with the simple essence of the beautiful, perfect floral structures around her. Maybe she had initially been motivated by the need to secure her job, but now it was much more than that. Her love of plants had led her to the end of a mystery that spanned millennia and the entire globe. Her love of plants had led her to Jack—who was still just as irritating and headstrong and wild-eyed as when she'd first met him, but still—no, damn it, she wasn't going to die here, in this garden.

Because this was *her* turf.

And then suddenly, she skidded to a stop, her feet digging into a section of soft, falanius moss. But it wasn't the moss that had frozen her in her tracks. It was the pair of towering plants behind the moss, rising up from behind a fallen deciduous limb.

The two stems were much too long, reaching almost a foot above her head, curving outward from each other, jutting out over a small clearing between the moss and the edge of more underbrush. And the quintet of leaves at the end of each stem were incredibly large—each as big as a man-hole cover, flat and heart-shaped. But the deep pink color and the colony of frond-like hairs around the interior of the lobes were unmistakable.

Sloane's breathing became steady as she realized what she was looking at. She quickly crossed the moss and crept beneath the two overhanging stems, standing with her back to the green stalks. Then she waited.

It was only a few seconds before she saw the woman sliding between the various trees and brush with the agility of a forest cat. The woman saw her at almost the same moment—and a smile broke across her narrow face.

She slowed her pace, her eyes scanning the area around Sloane for any nearby weapons. Satisfied, she stepped onto the carpet of moss, rising to her full height, a good inch taller than Sloane's five-foot-seven.

"That was a pretty good kick back at the pyramid in Mexico," she said in heavily accented English as she advanced carefully across the moss. "I almost broke my neck on the way down."

"That was you?" Sloane said, remembering the moment at the top of Chichen Itza. "I thought you looked familiar. You look much better on your feet, not tumbling down two-thousand-year-old stairs."

The woman grinned, taking another step forward. She was just a few feet away now. Her right hand moved to her belt and she withdrew the cruel-looking, serrated knife.

"You won't catch me by surprise again, bitch."

Suddenly she lunged. Sloane leaped backward, barely avoiding the blade, and smacked one of the stalks with the palm of her hand. Then she dropped flat to the ground.

The woman stood over her, a confused look on her face.

"Now why would you—" she started, but that was as far as she got.

The giant, heart-shaped leaf of the plant plunged downward, opening like a pair of bright pink jaws. It closed over the woman's head with a sudden snap, then sprung back upward, carrying her up into the air, her feet dangling four feet over the ground.

Sloane rolled away from beneath the woman's kicking legs, then rose slowly, brushing moss from her pants.

The woman was still struggling, her muffled cries emanating from beneath the bulging pink leaf wrapped around her head, but the plant was much too strong. Slowly, the kicking slowed to a sullen twitch.

"There's only one bitch in this garden," Sloane said. "And her name is *Dionaea muscipula*."

Then she turned and headed back the way she had come.

CHAPTER THIRTY

"I think we got off on the wrong foot," Jack tried as the killer named Vika advanced toward him, her javelin hanging ominously from her left hand. "I'm really not that bad a guy. In fact, most people find me charming."

A grimace moved across Vika's features, and Jack noticed she was both limping and favoring her left side. Even so, he didn't give himself much of a chance, one arm pinned to a tree, the other gingerly reaching behind his back.

Without warning, Vika lunged forward, the javelin aiming directly for his chest. Jack barely got the iták out in time to parry the ivory blow, simultaneously spinning his body away from the tree, using all his weight to tear free from where he was pinned—leaving a good portion of his sleeve still attached to the birch.

"Goddamn it," he said as he came to a stop with his back to the ivory steps, his fingers moving beneath the collar of his tattered coat. "That was my favorite jacket."

The woman spun around to face him, raising the javelin.

"You talk too much," she grunted, now in obvious pain.

Jack could see blood on her lips, and he wondered how much longer she could stay on her feet. Long enough, he figured, so he did the only thing that came to mind. He lowered his shoulders and charged.

He hit her low, just below the point of the javelin, driving his entire weight into her waist, and they both toppled toward the ground. Even before they hit dirt, she'd somehow spun him around so that he landed flat on his back, and then her impossibly strong thighs were around him, pinning him down, her left hand raising the javelin above his face. Then the ivory was flashing downward—and at the last second, Jack moved his head, the javelin flicking at his earlobe, sticking half a foot into the packed ground next to his skull.

Jack drove his left hand upward, catching her right below her bottom rib—and suddenly her face turned white and her thighs released. Jack rolled out from under her and got into a crouch. He felt the dirt shift under his heels, and when he looked down, he realized he was right on the edge of the deep moat. He could hear hissing and spitting from below. He gasped, trying to move forward, but suddenly Vika was right in front of him, another javelin coming out of the holster on her back.

"Your luck is about to run out," she said, coughing blood.

She raised the javelin over her shoulder, taking aim at the center of his chest—and then suddenly, she froze.

Her eyes went wide, and then her entire face seemed to go slack, her lips twitching above her teeth. A glaze swept across her pupils and she stumbled forward, the javelin sliding from between her fingers, dropping harmlessly to the ground.

Jack stepped to one side, watching as she took the last few feet in a blind stagger—and then she toppled forward into the moat. She landed with a thud, and then there was a furious hissing, followed by the sound of dozens of jaws snapping open and shut.

Jack slowly opened his left hand; between his second and third finger was the jagged scorpion stinger he'd taken from the pouch around his neck.

He tossed the stinger to the ground and retrieved his trusty iták. He was about to head into the garden to search for Sloane when he heard a loud creak from high above. He turned just in time to watch Jendari Saphra open the top of the bronze sarcophagus.

"It's really her," Jendari gasped.

Jack felt frozen in place.

"Jack!"

Sloane was rushing toward him. The second killer was nowhere to be seen, which meant Sloane had somehow beaten the woman. Still, there was no telling how many more of the dark-haired killers were on their way. Jack knew they should be heading into the river, trying to find a way out—but instead, he found himself transfixed by the billionaire on the raised platform.

As he watched, Jendari reached into the open sarcophagus and carefully cradled something heavy in both of her arms. As she leaned back, lifting the thing out of the bronze coffin, Jack saw that it was a body; small, almost childlike in size, encased in solid orange amber.

"It's her," Jendari repeated, her voice turned solemn. "The power—the infinite power. Just a single one of her trillion, trillion cells. To cure disease. To fix aging. Maybe even to live forever."

Jack swallowed, still frozen in place.

"The Tree of Life," he whispered.

He could feel Sloane staring at him, but he couldn't take his eyes off of the body.

"Every culture that has ever existed, every religion, every civilization on Earth—don't you see? The Tree of Life—it's based in reality."

"You mean the oak?"

"Not the oak. The body in the amber. The Tree of Life isn't a plant, it's her, it's—"

Before he could finish the sentence, a familiar streak of white shot upward from deep within the moat behind him. The javelin hit Jendari in the dead center of her chest. She staggered backward, still holding the body encased in amber. Then she looked down, and Jack followed her astonished gaze into the moat—

And there, lying on her back, covered in slithering asps, was Vika, her eyes momentarily clear, fighting the snake venom that would assuredly kill her and the scorpion poison that would lubricate the way.

From above, Jendari gasped, blood spattering from her lips.

"Why?"

"I have my orders," Vika said. "*Você é indigno.*"

This time, Jack understood the words. *You are unworthy*. He watched as Jendari collapsed backward beneath the amber and toppled directly into the open sarcophagus.

And at that precise moment, Jack felt a strange, cool change in the air.

"Sloane," he said. "I think we'd better—"

But he never had a chance to finish his sentence. There was an eardrum shattering crack, followed by a terrible gushing sound that seemed to come from everywhere at once. Sloane screamed, pointing to one of the stone walls of the chamber. Jack saw it too: The wall was bulging inward. He looked around and saw that the other walls were bowing inward as well. His stomach dropped as he realized what was happening. Jendari's fall had triggered something in the structure of the vast cavern. They had entered the cavern via a river, and now it appeared that the three walls around them were barely holding back three more rivers, making four. In a moment, they were going to be a the epicenter of a truly biblical flood.

"This isn't good," he gasped. And then he had a sudden idea.

He grabbed Sloane's hand and leaped forward through the jungle, running as fast as he could toward where they'd left the wooden sarcophagus. The sound was getting louder by the second.

"Faster," he screamed, leaping over a root. "Into the coffin!"

He half threw her the last few feet over the brush, and she clambered over the edge of the sarcophagus. He dove in after her, landing on top of her prone body, his weight sending the vessel straight back into the river. He pushed himself up, leaning over the edge, paddling furiously with both hands. As he worked at the water, he searched the far wall and finally spotted his goal: the small, tunnel-like opening he had seen on their way into the cavern. He had no idea where it led, or if it would be wide enough for the sarcophagus. But he also knew they didn't have much of a choice. They were running out of time.

"Come on, come on, come on," he hissed, using his hands and the current to guide them the last few feet—and then thankfully, the front of the coffin slid into the opening. He threw himself flat on top of Sloane, face-to-face.

"Stay down, keep your eyes closed. And for the love of Eve, hold your goddamn breath!"

And then there was a sound as loud as Armageddon itself—the three walls collapsing, the rivers rushing in, tsunami-high walls of water instantly filling the chamber. Suddenly the water hit them like a fist from behind, rocketing them forward through the narrow tunnel—and everything went black.

CHAPTER THIRTY-ONE

Two bodies clasped together in the bottom of a sarcophagus, tearing forward at a mind-numbing velocity, ricocheting through the narrow tube of solid rock, fountains of wood splintering off as they skidded through a half-dozen curves, and then, without warning, they were suddenly barreling straight upward on a geyser of pure liquid. For a brief, nauseating moment Jack felt completely weightless, and despite his own warning to Sloane, he opened his eyes and lifted his head. He saw that they were arcing up at breakneck speed toward what appeared to be a pane of pure, glowing crystal—

And then he frantically lowered his head just as they crashed right through, into blindingly bright daylight. Wind whipped across the wood beneath them, then there was a terrifying jolt as they made contact with the ground and skid forward on a sheet of sand, tossing up clouds of thick dust behind them. Jack lifted his head again and saw that they were speeding down the side of an enormous dune. Ahead of them, at the base of the dune, he could make out a wide glade of sand. There were shapes moving across the sand, and it took Jack a moment to realize the shapes were children: ten, maybe twelve kids kicking a soccer ball between them, laughing and shouting at each other in Arabic, running and playing—and then, as one, the children froze, staring up at the dune.

The sarcophagus slid the last ten yards down the slope, then shot out into the sandy glade—finally coming to a stop in the center of the children, inches from the forgotten soccer ball.

Jack coughed, spitting up water and dust, and he felt Sloane pushing out from under him. She peered out over the edge of the sarcophagus, saw the sun and the sand and the children, and then she smiled, maybe the first real smile he had seen from her. Still, the kids didn't move, rooted in place, staring in stunned silence.

Jack leaned out of the sarcophagus, grabbed the soccer ball, and tossed it toward the nearest kid. It bounced once, then landed at the kid's feet. The kid looked at the ball—then turned and ran. The other kids followed his lead, and a moment later, Jack and Sloane were alone in the water-logged coffin.

Jack looked at Sloane and shrugged.

"It's been that kind of a week."

"Jack, that body in the amber, it was—"

"Yes," he said. "I think so."

"And now it's gone."

He shrugged again. Amber was a pretty resilient material. There were samples of amber that had been dated back to many millions of years. A body encased in amber could survive millennia, perhaps even more, submerged beneath four rivers' worth of surging water.

"Everything, gone," Sloane said. "After all we've been through, we're left with nothing to show for it."

Jack thought for a moment. Then he reached into his jacket pocket.

"We've got this."

He pulled out his hand, and between his fingers hung the red leaf he had plucked from the ancient, thorned vine.

Maybe it wasn't an ancient corpse encased in amber, or a bronze segmented snake, or proof of a mythical culture. But it was certainly enough for a career-saving paper. Perhaps even enough to earn a botanist her tenure—or perhaps at least a transfer to an Ivy League institution, maybe one where the sweaters came in orange and black and the graduate students bickered like the bratty little prodigies that they were.

Sloane reached for the leaf, but Jack held it just out of range, so that she had to move closer, right up next to him—and he figured this was as good a time as any to do something stupid.

So he leaned forward and kissed her.

And to his surprise, she actually kissed him back

The man in the bright orange construction helmet wiped sweat off the back of his neck as he climbed into the front cabin of the eleven-hundred horse-power Komatsu D575A bulldozer, settling himself noisily into the oversize vinyl bucket seat. Even before he reached for the ignition key, he could feel the massive power beneath him; the two-hundred-and-eighty-nine-ton beast, nearly forty feet front to back from the corrugated steel blade on its articulated pneumatic arms to the posterior edge of the rear rubber treads, was by far the largest dozer in production. Certainly it was more than enough machine for the job ahead—and his ride was just one of seven matching D575s lined up next to each other at the edge of the deserted village.

Any moment, the man in the orange helmet knew, the order would come in and the phalanx of dozers would roar to life. Ten minutes after that and the village would be gone; in its place, nothing more than a flattened glade of mud. The man had no idea how long it would take the rainforest to remove all trace that the village had ever existed, but judging from the dense growth he'd seen on the way down to that shit-strip of a jungle air-field, he guessed months, rather than years.

As he waited for the onboard intercom to cough up the command, he half wondered what this little, insignificant speck of a place at the edge of the

Amazonian rainforest had done to deserve such an ignominious fate. But he didn't ponder the question for long, because things like that were way beyond his pay grade. He was simply there to do a job, and he'd learned long ago, when the orders came in, it was best not to ask questions.

Really, there wasn't anybody to ask, anyway. Just job contracts that came in, periodically, attached to envelopes loaded with cash. Delivered by couriers who knew even less than he did. Even the name at the bottom of the contracts raised more questions than answers.

The Euphrates Conglomerate. *And who the hell were they?*

Deep pockets, that's who they were. The kind of pockets that could afford seven of the biggest goddamn bulldozers on Earth for a simple demolition job in a sweltering corner of a billion-acre rainforest.

The man in the orange hat grinned, thinking of those cash-laden envelopes as the intercom finally crackled the single-word command through the humid air. Then he leaned forward in his bucket seat and reached for the ignition.